THE ARSENIC LABYRINTH

Daniel Kind is finding his relationship with Miranda going through a difficult time. Feeling isolated in their rural idyll in Brackdale, Miranda has itchy feet, and Daniel fears she may just get up and leave. She wouldn't be the first: ten years ago a woman called Emma Bestwick left her cottage and disappeared, an unresolved case which has always irked DCI Hannah Scarlett, head of the Cold Case Review Team. When someone starts dropping hints about Emma's death, Daniel and Hannah are drawn together again and discover that one person will preserve the secrets of the past at any price.

THE ARSENIC LABYRINTH

THE ARSENIC LABYRINTH

by

Martin Edwards

Magna Large Print Books
Long Preston, North Yorkshire,
BD23 4ND, England.

British Library Cataloguing in Publication Data.

Edwards, Martin
The arsenic labyrinth.

A catalogue record of this book is
available from the British Library

ISBN   978-0-7505-2748-4

First published in Great Britain in 2007 by Allison & Busby Ltd.

Copyright © 2007 by Martin Edwards

Cover illustration © Brighton Studios

The moral right of the author has been asserted

Published in Large Print 2007 by arrangement with
Allison & Busby Ltd.

Magna Large Print is an imprint of Library Magna Books Ltd.

Printed and bound in Great Britain by
T.J. (International) Ltd., Cornwall, PL28 8RW

Dedicated to
Carolyn, George, Gary and Karen

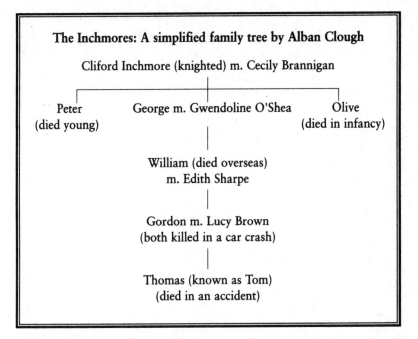

The Inchmores: A simplified family tree by Alban Clough

Cliford Inchmore (knighted) m. Cecily Brannigan

Peter
(died young)

George m. Gwendoline O'Shea

Olive
(died in infancy)

William (died overseas)
m. Edith Sharpe

Gordon m. Lucy Brown
(both killed in a car crash)

Thomas (known as Tom)
(died in an accident)

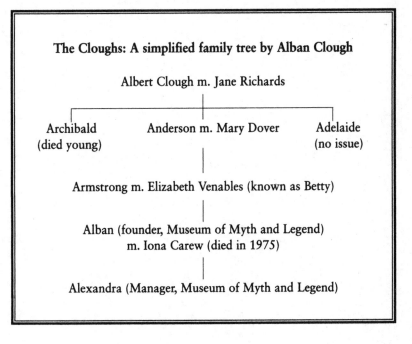

The Cloughs: A simplified family tree by Alban Clough

Albert Clough m. Jane Richards

Archibald
(died young)

Anderson m. Mary Dover

Adelaide
(no issue)

Armstrong m. Elizabeth Venables (known as Betty)

Alban (founder, Museum of Myth and Legend)
m. Iona Carew (died in 1975)

Alexandra (Manager, Museum of Myth and Legend)

JOURNAL EXTRACT

You'd never believe it to look at me now, but once upon a time I killed a man.

My calves ache with the effort of scrambling up the slippery fell. It is not too late, I need not carry out my plan. Murder is a choice, an act of free will. How easy to turn around and go back home. Nobody need ever know the wicked imaginings that twist my soul. It is within my power to let him live.

It is not merely his fate that lies in my hands this afternoon. It is my own.

My knees tremble. In the bag slung over my shoulder, I feel the sharp blade of the knife.

I didn't turn back, but passed beneath the large stone they called the Sword of Damocles. Long gone, destroyed like so much else that once seemed permanent and immune to change. I am ill at ease in the modern world. I shall not be sorry to bid it farewell. But before I leave, I shall share my secrets. I have this foolish superstition that, if they were buried with me, I should never find peace.

His back is turned, but when he hears my footsteps he spins round, leering with anticipation. He expected someone else. At the sight of me, his smile dissolves. The curl of his lip is familiar. I am accustomed to disappointing him.

'You contrived this.'

A nod of assent.

'*How long have you known?*'

What did it matter? When I did not reply, he let fly with a volley of abuse. I was jealous and selfish and sick in my head. The words glanced off me like arrows striking a shield.

When he reaches out and touches my arm, I recoil. A hungry gleam returns to his eyes. I can read his mind. We are alone and I am at his mercy. He looks about him, his attention caught by a rattle of stones.

I am dying now, withered and weary, but that afternoon I was so alive. More alive than ever before. Or since.

Slowly, he takes off his belt. Followed by his shirt.

I stand in front of him, motionless. He commands me to undress, just as I expected. My hands shake as I pull off my stockings and struggle out of my corselette. I take too long. Grunting with impatience, he strips quickly. When I start to fold my petticoat, he roars in disbelief.

'*For God's sake, woman!*'

I bend down and reach into the bag. I have obeyed him for the last time. He stands in front of me, naked and defenceless. I am almost naked too.

But I have the knife.

PART ONE

CHAPTER ONE

Who shall I be today?

Guy smiled at the landlady as she proffered a ballpoint pen with a bitten top. Her hands were chapped, her pink nail varnish flaking. He reached inside his suede jacket.

'Thanks, but I always write with my own fountain pen.'

He liked to think of the black lacquer Waterman Expert as an heirloom, though he'd picked it up less than eighteen months previously in a grubby little shop in Camden Town. The landlady opened the register with as much reverence as if it were *The Book of Kells*. Guy paused; hadn't Megan described him as a regular Jekyll and Hyde?

Today, no question – Dr Jekyll.

At Haverigg, he'd studied calligraphy, an agreeable means of passing the long days. No need for artistic skill, just patience and attention to detail. Before running out of both, he'd mastered the basics of an elegant script. Bending over the page, he wrote with a flourish.

RL Stevenson.

Perfectly safe, this flight of fancy. He'd once made the mistake of introducing himself as Guy Mannering to a woman who proved to be a closet Sir Walter Scott fan, but Mrs Welsby didn't strike him as bookish. Bed and breakfast places further

15

up Campbell Road rejoiced in names like Brides-head and Xanadu, but this house, squashed at the end of a three-storey Victorian terrace, was called Coniston Prospect. Not that the name lacked imagination. A tall man looking out of the attic window would need to stand on his toes to see beyond the trees and satellite dishes and catch a glimpse of Coniston Water.

Fanned out on the table were the *Daily Express*, opened at the gossip page, and a local tabloid. On a scuffed sideboard squatted a Pye transistor radio, so ancient it was probably fashionable retro chic. Through the interference, he discerned Lionel Richie's breathy enquiry, *'Is it me you're looking for?'*

'Welcome to Coniston Prospect, Mr Stevenson.'

The smell of fried bread and burned bacon lingered in the air. Guy gave a contented sniff. He preferred four-star luxury, a boutique hotel by Grasmere or Ullswater would have been more his style, but he didn't mind roughing it until he sorted himself out. No bad thing to keep your feet on the ground. He found it so easy to get carried away. After leaving Llandudno in a hurry, he was short of cash. Lucky he was adaptable – Megan's word was *chameleon*.

'Please, Mrs Welsby, the name's Robert.'

Her smile revealed teeth as crooked as the Hardknott Pass. Guy winced. Dentistry counted for a lot, in his opinion. In more affluent days, he'd spent a fortune on caps and straightening.

'My friends call me Rob.'

'I'm Sarah,' she said quickly. 'I do hope you'll

be happy here.'

Her eagerness to please was unfeigned and he found himself warming to this solid woman in turquoise tracksuit and down-at-heel trainers. Seizing her hand, he found her grip was weak, her flesh soft. Once she'd been pretty, but she'd put on too much weight and years of disappointment had faded her blue eyes. The fair hair was dyed, the roots greying. No rings on the fingers. She could use a little excitement in her life. He pitched his voice lower.

'I'm sure I will be.'

He meant it. A threadbare carpet wasn't the end of the world. All she needed was encouragement. There was more to life than wiping cobwebs from picture rails or scrubbing ketchup stains out of your pinafore.

'I suppose you'd like to unpack?'

He nodded. It wouldn't take five minutes. He travelled light, out of habit as well as need.

'I'll put the kettle on. A cup of tea is so refreshing after a journey. Have you travelled far?'

'I'm not long back in England, as it happens.'

No less than the truth. He'd spent too long in rain-sodden Llandudno, gazing out at wind-whipped waves. The tan came courtesy of a solarium in Deganwy. No matter; the sparkle of delight in Sarah Welsby's eyes told him that she was thinking south of France rather than the coast of North Wales. It would be unkind to disillusion her and Guy hated being unkind. He was about to murmur that the world was becoming smaller when his eye caught a headline in the local newspaper, above a blurry photograph of a face he would never forget.

What happened to Emma Bestwick?

'Detective Chief Inspector Scarlett!'

Hurrying towards the entrance of Divisional HQ, coat collar raised against the cold bite of February, Hannah heard pounding feet and someone shouting her name. She stopped in her tracks and swivelled.

A man was racing across the car park towards her. As he drew closer, his shoes skidded on the rain-greased tarmac and he lost his balance. With a stifled cry, he tumbled to the ground.

She walked over and helped him rise gingerly to his feet. He was about five feet seven, but lean and sinewy, with his clothes so slickly tailored that he did not seem small. She smelled cedarwood; he'd overdone the after-shave. He squinted at the streak of mud on his cream trousers with as much pain as if he'd broken his ankle.

'All right?'

'I'll live.' Scots accent, gritted-teeth smile. 'You know, this is the first time I've ever been picked up by a senior police officer.'

Early thirties, features as sharp as his suit. Gel glistening on coal-black hair. Despite his fall, not a strand out of place.

'Tony Di Venuto, I presume?'

'So you know who I am without being introduced. Proof positive you're a top detective!'

Di Venuto knew she'd recognised his voice from their phone conversation, but still treated her to a roguish smirk. Hannah groaned inwardly. A phrase of Les Bryant's echoed in her mind. *If he were a chocolate pudding, he'd eat himself.*

'What can I do for you?'

'When we spoke last Friday, you promised to consider reopening the Emma Bestwick file. You're in charge of cold cases. It's a perfect project for...'

'As I said, the moment you provide any new information, we'll be glad to study it.'

'Hopefully my piece in the *Post* will jog a few memories.'

'Hopefully. Now if you'll excuse me...'

'I realise you're very busy.'

'Uh-huh.'

'I believe she was murdered, Chief Inspector. Emma deserves justice. Her killer is still at large.'

He even talked in tabloid headlines. Hannah summoned the stonewall smile she reserved for press conferences when she had no titbits to offer.

'We never found any evidence she was dead. People disappear from home every day of the week. Plenty of them are never seen again.'

'Ten years have passed. Nobody has heard from Emma in all that time. It's inconceivable that she's still alive.'

Hannah cast around for the right words. She didn't want a casual remark to finish up as a sensational quote in a newspaper article. The media relations people would send her off on another press training day for punishment.

'Stranger things have happened.'

'Won't you let me take you through the facts?'

'That won't be necessary.' Hannah stepped away. 'One thing you ought to know. I was a member of the team that investigated Emma Bestwick's disappearance.'

Guy's new quarters occupied the basement at Coniston Prospect. He'd mentally rechristened it Coniston Glimpse. Mrs Welsby advertised en suite facilities, which meant he had exclusive benefit of a chilly toilet and separate bathroom on the other side of a short passageway. A yellowing spider plant drooped on the mantelpiece above the gas fire. The room reeked of damp, and as he lay on the stiff mattress Guy noticed patches of rot around the window frame. The radiator and pipes kept cackling, as though Macbeth's witches were trapped inside.

His lips moved but no sound came as he read once again the opening paragraph from the article in the newspaper that he'd cadged from the landlady.

This week sees the tenth anniversary of one of Cumbria's strangest unsolved mysteries. Thirty-year-old Coniston reflexologist Emma Bestwick vanished from home and was never seen again. Police were unable to establish whether she left of her own accord or was the victim of suicide, accident or murder. Perhaps the time has come for the Cumbria Constabulary's Cold Case Review Team to take another look at whatever happened to Emma.

How bloody typical. Talk about media irresponsibility. With so much strife in the world, how could it make sense to scour through the past, looking for trouble? People disappeared all the time, what was so odd about that? Why make a front page story out of one woman who went

20

missing long ago? Emma Bestwick was a troubled woman who might easily have given up her old life and gone in search of something new. It was perfectly plausible; he'd made a fresh start himself more than once. Why bully an over-worked police force into raking up old ashes?

A timid knock at the door.

'Only me! I brought your tea down.'

He tossed the newspaper to one side, scrambled off the bed and flung open the door. Mrs Welsby's face was pink, as though she felt like an intruder in her own home. He took the hot mug, blenching as it scalded his fingers, yet managing to preserve a grin of thanks.

'I meant to come back upstairs, but truth to tell, I needed forty winks. Travel can be exhausting, don't you find? It's wonderful to have the chance to put my feet up.'

'You do take milk?'

The mug bore a smiley face and he tried not to wince as he sipped. He loved leaf tea; his favourite was Assam, followed by Darjeeling, but this muddy mess was courtesy of two Co-op tea bags.

'Mmmmm. Lovely.'

He saw her eyes flicker in the direction of the newspaper. He'd left it on the bedside table.

'Thanks for letting me have a glance. Good to catch up.'

'You know the Lakes?'

'My favourite place in the whole world!' As soon as he said it, he realised it was the truth. Keep your Costa del Sols and your Corfus. Even the glory that was Rome was of another day. If he belonged anywhere, it must be here. The Lake

District felt like home, even in the rain. Especially in the rain. 'Mind you, this is my first time back in a decade. Too long.'

'Well, I mustn't interrupt.'

'Any time!'

They swapped smiles, and as the door closed behind her, he climbed back on to the bed. The journalist was called Tony Di Venuto. What had caused him to light upon the disappearance of Emma Bestwick? News must be thin, there was no other explanation. The tenth anniversary wasn't much of a peg to hang a story on.

Since he'd last walked the streets of Coniston village, Guy had stopped thinking about Emma. He had a gift for blocking out unpleasantness, found it as easy as closing a door on a draught. Yet memories lurked like invisible weeds beneath the surface of a tarn. After heading out of North Wales, he might have journeyed anywhere. But the Lakes pulled him back; he was a puppet on an invisible string. True, he'd given a promise never to return. But ten years was long enough. Nothing was forever.

Hannah switched off the tape recorder and yawned as Les Bryant lumbered into her room. She'd spent the past hour listening to interviews conducted by Maggie Eyre, a young DC in her team. Dip sampling of tapes was a tedious part of the job and some DCIs were quick to delegate it, but for her it was not a task to be skimped, however predictable the outcome. The idea was to check whether the interrogation techniques of junior officers were up to scratch and it was unwise to take much for granted. But it came as no surprise that Maggie's questioning of witnesses had been diligent, firm and courteous. Another tick in another box.

'Jobs they never tell you about at the student recruitment fairs,' she muttered.

Les shrugged and deposited his ample backside on a chair on the other side of her desk. 'Wouldn't know, I was never a student.'

She couldn't resist a grin. 'University of life, huh?'

'School of hard knocks, yeah.' He considered her. 'You look different today.'

'Thanks for noticing.'

He went through a pantomime of guesswork. 'Ummm ... your hair's not the same. More blonde than brown these days.'

'We'll make a detective out of you yet. And don't dare to say that you liked it the way it was. Now, have you squared things with Lauren?'

That morning the Assistant Chief Constable had scheduled a meeting with Les to review his conditions of service. He'd shambled out of retirement to lend his expertise to the Cumbria Constabulary's Cold Case Review Team. He was a dour Yorkshireman, a veteran of such fabled cases as the Whitby caravan shootings. The young DCs nicknamed him *In my day,* a tribute to Les's favourite phrase. But Hannah liked his morose humour as well as his nose for crime. He'd forgotten more about detective work than most cops would ever know. Once Lauren Self sorted out a few niggles about expenses, they could talk about extending his contract.

'Her ladyship was too busy. Press conference announcing that the force merger has been put on hold. I heard on the grapevine that some reporter asked if she thought the Home Secretary should be charged with wasting police time. By all accounts, she nearly jumped off the podium and slapped him.'

'Christ, I'll keep out of her way, then.'

The Home Office had decided that big was beautiful. Small forces must be gobbled up by larger neighbours, supposedly because terrorism and organised crime didn't recognise local boundaries, more likely because some number-cruncher in Whitehall imagined it might save cash. Goodbye bobby on the beat, hello regional call centre. Now the politicians were wetting themselves because they'd got their sums wrong. Most of Hannah's colleagues were praying that soon mergers wouldn't merely be shelved, they'd be dead and buried. If forces amalgamated, people in the countryside would lose out, as per usual. If it came to a choice between throwing resources into some urban sink estate or cosy Keswick or Kendal, there would only be one winner.

'Reason I'm here, I wondered if you wanted me to have a quiet word with this reporter who's been stalking you.'

'I can fight my own battles. He turned up here as I was arriving, but I sent him off with a flea in his ear.'

'What do you reckon to him?'

'Looks a bit like the young Frank Sinatra.'

'Christ. Is that good?'

'Not really. I never was that keen on "My Way".'

'Not what I heard,' he muttered. 'Any road, journalists are like pit bull terriers. Good idea to throw 'em a bone now and then.'

'Thanks, Les, but there's nothing you or I can do to satisfy Di Venuto. We don't have the resources to look into every case the force never managed to close. He's come up with nothing new. Emma was a mixed-up lady. In the end we had to go along with the SIO's gut instinct.'

'Which was?'

'He reckoned she didn't want to be found.'

'Recharged the batteries, Mr Stevenson?'

The landlady gave a shy glance of greeting and Guy wagged a finger in playful reprimand.

'Rob, please.'

'Rob.' She tittered. 'Sorry.'

'Wonderful what a nap can do.' He stretched his arms. 'I feel at home already.'

'That's marvellous.' Regret made the corners of her mouth turn down. 'The Lakes are full of hotels with spas, Jacuzzis and gourmet cuisine. Foreign chefs, glowing write-ups in the *Michelin Guide*. How can a woman on her own compete?'

'Don't beat yourself up over it, Sarah. Give me traditional home comforts any day.' In time he'd accustom himself to the sinister rumble of the central heating. 'Here I feel like a house guest, not an entry on some computer system. As for food, I'm very much a full English breakfast man.'

She brightened. 'Fried egg, two sausages,

baked beans, grilled tomato?'

'Perfect! I draw the line at black pudding, though.'

'Oh, me too.' A comical shiver. 'Blood frightens me.'

He drew breath. 'I'm looking forward to tomorrow morning already.'

'You move on in a week's time, then?'

'That was the plan.' So as to negotiate a discount on the daily rate. Always handy, even though Coniston Prospect must be the cheapest B&B south of Carlisle. 'But you never know. Seems like I've been on the road for years. Perhaps it's time to put down one or two roots.'

'Really? What do you do for a living?'

I live dangerously. The phrase trembled on his lips. It excited him, the glamour of adventuring into the unknown. But over the years he'd learned not to show too many cards too soon.

'Financial services. Internet-based stuff, mainly. Have laptop, will travel. That's me.'

'Goodness. Sounds very high-powered.'

A modest shake of the head. 'Not as glamorous as you might think. Money's all very well, but if it's all tied up offshore, it isn't much use in the short term, don't you agree?'

'I suppose not.'

'And then there's the hours. This 24/7 economy is terrific but we all need to sleep. Good people burn out too often. I tell myself, the simple pleasures are best.'

'Oh, you're absolutely right.'

'And where better to enjoy them than here, in God's own country – and in good company?'

Their eyes met. Blushing, she jumped out of her chair. 'I'd best be off to the supermarket. Stock up on eggs and bacon!' At the door she wavered. 'If you wanted an evening meal, it's no bother.'

'I don't want to put you to any inconvenience.'

'Not a bit of it. I'd be glad of someone to talk to apart from the cat. The German couple who have the room on the first floor, they don't say much. Only have eyes for each other.'

'Young love, eh?' He sighed in amiable reminiscence.

'Well, I'll see you later.'

When she opened the door, a Siamese cat stalked in. Svelte and snooty, with almond-shaped eyes, its demeanour suggested a commandant in *Bridge over the River Kwai*, sneering at a sweaty prisoner of war.

'Rob, meet Clooney,' the landlady said.

The cat gave a dismissive flick of its tail. Guy contrived a weak grin and kept his mouth shut. The animal looked as though it wouldn't believe a word he said. The landlady said how intelligent Clooney was and left Guy in peace.

After the door had closed behind Sarah Welsby and her pet, he settled into an armchair and flicked the TV remote. Half a dozen soldiers had been blown up by a suicide bomber in the Middle East and a minister was insisting that their sacrifice hadn't been in vain. Five turgid minutes of regional news focused on wind farms and planning permission for affordable housing. The weather forecaster promised squally showers. Nothing about Emma Bestwick. No surprise;

27

there simply wasn't a story.

Against expectation, this irked him. A ten-year anniversary ought to mean something to someone. At least Tony Di Venuto remembered. It was plain from the article that he'd done his homework. He'd mentioned stuff that was new to Guy.

Emma's sister and her husband, Karen and Jeremy Erskine, have lived with the torment of not knowing Emma's fate for a decade. Mr Erskine, who teaches history at the exclusive Grizedale College, was one of the last people to see Emma before she disappeared. Yesterday, however, he stated that his wife did not wish to make any public comment. 'This is a private family matter,' he insisted, before adding, 'My wife has lost hope of seeing her sister again. Ten years is a long time, we don't believe she will ever come back. Karen needs to move on.'

Jeremy Erskine. Interesting that Di Venuto had made the point that he was one of the last to see Emma – *alive* was the implication. How could Karen get on with her life if she had no idea whether Emma might turn up? Always there was the tantalising chance that one day the doorbell would ring and she'd open up to stare into a familiar, much-loved face. Guy's heart went out to her.

He made a note of the phone number of the editorial office and slipped on his wet weather jacket, tying the knot of his hood tight beneath his chin. Outside, the sky was the same colour as the slate buildings and passing cars had their headlights on. Opposite the Glimpse stood a chip shop, its lights dazzling in the murk, and a shuttered fudge emporium that specialised in clotted cream and rum 'n raisin flavours. No wonder Sarah Welsby was running to fat.

Rain spat into his eyes, but he blinked hard and kept moving, scanning the streets for somewhere to phone from. He didn't have a mobile – who would he ring, who would want to get in touch? Besides, this wasn't a call he could allow to be traced.

When he saw the phone box, he remembered the last time he'd used it. To ring up Emma Best-wick.

The kiosk was empty and he was in a hurry. No point in ignoring it out of some kind of super-stition. He stepped inside and dialled. The switchboard girl at the newspaper office put him straight through.

'Tony Di Venuto?'

Of course, he disguised his voice. A whisper does not have a recognisable pitch, hadn't Nicole Kidman said so in *The Interpreter?*

'Speaking.'

The Scottish accent didn't match the name. Guy pictured a hawk-eyed newshound, bristling with ambition. Dreaming of the scoop that would carry him into Fleet Street, or Wapping or wher-ever the modern Press congregated.

'You wrote the piece about Emma Bestwick.'

'Who is this?'

Guy's heart was beating faster. Why was he doing this? A question he often had cause to ask himself. Not all his instincts were sound. He was apt to act on a whim, he made too many mistakes.

'Are you still there?' Tony Di Venuto asked.

Grinding his teeth so hard they might crack, Guy forced himself to focus on the here and now. This clammy kiosk with steamed-up windows, heavy with the reek of chips and battered fish, disfigured by graffiti extolling the sexual tastes of Bazzer and Kylie. He dared not let his mind roam.

'Don't hang up.'

One, two, three, four, five, six, seven, eight, nine, ten. Guy counted silently, fighting for calm.

'Who – who are you?'

Guy breathed out. Di Venuto deserved a crumb. Something to pass on to the sister. It was the least he could do. Where was the harm, where the risk?

'Jeremy Erskine is right,' he hissed, 'Emma Bestwick won't be coming back.'

'How do you know?'

Guy slammed down the phone. He knew better than to give away too many secrets.

CHAPTER TWO

Daniel Kind pushed the oak door of Tarn Cottage and it swung open in silence on newly oiled hinges. In the hall stood his partner Miranda, dressed for a journey in new Barbour coat and Timberland boots. She was smiling at her reflection in the mirror. *Another dab of lipstick? No, it's just right.* At the sound of his footsteps, she spun to face him. Holding up her hand like a traffic cop, so that he stopped in his tracks. The smile vanished, her mouth compressed into a thin red line.

'Before you say a word, I don't have time now. I need to catch my train.'

'Relax, it doesn't leave Oxenholme for another hour. Even if it's on time.'

'I daren't think what will happen if I'm late arriving at Euston. Ethan called while you were out. He wants to meet over dinner this evening.'

'Let me drive you to the station, it's no trouble. We can talk on the way and there'll be time to spare for a cup of tea in the buffet.'

'Too late, I've ordered a taxi.'

'Ring up and cancel.'

'No, I hate unpicking arrangements, don't you think it's inconsiderate? Besides, you have work to do. That book proposal, is it ready to send to your agent?'

'Not even close,' he said, risking a sheepish grin.

'Oh, for God's sake! It's not good, Daniel, you can't afford to lose your edge. This is the twenty-first century. The Lake District may potter along in the slow lane, but the rest of the world won't wait for it to catch up.'

'Don't you want to talk about last night?'

For reply, Miranda raced off up the stairs, those posh new boots crashing on the wooden treads like drum beats. Next to the doorway, her suit-case bulged complacently. By the look of it, she'd packed for a fortnight. He realised she hadn't said when she was due back. A question slunk into his head.

What if she doesn't come back?
Don't be stupid, he told himself.
Would it matter if she didn't?
For God's sake. A single quarrel couldn't destroy everything that bound them together. It was Miranda who had wanted them to escape to this closed-off valley, shoe-horned between the fells. It was Miranda who'd persuaded him to give up teaching history at Oxford and abandon a career that had taken him on to TV screens on both sides of the Atlantic. Fame meant nothing to him and he didn't regard it as a sacrifice; it thrilled him to think they could start afresh, make everything new. When he'd brought her to the Lakes last spring, she'd fallen in love with Tarn Cottage and they'd snapped it up on the spur of the moment. He'd resigned his college fellowship and sold his old house. But Miranda wrote a column for a glossy magazine and the time never seemed quite right to give up her flat in London. Now she was setting off for an editorial conference at Canary Wharf. These dark winter days, she got away from it all by heading for the bright lights.

She came back down the stairs, clutching her Gucci bag like a favourite child. Her hips swung like a samba dancer's and his heart lurched with desire.

'The car will be here any minute.'

'What you said last night...'

'Forget it, Daniel. I should never have opened that second bottle. I was pissed, no way should I have ranted like that. I mean, yes, the Lakes are quiet. But of course Brackdale's not a *graveyard.*

32

I can't believe I said that! And I don't feel trapped, I'm not really lonely. How could I be, in such a gorgeous spot?'

'So you still want to live here?'

''Course I do.' She pecked him on the cheek. 'And with you. In case you were wondering.'

At least she was ready to kiss and make up. One thing he loved about Miranda, her bad moods sped past like scurrying clouds. Last night they'd shouted at each other; a watershed, not soon to be forgotten, their first fierce row. No plates thrown, but she'd locked the bedroom door on him. The scrape of the turning key echoed in his brain for hours. He didn't undress, spent all night lying on the bed in the spare room.

Through the small hours, the downpour battered the new roof tiles. Miranda hated winter, she hated the cold and above all she hated rain. She'd scoured for statistics to prove that Tarn Fold was the wettest place in England. Daniel didn't believe it, if only because Seathwaite over in Borrowdale was deluged by 120 inches a year. Brackdale probably got no more than 119. But what did that matter? Close the door, stoke the fire, and everything was fine. Miranda said her London flat was a bolt-hole, nothing more. But wasn't that the point of Tarn Cottage?

He'd breakfasted early. The coffee tasted bitter and he didn't finish his toast. The bedroom was still a no-go area and she didn't answer when he rapped on the door and called that he was leaving for Kendal. He was giving a talk at Abbot Hall: *Victorian Eco-Warrior – John Ruskin and Climate Change.* Ruskin's green campaigning was the first history he'd researched since his last lecture at Oxford and the applause proved he hadn't lost his touch. But his mind was elsewhere as people pumped his hand and he barely glanced at the praise on the feedback forms. He'd driven too fast all the way home and scraped his wing mirror against a tree as he swung into Tarn Fold.

'I'll call you tonight.'

'No need,' she said hastily. 'I expect I'll be out late with Ethan.'

Ethan, bloody Ethan.

'OK.'

'Don't look like a wet Wednesday in Wasdale, huh? I'll catch up with you as soon as I've got a minute, all right?'

A horn tooted outside and she'd gone before he could utter a word.

'Now will you take this seriously?' Tony Di Venuto demanded.

Hannah Scarlett squeezed her fingers tight around the phone. Did strangling a troublesome journalist count as justifiable homicide? 'Trust me, we always take our work seriously.'

'In that case, how will you respond to this amazing development?'

'You've not given us much to go on. An unknown person calls you, presumably because of the article...'

'He mentioned it specifically.'

'...and tells you Emma Bestwick won't be coming back. He doesn't even say she is dead. How do we know he isn't a time-waster? You haven't even got his name.'

'For God's sake, he rang off before I could question him.' The tightness of his voice told her that the rebuke stung. 'Hey, this wasn't some boozed-up teenager having a laugh at my expense. I was quite clear what he meant. She is dead.'

Hannah's gaze flicked to her computer screen as an email from Lauren Self jumped into her inbox. The ACC was moaning because Les had skived off the diversity training workshop. The fact that he was on a fixed term contract was *not* an excuse. The need to implement good practice applied to everyone, no exceptions. Yawn.

'You don't tape incoming calls?'

'Not routinely.'

She punched *delete* and Lauren's message vanished. The tiny act of defiance cheered her. 'So what can you tell me about him?'

'Man of my age, or thereabouts. Local accent, but he only said a few words.'

'Was he calm?'

'Curt, perhaps a bit flustered.'

'You've interviewed people close to Emma in connection with your story. This wasn't a man you've spoken to before? Jeremy Erskine, for instance?'

His laughter had a mocking edge. 'No way.'

'Before she bought her own house, Emma lodged with a couple called Francis and Vanessa Goddard. They became good friends. Might your caller have been Francis Goddard?'

'I spoke briefly with Mr Goddard on the phone when I was researching my article. It wasn't him. Or her old boss, Alban Clough.'

'Who, then?'

'Not a former boyfriend, that's for sure.'

'Stranger things have happened, Mr Di Venuto.'

'Forget it, Chief Inspector. Emma wasn't interested in men, everyone knew that.'

A thought tiptoed into Hannah's head. 'Did you know her?'

After thirty seconds of silence he muttered, 'We never met. Why do you ask?'

'Just wondered. You're taking such a close interest in one old case. There's not a shred of proof Emma didn't leave the Lakes of her own free will. But if you had some personal involvement with her...'

'Aren't you listening, Chief Inspector? I said I never set eyes on her. It's not so surprising the *Post* should revive the investigation. We covered her disappearance in depth ten years ago. Look at our files if you don't believe me.'

'And Mr Erskine?'

'What about him?' Sharp, defensive.

'Reading between the lines, you don't care for the way he's writing off Emma's disappearance as old news.'

'She was his sister-in-law. He ought to be concerned.'

'Presumably his loyalty is to his wife. That's why he wants her to move on.'

'Very commendable.' Sarky sod.

'But you've never met him before?'

'Not until I talked to him a week ago. Listen, Chief Inspector. I'm not the story here. This is all about Emma Bestwick, nobody else.'

'Of course,' Hannah said.

But she didn't believe him.

Daniel closed down his computer and slung on a fleece before wandering outside for a breath of Lakeland air. This corner of Brackdale was as peaceful as anywhere in England, but it was never entirely silent. Stop and listen and you could hear faint rustlings in the undergrowth, the distant cough of an invisible raven. He'd fallen for the Lakes as he had for Miranda, swept away on a tide of passion. Now he couldn't contemplate living anywhere else. The beauty entranced him, and the history too. The only thing he knew for sure about his next book was that it would be rooted in the Lakes. Historians needed to soak up the spirit of the places they studied. Sitting in a library wasn't enough.

As he wandered by the tarn, a pale light filtered through the dripping trees, spreading patterns on the dark water. Mist curtained the upper reaches of the hillside; dusk was gathering and he could barely make out Priest Edge and the grim bulk of the Sacrifice Stone. He could not guess how many men, women and children had met their death on the Stone in pagan times. Lives given up in the hope of buying salvation.

Few people came to Tarn Fold, but it was never as still as Miranda said. A fox hurried through the undergrowth, in search of food. The air smelled of damp earth and fallen leaves. His path twisted this way and that before arriving at an inexplicable dead end. The garden of Tarn Cottage had tantalised him for months until he discovered its melancholy secret.

He hadn't seen Hannah Scarlett since the end

of summer, when they'd both been caught up in the violent climax to one of her inquiries. In its stunned aftermath, they reached an unspoken understanding that they needed time apart. Daniel's late father, Ben Kind, had been Hannah's boss for years and she reckoned he'd taught her all she knew about detecting crime. A bond had formed between her and Ben's son. But they were both in relationships and it was unwise to grow too close. Once or twice during the past six months, Daniel had picked up his mobile, wanting to hear her cool voice again. He'd deleted her number from the quick dial menu, but the digits had lodged in his brain, like squatters determined to stick it out. So far he'd never made the call.

Safer to take refuge in history. At auction last October, he'd bought a yellowing set of letters, in which an acquaintance debated Ruskin's dread of industry encroaching on the glory of the Lakes. That horror of the smoke-belching steel-works of Barrow-in-Furness became the starting point for the Kendal lecture. But Daniel didn't have enough fresh material to justify a full-length book, and much as he loathed the treadmill of contracts and deadlines, he could use the cash. Since leaving Oxford, he'd lived off royalties from the TV series he'd presented, while the profit from selling his old home was swallowed by the cost of renovating Tarn Cottage. Following the death of his partner Aimee, he'd needed to break from the past, even just writing about the past. But Miranda was right: a sabbatical was one thing, opting out altogether quite another.

There is no wealth but life, Ruskin said. True, but you still had to pay your grocery bills.

Daniel retraced his steps and sat down on a bench looking over towards the lower slopes of Tarn Fell. Fishing his mobile out of his pocket, he punched in a familiar number.

'Amos Books.'

He recognised the girl's smoky voice. 'Trecilla? This is Daniel Kind... Fine thanks, how are you? Is Marc around?'

'He's scouting for new premises in Sedbergh.'

'Don't tell me you're moving?'

'No, they're talking about opening another branch. Can I help?'

'I'm interested in finding out more about John Ruskin's life in the Lake District. His battles with local industrialists, that sort of thing.'

'You'd be best speaking to Marc. I'm afraid I've never got into Ruskin, but Marc's a fan. He's back in tomorrow.'

'I'll drop in, see if I catch him.'

Why not? It couldn't do any harm. Ruskin had made his home in the Lakes for thirty years, there was always the outside chance that some rare treasure might lurk on a dusty shelf in Marc's rambling emporium, casting fresh light on Ruskin's life and work. Yet as he ambled back towards the cottage, Daniel admitted to himself that this wasn't really about research. Marc Amos lived with Hannah and tomorrow he'd have the chance to ask after her. Out of curiosity, nothing more.

Les Bryant wiped the froth from his mouth and

said, 'Better dig out the old files.'

'They're already on my desk,' Hannah said.

They were closeted in a sepulchral corner of the mahogany-panelled bar at the back of the Woollen Shroud, a pub on the outskirts of town. As usual it was deserted save for a handful of grizzled regulars who seldom spoke or even moved. For years, Hannah had met informants here, people who didn't want it known they were talking to her. The privacy compensated for the graveyard ambience. She wondered how the landlord earned enough to live on. Probably best for a police officer not to know.

Proving that miracles do happen, Les had blown the dust off his wallet and bought the first round. His way of making up for exposing her to criticism from the ACC. He'd even promised to move heaven and earth to attend the next scheduled seminar on dignity at work. Though his snoring might distract the other attendees.

'So you're more interested than you let on to Di Venuto?'

'It's not about whether I'm interested. As it happens, I hated it when we gave up on the case. The snag is, Di Venuto has no new info for us and the files don't hold any clues.'

'Give me a flavour.'

She savoured the nip of her wine. 'Emma Bestwick vanished off the face of the earth without forewarning. What happened to her, nobody knows. She lived alone and several days passed before her disappearance was reported to the police by a neighbour. We searched her home, but didn't find any indication of where she might

40

have gone. Wherever it was, she hadn't taken her passport with her. She kept her credit cards in her wallet and that was missing, but they were never used.'

'What did she do for a living?'

'Self-employed reflexologist.'

'Oh yeah?'

His leathery features crinkled in scorn. Les didn't hold with touchy-feely crap like reflexology. He'd once revealed that his wife was passionate about yoga and gave the impression that one of his motives for joining the Cold Case Review Team was to avoid watching her tie herself in knots on a mat in the living room when all he wanted was to switch on the football.

The temptation to tease was irresistible. 'Yeah, Reiki and sekhem healing, chakra colour balancing, metamorphic techniques, Indian head massage...'

'For Chrissake,' he said in disgust.

'Listen, hasn't Mrs Bryant recommended it for your sinusitis? Hopi ear candle therapy could work wonders, removing the impurities...'

'Get on with the story, eh?'

Hannah grinned. 'All right. Emma worked from home. A bungalow she'd bought a few months earlier, down the road from Coniston Water.'

'Local woman?'

'Grew up in the Eskdale Valley with a younger sister. Spent a few years working in Merseyside before coming back to Cumbria. At first she lodged with a couple called Goddard who lived in Coniston. At the time she was working at the Museum of Myth and Legend. Ever visited it?'

41

Even in the gloom, Les's derision was unmistakable. On second thoughts, Hannah realised it was a silly question. The old curmudgeon would have no time for such flights of fancy. Impossible to picture him traipsing round museums and galleries, guide-book in hand, camera primed for action. His idea of interactive entertainment was sitting in the stand at Elland Road, yelling at Leeds United's shot-shy strikers to have a crack at goal.

'Never heard of it.'

'The museum's at Inchmore Hall, off the Ambleside Road. A baroque mansion, all turrets and crazy gables. Think Hogwarts. The owner was – still is, I checked – a wealthy eccentric called Alban Clough. He's obsessed with Lakeland legends and he's devoted his life and most of his fortune to keeping them alive. His daughter, Alexandra, manages the museum, and both of them live at Inchmore Hall. Emma helped on the counter and took visitors round. Interesting job, but poorly paid.'

When he leaned towards her, she could smell tobacco. Les was an unrepentant heavy smoker. There was probably more tar on his lungs than on the A49. He coughed, as if in confirmation.

'Was her pay relevant?'

'As part of the puzzle, yes. There was so much we couldn't explain about Emma Bestwick. When she returned to the Lakes from Liverpool, she'd scarcely a penny to her name. Within a year, she was putting down a deposit on a nice little bungalow and buying herself a brand new Fiat.'

'Lottery win?'

'So she told her sister and Alban Clough. We checked and found she'd lied. And she didn't always tell the same tale. She led Francis and Vanessa Goddard to believe that the money was inherited. But who from? Not a family member, otherwise Karen would have known about it.'

Les took another swig from his tankard. 'Young woman comes into money for the first time in her life, then disappears for no apparent reason. No wonder we didn't write her off as one more runaway.'

One thing about Les: he never forgot that all police officers were on the same side. He always talked about *we* and *us*, not *them*.

'But how long can you keep banging your head against a brick wall? The file may not have been closed, but nobody was begging us to keep it open.'

'Not even her family?'

'There were no near relations except Karen and she seemed certain that Emma would turn up again one day.'

'But she never did.'

'Karen's husband, Jeremy, went to see Emma just before she disappeared. His story was that he had back trouble and she'd offered to help.'

A sardonic chuckle. 'Spot of massage?'

'We found no evidence of any affair. To all appearances the Erskines were happily married.'

Les's face made it clear that happy marriages were as common as fairies at the bottom of the garden. Come to think of it, would Mrs Bryant be content for him to stay on this side of the Pennines for another twelve months?

'How about her friends?'

'Vanessa Goddard seemed cut up about her disappearance, but she was Emma's only close friend. Emma wasn't interested in men and although she'd had an affair with Alexandra Clough while she worked at the museum, that came to an end months earlier. No hard feelings, according to Ms Clough.'

'Did you believe her?'

'Do me a favour. How many relationships end with no hard feelings? But there was no evidence to link Alex Clough – or anyone else – with Emma's disappearance. Every avenue turned out to be a dead end.'

'So over the years nobody has bothered too much about her.'

'Until Tony Di Venuto.'

'And then, someone rings him up and implies that Emma is dead.'

'All he said was that Emma wouldn't be coming back. Which leaves us no wiser.'

'You think Di Venuto made it up?'

'Perish the thought that a journalist might tell porkies.' He burped and patted his belly. 'So what was your take on the case? What did you think happened to Emma?'

Hannah sucked in her cheeks. 'You have to remember, I was wet behind the ears.'

'Even so.'

'The SIO was Sid Thornicroft. Decent detective, but he was coming up for retirement and he was more focused on collecting his pension than clues. The investigation ran out of steam as soon as he decided that Emma had done a runner. I

44

didn't agree, but so what?'

'You thought she was dead?'

She nodded. 'Like Di Venuto. My hunch was that she'd been murdered. But without evidence...'

'Lauren will want us to delve. Make sure we're on the right side of the Press.'

'Christ, Les, don't tell me you're becoming media-savvy in your old age.'

He propped his elbows on the table and cupped his chin in his hands. 'It's you I'm thinking of. Cold case work is a cul-de-sac, ideal for boring old farts like me. You were shunted into it after you screwed up on a trial, but soon you'll be ready to get back in the swim. Which means giving the ACC an occasional stroke, even if you'd sooner shove her statistics up her bum.'

Hannah wanted to argue, but if she said she was happy to paddle in a backwater forever, he wouldn't believe her.

'All right. We start at nine tomorrow.'

She made it sound as if she didn't care, but her heart was beating faster. This wasn't about keeping Lauren sweet. Hannah had never been able to forget the photograph of Emma Bestwick in the old file, the same picture that accompanied Di Venuto's article. Her looks would never stop traffic. The face was round and pleasant, but flabby at the jaw-line, and instantly forgettable. Yet the puzzled frown and parted lips had stuck in Hannah's mind. She imagined Emma searching for something just beyond the horizon, could almost hear her murmuring *what's it all about?*

How had she come to vanish in an instant? If Hannah understood the woman, she might

45

understand her fate. Emma seemed so ordinary, but she'd proved elusive in more ways than one. Hannah had never managed to wriggle inside her head.

A sense of failure had nagged at her over the years like an arthritic joint, yet to devote precious resources to a hopeless case would have seemed self-indulgent. Hannah didn't care for Tony Di Venuto, but he deserved her thanks. He'd given her a second chance to do right by the woman everyone else preferred to forget.

Guy's landlady made a conspicuous effort with the dinner. Sarah Welsby might not specialise in exotic cuisine, but the roast chicken was wonderfully tender, the potatoes and carrots cooked to perfection. He'd invested in a decent bottle of Soave and she poured them each a generous measure of Harvey's Bristol Cream before they sat down to eat by candlelight. Cosy, verging on intimate. Too bad his mind kept wandering. Ever since speaking to Tony Di Venuto, he hadn't been able to concentrate on the here and now.

Sarah did most of the talking. Probably she wasn't accustomed to having anyone listen to her. Even Clooney the cat took no notice, endlessly washing his paws. There had been a husband called Don, a building society manager. On their fifteenth wedding anniversary, a jealous colleague tipped her off that Don and his secretary were having an affair. Five years after the divorce was finalised, Sarah was still raw at his betrayal.

'You never had children?'

She lifted her coffee cup with a trembling hand.

'His decision. I accepted it, in my book it's wrong to bring a baby into the world if you aren't both keen. But by the time they tied the knot, she was six months pregnant. What did she do for him that changed his mind, I wonder?'

Just as well they'd drained the bottle. Any more wine would make her maudlin and Guy found that unattractive in a woman. But he had a talent for sympathy.

'He hoodwinked you. A respectable professional man. Disgraceful.'

A timid smile. 'Sorry. Listen to me, pouring out my woes. You must be bored stiff.'

He leaned across the table. Not quite invading her personal space. 'On the contrary. This whole evening has been – so delightful.'

A little giggle. 'You know, the German couple are always late for breakfast. I think I might leave the washing-up until tomorrow morning.'

'Splendid idea.'

The silence lasted half a minute before she stretched and said, 'Well, I suppose I'd better be going up.'

She ventured another smile, bolder this time, and he smiled back. But he didn't move closer. *Timing is everything.*

'You know something, Rob? I'm afraid I'm a bit tipsy. Hopeless, aren't I? Normally I don't have more than a single glass with my meal.'

'You'll sleep all the sounder tonight.'

'Yes.' She rose clumsily to her feet. The pale blue eyes weren't focusing. 'Well, goodnight.'

'Goodnight, Sarah.'

He ambled back downstairs. This was one of

his Garbo moments; he could do sociable, but he did love being on his own. Flinging himself on to the bed, he couldn't help congratulating himself. Moving into Coniston Glimpse might seem counter-intuitive, given his taste for the *dolce vita*, but he could make a virtue out of a necessity. Sarah was sure to refuse to take his money when he offered it. Already they were becoming friends, they could do each other a good turn.

He buried his face in the pillow, to shut out the noise from the pipes. He wanted to replay in his head that conversation with the journalist. The moment he'd put the phone down, his stomach lurched – with excitement, not fear. Over the past ten years, he'd travelled far and wide and spent a great deal of money, some of it his own. Yet it was as if he'd been sleepwalking, all that time. It had become an article of faith, that he must forget Emma Bestwick, scrub the memories out of his mind. Guilt was a passing phase, like the quarters of the moon, he should have learned that at Haverigg.

But the truth was, you couldn't undo the past.

CHAPTER THREE

Guy was stretched out in a coffin, but he wasn't dead. Prising his eyes open, he saw nothing but darkness. He was cold and naked save for a coverlet of coarse cloth. The air was foetid and he found himself fighting for breath. His mouth

48

tasted of wet earth and he knew he'd been buried six feet under. He banged on the lid until his knuckles bled, but there was no way out. He screamed for help, but nobody heard. When he prayed for rescue, nothing happened.

He awoke drenched in sweat. Relief at the sight of the white walls of his room and the rumble of the basement plumbing was soured by dismay. So many years had passed since he'd last had the nightmare of being buried alive. He'd persuaded himself that it had gone forever. On his first night back in the Lakes, memories swarmed like mosquitoes to torment him.

Forcing himself to quit the warmth of the bed, he padded across the corridor to the bathroom. The shower was temperamental. When he jiggled the switch, it did not respond. He tried again and, all of a sudden, was half-drowned by a hot gush. It reminded him of Megan.

He wasn't sorry Megan never wanted to see him again. She'd saved him the trouble of ending their relationship. He hated causing sadness and upset, hated it. Far better to steal away in the night without a word. That was more romantic; she could read into his departure whatever she wished. He never hurt people with malice aforethought. Nobody seemed to appreciate it, but he had his own moral code.

Towelling himself dry, he heard the ceiling bumping under Sarah Welsby's footsteps. For a moment he became Michael Caine in *Get Carter*, ringing Britt Ekland for a lurid chat while his eavesdropping landlady rocked in her chair. Guy could do with a Britt in his life, but for the time being Sarah would have to do.

When he arrived at the breakfast table, she was frying bread in the kitchen while Clooney scratched at a post in the corner of the room. The cat threw Guy a derisive glance and then carried on. Guy was an equable soul, but nobody likes to be patronised. He was scowling at Clooney's hindquarters when Sarah walked in, bearing a plate of hot toast.

'You do like cats?'

Guy nodded with vigour and attributed his grimace to a spasm of indigestion. No reason to miss out on his full English, though. They agreed that cats were wise and sophisticated creatures and Sarah confided that she'd spent a small fortune installing a state of the art infra-red cat flap in the back door. Guy wished she'd invested in better plumbing. The love and money she lavished on the animal was out of all proportion, in his opinion. She needed a man in her life.

Pity that even the meekest women were as unpredictable as weather. He'd blundered with Megan, telling her how his grandma believed a woman could ensure her partner's undying devotion. Be a maid in the living room, a cook in the kitchen and a whore in the bedroom. This was a quote from a celebrity that he'd read in a newspaper – the bit about his grandma was just for colour, for he'd never known a grandma – but it made good sense. Unfortunately, Megan kept reading magazine articles about assertiveness and being your own person. Guy had no time for that stuff; he loved being *other* people. Their quarrel marked the beginning of the end.

50

As Sarah chattered nineteen to the dozen, he contented himself with an occasional murmur of assent while concentrating on his food. The first mouthful of fat, succulent, pork and leek sausage, smeared with runny egg, made him sigh with pleasure and when he complimented her on the quality of her home-made marmalade her round face glowed.

'The Germans aren't up yet.' She put on a half-shocked look.

'Young love, eh?'

She fiddled with strands of her disorganised hair. 'A distant memory for me, Rob, I'll be honest.'

He put down his knife and fork and bestowed on her his undivided attention. 'A woman like you must have – um, admirers, I'm sure.'

'Admirers?' She gave her habitual, self-deprecating, tinkly laugh. 'Joking, aren't you?'

He shook his head and neither of them said anything for a while. He felt an urge to resume eating before the bacon rashers cooled, but at last she said in a tone of contrived brightness, 'So what will you be up to today?'

'Catching up with the past.'

He said it on the spur of the moment. He'd returned to the Lakes in haste, without an agenda in mind. Life was a fast-flowing river, you could never guess where the current might take you. Yet the moment he uttered the words, he knew where he had to go.

'You were late back last night,' Hannah mumbled as she chewed the last of her breakfast.

51

Marc Amos pulled a stool from beneath the breakfast bar and sat down beside her. He was still in his white gown, smelling of lemon soap; she was aware of his nakedness underneath the towelling. After all these years, he still turned her on. When he'd joined her under the duvet at midnight, she'd been half asleep, but she relished his warmth next to her and she'd have responded if he'd been in the mood. At one time his lust was as predictable as sunrise. But all he did was whisper goodnight and roll over and away from her. Within two minutes he was snoring.

'Sorry, should have phoned. Leigh and I got caught up talking to the agent. By the time we'd got rid of him, the two of us were dying for a bite to eat, so we went to a bistro and chewed over the business plan. Next time I looked at my watch, it was half past ten and I didn't want to disturb you. Thought you might be in bed. Don't suppose you made any more toast?'

She shook her head. Marc had a flair for camouflaging thoughtlessness as care and consideration. 'I'll be off in a minute. You know where the toaster is.'

'Don't you want to hear about the business plan?'

She spotted the trap. If she reminded him that police officers started work long before second-hand bookshop owners with obliging staff, he'd put on his mournful look and say she was always too busy, and they needed to talk more. One thing *he* never wanted to talk about was her miscarriage at the end of last summer. She'd become pregnant by accident, but after losing the baby she felt

52

suffocated by grief. While he'd never said as much, she knew the prospect of fatherhood frightened Marc. Or perhaps it was the prospect of taking on responsibility for another human life.

'Fire away.'

His eyes widened; he'd not expected her to show interest. She ought to do better, she told herself with a pang of guilt, instead of getting hung up on Marc's blind spots. A relationship was a two-way thing.

'Sedbergh's close to the motorway and developing a reputation as England's book town. Leigh's doubled her turnover in eighteen months, so an upmarket café is crucial. We'll formalise our partnership and divide the premises between us. Half for books, half for people to browse over coffee and a snack.'

They chatted for five minutes before she had to go. It was a long time since she'd seen him so energised about the fortunes of the shop. For Marc, books were objects of beauty, to be loved, not just read. Catching up with tax returns and stock inventories came a poor second to the surge of joy at finding a rare first edition at a fair. Leigh Moffat had, beneath her demure exterior, a shrewd brain; he was right, together they made a good combination. But Hannah caught herself wondering whether that was all they made.

Listening in her Lexus to Rufus Wainwright's mournful vocals on 'Go Ask Shakespeare', she told herself not to be so stupid. Jealousy was Marc's vice, not hers. For years he'd suspected her sergeant, Nick Lowther, of lusting after her. Wrong and unfair. And it wasn't as if Marc had always been a one-woman man. In the early days of their relationship, he'd had a fling with Leigh's younger sister Dale.

These last few weeks, Marc seemed to have lost interest in sex, which was akin to Casanova taking up celibacy. She'd experienced a flutter of paranoia when he passed on gossip that Vicky, a skinny graduate who was working in the shop supposedly to pay off her student debts, had squandered her earnings on a spectacular boob job. Was he secretly hoping she might follow suit? All things considered, she'd rather worry about his running off with Leigh.

A red light loomed and she stamped on her brake. That was the trouble with being a detective. You wound up suspecting everybody and everything.

The rain had died away overnight, but Guy knew the Lakes well enough to wrap up warm and prepare for the worst. A fortnight before their final row, Megan had paid to kit him out in the wet-weather gear that walking in Snowdonia demanded. He'd said he would reimburse her when the big futures deal came through, but obviously her behaviour rendered the promise null and void. It served her right that there was no big futures deal. When he said he planned on going for a walk, Sarah filled a flask and insisted on lending him her mobile phone and a torch.

Outside, the wind's edge scraped his cheeks like a blade. At the head of the lake, he sat on a bench and read a couple of chapters from a dog-eared *David Copperfield* that he'd picked up from a charity shop. Small children squealed while their anorak-clad mothers prattled about soap operas and celebrity scandals.

This time last year, he'd still been in Rome, squashed into a one-bedroom apartment with Farfalla and her one-year-old, Bianca. He'd met her the day Maryell, the wealthy American widow whose suite at the Boscolo Palace he'd shared, discovered that he wasn't a celebrated English artist after all. He'd told Farfalla that he was a spy working for the British government. At the time he was reading *The Woman in White* and he amused himself by telling her that it was his sourcebook for deciphering top secret codes. Trouble was, he discovered that he wasn't the only one leading a double life. Farfalla meant 'butterfly' and she lived up to her name. All the time she was supposedly waitressing on the Via Cavour, she was sleeping with a minicab driver who made a fortune fleecing tourists new to the city. Guy knew it couldn't last. Language was a barrier, and then there was the child. Farfalla decided to move in with her fancy man, and forty-eight hours later Guy was chatting up Megan by the check-in desk at Fiumicino airport. She'd walked out on her job as a nanny when the kids' father wanted her to perform services never mentioned in the contract she'd signed with the agency.

Guy stuffed the book into his pocket and contemplated the inky water. Those cold depths had been the resting place of Donald Campbell, who sacrificed his life in quest of speed, his boat somersaulting as he strained to reach 300 miles per hour. Guy remembered seeing black and white footage of Campbell before the accident. A suave, Brylcreemed Englishman, cigarette in hand. A charmer, a ladies' man, the sort of chap Guy might have become, had he been a couple of generations older. After thirty-odd years, the wreck of *Bluebird* was found and lifted from the bottom of the lake, tail fin intact, still proudly bearing the Union Jack. Campbell's remains were recovered at last. It was right and proper that the dead should receive a decent burial.

Emma Bestwick would be forty now, older than the gossiping women. He wouldn't speculate on what course her life might have taken. What was done was done. But he ought to pay his respects.

The wind had dropped as he ambled into the village, past the deserted bowling green and tennis courts, glancing in windows of shops that sold fishing tackle and Kendal mint cake, hiking boots and waterproof gear. When he glanced over the roofs towards the bracken-covered slopes, his stomach lurched. The road bent at the bridge and he stopped to take a deep breath and listen to the rush and gurgle of the beck. Across the road the bell tower of the church of St Andrew loomed above a small burial ground dotted with clusters of snowdrops. A sign pointed to the tall carved cross that marked John Ruskin's grave. Ruskin had opted to be buried here, in preference to Westminster Abbey. What a waste. Guy couldn't understand why Ruskin hadn't wanted to finish up in splendour. One day he'd have his own fifteen minutes of fame, and he'd make the most of them.

56

He consulted his watch. A 14 carat Rolex Oyster Perpetual, benefiting from a champagne dial and gold index markers, picked up in a dodgy bar off the Via Veneto. On the stroke of noon he strolled into a low-beamed pub and ordered a pint of strong bitter beer, brewed on the premises. He didn't need to slake his thirst. But the alcohol made his head buzz, eased the memory of the last time he'd climbed the fells behind the pub, on his way to meet Emma Best-wick.

Hannah and Lauren Self should have had a lot in common. Two senior women in a man's world. Loosening up after a couple of drinks, Lauren liked to talk about girl power and how women in the force needed to look out for each other. A politician to her beautifully manicured fingertips, she'd been fast-tracked to the giddy rank of Assistant Chief Constable by dint of relentless focus on telling councillors on the police authority precisely what they wanted to hear. Hannah preferred to keep a safe distance from the ACC. But, when she wasn't schmoozing with the great and the good, Lauren wasn't a bad detective. If she wanted to find you, there was no hiding place. She cornered Hannah by the water cooler.

'Hannah, just the person! This news coverage of the Emma Bestwick case, what is CCRT's action plan?'

Lauren loved acronyms as much as Home Office statistics and high profile campaigns against institutional discrimination. It was a safe bet that she had never heard of Emma Bestwick until the press office had served up the cuttings, but Tony Di Venuto's piece must have concentrated her mind.

Hannah gave a butter-wouldn't-melt simper and said, 'I've requisitioned the old papers and prioritised a formal review. Let's see if some joined-up thinking can produce a few outcomes.'

If Lauren realised she was being sent up, her glossy smile betrayed nothing. 'Terrific. We need to stay ahead of the game on this.'

'We're short-handed at present. Nick Lowther will be in court for another week, and Linz Waller and Gul Khan are working on a possible DNA match in the Furness rapist inquiry. The Bestwick case is the longest of long shots. You're happy to devote resources to a review?'

'We need to respond to public concern, Hannah. You still have Les, Maggie and Bob Swindell at your beck and call. I'm surprised you haven't organised a formal press briefing. CCRT is a high-profile unit and we want journalists to understand the value of local police work, benefiting from our can-do culture. Plus our commitment to working in close partnership with the community.'

In other words, we need to position ourselves for the day when a force merger comes back on the agenda. Hannah assumed an obedient expression as she filled her cup to the brim.

'Understood.'

Lauren smiled. 'Excellent. Keep me in the loop.'

'Will do,' Hannah said, sticking her tongue out

58

at the ACC's elegant, retreating back.

At least she had an excuse to put the dip sampling tapes back in a drawer. She'd never wanted this job; Lauren had sidelined her after the Rao trial went pear-shaped. In part a rebuke, in part a convenient way of making sure that Hannah didn't start getting above herself or – Heaven forbid – grabbing a share of the girl power. Hannah couldn't care less about status; something Lauren would never understand.

At last, Hannah was appreciating the positives of cold case work. She liked the people in her team, enjoyed making up her own rules. Above all, she relished becoming a detective again, rather than telling other people what to do and worrying about how well they would do it. If the choice was between interviewing suspects and attending endless meetings to discuss the latest measures of police service efficiency, it was a no-brainer.

Back in her office, she leafed through old statements. Might Tony Di Venuto have figured in the original investigation? She found no mention of his name.

'Solved it yet?' Les asked.

She'd been so engrossed, she hadn't even heard him lumber into the room. 'If only.'

He peered over her shoulder at the file photograph of Emma and sniffed. 'Ms Ordinary, eh?'

Harsh, but fair. Emma wasn't plain, but neither were her looks special. The only extraordinary thing to have happened in her life was that she had disappeared without trace.

'I don't think she was a warm woman. Hardly

any close friends.'

'Boyfriends?'

'She preferred other women.'

'I suppose you're expecting me to say that was just because she'd not met the right feller?'

Hannah laughed. 'Sid Thornicroft wondered if her disappearance was connected with her sex life.'

'She'd met someone new and gone off with her?'

'It was a theory. But we found no trace of any new friendships after she split up with Alexandra Clough.'

He parked his rear on a corner of her desk. 'No suggestion she was being stalked?'

'Not by Alex Clough, if that's what you're thinking.'

'I was wondering about men. Just because a woman isn't available, doesn't mean some dickhead won't obsess about her.'

'Sid Thornicroft thought that if she had been murdered, the likeliest candidate was a chap called Tom Inchmore. He worked as a handyman at the Museum of Myth and Legend and mooned after Emma. According to the Cloughs, it was simply because she treated him with kindness. But when Sid found he had a record of minor sexual offences, a lightbulb flashed in his brain.'

'I'm guessing you weren't Sid's number one fan.'

A throwaway remark by Ben Kind, in the pub one night, surfaced in her mind. *Sid Thornicroft? So pedestrian, he never steps off the pavement.* She shrugged.

60

'What did Inchmore do?'

'Two cautions as a teenager. Once for stealing an old woman's undies off her washing line and once for peeping into a girls' changing room at the gym of a local school. In Sid's opinion, steps on the road to rape and murder.'

'It wouldn't be the first time.'

'Yeah, well, I was sent to tease a confession out of Tom Inchmore.'

She could see him now, an acne-ravaged young man with scruffy black hair and a furtive demeanour who spent too much time peering at her breasts and not enough mumbling answers to her questions. Tom was one of life's losers; she couldn't help feeling sorry for him. His mother was dead and he lived with his grandmother, Edith Inchmore, a warty, bad-tempered old hag straight out of *Grimm's Fairy Tales*. But Edith had more guts in her little finger than Tom had in his whole body. She simultaneously despised and protected him, engaging a lawyer to warn him not to answer questions and seize every opportunity to complain about police harassment. Hannah had conceived a grudging respect for her determination to safeguard what little was left of the family name. Edith was convinced the police were intent on stitching the lad up. And maybe the old witch wasn't so far off the mark.

'Any joy?'

'None whatsoever. So Sid brought in the nastiest DC in the force to give Inchmore a hard time. But even he didn't manage to beat out a confession.'

'Run a criminal records check. See if Tommy's

61

been a good boy over the past ten years.'
'Over the last five years, certainly.'
'You reckon?'
'He's been dead that long.'
'Oh yeah? How did that happen?'
'Accident. No suspicious circumstances. He fell off a ladder while he was fixing a tile on the roof of the house where he lived.'

Yes, poor Tom Inchmore had been a loser right to the end.

'So, if he did kill Emma, not much chance of finding what he did with the body.'
''Fraid not.'
'No wonder Thornicroft gave up the unequal struggle?'
'To concentrate on improving his golf handicap.'

Les belched to show what he thought about golf. 'Other theories?'

'Emma might have gone for a walk and fallen into a tarn or down a ravine. It happens. But usually to over-adventurous visitors. Not to people born and bred in the Lakes.'
'The usual checks were made?'
'Mountain rescue, helicopters, the lot. An elderly neighbour gave us a lead. Her kitchen looked out towards the fells and when she was taking her washing off the line one afternoon, she said she caught sight of Emma, making her way up a rough track that meanders towards the fells. When we couldn't find any wet-weather clothes in the bungalow, we thought we were on to something. She might have got into difficulties and broken a leg or worse. But the witness was scatty

and couldn't put a date or time on the observation. Besides, Emma was more into yoga than yomping. Nobody knew what was in her wardrobe, so we couldn't check what might be missing. The search of the fells came up with zilch. It's hard enough seeking a needle in a haystack when you're sure the needle is waiting to be found. The weather was against us too. Gales, thunderstorms, landslides, the whole apocalyptic bit.'

Les sighed. 'What about Emma's dark secrets?'

'Her cupboard seemed bare of skeletons.'

'That's suspicious, for a start. Everyone has dark secrets.'

'Even you, Les?'

He scowled. 'Never you mind. How about yourself?'

'If only. They might make me more fascinating.'

'What's up, Hannah?' He bent towards her. 'Feeling unloved?'

His insight shocked her. Swallowing hard, she told herself to take care. This was the danger of working with good detectives. Time for a diversion.

'Lauren bollocked me for not alerting the media about our continuing active interest in Emma's case. To appease Di Venuto, of course.'

He sniggered. 'So she's happy for you to reopen the inquiry?'

'You know what she's like. If something photographs well or merits briefing the media, she'll throw resources at it like confetti.'

He slid off her desk. 'Best let you get on with it, then. Shout if you need me.'

As the door closed behind him, Hannah

groaned. She mustn't let her problems with Marc spill over into her work. Things would sort themselves out. Into her head came the voice of a dead man, Ben Kind, when a row with an odious colleague the week after her promotion to DS drove her to the brink of tears.

'Stop putting yourself down. All you need is more confidence in yourself. Trust me, I'm a policeman.'

Remembering Ben led her to thinking about his son. What was Daniel Kind up to these days? The other night, with Marc out book-hunting and nothing worthwhile on the box, she'd searched against his name on the internet, but found no recent mention of him. Presumably he'd settled down with his pretty girlfriend to live the dream in Brackdale. Maybe one of these days they'd bump into each other again.

She picked up Emma's photograph again and forced her mind back to the unfinished business of the misper investigation. She still believed Emma to be dead, but yearned to be proved wrong. Maybe if they ever met, the two of them would find they had things in common. Things bubbling beneath the surface that nobody else suspected.

CHAPTER FOUR

Families fascinated Hannah. She studied them as others might scrutinise exotic fish in an aquarium. Some glittered and charmed, others bared sharp teeth, all seemed mysterious to her. Supposedly, your sister should be your best friend, but she'd met dozens of sisters who hated the sight of each other. First time around, Hannah hadn't met Karen Erskine. This time she intended to speak to her and her husband – but not yet. She wanted to feel her way back into Emma Bestwick's life and it made sense to start with people she'd interviewed before.

Last time, she'd spent hour after hour trawling through lists of Emma's school contemporaries, teachers, people she'd worked with. Most of their recollections of her were fuzzy. She hadn't made a lasting impression, nobody had bothered to keep in touch. Les was right. Ms Very Ordinary Indeed.

Francis and Vanessa Goddard had given Emma a roof over her head before she came into money. In the early days of the inquiry, Hannah had wondered if Francis had developed an unhealthy interest in their paying guest. Ben Kind had trained her to suspect everyone, but there was no evidence to justify pointing a finger at Francis and in the end Hannah had concluded that what you saw with Francis was what he was. A man in love with his wife. As for Vanessa, she'd been married before. And Jeremy, her first husband, had left her to marry Emma's sister. The Lake District, for all its millions of visitors from the four corners of the globe, remained at heart a gathering of tightly knit communities with everyone seemingly connected to everyone else.

The Goddards hadn't moved house in the past decade and Hannah phoned to make an appointment. With druggies, you never gave advance warning, because by the time you showed up they would have disappeared. But the Goddards were going nowhere and it made sense to observe the courtesies. Hannah needed witnesses on her side if this was to be any more than a wild goose chase.

Vanessa Goddard snatched up the receiver on the second ring. She sounded relieved when Hannah announced herself. Not a universal reaction.

'I thought it might be the school,' she explained in the breathless voice that Hannah remembered. 'Christopher, my boy, was under the weather this morning, a tummy bug. He attends the prep school at Grizedale College, you know. I wasn't sure whether to send him, especially in such dreadful weather, but Francis keeps saying we can't wrap him up in cotton wool. When the phone went, I thought it might be the nurse, to say I needed to bring him home and put him to bed.'

Obviously I've never lived, Hannah thought, never having been a doting mother. Though if I hadn't miscarried...

She said quickly, 'It's ten years since Emma Bestwick disappeared. You may have seen the coverage in the local press.'

A sigh. 'Yes, it brought the memories flooding back. We've been expecting someone would get in touch.'

'You won't remember, but I was the officer who interviewed you and your husband.'

'It's not something you forget in a hurry. We're just normal people, we don't have much to do with the police. So they've made you a Chief Inspector? My goodness. I suppose I should feel honoured.'

Hannah didn't think Vanessa Goddard was taking the mickey. She remembered her as a friendly, talkative woman who lived on her nerves, but she'd have felt more flattered if Vanessa hadn't sounded startled by her promotion.

'These days I'm in charge of the county's Cold Case Review Team.'

'I read about it. Don't you specialise in unsolved murders, DNA, that sort of thing?' An intake of breath. 'Has a body been found?'

'No, no. We are taking another look at the case, that's all. First things first. I presume you never heard anything from Emma after we last met?'

'Not a word.' The answer was so quiet that Hannah had to strain to hear.

'I wonder if I could come over and speak to you and your husband about Emma.'

'What for?'

'We have to consider if anything was overlooked last time.'

'Such as?' Not frosty, just puzzled.

'Anything that might lead us to Emma.'

'But what good will it do?'

67

Hannah stifled the urge to snap. 'Don't you want to find out what happened to her, Mrs Goddard?'

'I'm not a detective,' Vanessa said. 'Do you recall, when we last met, I told you I believed she was still alive?'

'I remember.'

'I've changed my mind. Ten years is a long time. Too long for Emma to disappear without making contact with anyone she cared about. I've had to come to terms with the fact that she won't be coming back. She must be dead, nothing else makes sense.' A pause. 'To be honest, Chief Inspector, I'd rather not know the horrid details of whatever happened to her. I prefer to remember her as she was.'

Hannah gritted her teeth. *Perhaps you do. But that option isn't open to me.*

As Guy strode out of the pub, the sun sneaked out of hiding. He followed the steep and narrow road by the side of the building. Beyond the fell gate, the road became a rough cart track, running alongside the deep gill of Church Beck. Rain had swelled the stream and below the old stone miners' bridge the crash of the waterfall was louder than he remembered. Light skipped on the cascade.

The sun scurried back behind a dark cloud as he surveyed the broad plain. How bleak was his valley. Heaps of spoil from the quarries reared up beyond the trickling stream. On the right, a row of old labourers' cottages; above them the red-grey Yewdale Fells. The whitewashed buildings, once occupied by officials of the mining companies, were now given up to a hostel and a centre for mountaineers. Ahead, the fells towered above patches of wilderness. Their names drifted back to mind. Raven Tor, on the left, and further on, splitting two troughs of land, Kernal Crag and Tongue Brow.

Men had quarried here since Roman times and the fell-sides bore the wounds to prove it. Coppermines Valley fascinated him, every pock-marked inch. He imagined explosions echoing around the fells when gunpowder blasted a fresh tunnel or shot-hole. Megan had complained he was superficial, thinking of his taste for little luxuries, but she was mistaken, as usual. He liked to look beneath the surface of things, every now and then. He'd trade a dozen pretty Buttermeres, a score of jam-packed Amblesides, for the moody desolation of this acned valley.

Even on a February afternoon, a few diehard walkers were out and about. Not wanting company, he zig-zagged away from recognised pathways and through the bracken. His boots struck a fragment of rusty track on which mine wagons once trundled and he stopped to rub his aching calves. Christ, he was out of condition. Once he'd roamed the fells for hours without so much as tweaking a muscle. How many times had he scrambled over these ice-smoothed rocks and the scree, clambering along the hidden trails leading to the blackness of Levens Water?

Blobs of rain spattered his jacket. He stumbled on the slippery ground and realised he was out of practice at drinking strong beer. His throat was sore, his head buzzing. It had drizzled that afternoon ten years ago. He could see the stone cairn where he had met Emma Bestwick for the one and only time.

In his mind, he pictured her, a tall, solidly built woman encased in a wax jacket. Fine strands of hair escaped from her hood; in other circumstances he might have caressed them. The long pull up the old track had left her short of breath and she didn't speak when he apologised for bringing her out on such a miserable day. Until he saw her approaching, he'd feared she wouldn't come. She was taking a risk, meeting a man she didn't know in such a quiet spot. Nobody else was in sight. Perhaps beneath the quiet exterior she had a wild and reckless streak. Of course she understood his insistence on secrecy. When he offered his hand, she didn't respond, but her tense half-smile never flickered as he explained what he believed she ought, in all conscience, to do. For five minutes he convinced himself that he could persuade her to change her mind and make everything all right.

'Sorry.'

Her voice was as sharp as a shard of glass. He'd miscalculated, this woman was determined not to compromise. She was immune to reason, let alone charm. He'd taken such pains to be sympathetic. OK, there was something in it for him, but he wasn't simply doing this for his own selfish ends. For once in his life he was playing the Good Samaritan and repaying past kindness. She ought to meet him half way, surely that wasn't too much to ask?

'But if...'

'I promised to listen, it was the least I could do. But I've made my decision. There's no going back.'

'If you'll only...'

'No more, please. Arguing will only make matters worse.'

'You gave your word!'

She shrugged: *so what?*

The sheer bloody unfairness of it made his temples throb. He hated being rebuffed, especially by a woman. Growing up without parents had made him want to be wanted, but despite his taking such trouble, she hadn't moved an inch. Not a fucking inch.

He seized her arm, but she was stronger than he'd expected and she shrugged free of him with as much scorn as if he were one of those beggars who used to hang around the Colosseum, pestering for cash.

'How dare you touch me!' She hissed with disdain.

Even in the cold and wet, his skin burned with outrage. Who was she to treat him like a piece of shit? She ought to be glad to do as he asked. That was the deal with women. You acted kind and sensitive and they owed you something in return.

He strove for calm, despite her provocation. 'You made a promise. There's no going back on it.'

She stared at him, defiance mixing with a grimace of triumph.

'I won't be bullied. Can't you understand? I changed my mind. It's that simple, there's no more to be said.'

She turned to leave and he reached for her again. This time she was ready to dodge his grasp, but in twisting away she caught her toe on a stone and lost her footing. A moment later, she was lying on the floor and he was bending over her. It was akin to conquest. Adrenaline surged through him. She was at his mercy, he could do whatever he wanted.

'Wait. I haven't finished talking.'

She didn't utter another word as she lifted herself up. All she did was show her teeth in contempt, as if he were a flea-ridden mongrel. That said everything. To her, he wasn't a smart, sophisticated intermediary, someone with whom she could do business. She could see right through him, see the man he was, deep inside.

'Listen to me!' he shouted.

She spat in his face.

He brought his hand down to slap her, but she dodged out of reach. In so doing, she slipped on the icy ground. As she tumbled, she hit her head on a small boulder. The cracking of her skull sounded like a rifle shot.

Guy blinked the dampness away, told himself it was rain, not tears. For a decade, he'd blocked out every detail of his brief encounter with Emma Bestwick. But here there was no escaping her.

He couldn't see a living soul. Even in summer, when the hills were alive with the sound of walkers, few people bothered with this unlovely cleft in the landscape. Within a radius of two or three miles, there were so many more rewarding walks and climbs. No shimmering tarns and breath-snatching vistas at Mispickel Scar. Even in the height of summer, it was chill and eerie. After the miners left, nobody else had much reason to explore its nooks and crannies, seldom lit by sun filtering through the crags. Ten years ago, he'd loved coming here on his own, it was the one place where he wasn't seized by the compulsion to become someone else. And then Emma Bestwick stole it from him, transformed it into forbidden territory, a place to which he dared not return. Until today.

Picking his way with exaggerated care, he crossed a centuries-old packhorse way, chiselled by hand from solid rock. Breathing hard, limbs hurting. He felt like one of those lumbering beasts of burden, saddle-bags stuffed with ore, though he'd barely climbed a thousand feet. A gash in the rocks loomed up. A sign bore the word DANGER in tall red letters. He read the warning underneath.

Proceed no further. This route is unsafe and fatal accidents have occurred.

Fatal accidents? Too right.

Impossible to stop now. How had he managed to drag Emma here? Fear and terror must have endowed him with strength.

Something puzzled him. He halted in mid-stride, trying to fathom what was wrong. The profile of the landscape was not as he remembered. At first he thought he must be lost. Ten years was a long time, it was easy to become confused in the absence of landmarks. The stone cairn was far below and out of sight.

Every inch of his last journey to Mispickel Scar was logged in his brain. From a distance, the crags and the ground below looked unchanging, eternal. But nature kept moving on. Nothing stayed the same forever.

There had been a landslide. Part of the rock-face had collapsed, burying a section of the old track. Mispickel Scar was notoriously unstable. From the archives of memory, he retrieved climbers' talk of a terrifying landslip engulfing the site of the old works, half a century or more ago. History had repeated itself.

A pile of debris, crude and unstable, covered the ground in the depression between the sheer faces of the crags. As he clambered up and over the obstacle course, he peered round, trying in vain to spot a familiar pillar of stone, perched so precariously beside the pathway that nobody could ever be sure what kept it standing. Walkers knew it as the Sword of Damocles.

Shit, where's the Sword gone?

The first time he'd reached this point and stepped past the Sword, he'd thought of the scene in *Lost Horizon,* when in the midst of the snowy wastes, the travellers suddenly pass into the green and pleasant land of Shangri-La. But Mispickel Scar wasn't somewhere people lived forever. Quite the reverse. He hauled himself up on to the slippery stone connecting the rocks and gazed down towards the ancient workings.

Jesus Christ.

The sight snatched his breath away. At last he'd solved the puzzle that had tormented him ever since reading Tony Di Venuto's article – *why hadn't she been found?* Even in this God-forsaken spot, people would descend the most dangerous holes in the ground. After he'd done what he had to do, he'd lugged chunks of rubble to block the access to the shaft, but none would have deterred anyone intent on entering the old miners' tunnels. He'd assumed it was inevitable that Emma's body would turn up eventually, discovered by some adventurous explorer. Her death would be put down as an accident. Now the reason why her disappearance remained a mystery lay before his eyes.

The Sword had collapsed into the midst of the stones scattered below, breaking into two and bringing with it a mass of smaller rocks. The opening of the shaft was no longer visible. There wasn't a clue to suggest it had ever been there.

He stood rooted to the spot, letting the wind graze his cheeks. His nose was running and he wiped it with his sleeve. If someone wanted to know why he'd come back here, he could offer no answer. So often he did things that seemed logical at the time, but impossible to rationalise later. Yet he was sure it was right to return. He needed to pay his respects.

At last he tore himself away and began to retrace his steps. It felt colder and the mist was coming down. Soon darkness would fall. He must get back to the village. He'd lingered too long, careless of the rules of walking the fells. Not a soul knew where he'd wandered. His boots slid on a patch of ice and his legs gave way.

He raised his arms to break his fall. As he hit the ground, he scraped his hip and hurt his hands. The shock left him gasping.

Shit, shit, shit. If he hurt himself so badly that he could no longer move, nobody would come running to the rescue. Hours would pass before Sarah raised the alarm. It would not take long to freeze to death.

Gingerly, he struggled to his feet. Thank God, nothing was broken. No harm done except for bruising. He forced himself to move, intent on beating the mist and the twilight. The cold chewed at his face and his limbs were throbbing. He shut out the pain and the memories, shut out everything except the need to keep slithering down the fell.

At last he reached a shelf of rock above Coppermines. He gazed towards the village of slate and the broad sheet of water beyond. He'd made it. So what if he'd been foolhardy? He'd be all right now, he'd got away with it. As usual, Megan would say.

He could hear it now, that familiar lilting reproach, tinged with reluctant admiration.

'You're such a lucky devil.'

Amos Books occupied a converted mill, and even with the windows shut to keep out the winter blast you could hear the water crashing over the weir. Daniel spotted Marc Amos in the local history section on the first floor, talking into his mobile, running a hand through untamed fair hair. In checked shirt and patched denim jeans, he was a carelessly attractive man, his looks marred only by a spoiled-boy pout when something didn't suit him. When he noticed Daniel, he

76

mimed impatience to get off the phone. Daniel leaned against the shelves that stretched from floor to ceiling, inhaling the aroma of old books. Musty, yes, but an addictive fragrance.

'Sorry, but we haven't seen a first edition of *Cards on the Table* in wrapper for years. If we found one, it would cost an arm and a leg, given the money the Japanese collectors are splashing around. All we have left is a scruffy reading copy of a first edition. Ex-library, dampstains, foxing, weak hinges, every disability known to man. I'll carry on searching, but... OK, keep in touch.'

Marc switched off the phone and bounded down the aisle between the shelves like an enthusiastic mongrel. The ancient wooden floorboards squawked in protest under his feet. His grin of welcome was warm. He made customers feel good about indulging their bibliomania, perhaps because the disease afflicted him too.

'Long time, no see. How's the writing going?'

'Slow progress. Don't let me interrupt if you're busy.'

'My trouble is, I like interruptions too much. I'd be better off if I didn't, but it can't be bad for business to pass the time of day with a customer. Do you fancy a coffee?'

In the café downstairs, they exchanged pleasantries with Leigh Moffat, serving behind the counter. She was dark, attractive and self-contained. Daniel noticed the delicacy with which she wiped away a sliver of cake that slipped onto Marc's smooth wrist. She and Marc seemed so at ease with each other, he was tempted to wonder if there was more between them than a strictly business relationship. Wishful thinking, he told himself as they found a table beside a window looking out on the stream. He was casting round for reasons not to feel bad about being fascinated by Hannah Scarlett.

Sipping the froth on his cappuccino, Marc murmured, 'Trecilla told me that you're interested in John Ruskin and local industry.'

'I've been reading a lot of Ruskin lately.'

'There's a lot of Ruskin to read. I sold a complete set to an American collector last year. Thirty-odd volumes, nine million words, something like that.'

Daniel grinned. 'I may skip a bit. He was an opinionated old bugger. Even so, I'm getting hooked.'

'You're not the only one. Tolstoy was a fan, along with Proust. They say Mahatma Gandhi's life was changed by devouring Ruskin on a train trip across Africa. Are you thinking of writing about him?'

'Who knows? Now the cottage renovations are finished, Miranda's on my case. She doesn't want me to vegetate. But I'd have to do more than simply dig over old ground. I'm casting around for ideas that haven't been done to death. By the sleepy standards of nineteenth-century Cumberland, Coniston was an industrial metropolis. What did Ruskin make of what was going on in his own village, I wonder? Did he lecture the men who owned the slate mines across the lake, or was he afraid of upsetting his neighbours?'

'He was never famed for his diplomacy.'

'Exactly, but I'm short of sources. Without

them, you can scrabble around forever like a hen in a yard, looking for scraps to feed off. So where better to look than this Aladdin's cave of yours?'

Marc waved at the thousands of books surrounding them. 'Be my guest.'

'Maybe one of these days I'll drop lucky again. Last year I picked up a set of letters at an auction which gave a contemporary account of Ruskin's arguments with the steel barons of Barrow.'

'He'll rest easier in his grave, with the steelworks closed down. Shame it took a hundred years. People used to say he was mad, didn't they? Especially when he retreated to Brantwood and never wrote another word. All those dangerous heresies they feared would bring the nation to its knees. The welfare state, corporate responsibility, campaigning against industrial pollution.'

Daniel grinned. 'I hear you're opening in Sedbergh.'

'Nothing is definite. Leigh's excited about branching out and so am I. The real challenge is persuading Hannah that another business loan wouldn't take us down the road to perdition.'

'She isn't keen?'

A shrug. 'Who can blame her? She brings in more money than I do. And there's no index-linked, tax-payer funded pension for second-hand bookdealers. Like all police officers, she's a dyed-in-the-wool cynic. You don't realise how lucky you are with Miranda.'

'Lucky?'

'Wasn't it her idea to downshift to the Lakes? A bold move, to throw up tenure at Oxford. Going

79

for the dream. But I guess you've never regretted it.'

'Too right I haven't.' *Though maybe Miranda has.* 'So – how is Hannah?'

'Overworked, otherwise fine. Speaking of Coniston, she's over there today, something to do with one of the cold cases.'

'Give her my best.'

Marc nodded. 'That business at Old Sawrey...'

'Uh-huh?' Even now, he flinched at the memory of the way he'd blundered into Hannah's investigation.

'I know she's wondered how you coped with it all. She knew your father, I guess she felt a kind of responsibility for you.'

'I shouldn't have poked my nose in.'

Marc drained his cup. 'What happened wasn't your fault. She told me how much you helped her.'

'She did?' Daniel felt an embarrassing surge of pleasure, like a hapless schoolboy complimented on an unexpectedly good report.

'Yeah. According to her, you'd make a good detective. After all, it's in your blood.'

Hannah hadn't encountered either Alexandra Clough or her father during the original inquiry, but from all she'd heard, Emma's former lover was an ice maiden. The impression was confirmed as soon as she rang to ask for a meeting.

'It was ten years ago, for goodness' sake.' A cool voice, superior, doubtless the product of a pricey education. 'Why rake over old coals?'

It took Hannah five minutes to persuade her to

agree to an interview. Today was impossible, Alex insisted, she and her father were far too busy. It sounded like an excuse, the delay a reprisal for having to surrender to the inevitable. Hannah was left in no doubt that this whole cold case nonsense was some form of PR guff, so that the police could curry favour with a journalist who had column inches to fill.

'I must ask you not to bother my father excessively. He's seventy-five, you know.'

'I understand that he still runs the museum?'

'You may have forgotten, I've been the manager here since he turned sixty. My father founded the museum; naturally he continues to advise me. But I put you on notice, he has a heart condition. Last year the doctors fitted a pacemaker. A police interrogation is the last thing he needs. If anything should happen to him...'

'I'm not proposing an interrogation, just to ask a few questions.'

An elaborate sigh. 'I can assure you, Chief Inspector, that at the time Emma Bestwick disappeared, we told your colleagues everything we knew.'

Not quite, Hannah thought. True, you did both say a great deal. But you didn't actually *tell* us very much at all.

Suppose I did no more than stumble across her body? If only I hadn't panicked. Emma wasn't murdered, there was no intent. She died a natural death.

As Guy walked down Campbell Road, a narrative took shape in his brain. This was his gift, to reinvent his life so as to wipe away the petty

81

mishaps and misdemeanours. They confused so many people. Too often folk saw him as a liar and a cheat rather than a man misunderstood. By the time he sauntered into Sarah Welsby's kitchen, he was brimming with good cheer.

'Had a good day, Rob?'

His full-wattage smile encouraged her to start jabbering away while she loaded the dishwasher. Shopping, a conversation with the German guests, a rambling anecdote about an elderly neighbour whose poodle had been put down.

When she paused for breath, he said, 'Tell you what. Why don't I take you out for a meal tonight? There are a couple of good restaurants close by.'

'Oh, but I couldn't possibly...'

He raised a hand. 'No objections, please. Do we have a date?'

She blushed. 'I suppose we do.'

As he left the kitchen, his eye caught today's copy of the *Post* on the work surface. Emma's sister must be tormented by the not-knowing, if the journalist was to be believed. Without closure, she could not move on. Why not bring the story to an end? Time was a healer, it was safe now. Nobody could prove anything against him. He was ready to draw a line under the tragedy. How better than by telling a little of what he knew?

Compassion seized him. *The tragedy.* That was precisely the phrase he'd been groping for all these years. To call it murder was foolhardy and wrong. OK, he'd blundered, but to err was human. He wanted to make amends, to do the right thing. Redemption lay in putting Karen out of her misery and ending the years of uncertainty and despair.

Yes, Karen deserved closure and he had the power to grant it to her. He would be wise and gracious. He would reveal where Emma had been lain to rest.

CHAPTER FIVE

Thurston Water House, residence of the Goddards, was a double-fronted Victorian villa. Set back from the road, it was a stroll away from the steamship pier, but guarded from the trippers' gaze by spreading oaks and a hawthorn hedge. Ten years ago, Hannah had asked herself how a nurse and a librarian could afford such a place on public sector pay. Sinister speculation was dashed when Francis explained that Goddards had lived in these parts since the days when the lake was known as Thurston Water. His great-great-grandfather had owned a gunpowder works at Elterwater and made a fortune out of those who blew holes in the hillside. This house was the fruit of all that destruction.

Francis answered the door. Ten years hadn't aged him. Tall and gawky, he still resembled an overgrown schoolboy in a sleeveless cricket sweater and paint-splashed corduroy jeans. Hannah remembered her surprise at learning that he and his wife shared a passion for dancing; he looked as though he had two left feet. But she'd found his awkward eagerness appealing, even as she wondered if he was capable of murder.

'Good to see you again, Chief Inspector. Sorry I'm in my scruffs. I'm on a day off from the hospital and Christopher's room needs repainting. Goodbye Rupert Bear and Nut Wood. Hello Dr Who and scary aliens from outer space.'

The smell of coffee wafted from the kitchen at the rear into the hallway as Francis led her into the front sitting room. The leather furniture was stained where a ballpoint pen had leaked, a dozen children's DVDs tottered in a tower beside the home cinema system. Bookcases groaned under Folio Society editions of classic novels, on the mantelpiece a small silver cup inscribed *Come Cumbrian Dancing – runners-up 2004* was surrounded by photographs of Vanessa, Francis and their boy. *Shrek* was playing soundlessly on the TV. Francis flicked the remote, and the green ogre and skinny grey donkey vanished.

'Take a seat, Chief Inspector. Vanessa won't be long, she's just helping Christopher with a project for school. Can I offer you a coffee, do you take milk?'

Whilst he slipped out of the room, Hannah sank into the embrace of a cavernous armchair. Facing her was a photograph of the three Goddards standing next to a gigantic Mickey Mouse under a Californian sun. The boy was lanky, the image of his father. He was clasping a sleek white iPod, staring proudly into the camera lens while his parents smiled fondly down at him.

'Christopher was a babe in arms when I last

saw him,' Hannah said as her host returned bearing two steaming mugs.

'Amazing how time flies. We went to Disneyworld last summer and he's shot up since. But you wanted to speak to us about Emma?'

'Thanks for seeing me. You spoke to Tony Di Venuto, I gather?'

'I should have refused to say a word,' Francis said. 'I told Vanessa it was only a matter of time before the police came knocking on our door. If only to keep that bloody journalist off their backs.'

Hannah remembered the patience with which he'd answered her questions the first time they'd met. Remembered wondering if he'd killed Emma after she'd turned him down, and dumped the body in the lake. He'd lived cheek by jowl with her throughout his wife's pregnancy. Suppose he wasn't getting enough sex, might he have turned his attention to the lodger? But by the time she'd finished questioning him, the theory had lost its lustre. Perhaps Emma was dead, but surely Francis was too decent a man to have killed her?

'Even after all this time, people may recall something they didn't mention during the original inquiry.'

He scratched his head. 'We did our best to help before. I'm not sure what more we can say.'

'You and Mrs Goddard were among the last people to see Emma before she disappeared. She called here the afternoon before the last sighting of her.'

'She was a friend. The three of us kept in touch even though she wasn't living here any more.'

85

'Anything to suggest that she might be unhappy in Coniston, ready to move on?'

He shook his head. 'Don't forget, Christopher was only a few weeks old. We were both preoccupied with our baby, not visitors. Emma was sweet, she came to drop off a couple of things that she'd knitted for him. She was here for no more than half an hour. She may have mentioned how business was going. Slowly, I think.'

'Did that worry her?'

'She was disappointed, but there was no need to panic. She'd spent a fortune on advertising, but it takes time to build up a reputation and a clientele.'

'She was enjoying such work as she had?'

'As far as we could tell. After she went missing, Vanessa and I wondered if we should have offered more help. But if you have a family, Chief Inspector, you'll know that nobody is as self-absorbed as a first-time parent.'

'You never had any other lodgers?'

'No, Emma was our one and only. The upkeep on this place is pretty heavy, so a few extra pounds came in useful. Emma and my wife had made friends and when she said she didn't like the room she was renting in Hawkshead, we decided to do each other a bit of good. It was never a long-term arrangement. After Christopher was born, we wanted the house to ourselves.'

'How did you cope with the loss of income?'

'I left the NHS and started nursing at the private hospital over in Newby Bridge to help make ends meet. We're not rolling in it, but we get by.'

'How long did she stay here?'

'Not far short of a year. She was never any trouble. The perfect guest, if you like.'

'Did she ever bring friends back here?'

'Alexandra Clough, yes, a couple of times, before they split up. Nobody else. Emma was a very private person. Content with her own company.'

'The last time you saw her, did you pick up any suggestion that she was under financial pressure?'

'None. Even if holistic therapies weren't a money-spinner, she was better off than ever. Don't forget, she'd inherited enough to buy the bungalow and a new car.'

'The inheritance, yes.' Hannah crossed her legs. 'It's rather mysterious. We never found any evidence that Emma had inherited a penny. Karen Erskine knew nothing about a legacy, the sisters didn't have any rich relatives who'd shuffled off this mortal coil. What did Emma tell you about this windfall?'

'Only that she'd come into money unexpectedly. We were delighted for her and of course it did salve our consciences. With a child on the way, we wanted to turn Emma's rooms on the top floor into a playroom with a store area for the baby's things, but we dreaded having to ask her to leave. But everything worked out for the best.'

'Her sister couldn't think of anyone who might have left her a sizeable bequest.'

'The two of them weren't close, it might be somebody Karen knew nothing about.'

Hannah sipped her coffee. An Arabic blend, too strong for her taste. 'When she put down the

87

deposit on her bungalow, she paid cash. Same with the Fiat she bought. A probate solicitor would pay out legatees by cheque, but her bank account didn't reveal a significant payment in during the twelve months before she disappeared.'

'Odd.'

'Emma told her sister and Alex Clough that she'd won a big prize on the lottery. When we checked, that wasn't true. Why would she lie to them, do you think? Or to the two of you?'

He stared at her. 'Emma had no reason to deceive us. We were glad for her. After years of not having two pence to rub together, finally she could please herself.'

The door opened and Vanessa Goddard bustled in. Small and buxom with frizzy red shoulder-length hair, she wore a black tee shirt and denim jeans. Her plump arms were freckled, her lipstick vivid. A port-wine birthmark the shape of Africa spread across her left cheek. When they'd first met, Hannah's eyes kept straying to it and she'd felt hot with embarrassment. But Vanessa had taken no notice; she'd had a lifetime to acclimatise to people staring on first acquaintance. She sat beside her husband on the sofa, their bodies touching. Francis's hand strayed to her knee, her shoulder rubbed against his.

'Sorry to keep you, Chief Inspector, but Christopher needed help with a Google search. Homework's changed since the three of us were at school. Now, what can we do for you?'

Hannah wasn't flattered by the implication that they were much of an age. Vanessa must be fifty now, her husband a few years her junior. Perhaps

88

having a child later in life made you feel younger. How would Marc react if she told him she was expecting a baby again? Would she see that same trapped look on his face?

Jesus, this was no use. She needed to concentrate.

'Did Emma ever talk about her time in Liverpool, mention the people she knew there?'

'She flitted from job to job. Temping for accountants and lawyers, a spell working on reception at a hotel, another as a PA at the Women's Hospital. She never found her niche, that's why she came back to the Lakes.'

'Why did she leave in the first place?'

'She'd had a series of dead-end jobs since leaving school and the bright lights lured her. Liverpool was an exciting city long before they called it the Capital of Culture, and she'd always been a Beatles fan. Her parents died when she was sixteen or seventeen, and she and her sister didn't get on too well.'

Hannah said, 'You said before that, according to Emma, when she came out as a lesbian, Karen gave her the cold shoulder.'

Vanessa nodded. 'We think of the Lakes as cosmopolitan, don't we? Because people from so many countries come here to work, as well as to visit. Go into a café in Bowness and you can be served your cup of tea by someone from anywhere in the world. But the fact is, some of the locals are deeply conservative. I've never met Karen, Chief Inspector, but Emma gave the impression she was rather narrow-minded.'

'So Emma decided to get away from here?'

89

'I suppose she wanted to find herself, if you like.'

'But she didn't find herself in Liverpool, did she? She doesn't seem to have formed any meaningful ties there. That's why she came back.'

Vanessa sighed. 'I was very fond of Emma, Chief Inspector. But she didn't open up easily. That's why she didn't make many friends. Living on her own suited her. Even when she was staying with us, we might not see her from one day to the next.'

'You weren't aware of any lovers in Liverpool? Or anyone who might have left her a lot of money?'

'No one.'

'How did she set about finding herself back home in the Lakes?'

'She liked working at the museum. She and Alex were happy enough for a while, but then their relationship hit the rocks. Emma took it badly and was off work with stress for months. Then she came into this money and it gave her the opportunity to start afresh.'

'According to Alex Clough, their relationship simply ran out of steam.'

Vanessa shrugged. 'I don't know the whys and wherefores. I never wanted to intrude. But you can take it from me that Emma was devastated.'

'You were her friend, she must have given you a hint about why her affair with Alex Clough fell apart. Was there a row?'

'I told you before, I've no idea. Emma and Alex had a lot in common, but it's hard to work for someone you're personally involved with. Alex

90

was the boss and I don't think Emma could get that out of her head. If you ask me, you have to treat each other as equals if you want to keep a relationship flourishing long term.'

She smiled at her husband and squeezed his hand. Last time Hannah had wondered whether the lovey-dovey stuff was put on for her benefit. Perhaps when the door closed behind her they would start bawling at each other. But their intimacy struck her as instinctive, these were two people at ease with each other. Was there such a thing as a genuinely happy marriage? If so, this might just be it.

'Might the money have been a pay-off from Alban Clough? Or his daughter?'

Vanessa raised her eyebrows. 'Why give her such a large golden handshake?'

'An affair with her boss had gone wrong. Some people might conjure a sexual harassment suit out of that scenario.'

'But she was a willing partner in the relationship.'

'Even so. She was off with work-related stress.' A burning topic in *Police Review*. 'The pay-outs in litigation can be sky-high.'

Francis said, 'You'd have to speak to Alex Clough or her father about that. But Emma never gave us the impression that she meant to bring a claim. She just couldn't face going back to work for Alex after they split up. The Cloughs paid her wages till she resigned, but we never heard about anything more generous.'

'You're a nurse, Mr Goddard. How sick was she?'

91

'Depression is a tricky illness, Chief Inspector. She was genuinely ill, but I was confident that eventually she would make a full recovery, and so it proved. Last time we talked, you asked if she might have become suicidal. I still can't believe she would have killed herself.'

'And coming into money perked her up?' Hannah asked drily.

'Well, it would, wouldn't it?' Francis was earnest; he didn't do irony.

'So she set up as a reflexologist. Lifelong ambition or impulse decision?'

'She was searching for something new,' Vanessa said. 'A deeper meaning in life. She celebrated her thirtieth birthday whilst she lived in this house. We went out for an Indian together in Bowness and she told us that she fancied being her own boss. Having no one to answer to except herself.'

'Was this interest in holistic therapies new?'

'Yes, they seemed to assist her own recovery and she wanted to help others to feel better. Making her plans gave her a new lease of life. She'd been putting on weight, stuffing herself with comfort food while she was down in the dumps. But she worked hard at dieting and shed more than a stone. By the time she left us, she really looked quite trim.'

'When we spoke before,' Hannah said, 'you believed she'd left the Lakes of her own accord. But if she relished running her own business...'

Vanessa bowed her head. 'You're right, Chief Inspector. I've had time to come to terms with the inevitable. When you and I first met, I'd not long had Christopher and I wanted to believe everyone was as happy as me. I hated to think that something dreadful might have happened to my friend. So I persuaded myself that she'd fallen for someone and followed her on the spur of the moment. I liked to think that one day she'd come back. But as the years passed...'

'Seems unlikely that Emma would have thrown up her new home, her new car, for the sake of a flight of fancy.'

'I was deceiving myself, I see it now.'

'So what might have happened to her – any ideas?'

Francis Goddard said, 'Your guess is as good as ours, Chief Inspector. An accident of some kind?'

'Then why has she never been found?'

'If we rule out suicide, that only leaves the possibility of murder.'

In her best press conference police-speak, Hannah said, 'We're keeping an open mind.'

Vanessa touched the mark on her face, as though it were sore. A habitual gesture, whenever she was troubled. 'Who would want to murder Emma? It doesn't make any sense. She was a caring person, she never did anyone any harm.'

'How did she get on with Karen and her husband?'

Francis said brusquely, 'I'm sure you haven't forgotten that Jeremy Erskine was once married to Vanessa.'

'To be honest, I found that curious, Mrs Goddard.'

'Vanessa, please.'

'Well, Vanessa. Your husband leaves you for

93

someone else. And then you take that someone else's sister in as your lodger.'

A long silence. Husband and wife exchanged glances. Vanessa cleared her throat.

'I didn't like to say this to you before.'

Hannah leaned forward. Her heart was thumping.

'Yes?' she whispered.

'As you know, I met Emma when I led a workshop at the museum. She'd just started working there and we hit it off from the start. Whilst we were talking, I realised she was the sister of the woman who'd married my ex. The truth is, I was fascinated. I liked Emma, but of course I was curious. I wanted to find out more about Karen. Hopefully to reassure me that Jeremy had made a terrible mistake.' Vanessa was talking quickly, her hands were trembling. '*Schadenfreude*, I'm afraid. Dreadful confession, but there's something of the voyeur in all of us, don't you agree?'

I'm a detective, how could I not agree?

'For three years, I'd loathed Karen Bestwick, and I'd never even set eyes on her. I didn't have a clue whether she was blonde or brunette. In my mind I christened her Miss Piggy. Nothing personal, she was skinny as a stick-insect, according to Emma. I don't mind admitting, I'd have resented anyone that Jeremy went off with. And now I'd stumbled across someone who knew her intimately – and who didn't think the sun shone out of her backside. Far from it. I'm ashamed to admit it, but I loved hearing what a selfish, superficial woman Karen was.'

Hannah risked another sip of coffee, but she'd

94

ignored it for too long and it was cold. Before coming out here, she'd refreshed her memory from the old statements. Out of the blue, Jeremy had walked out on his marriage to Vanessa to go and live with Karen, a secretary at the school where he taught. Vanessa's morale must have been at rock bottom when she learned Karen was pregnant, but within weeks of the decree nisi landing on her doormat, she met Francis Goddard while running a reading group for patients at the hospital where he worked. Three years later, she was married to a man apparently besotted with her and living with their new baby in a lovely home near Coniston Water. Talk about falling on your feet. Hannah couldn't find it in her heart to blame her if she got a kick from learning the faults of her ex's new wife.

'Why didn't the sisters get on?'

Vanessa shrugged. 'All they had in common was their genes. If you ask me, the idea that blood is thicker than water is rubbish. Emma was quieter, more serious. Karen's main interests were men and make-up. She was looking for someone to take care of her, shower her with flowers and chocolates.'

'Was Emma jealous of her?'

'Nothing to be jealous of.'

'Had she ever had a boyfriend?'

'You'd need to ask Karen.' Vanessa stroked her husband's hand. 'In case you're wondering, I didn't feel I was taking a risk if ever I left her alone in the house with Francis.'

Hannah turned to him. 'You and she were on good terms, though?'

Francis Goddard gave her a wry smile. 'Certainly. And as I said last time we met, it went no further than that. You put me through the mincer ten years ago, Chief Inspector. I'm sure you suspected that Emma and I were lovers.'

Oh God. She felt herself colouring. Ten years ago, she'd lacked experience as a detective, but she'd never realised she'd been so transparent.

'I had to ask.'

'Only doing your job? I understand. I'm sure if I'd had something to hide, you'd have unearthed it. Sorry to disappoint you in this cynical day and age. But I only ever had eyes for Vanessa. There was no affair between Emma and me.'

A thought leapt into Hannah's mind. *How about between Emma and your wife?* Ten years back, the possibility hadn't even occurred to her. Vanessa was wrapped up in her new baby and the idea of her embarking on a covert lesbian relationship during pregnancy would have seemed absurd. Probably it still was. Chances were, friendship flowered between Emma and Vanessa due to nothing more than mutual convenience. It provided Emma with a roof over her head. And Vanessa with the reassurance that Jeremy Erskine had betrayed her for a Muppet.

If Emma had been murdered, Hannah reflected as she drove, there was no evidence as to when she might have died, so alibis were pretty much irrelevant. Chances were, it was a sex crime. If so, the killer was probably someone previously unknown to her. The likeliest exception was Tom Inchmore, the Cloughs' handyman. His family had once owned the biggest mine-works on the Coniston fells, as well as the mansion that housed the museum, before falling on hard times. But that inadequate under-achiever had maintained his innocence even in the face of questioning from a DC later kicked off the force for beating up a teenager in Millom under the gaze of a CCTV camera.

By the time she arrived home, Hannah had resolved to give the revived inquiry no more than a week. Much as she wanted to understand Emma's fate, not every file could be tidied into the 'case closed' cabinet. It was too easy to chuck resources into a bottomless pit. The *Post* wouldn't keep the story on the front page for long. She'd speak to the Cloughs, and to Emma's sister and brother-in-law, then review progress.

Marc had beaten her home and switched on the oven. He wasn't a bad cook and she enjoyed being waited on. His good humour was explained by the fact that a customer from Tokyo had paid a small fortune for a book he'd picked up for a song in a house clearance and first advertised on the internet forty-eight hours ago.

'And a friend of yours dropped in. Daniel Kind.'

'What was he after?' Her voice sounded ridiculously gruff.

'Researching John Ruskin. He asked after you and I told him how glad you were of his help over that business in Old Sawrey.' He shut the fridge door and reached out to stroke her hair. 'So, how was your day?'

Did he really want to know? She murmured

something indistinct and that seemed enough. He was at her side now, caressing her neck whilst he kept his eyes fixed on the oven's temperature dial.

'Time to relax,' he whispered.

His hand strayed, as if by chance, to her breast. She closed her eyes as his lips brushed her cheek. To her dismay, a picture sprang into her mind. Not Marc but Daniel Kind, leaning close to her, his expression intent. She felt a tightness in her stomach, as if she were hungering for his touch.

Guy slipped out of the Glimpse and set off for the call box. It was after five o'clock and Tony Di Venuto had left, but he got through to a colleague and soon wheedled the journalist's mobile number out of her. All it took was a little persuasion, and Guy was very good at persuasion.

'Is that Tony Di Venuto?'

'Who is this?'

Idiotic question. Di Venuto must have recognised Guy's spectral whisper from the previous call. He ought to give Guy credit and not take him for a fool.

'We spoke yesterday. About Emma Bestwick.'

'You told me she wouldn't be coming back. Is she dead? Look, why don't we get together for half an hour? Over a coffee, how about it? You could...'

'No coffee,' Guy interrupted. 'All I want to do is to tell you something.'

'Who are you?' Di Venuto's voice rose. If he was trying to contain his excitement, he was failing.

'You don't need to know.'

'Why have you called me?'

'For Karen's sake,' Guy said.

Christ, he might have been a cheesy cabaret singer dedicating 'The Lady in Red' to his latest squeeze. But he meant it, he was doing this for her.

'*Karen?*'

'Yes, she needs closure.'

The journalist sounded mystified. 'Did you kill Emma?'

'That's disgusting. I swear to you, she was alive the last time I saw her.'

It was true, that was the wicked irony.

'Then how can you be sure she's dead?'

'I know where the body is buried.'

All at once, Guy was sweaty and shaking, as if stricken by fever. He fought to compose himself, gulping in the stale call box air. *I'm not a murderer, I'm not a murderer, I'm not a murderer.* It was all a terrible mistake, though nobody would believe it. But he'd come this far. He couldn't slam the phone down yet.

'Where?' Tony Di Venuto said in a hoarse whisper.

'Below the Arsenic Labyrinth.'

CHAPTER SIX

Over breakfast the next morning, Guy felt a calm that not even Mariah Carey warbling from the transistor radio could disturb. Calling the journalist had been tough, but courage had brought him peace of mind. He'd slept without dreaming and done justice to a full English breakfast guaranteed to fur the arteries. Sarah had cooked mushrooms, as a little treat. With a conspiratorial wink she indicated that this was to celebrate the departure of the German couple. They'd been up at the crack of dawn, feasting on toast and marmalade before setting off back to Heidelberg.

'I'm not sure I'll advertise vacancies until it's time for you to leave. It's been non-stop for the past fortnight and I fancy putting my feet up for a few days.'

'You deserve a break.' He considered the bags under her eyes. 'You look tired, you must be working too hard.'

She shook her head. 'My own fault. I spend too much time upstairs on the computer.'

He tutted. 'All work and no play? You need to grab a bit of enjoyment as well as looking after your guests. Mind, you'd better be careful. You may not get rid of me as easily as all that. I've made myself so comfortable here that I was wondering...'

'Yes?'

She leaned across the table and he caught a fragrance that revived memories of a happy few months in Paris three years back. Chanel Number Five. So she was making a special effort. He could scarcely resist the urge to preen.

'I might like to stick around for a while. If it's not too much trouble.'

'Trouble? Nothing of the kind, it's an absolute pleasure. How long would you like to stay?'

'Depends on arrangements with my associates in Geneva.' He sighed, a fast-moving executive at the mercy of tedious colleagues. 'You'll have to promise to kick me out the moment you want a bit of peace and quiet!'

'No danger of that.' As she reached over for the teapot, her hand grazed his. 'Two's company, as they say.'

He allowed her to pour him a second cup. In time you could acclimatise to anything, even Co-op tea bags. He was a man at ease with himself, as relaxed as though he'd been luxuriating in a jacuzzi. As it happened, the water heater in the basement was on the blink, but never mind. His luck was on the turn. Maybe tonight he'd be bathing upstairs, together with Sarah.

Guy recalled Megan, head lifted as she announced her ultimatum. If he wanted any more of her cash, things would have to change. They would get engaged, start behaving like a normal couple. If he didn't like it, he could lump it. And repay what she'd lent him. And, and, and ... well, he'd stopped listening. At last he saw Megan for what she was, a self-righteous young woman with a scrawny neck. For a fleeting moment he'd been tempted to put his hands around the pale pink flesh. It would be so easy to squeeze the breath out of her.

If she could see him now. Sarah was much more accommodating, in every sense. He deserved a bit of good fortune. As a boy in the Home, he'd imagined himself as a prince, immensely popular and possessed of untold wealth, yet condemned to penury and loneliness through a spell cast by a jealous wizard. The fantasy stayed with him for years, but when at last he was granted the freedom and riches he'd yearned for, all too soon he'd frittered them away.

He was ready for a second crack at the good life. By calling Tony Di Venuto, he'd done the right thing. Paid his dues. The authorities would set wheels in motion. He was hazy about official procedures, but before long Emma's body would be found and she could be given a belated Christian burial. Karen Erskine could get on with the rest of her life while the journalist earned kudos for breaking the story. Leaving Guy to make the most of his new life in which everybody was a winner.

Just like the endings to the stories he'd made up as a kid. Happy ever after.

Inchmore Hall, home to Cumbria's Museum of Myth and Legend, stood on the edge of the village in grounds extending over six acres, up to the lower reaches of Wetherlam. The hall was a grey monstrosity of Victorian Gothic, boasting turrets, tall chimneys, and black and white gables, the whole edifice surmounted by an extravagant tower with a copper top. Blinds were drawn at the ground floor windows, protecting the exhibits from non-existent sunlight. Copper beeches and dank rhododendron bushes masked the curving drive. A signboard beside the stone gateposts cautioned that during the winter season, opening hours were by appointment only. Hannah parked outside the canopied front door and ran up a flight of worn stone steps to ring the bell.

'Yes?'

The woman framed in the doorway wore a black trouser suit, so simple and chic that it must have cost a mint. Short dark hair contrasted with luminous skin. Her forehead was high, her chin sharp. She wore dangly sun and moon ear-rings and a crucifix of ebony and silver hung from her neck. Alexandra Clough's signed statement suggested intelligence and a calm reluctance to give more away than she wished to reveal. So did her unflickering gaze as Hannah flourished her ID.

Alex led the way with dainty, precise steps into a galleried entrance hall. The ground floor was crowded with pots of dusty palms and aspidistras. Carved pitch panelling covered the walls and an arch-shaped stained-glass window at the far end of the hall depicted a purple sunset over brooding fells. The air was so cold that Hannah expected to see icicles on the huge brass candleholders. She shivered.

'Sorry we don't keep the heating on when we're not open to the public. We don't receive any funding from the council, so we need to make economies.' Alex unlocked a heavy door. 'We can talk in my office. It's a little warmer there.'

103

Only by a couple of degrees, Hannah discovered. Alex waved her into a leather-backed chair and sat behind a desk large enough to massage the ego of a tycoon. The electric reading lamp and computer squatting in front of her were the only concessions to the twenty-first century. Bookcases stuffed with calfskin-bound tomes lined the walls, two gilt-framed oil-paintings occupied the corner alcoves behind her. A middle-aged man with a clipped moustache leaned on a walking stick in one picture. He wore a pin-striped suit and a frown suggesting that he didn't suffer portrait painters gladly. In the other, a young woman with high cheekbones and an evening dress of pale blue tulle displaying plump milky-white breasts. Was it mere fancy to detect a resemblance between this woman and Alex Clough?

Alex Clough caught Hannah's gaze. 'My grandparents, Chief Inspector. Armstrong and Betty Clough. She was rather beautiful, don't you agree?'

Hannah nodded. 'Did you know her?'

'Oh yes. My grandfather died soon after I was born, but she lived until she was eighty-six. A remarkable woman, we were very close. Now, you are reviewing Emma's disappearance. How can I help?'

Hannah shifted in her chair. It was old and uncomfortable, like everything she'd seen of Inchmore Hall. 'I'd be grateful if you could tell me about your relationship with her. How it began, why it ended.'

Alex took a breath and Hannah guessed that she'd rehearsed her answer. 'She joined us twelve

104

months before she vanished. At this time of year, we look to recruit in good time for the season. Apart from temporary staff and maintenance people, we only have one clerical post. Our previous administrator deserted us for a better paid job in Carlisle and so there was a vacancy. Emma had flitted from job to job. At one point she was employed on a short-term contract at the Liverpool Museum. Inchmore is scarcely in that league, but at least she had relevant experience and my father liked that.'

'It was his decision to take her on?'

'Then, as now, I was the manager here. But my father created this museum, Chief Inspector. He remains passionately committed to it and I consult him on all business matters. If you are wondering whether I recruited Emma because I was attracted to her, the answer is no.'

'She'd tired of city life?'

'Growing up in the countryside, she thought she was missing out on the bright lights. When the lights stopped dazzling her, she saw all the urban grime. Eventually she realised that the grass really was greener back home in the Lakes.'

'Did she keep in touch with anyone in Merseyside?'

'Not to my knowledge. Emma never kept up with people she went to school with, either. She didn't make friends easily.'

'Even so, the two of you became close. How did that come about?'

'How do these things ever come about?'

Hannah glared at her watch. She was in no mood for fencing.

Alex fiddled with her ear-rings. 'I suppose ... Emma excited my curiosity.'

'Well, this is a museum. A place to study exhibits.'

Tiny teeth showed in a mirthless smile. 'Do I sound cold-blooded? I'm paying you the compliment of telling the truth, rather than fobbing you off with a self-serving lie. On first acquaintance, Emma seemed quiet and timid. I thought she was pretty, but she lacked confidence. When she was a teenager, she put on puppy fat and she used to say that she only had to look at a bar of chocolate to put on weight.'

Hannah thought of Emma's puzzled look, captured by the photographer. 'She was unsure of herself.'

'Yes, her self-image was poor. She compared her looks unfavourably with her sister's and her solution was to fade into the background. Yet the more I got to know her, the more I became convinced she was as capable of passion as my father. The difference was that she'd never found anything to become passionate about.'

'Did she care about her work here?'

'At first, yes. Even if she did leave school at sixteen with few qualifications to her name, she was bright. I'm afraid our universities these days are overflowing with students with far less native intelligence than Emma. The trouble was, she had a lazy streak. Once she lost interest, she didn't put in the effort. She gave up too easily, that was why she kept changing jobs. She was looking for something she could commit to, long term. Something special.' Alex sighed. 'But with

Emma, nothing lasted. Her moods kept swinging.'

'When did the two of you first get together?'

'Within a month of her starting. She was helping me one night with an application for a grant towards our running costs. Tiresome, long-winded form-filling, but important. The upkeep of this building costs an arm and a leg and the paying customers contribute buttons towards our overheads. Any scraps of outside funding are welcome. The cleaners had finished for the day and Father was speaking at a black tie dinner in Leeds. I told Emma how as a young man he'd dreamed of creating a museum to celebrate his fascination with the legends that swirl around the Lakes like fog. It was our first intimate conversation. Once we'd finalised the figures, I dug a bottle of rather nice wine out of Father's private cellar. He and I have our quarters upstairs and in those days my grandmother lived here too. After I invited her to my sitting room, one thing duly led to another.'

Hannah glanced at the portrait of Armstrong Clough. For a moment she fancied she caught him scowling at the way feckless young women behave nowadays. His demeanour suggested it would have been different in his day. Poor, pretty Betty probably led a dog's life.

'You weren't in a relationship at the time?'

Alex shook her head. 'After a couple of years of living like a nun, all the pent-up emotion came flooding out. For Emma it was much the same that night, I think. When she told me that she had very little experience of sex, I believed her. Let

107

me speak bluntly, Chief Inspector. There was a – a clumsy innocence about her love-making that I found captivating. Her enthusiasm compensated for any lack of sophistication.'

'Did she speak about her own previous relationships?'

'Never. We assured each other that there hadn't been anyone serious before and that was all that mattered. For myself, it was true. I suspect it was the same for Emma.'

'Had she ever had a boyfriend?'

'She'd experimented with boys in her teens. Because it was the done thing, rather than from genuine lust. No one lit her fire.'

'Except you?'

A smile as frosty as February. 'I should not flatter myself, Chief Inspector. I thought we had a match made in heaven, but this time I was the naïve one. I'm not sure Emma was cut out for relationships. At first she was intensely possessive, wanted to be with me every hour of every day. But that soon waned and before long she was happier with her own company. Sex mattered even less to her than to me. I lost the ability to excite her.'

'And how did you react to that?'

'Looking back, I see the mistakes I made. When an affair is crumbling around your ears, it's difficult to be objective. We worked side by side all day, every day, and it wasn't healthy. It is possible to be too close, don't you agree?'

Hannah said nothing, waited for her to continue.

'I pushed too hard, and soon she was keeping

me at arm's length. On good days she was delightful company, but she could be moody and uncommunicative. It hurt that she'd rather scuttle off back to her rented room than stay here with me, in my marvellous home.'

Hannah could understand what drove Emma off to the sanctuary of Thurston Water House. Inchmore might be marvellous, but it was also dark, vast and intimidating. The architect must have read too many Gothic novels. After a day closeted in here, a rented room surrounded by people who made no demands might become a longed-for haven.

'Did you remain friends?'

'I couldn't accept that our affair had passed its sell-by date. Working so closely together made matters worse. Each day I was giving her instructions, and she wanted to be left to her own devices. It was bound to end in tears.'

'And did it?'

Alex Clough said softly, 'The last day she worked here, she cried her heart out.'

She hadn't mentioned this during the original inquiry. That was an upside of cold case work. Interviewed after a gap of years, people forgot past evasions, as well as details of the lies they had told.

'Why?'

'She'd taken a couple of days off sick and was falling behind with her jobs. I asked if she was working to rule. Not very witty, but I was shocked when she burst into tears, and devastated when she accused me of bullying her because our affair had hit the buffers. I was sure she didn't mean

109

what she said, and I tried not to let my feelings show. I told her to go home and get over it. She never came back.'

'How did your father take all this?'

'We didn't discuss the situation. Too embarrassing. But he understood what I was going through and he was always sweet to Emma. There was never a cross word between them.'

'She went off sick with stress.'

'According to the doctor's certificate.'

'You don't sound convinced.'

'Come on, Chief Inspector. How difficult is it to get a busy GP to sign you off if you don't fancy turning in for work?'

'You think she was shooting you a line?'

Alex shifted uncomfortably. 'If Emma was suffering from stress, it wasn't my fault. There was no question of my victimising her because she didn't want to sleep with me any more.'

'She was off work for half a year. That must have caused you enormous difficulty. Not to mention cost.'

'You exaggerate. As for expense, I'm afraid our sick pay scheme is not exactly generous. We pay the statutory minimum. A temp came in from an agency and Father and I put in long hours to make sure the museum wasn't affected by Emma's absence. I won't pretend it was ideal, but we got by.'

'I read in your statement that you asked her to undergo an independent medical examination.'

'I didn't want her to feel under pressure to rush back before she was better, so for months I was patient. But how long could I be expected to wait? In the end, I wrote to Emma, suggesting we pay for a check-up. Before that, I'd phoned the Goddards more than once and asked if I could arrange to visit her, but they said Emma had asked not to see me. That hurt, all I was interested in was her welfare. Vanessa was apologetic and said she and her husband still hoped Emma would come round.'

'But she didn't.'

'On one occasion I spoke to Francis and suggested that Emma consult a psychiatrist. I didn't doubt that, as a nurse, he was caring well for her, but I was sure she needed specialist help. To his credit, Francis agreed. He said he'd already persuaded Emma to see someone. But before an appointment could be arranged, I received a letter from her, tendering her resignation and proffering apologies for having messed me about. I gave a copy to your colleague who interviewed me.'

'So you didn't have to pay her any compensation?'

'Compensation for what?'

Hannah shrugged. 'Constructive dismissal, sexual harassment, damage to emotional well-being. Employing people is a minefield, isn't it?'

'We've never had a problem.' The temperature in the room was dropping with every sentence. 'Not with Emma and not in the ten years since. I hear there's a compensation culture in the police service, but the private sector is different. Small employers like the museum don't fork out large sums to pacify disgruntled workers, they can't afford it.'

111

'Litigation lawyers conjure claims out of nothing.' Hannah chose a more-in-sorrow-than-in-anger smile. 'A boss who has an affair with a worker that turns sour is vulnerable to all kinds of unfounded allegations.'

Alex clenched the computer mouse as if it were a stress ball. 'It's academic. Emma never threatened legal action. We paid her up to the end of her notice period as a goodwill gesture, that's all.'

'No golden handshake?'

'Not a penny more than she was due.'

'Then where did she get the cash to buy a house and car and start her own business?'

'Your guess is as good as mine.'

'She told different tales. An inheritance, a lottery win. Neither was true.'

'She said to Father it was lottery money. I knew she picked the same numbers each week, it was the closest she came to a religious ritual. When I heard it had paid off, I was genuinely thrilled for her.'

'No bitterness?'

'Like my father, I adhere to the philosophy of Edith Piaf. No regrets. Yes, I was bruised, but I got over it. After Emma resigned, we stayed in touch. Which is why your theory that she held us to ransom over an employment claim is absurd. The flame may have died, but there was no ill will between us.'

'When did you last see her?'

'I visited her bungalow a couple of days before she disappeared. She seemed fully recovered. I was so glad to see her happy. I told her I hadn't been sleeping well and she lectured me on herbalism, holistic therapies and maintaining the body's natural equilibrium. Guff, perhaps, but she was brimming with zest. It reminded me of her early days at the museum.'

'You went for a massage?'

'Please don't look so prim, Chief Inspector, I'm sure you've encountered more shocking confessions. She offered me a free initial consultation and we both kept our knickers on.'

'Uh-huh.' Hannah had worked out that Alex's conversational m.o. was to use frankness as a weapon. Was the candour more apparent than real, a device to conceal what was really going on in her head?

'Emma applied pressure to my feet with her hands. She was good at it. I always loved to be touched by her, but of course nothing sexual took place.'

'Were you disappointed?'

Alex Clough shuffled a couple of sheets of paper on her desk, aligning their corners so that they were neat and tidy. Without looking up, she said in a voice of infinite calm, 'On the contrary, I had a glow of well-being and relaxation. You should try it, Chief Inspector.'

'Did you book another appointment?'

'Yes, it was scheduled for ten days after the first. But by then Emma had disappeared.'

'Had you hoped to rekindle the affair?'

'Reflexologists have their own code of conduct, I presume. Emma wouldn't have behaved unprofessionally.'

'Forgive me, Ms Clough, but that is hardly an answer.'

'Very well. I wanted to see how she was. We'd been so intimate – I couldn't pretend to myself that she'd never existed. As for what might happen in the future, I was philosophical. Events must take their course. No pressure, to coin a phrase.'

Oh yeah? Alex Clough was a rich man's daughter, she'd probably had pretty much everything she'd ever wanted. She was accustomed to being in control, would dread surrendering to the mercy of Fate.

'And how did she respond?'

'The only time I put a foot wrong was when I complimented her on how well she looked. It was nothing but the truth. She'd lost weight after the illness, and she was very trim. But she suspected I was having a dig, implying that she hadn't really been sick. I assured her nothing could have been further from my mind and after that she was fine.'

'When we interviewed you before, you couldn't account for Emma's disappearance. Has anything occurred since then to explain it?'

Alex Clough shook her head. 'Things were looking up for her. Why would she run away? It makes no sense.'

Ten years back, Hannah had thought the same. Today, trapped in the cage of calendars and chloroformed by bureaucratic routine, she could see the appeal of starting again, somewhere nobody knew a thing about her. She'd even dreamed of it a few nights back, dreamed of waking one morning in a strange hotel room. When she looked in the mirror, she'd gone strawberry blonde, when

114

she went downstairs, the man at the desk greeted her by an unfamiliar name. Everyone spoke a foreign language she couldn't understand, yet she wasn't frightened. The weirdness of it was exhilarating. She felt free.

'What do you think happened to her?'

'Who knows? An accident?'

'Or perhaps she was murdered?'

'By whom?' Alex Clough wasn't the sort to let her grammar slip, even when asked about the possible homicide of an ex. 'And for what reason? Unless she had the bad luck to fall prey to a rapist who throttled her and somehow disposed of the body.'

'You speak of her in the past tense. Presumably you believe she is dead?'

'Nothing else makes sense, does it? I did my grieving in private long ago. I have had to move on.'

'Aren't you curious about your lover's fate? Sad that you never had a chance to say goodbye?'

A brisk shake of the head. 'Like I said, no regrets.'

'I'm surprised, Ms Clough. Museum folk, they're supposed to have a thirst for knowledge. Do you really not want to find out what happened?'

Alex Clough folded her thin arms. Her pale face had turned grey. 'You have your job to do, Chief Inspector, but I've decided ignorance is bliss. Some things are too painful. I can only pray that the end, when it came, was quick. That she didn't suffer.'

'Your relationship with Emma still means a

great deal to you, doesn't it?' Hannah said in a quiet voice.

A long pause. Alex Clough bowed her head, but Hannah could still see the single tear trickling down her cheek. When she spoke, she no longer sounded glacial. Just hoarse, and old before her time.

'Everything. You must understand, Emma Bestwick meant everything to me.'

When the phone trilled, Daniel was in his study, leafing through the correspondence that he'd bought at auction. Letters written by a neighbour of Ruskin who had been an occasional visitor to Brantwood in the years before genius yielded to mental collapse. Already Daniel was regretting his failure to buy more of the lots. The old story. You always regretted the ones that got away.

He picked up the receiver. 'Hello?'

'It's Louise.'

His sister. A corporate lawyer, currently working in academe. Even in a social call, she was as brisk and no-nonsense as a textbook on insider trading. When he explained that Miranda was away in London, she tutted.

'Not again?'

He pictured her mouth tightening in disapproval. An expression she'd inherited from her mother, worn whenever he made the mistake of mentioning the father who had left them all for another woman.

'She needs to see her editor face to face.'

'I'm amazed she can tear herself away. I read her article about how trendy the Lakes have become. *"A fantastic destination for the loft and latte set. You may not realise after glancing at the temperature gauge, but the Lake District is hot."* 'The breathless take-off was so accurate that Daniel winced. 'Haven't they heard of video conferencing?'

'They're journalists, not company executives. They'd rather interact face to face.'

'Well, you know what I think.'

'Uh-huh.'

Daniel didn't want to go there. The two women had nothing in common. He hated having to defend Miranda to Louise. Trouble was, his sister was a lawyer to her fingertips. She specialised in chilly logic, and giving unwelcome advice.

'I mean, I hope it works out for the two of you, but...'

'It will,' he interrupted.

'Let's face it. You met her when you were bereft after Aimee's suicide. Oh, she did you good, I don't deny it. None of us could get through to you until she came along. But the two of you are so very different. You used to be so funny, so laid-back. You're not cut out for a roller-coaster ride with a drama queen.'

'She's not...'

'You know what I mean. Escaping your old lives suited you both for a time, but you can't live a dream forever. Passion is fine, but it isn't enough long term.'

What makes you an expert? he was tempted to ask. But that would be cruel. Louise's own relationship had fallen apart last summer and he wasn't sure she was over it even now. She'd never

117

rung him without a reason until she started living on her own. But she'd never admit she was lonely. Too much pride.

'We'll be fine.'

'Listen, you're not as accustomed to failure as the rest of us. But sometimes it's better to...'

'When I want an agony aunt, I'll give you a ring.'

She gave a *have it your way* sigh and said, 'Started that book yet?'

'Waiting for inspiration.'

'You once told me that nobody who writes should ever wait for inspiration.' A note of curiosity entered her voice. 'Seen any more of that police officer friend of yours?'

'No.' Did he imagine a touch of innuendo in the word *friend?* 'Why do you ask?'

'I just thought ... oh, nothing.'

After she'd rung off, he dialled Miranda. Was it selfish to hope she was missing him? She was in a restaurant, surrounded by a wailing saxophone and people laughing. Glasses clinked, someone whistled for a waiter. American football was playing on TV in the background, the commentator shouting himself hoarse. Miranda was joining in the laughter and a couple of times she asked him to repeat what he said. Even when he did, he wasn't sure she was paying attention.

'Was there anything particular?' she asked in the end. 'The roof isn't leaking, the electrics haven't gone up in smoke?'

'Nothing special,' he said. 'Didn't mean to interrupt.'

'No problem,' she assured him. 'Talk soon.

Love you.'

She made a loud kissing noise and the phone went dead.

'The woman intrigued me.'

Alban Clough was leaning back in his ancient leather chair, eyes shut and hands behind his head. He might have been speaking of an exhibit on display downstairs and not his daughter's vanished lover.

'Why?' Hannah asked.

He'd invited her up to the small sitting room at the top of Inchmore Hall. The only access from the living quarters on the floor below was by a perilous spiral staircase lit by candles in wall-holders that would have a health and safety inspector frothing at the mouth. But Alban Clough clambered up the steps like a mountain goat rather than a man of seventy five with a heart condition. As she followed, Hannah took care not to look down and tried not to think about the cop who feared heights in that Hitchcock movie.

The small table that separated them was piled high with books and foolscap sheets of closely written text, with more papers scattered across the carpet; Alex's tidiness gene couldn't have been inherited from her father. Looking through the single mullioned window, Hannah watched slivers of mist curling down from the heights. At least there was one hotspot inside Inchmore Hall. A log fire crackled and the air was heavy with the smell of burning wood.

Alban Clough jerked upright and opened his eyes. As he shifted his weight, the armchair squeaked. 'She was a sweet girl, but secretive.'

'What about?'

'I could not discover that. Which is why I was intrigued.'

'Her sexuality? The relationship with your daughter?'

He pooh-poohed the suggestions with a flourish of an age-spotted paw. 'I might claim, Chief Inspector Scarlett, to be worldly wise. It was apparent from our first meeting that Emma was a lesbian. A man of sensitivity and experience can recognise the signs, let me assure you.'

How easy to take a serious dislike to Alban Clough. Six feet three and broad as a bull, with self-esteem to match, he had the unruly white hair, hooked nose and booming voice of a hellfire prophet, but his most profound conviction was evidently of his own infallibility. He didn't have his daughter's dress sense; there was a button missing from his cuff, and his shirt wasn't properly tucked into his elderly slacks. Yet he struck Hannah as a man to be reckoned with.

'Did you approve of the relationship?'

'For as long as it brought Alexandra pleasure, most certainly. I feared it would not last, but a parent's lot is to worry about their offspring's happiness. Do you have children, Chief Inspector? If so, you will understand.'

Hannah let that whistle past. 'You questioned Emma's motives?'

'Because she saw sleeping with my daughter as a passport to a life of comfort of plenty? By no means. I believed her affection for Alexandra to be genuine, though falling short of undying devotion. In my presence, she was good-natured and deferential.'

I bet, Hannah thought. Emma might be an elusive character, but she was no fool.

'Then what?'

'My daughter is a highly intelligent and remarkably sensible woman, but in personal relationships apt to wear her heart on her sleeve. That wasn't Emma's way. It seemed significant to me that her only other friend was the woman from whom she rented a room.'

'Not her sister?'

'Karen Erskine and her husband visited the museum, I suspect out of curiosity rather than any deeply felt interest in my life's work. Jeremy Erskine made it clear that a history master at Grizedale College could not approve the unsourced speculation in which I indulge concerning the origins of local myths and legends. Alexandra took pains to make them welcome, but Emma had little in common with Karen. I wondered if Erskine had taken a shine to Emma, and that was a cause of *froideur*. If so, he was wasting his time.'

'Are you sure?'

'Positive. Emma was not interested in men.'

For a wild moment, Hannah wondered if Alban Clough had first-hand experience of rejection by Emma. Or maybe it wasn't so wild? The way he'd considered her appearance when his daughter introduced them downstairs verged on the lascivious. An age gap of thirty-five years might not have deterred a man in the habit of getting his own way. Hannah's closest friend, Terri, had

121

decided after three failed marriages to try her luck with internet dating and she'd reported with glee that one of the men she'd met, though old enough to be her father, had the stamina and lust of a nineteen-year-old. He also turned out to be an undischarged bankrupt with three convictions for false accounting.

Suppose Alban had propositioned Emma after she'd broken up with Alex, that might account for the stress she'd suffered. What if they'd had a surreptitious affair? And if Emma had indulged in a little quiet blackmail...

'What about Tom Inchmore, did he realise that?'

'Alas, poor Thomas. To adopt the modern idiom, he wasn't the sharpest knife in the block. He took a shine to Emma while she worked here, she was always very good with him. As you may be aware, he's dead now, so he cannot defend himself. But let me say this on his behalf. He may have been a Peeping Tommy, but he was no murderer.'

'Suppose he made overtures which she rejected. It's a situation that often leads to violence.'

'Your colleagues explored that hypothesis in – shall we say, considerable depth? – ten years ago. Frankly, I was surprised that they failed to thrash a confession out of him. He was pitifully weak. That he steadfastly denied guilt proved that he found the notion of harming Emma horrific.'

'I presume he was descended from whoever built this place?'

'Indeed.' Alban puffed out his cheeks and Hannah realised that she was in for a lecture.

Presumably in winter he pined for the chance to pontificate to tourists with time on their hands. 'During the nineteenth century, Clifford Inchmore ran a successful business, mining the Coniston Fells and earning a knighthood to accompany his fortune. My great-grandfather, Albert Clough, joined the firm as a young man and rose to become a partner in the firm. But Clifford's son, George, was not cut from the same cloth. Albert left to set up on his own and George set about squandering his inheritance with unwise commercial ventures. Long before the influenza epidemic of 1919 carried off Albert, George had been made bankrupt. He lived long enough to suffer the indignity of seeing his son William go cap in hand to Albert's grandson for work. Armstrong Clough, my father, took him on and was rewarded by William absconding after the war ended. He stole one thousand pounds, and we heard he died in Crete five years later without a penny to his name. Nonetheless, my mother insisted that we had a duty towards the family that gave Albert his first opportunity in life.'

'That's remarkably forbearing.'

'My mother was a remarkable lady.'

'So you gave Tom Inchmore a job out of the goodness of your heart?'

'Because my mother had a good heart, which is not quite the same. Tom's parents both died young, in a car crash twenty-five years ago, and from then on he was looked after by his grandmother, William's wife. Edith Inchmore was herself a formidable woman. She died only last year at the age of ninety.'

'The two old ladies were friends?'

'They kept their distance from each other. While the Inchmore residence was a cramped two-up, two-down riddled with dry rot, my mother was chatelaine of this magnificent hall. It cannot have been easy for Edith Inchmore to bear, but she had only her husband's family to blame. As for my mother, she had a fanatical sense of duty towards others less fortunate than herself, even if she disliked them. *Noblesse oblige*, if you like. It is a mark of my devotion to her that I resisted the temptation to sack Tom Inchmore, despite his being one of the least competent young men I have ever met. That explains why he fell off a ladder when repairing a leaky roof. To suggest that he became cunning and successful for the first time in his life on resorting to murder is sheer fantasy.'

Not the most generous character reference Hannah had ever heard, but it was time to change tack.

'You know Francis Goddard, I take it?'

'Indeed. I cannot pretend that we have much in common. The meek may well inherit the earth, but that does not make them interesting.'

'Emma lived under his roof. Might something interesting have occurred between them?'

Alban laughed so hard that his eyes started watering. 'A deliciously sordid speculation, Chief Inspector! But regrettably wide of the mark, if I am any judge. Moreover, I have known Vanessa Goddard for many years. She is dedicated to outreach work, establishing partnerships between the libraries and other agencies. She lost her first husband to another woman, but Francis is well and truly under her thumb. I cannot conceive that he would have the spunk for a dangerous liaison with Emma, even were he not devoted to his wife.'

'And you don't have any reason to doubt that devotion?'

'Certainly not. Vanessa and Francis have always had eyes only for each other. Emma herself confirmed it.'

'What did she say?'

His wicked smile made him look like a gleeful old troll. 'In the first flush of happiness after she embarked on a relationship with my daughter, I overheard her saying to Alexandra that she would be glad when she could afford to move into a place of her own. She indicated that, although the bedroom walls at Thurston Water House were by no means thin, Vanessa and Francis were raucous as well as uninhibited in their love-making. I find it pleasing to hear of a genuine love match, they are so very rare these days, but Emma found it embarrassing to be forced to eavesdrop on their passion. Poor girl, at heart she was something of a prude.'

Did this prove that Vanessa and Francis were incapable of straying? Hannah dabbed at a smear of sweat on her forehead. The heat and the old man's salacious humour were overpowering.

'Very well, Mr Clough. I'm grateful for your help.'

Her host treated her to a wicked smile as she hauled herself to her feet.

'You're not going so soon, Chief Inspector? Oh dear me, please linger for a few minutes more. Let me explain to you what it is that women most desire.'

CHAPTER SEVEN

Daniel was in the kitchen, looking out over the cottage garden and tapping notes into his laptop. John Ruskin's life story proved that having it all was an illusion. Artist, critic, social philosopher, he was 'the pre-eminent intellectual genius of Victorian England'. Yet his marriage was annulled due to non-consummation, he spent years lusting after a girl who lost her mind and died young, and he proposed to another teenager when he was seventy. After Whistler sued him for libel and won the princely sum of a farthing in damages, depression defeated him and he spent his last years in Coniston leading a reclusive and child-like existence, cared for by his cousin Joan.

Daniel switched off the laptop and read a few more pages of *Unto this Last*. He found the title haunting. Ruskin never finished the book, but failure to complete wasn't an option for a twenty-first-century author who needed to keep the publisher satisfied and Daniel had started and discarded a couple of synopses. The malady was easy to diagnose. A historian was, by definition, an archive rat. But he still lacked documentary sources to provide a backbone for a book. He needed something he didn't yet possess.

His thoughts wandered to Hannah Scarlett.

I could call her, why not? Where's the harm?

He dialled Hannah's number without answering his own question. Straight through to voice-mail. It would have been so easy to hang up, but he heard himself speaking.

'Hannah, this is Daniel Kind. I was wondering ... how are things? Maybe we could talk some-time. Perhaps meet up.'

'So,' Alban Clough demanded, 'do you know what it is, Chief Inspector, that women most desire?'

'Break it to me gently.'

They had retraced their steps from Alban's eyrie in the tower to ground level and she'd started shivering again. Alexandra Clough was nowhere to be seen and everything was still except for their footsteps echoing on the floor. For all his age and supposed infirmity, Alban strode briskly across the main hall and Hannah could do no more than glance at the dusty displays featuring the phantom army of Souther Fell and the fabled wizard of Burgh under Bowness.

She ought to escape from this grotesque old man and his cobwebbed world and get back to Divisional HQ. But he intrigued her more than any exhibit in his museum. A few more minutes would not hurt. And she might learn something while he lowered his guard, showing off his expertise in Lakeland lore.

'Do you not know the tale of the Loathly Lady?' When Hannah shook her head, her host har-rumphed and said, 'I take it you are unfamiliar with the ballad of "The Marriage of Sir Gawain"?'

Hannah thrust her hands deeper into the pockets of her coat. After so many years living

127

with a bookseller, she ought to be well-read, but there were limits, and medieval ballads strayed far beyond them.

'Remind me.'

Her host led the way into the King Arthur Room. 'Few parts of Britain do not lay claim to a connection with the old monarch but my belief is that the old counties of Cumberland and Westmorland were as rich in Arthurian associations as Glastonbury or Tintagel. Take a look at that map. Each yellow crown represents a location boasting a story about Arthur, Merlin, or one of the Knights of the Round Table.'

Why were men so obsessive about their interests? If it wasn't football, fishing or philately, it was old books or even older legends.

'Fascinating,' she murmured.

His beam confirmed it was a good lie. 'I could tell the moment we met, Chief Inspector, that you were a woman of discernment.'

She ought to point that out to Marc tonight. Giving her host an enigmatic smile, she looked about her. Below the high ceiling, and running all around the room, an elaborate hand-painted frieze depicted gorgeous hills and shimmering tarns. Shameless really, when you remembered that Clifford Inchmore had built this house out of the profits made from scarring the landscape with mines.

'You were going to tell me what women most desire?'

'Indeed.' Alban Clough cleared his throat. 'In the days when King Arthur held court at Carlisle, he was riding out by Tarn Wadling when he encountered a bold baron with a club. The baron said that if the King was to avoid combat, he must answer a riddle.'

'Namely?'

Her host raised bushy white eyebrows and hissed, *'What is it that women most desire?'*

Despite herself, Hannah felt her body tensing. In her mind, she'd nicknamed the old man King Leer – but he was a born story-teller.

'Arthur chose the riddle and in his search for the answer, he encountered a woman as ugly as sin, sitting between an oak and a green holly. She offered to help him and he promised her the hand of Gawain in marriage if she told him the answer. She assented, and when Arthur returned to Tarn Wadling, he informed the baron that what women most desire is to have their own will.'

'Don't tell me. This legend was dreamed up by a man, right?'

Alban Clough bared yellowing teeth in a fearsome grin. 'The lore of our land, Chief Inspector, reaches far deeper than superficial notions of sexism and political correctness. Gawain was celebrated for his courtesy and expressed his willingness to marry the hag. Upon hearing this, she transformed into a woman of peerless beauty. Alas! Her looks endured either by day or by night – but not both. Gawain said he would prefer to enjoy her beauty while they were in bed at night. In distress, she said that then she must hide away, for it would humiliate her to appear at court, warts and all. Good and gentle Gawain said she must choose whatever suited her best. His compassion broke the curse put on her and her

brother, the baron, by their wicked stepmother –
he to challenge passers-by to solve his riddle, she
to remain ugly until a fellow took her hand in
marriage and permitted her to have her own
way.'

Hannah said nothing, but shifted from foot to
foot. Alban Clough noticed the movement.

'You are a busy lady, Chief Inspector. Enough
of Gawain. Follow me to the Room of Spirits and
I will tell you about the boggles and barghests
that populate our land of lakes. Stories that go
back centuries and yet have resonance in this
grubby, sterile age. The eternal nature of our
legends, their ageless qualities, are integral to
their enduring appeal.'

Hannah shook her head. 'Thank you, but I
must go.'

He bowed his head. 'A pity. If I may say so,
Chief Inspector, I hope that you will come back
to keep me company again before long.'

His wink was so roguish as to leave Hannah lost
for words.

Money was tight, that was the only fly in the
ointment. Guy had identified a nice little
restaurant where he was going to take Sarah this
evening. It would be a night to remember for her,
all the more delightful because they had not
yielded to temptation at the first opportunity. But
he liked his wallet to bulge with high denomin-
ation notes – women always found that impressive
– and as he checked his wallet while studying the
menu in the window of the restaurant, he realised
there would be no more treats without a further

injection of funds.

Striding back towards the Glimpse under a sky the colour of lead, he told himself his lack of cash was Megan's fault. In the days leading up to their break-up, she had become increasingly stingy, no longer so quick to whip out her credit cards when something needed paying for. Guy's preferred lifestyle relied on his companion of the moment matching his generosity of spirit with a willingness to foot the bills. Although he'd raided Megan's purse before leaving Llandudno – she shouldn't begrudge him a few quid after they'd shared so much – it had yielded measly pickings.

He turned into Campbell Road. Casual inquiry about Sarah's finances had revealed that her only substantial asset was the Glimpse. Her husband had transferred it into her name under the divorce settlement and paid off the mortgage, but he contributed a paltry sum in alimony and the money she made out of tenants was largely off-set by living costs. Shame. Guy was confident that he could persuade her to follow his expert advice and entrust a decent sum to him with a view to establishing a diversified portfolio of equities and bonds, if only she had something worthwhile to invest. This lack of ready funds explained why she hadn't spent much on her home. Apart from a surprisingly swish PC, she didn't seem to have much of value and the building needed maintenance. The good news was that, with property prices in the Lakes sky high, the equity must be worth a packet. He'd fallen on his feet. Sarah was worth more than she realised.

131

Back in her car, Hannah checked her mobile. Two messages: one from Les Bryant, the other from Daniel Kind. Which first? No contest.

'Daniel, this is Hannah.'

'Thanks for returning the call. Hope you don't mind my...'

'Of course not.' She answered too quickly, not wanting him to think her precious. 'Marc said he'd seen you at the bookshop.'

'How are things?'

Last time they'd met, she'd mentioned the miscarriage. Marc and her best mate Terri were the only other people who knew. She was usually so wary about imparting confidences, she could scarcely believe she'd told him. He was still almost a stranger, and yet because he was his father's son, it was as if they knew each other intimately.

'Fine. And you? Marc tells me you're researching a new project.'

'An excuse for mooching round bookshops.' He took a breath. 'Hannah, it would be good to catch up with you. I was wondering if we might meet sometime.'

'I'd like that.'

'Then...'

She didn't stop to think, or worry about seeming eager. 'Do you have any free time in the next few days?'

'Miranda's down in London at present. My time's my own. You're not around tomorrow, by any chance?'

'Do you know Café d'Art in Kendal?'

'I'll find it.'

'If you can make it for six-thirty, we could have

half an hour before I dash off home.'

'Perfect.'

As she dialled Les Bryant's number, she felt dizzy with elation. It took her back to schooldays and the excitement of a date. Stupid in a woman of her age, let alone a woman committed to a long-term relationship.

'You're going to love this.' Les, at his dourest.

'Don't tell me. Lauren's over-spent on media relations and run out of funds for the team's competency payments?'

'I'd put nowt past her ladyship, but actually it's your mate, Di Venuto.'

'No mate of mine.'

'He's determined to get you to review his favourite cold case. Three times he called asking for you before he condescended to speak to yours truly.'

'What's he want?'

'To share his latest scoop. He reckons he knows where we can find her.'

'On the check-out at Asda, where Elvis Presley stacks the shelves?' She wasn't usually facetious, but talking to Daniel had left her on a high.

'Not exactly. According to Di Venuto, she's buried beneath the Arsenic Labyrinth.'

'The what?'

'The Arsenic Labyrinth. It's only a mile or two from where Emma lived. So Di Venuto's like a dog with two dicks. Even if he is barking up the wrong tree. He wants to see you today.'

'Yeah, right. I'll see if I've got a window in my busy schedule.'

'Something you ought to know. He happened

133

to mention that his editor is vice-chair of Cumbrian Women in the Professions.'

Hannah groaned. Lauren had recently been elected to the committee of CWIP. Her networking skills were legendary.

'Hear that creaking noise? The window just opened.'

Hannah put down her teacup and said, 'So tell me about the Arsenic Labyrinth.'

Tony Di Venuto stretched out in his chair and lifted his legs. For a moment Hannah thought he was going to put his feet on the meeting room table, but he caught the look in her eye and decided against. She was determined not to let him get above himself.

'Never heard of it? Well, no disgrace in that. Neither had I and I've lived in the Lakes for twenty years since my parents moved down from Glasgow. After taking the call last night, I did some research. There are Arsenic Labyrinths dotted around the country, mainly in the south-east, but only one in Cumbria. Up in the Coniston fells.'

This was a man who liked listeners hanging on his every word. He paused to allow her to press him for details. When Hannah zipped her mouth, he was too pleased with himself not to carry on talking.

'Back in the nineteenth century, Coniston had its very own arsenic works. Imagine – a poison-making business, hidden in the hills.'

'In demand, was it, by Victorian gentlemen who fancied disposing of their wives?'

'Or wives who wanted rid of their husbands, who knows? The works were tucked away up on Mispickel Scar.'

Despite herself, Hannah leaned forward. 'And the labyrinth?'

'A zig-zagging flue that drew the arsenic off in saleable quantities. But the project flopped, maybe there weren't enough wannabe spouse-killers in Cumbria. By the time the arsenic works closed down, it had bled the main business of cash. The buildings were pulled down, along with the chimney. All that remains are a few stone footings from the Arsenic Labyrinth.'

'And your caller claims that Emma is buried beneath it?'

'The labyrinth was on ground level, but there are shafts and tunnels from the mines winding around the length and breadth of the Scar.'

'So the body might be anywhere?'

He stifled a yawn. 'Forgive me, Chief Inspector, I don't mean to be rude. I spent most of the night trawling for information on the net, and by seven this morning I'd arrived in Coniston. It's a tricky walk to Mispickel Scar in icy conditions and I have gashes on my knees to prove it. But the labyrinth doesn't cover a large area. If the man who phoned me is telling the truth, you won't have too far to search for Emma's remains.'

'If.'

'He didn't sound like a nutter. I'd guess that her death has preyed on his conscience, all these years. My story about the tenth anniversary was the last straw. He needed to tell someone, to do the right thing.'

135

'You believe he murdered Emma?'

'Not necessarily. He didn't admit to killing her, for what that's worth. Perhaps the culprit confided in him. Or he may have been a hired hand. Paid to murder a woman someone wanted dead.'

Did Di Venuto have a suspect in mind? Sooner or later, she'd find out who, or what, egged him on. 'Thanks for your statement. We'll give it careful consideration.'

'Please tell me you won't waste time. The man who rang me did so for the sake of Emma's sister. Karen's waited ten years, Chief Inspector. She doesn't deserve to be kept waiting any longer.'

'We'll let you know.'

His face reddened and she could tell he was fighting to choke back a furious retort. When he fixed her with his gaze, she refused to blink. He was the first to look away.

'Go for it,' Lauren Self said.

'We don't have anything to go on other than this message to the journalist. This *alleged* message. It wasn't taped.'

Lauren's eyebrows jumped. 'You're surely not suggesting that Tony Di Venuto is fibbing, simply to keep the story alive?'

'No, but...'

'As it happens, I know his editor. We've had a discreet word. She speaks highly of him as an investigative reporter.'

'Sure, but the caller may be a crank.'

'I don't think the editor of the *Post* would take kindly to the suggestion that her readers include cranks. Here we have two messages, entirely

136

coherent if a tad cryptic. No hint of self-aggrandisement. Sounds to me as though someone's conscience is playing him up. This is the beauty of cold case work, isn't it? Time works in our favour.'

'But to dig up half a hillside on the strength of an anonymous call...'

'No need to exaggerate, Hannah.' The ACC always said that her aim was to achieve consensus, by which she meant getting people to agree with a decision she'd already taken. Denied obedience, she was quick to bring out her claws. 'The investigation was dead, but Di Venuto has brought it back to life. We can't ignore what he's told us. If it turned out that he'd given us a vital lead, but we binned it, we'd be in the firing line. And I'm not just talking about flak from the leader column and letters page in the *Post*.'

'The budget may not stand a full...'

'Leave me to worry about the budget.'

Words to die for, when spoken by an ACC to a DCI. A streak of contrariness tempted Hannah to look the gift horse in the mouth.

'I'm really not sure...'

The ACC switched to action-woman mode. 'Sorry, Hannah, but if you're prepared to risk your reputation over this, I'm not. I owe it to you not to let you mess up a delicate relationship with an important branch of the media. Remember, the *Post* is the voice of the people we serve. We need them on our side. I think we've knocked around the pros and cons, don't you? Let's get weaving. And I don't mean tomorrow, Hannah. Right now, please.'

137

'Money no object, eh?' Les grimaced. 'For crying out loud, she wasn't talking that way when we were discussing my expenses.'

Hannah swung on her chair. 'Well, there are limits.'

'Listen, it's not cheap renting on this side of the Pennines. Everything round here's a rip-off compared to back home. You need a bank loan to afford a cuppa in some of these posh tea shops. Any road, what's the plan?'

'We'll start by dropping a camera down the shafts at Mispickel Scar. If that turns anything up, the next question is how to access the old workings.' Hannah jumped up and started doodling names on the whiteboard in the corner of her room. 'I'll talk to the South East Cumbria Mining Trust as well as a specialist in forensic archaeology. Maggie can look into health and safety issues and talk to the Mountain Rescue people. Bob Swindell will hunt out old maps and plans to save time and cost if we make a detailed underground search.'

'Not if,' Les said. 'When. You know the ACC better than I do. She won't leave any stone un-turned when it comes to keeping Mr Di Venuto happy.'

'There are a lot of stones up on Mispickel Scar.'

'That won't bother the ACC. You watch, she'll insist on being photographed wearing mountain gear and a hard hat.'

Tonight Sarah was a different woman. Her hair was done in a shaggy perm – rather 1980s, but never mind – and the jewelled tunic and black fitted trousers made her figure look svelte. The eye shadow and blusher were laid on with a trowel, but gold peep-toe shoes with kitten heels gave her feet a dainty look. Her toenails were painted a delicate pink. Relief washed through Guy as she locked the front door of the Glimpse and took his arm. This meal was a worthwhile investment – you had to speculate to accumulate – but it was a welcome bonus that she looked good on his arm.

The age difference didn't bother him, he was ready for a mature woman after the let-down of Megan. Once he'd lavished compliments on her appearance, Sarah did most of the talking. She'd long fancied a makeover, she said, she was fed up of being a couch potato and feeling hot with embarrassment whenever she listened to style gurus on *What Not to Wear.* Next week she might sign up with an exercise class

She's excited, he thought, she knows what's going to happen. The evening air was cold and crisp, the moon high. Words from a song bobbed in his memory. *Tonight's the night, everything's gonna be all right.* As he hummed the tune, he couldn't help congratulating himself on his decision to return to Coniston. He'd laid Emma's ghost and soon he'd lay Sarah. If he played his cards right, he could set himself up very nicely, thank you. How wise he had been not to take things in a rush. He'd hate Sarah to think that he was interested in nothing more than a quick bunk-up, or how much money he might sponge off her before it was time to move on. This was a

139

two-way thing, he was putting the fun back into her life.

The restaurant was owned by a chef with attitude and staffed by kohl-eyed blondes who shimmied between the tables as though on a catwalk. Guy commented on the finer points of the menu with just the right amount of *savoir faire;* his final touch was to order a bottle of Bolly. Sarah's protest that champagne always went to her head he dismissed with a masterful smile.

'The pleasure is mine,' he said, as they clinked glasses and toasted friendship. 'It's so good of you to sacrifice your evening to keep a lonely businessman company.'

'I'd only be watching *EastEnders.*'

When he shook his head in amiable disbelief, she said, 'Well, actually, some nights I spend quite a lot of time on the computer, rather than watching the telly.'

'Doing your accounts?'

'Not really.' She sipped the champagne. 'To be honest, I used to go in for internet dating.'

'My goodness.'

'Don't look so startled. It was a complete washout. The lies that people tell, you wouldn't credit it. Strapping six foot tall company directors turn out to be fat little bald blokes with bad breath.'

He clicked his tongue at such flagrant deception. 'You've given all that up?'

'Mmmmm.' She gulped down the rest of her drink, watched happily as he poured her some more. 'My guilty secret these days is that I like a bit of a flutter.'

'A bit of harmless fun.'

She fingered the rim of her glass. 'You know something, Rob? I've never seen the inside of a bookies' or a casino in my life. But betting is different online. I mean, it's so much less threatening. After all, nothing's certain in life, is it? Life is one big gamble, really.'

This struck him as rather profound, as well as a thought process to be encouraged. He steered the conversation adroitly to the world of business, and how much money might be made by combining investment know-how with access to ready cash. She explained that she'd never done anything more adventurous with her cash than open an account with the Halifax. His intake of breath made her turn pale.

'Whatever you do with your money carries a degree of risk. Even stashing it under the floorboards isn't as safe as you may think.'

Her eyes widened. 'I don't understand.'

'Forget the danger of burglars.' He leaned across the table, wagging a finger to emphasise his warning. 'What if inflation slashes the value of your nest egg? It's like putting a match to a wad of twenty pound notes.'

'I never thought of it like that. But you're familiar with investments. I wouldn't know where to begin.'

'It's not that difficult. The secret's in the timing. Trust me, I'm a financial adviser.'

They were both still chuckling when the starters arrived. Tucking into his devilled oysters, he let the conversation slide to the topic of Sarah's grievance about her divorce settlement. Her former husband's lawyer had been smarter than hers and while Don's earnings must be handsome these days, she was left to scrimp and save. Or rather, just scrimp. No problem, he decided as the pigeon marinated in liquorice was served. The Glimpse had potential for conversion into flats if she ever needed to downsize. She could fund a foray into the futures market by taking out a second mortgage.

He settled back in his chair. Sarah's round face looked pretty in the candlelight. He felt her knee touch his and returned the pressure. Everything was working out fine.

Sarah had already made one notable investment. New black lingerie. Basque, suspenders, the full caboodle. Once Guy had stripped her of it, she wanted him to turn off the bedroom light, but he refused.

'I like looking at you.'

Her skin was white, her face pink with champagne and excitement. 'You don't mean that.'

'Promise.'

She started to say something self-deprecating about her bulging tummy and the sag of her breasts, but he put a hand over her mouth and whispered in her ear.

'No more words, OK?'

Happiness lit the pale blue eyes as her head moved in assent. He felt her lips moisten his palm as he surveyed her body with the care of a great artist examining a model. Of course she could not compare to Megan, let alone lithe Farfalla, but the soft undulations of her doughy flesh were not unappealing. He meant to give her a night to remember. Gently, he took hold of her wrists and brought them up over her head. She made an inarticulate sound as he manoeuvred her into position. It was a rattle of contentment, she was ready to submit to whatever he wanted.

He smiled down at her. For a moment he was tempted to take advantage of her defencelessness and wrap his fingers around her white throat, just for the hell of it, just because he could. But he wouldn't do it. Tonight she was the safest woman in the world. He wouldn't betray her trust.

He'd been lying in the coffin again and when he woke, it was pitch dark. Sarah's plump buttocks were hot against his. He eased away from her and squinted at the digits on the clock radio.

Christ, still only 3.25. A long time until sunrise. Even lying here next to his newly acquired lover, he felt so alone. This must be how Al Pacino felt in *Insomnia*. He'd often wondered about the life of a detective. Maybe he could try it out after he moved somewhere else. How about checking into a country retreat as an ex-cop, someone who'd left the force under a cloud after being framed by a ruthless enemy? On second thoughts, perhaps not. Better to spend a few weeks blending in with the scenery.

His mouth was dry, his head throbbed and there was an uncomfortable nagging in his gut. Too late he'd remembered that although he liked champagne, it didn't like him. The sex had been good, but the trouble with pleasure was that it was over in a trice. Only pain lingered.

He closed his eyes and tried to sleep, but he

143

knew he would fail. Hard as he tried to shut them out, images from the past were crowding into his head. In his mind, he was back up on the Coniston Fells, standing over the prostrate form of Emma Bestwick.

After hitting her, he only had one thought. How to dispose of Emma, so that she would not be found. It was one thing for her to go missing, quite another for the corpse to be discovered and a murder inquiry launched. In the hue and cry, his name would soon come up on the list of suspects. Emma had agreed to keep their meeting secret and he'd taken care to avoid being seen on his way to Mispickel Scar, but the police's first step would be to check on local people with a criminal record. None of his convictions were for violence, but that would cut no ice if he lacked an alibi for the time of death. He needed breathing space, time to plan his escape.

Emma must disappear. The fells were pitted with mine-workings, but he needed to choose a place off the beaten track. Not easy, since pot-holers rushed down where wise walkers feared to tread. His options were limited, he didn't have the strength to carry her far. His only hope was to hide her in one of the shafts close to the Arsenic Labyrinth.

Even after ten years, the memory of that dreadful journey made him sweat like a pig. Tears had half-blinded him and he'd shivered with cold and fear as he lugged the dead weight of the woman along the rocky terrain. His heart was pounding, his muscles screamed, he wanted to fling himself down and weep and wail and beat his fists against the stony ground. He'd come here hoping to do good, but everything had gone wrong.

God knew how he'd managed it, but at last he'd reached the old footings, all that remained of the old labyrinth. Not far away was a narrow slit in the ground, barely large enough for the body of a full-grown woman. A deep, dark hole – he'd once dropped a stone down it and never even heard it hit bottom.

His knees were ready to buckle, but with a last effort he thrust Emma into the gap at his feet. He had to ease himself into the opening and use his boots to force the body past a rocky ledge that obstructed the shaft below ground level. He needed to make sure that she could not be seen from above. One more heave and the job would be done. He heard a crack, perhaps a bone in the leg breaking.

Suddenly, a faint sound came from the depths beneath his feet.

'Aaaaaaah.'

Oh sweet Jesus.

Sitting on the edge of the bed in Sarah Welsby's darkened room, the same horror clutched his throat as ten years before, at the moment he thrust Emma Bestwick out of sight.

She hadn't died when she banged her skull on the ground. It was a terrible mistake. She was still alive as he pushed her down, down, down. Into the blackness of her underground tomb.

CHAPTER EIGHT

'Blame it on the boll weevils,' Giselle Feeney said. 'There was a huge outbreak of them in the States. They decimated the cotton crops and all at once, arsenic was the most popular poison you could find. In the late nineteenth century, it became the key ingredient in lethal pesticides. Farmers couldn't get enough of it to control the boll weevils. And that wasn't all. William Morris used it to create new dyes and paints. The military used arsenic to make their bullets more brittle. Before penicillin, doctors prescribed arsenical compounds for the treatment of syphilis – yuck. As for arsenic's aphrodisiac properties, you really don't want to know. Or do you?'

Hannah laughed and dodged the question. 'Versatile stuff.'

They were lounging on the L-shaped leather sofa in Giselle's fourth floor apartment, high above the River Kent. Her living room was so high-tech, with its plasma screen home cinema and gleaming sound system, that it wasn't easy to guess that she was a forensic archaeologist. At least until you spotted the framed photograph of Giselle in Wellington boots standing in the middle of a mediaeval burial chamber on a Scottish island.

For a woman who liked to joke that her career lay in ruins, Giselle was doing fine. She might be wearing her boyfriend's Newcastle United shirt and a pair of Primark loafers, but she could have afforded Calvin Klein. Big-boned, bouncy and ferociously bright, she'd given up university lecturing to set up her own consultancy. Her clients ranged from regeneration planners, required by law to survey ancient sites about to disappear forever beneath housing estates or retail parks, to police forces and the Ministry of Defence. She and Hannah had worked together once before, when fragments of a dead man kept turning up in different parts of the north of England. Giselle had reconstructed the body much as her colleagues might reassemble a clay pot. Her skill she ascribed to a youth spent putting together two-thousand-piece jigsaws. She was a nationally renowned authority on burial practices through the millennia and possessed an encyclopaedic knowledge of pretty much everything else, but Hannah liked the way she didn't allow her academic expertise to blind her to the priorities of criminal investigation. She'd expected Giselle to know about arsenic labyrinths, and she wasn't disappointed.

'Mine owners down in Devon and Cornwall couldn't believe their luck. All of a sudden, a by-product they'd struggled to dispose of was in big demand. They heated up the arsenic to extract it from the ore and made a fortune in the process. A hundred feet in, the arsenic would have cooled and left dirty white crystalline deposits on the wall. Each month the works would be shut down and the door into the labyrinth opened. They'd send boys in to scrape the arsenic off the walls. As

147

for health and safety, the kids shoved cotton wool up their nostrils and smeared clay over their skin.'

'Lovely.'

'The good old days, huh? You can imagine a mine owner in Coniston might fancy breaking the monopoly of the Cornish businesses. Never mind the plumes of sulphur spewing out of the chimney, or the occasional death by poisoning. Occupational hazards. But the arsenic wasn't plentiful enough. The venture failed and brought down the copper-mining business with it. After that, everyone gave the place a wide berth.'

'Excellent place to hide a body.'

'Do you really expect to find this woman at Mispickel?'

Hannah shrugged. 'Your guess is as good as mine. So you're on board?'

'Listen, arsenic may have gone out of fashion with murderers who want to get away with it. Too easy to detect with Marsh's test. But it's lethal stuff. One level teaspoon will kill four people. Six, if the arsenic's refined. Taxidermists used to love arsenic, because it kills off the bacteria that hasten decomposition. But I've heard of museums that have to keep preserved rhinos stored under lock and key, because the toxicity of the arsenic makes them too dangerous to display in public. Dumping a body underneath the Arsenic Labyrinth strikes me as a pretty good idea. Creepy, too. Am I on board? Try and keep me away.'

Jeremy Erskine frowned at Hannah, as though she were a dense pupil who had handed in the

148

wrong homework. His voice was loud and musical and she was sure he loved the sound of it.

'Candidly, Chief Inspector, this is shoddy journalism. The reporter simply wants to make a name for himself. There was no good reason to write about my sister-in-law's disappearance, he didn't have a shred of fresh evidence. All he's done is tear open old wounds. It took years for my wife to come to terms with what happened, and now thanks to this ghastly publicity, she's back to square one.'

They were in the conservatory at the back of the Erskines' immaculate home. From their armchairs, Hannah and Maggie Eyre could see a neatly kept winter garden bounded by a ring of oaks and sycamores. A ladder led up to a wooden tree house and the misty tops of the Langdale Pikes loomed in the distance. Outside it was freezing, but the conservatory was so snug it might have been midsummer. On the other side of the sliding doors to the main house, a boy and a girl in matching tee shirts and Nike trainers sprawled on the Axminster carpet and watched TV.

Jeremy was sitting with his wife on a wicker sofa. They were a good-looking couple, tanned and trim after a New Year spent sand-skiing in the dunes of Dubai. Jeremy was in his early forties, tall with a long jaw and flecks of grey around the temples, Karen a cool blonde in a pink short-sleeved shirt and black leather trousers. The bronzed skin was stretched tight over her cheekbones; unlike her sister, she didn't carry a surplus ounce. Jeremy took hold of his wife's hand, as if to

149

comfort her in a moment of distress, but Hannah guessed it would take more than a newspaper article to rattle Karen Erskine.

'You gave Tony Di Venuto short shrift when he spoke to you about Emma.'

'You'd do the same in my shoes. He was appallingly persistent, wanted to come here to interview us, if you please. I said it was out of the question. A disgraceful intrusion. Frankly, I was on the point of making a formal protest to his editor. I thought there were laws to protect us from that sort of behaviour these days. Don't hard-working middle class people have a right to privacy?'

Hannah stared at Karen. 'Aren't you curious about what happened to your sister?'

'Of course,' she said. 'But this publicity isn't about discovering the truth.'

'If the anonymous caller is telling the truth, then...'

'What evidence do you have that he isn't a figment of a fevered imagination?' Jeremy interrupted. 'My understanding was that a court of law requires proof.'

'We're not in a court of law.' Hannah fought the instinct to snap that he wasn't teaching Year 8 kids either. 'Mr Di Venuto has no reason to lie to us. Wasting police time is a serious offence, as he and his editor are well aware.'

'He's out to cause trouble and sell newspapers. Quite irresponsible.'

'It would be irresponsible for us to ignore what he has told us.'

'Is this what we pay our taxes for?'

'We'll survey the site before deciding what action to take. Of course, we'll keep you both informed. DC Eyre will act as liaison officer.'

Maggie gave a brisk nod. The Eyres were a farming family and Hannah knew few people as down to earth as her DC. Jeremy's pomposity was perfectly calculated to get up Maggie's nose, but her equable expression yielded no hint of distaste. Learning to hide your true feelings when interviewing witnesses was a step on the road to becoming a good police officer.

Jeremy turned to his wife. 'Sorry, darling. Seems as though we have no say in the matter. All we can do is let events take their course.'

Karen's sharp chin jutted forward. 'This isn't ever going to end, is it, Chief Inspector? If you don't find a body, we'll be at the mercy of anyone who wants to speculate about Emma and make a few quid on the side. And if by some miracle you do, that will just be the start. There'll need to be an inquest, a funeral, you'll be looking for this man who made the phone call. The media will turn it into a circus. It will be impossible for us to grieve in private.'

Would Karen grieve? She was certainly restraining her curiosity about her sister's fate.

'You have nothing to fear from the media, surely?'

'That's just where you're wrong!' Karen grasped her husband's hand. 'The head at Grizedale retires in the summer. The deputy isn't up to the job and the Governors have made it clear they would prefer to recruit internally. Jeremy is the obvious choice. He's a first class historian and the results of his students are outstanding, half of them stroll into Oxford or Cambridge. He has marvellous ideas for raising the College's profile, making it the leading independent in the North. But how will the governors react if our name features in a murder case? Parents care about these things. The sort of people who pay for their children to attend Grizedale don't want to be associated with a high profile criminal investigation, even indirectly. This could ruin Jeremy's career progression. Have you stopped to consider that?'

No, it had never crossed Hannah's mind. Her mother had taught in the state sector and Hannah went to the local comprehensive. Hannah didn't begrudge others the right to educate their kids privately, but she couldn't imagine doing it herself. Combing through rival prospectuses, weighing up which school might offer the best prospect of glittering prizes, treating education as one more luxury purchase, along with the Scandinavian hi-fi and designer kitchen?

'What do you believe happened to Emma, Mrs Erskine?'

Karen must have anticipated the question, but its bluntness threw her off balance. As if to cover her discomfort, she mimicked her husband's truculence.

'Well ... don't you think that if I knew that, I'd have mentioned it sooner?'

'I'm not asking for hard evidence. Supposition is fine. You must have a theory?'

'Emma was an unhappy person,' Jeremy said before his wife could answer. 'Don't get me wrong, I deplore homophobia as much as the next man, but it's a sad fact that many gay men and women lead unfulfilled lives. My impression is that she'd never found love. Above all, she was jealous of Karen.'

'Is that so?'

'Karen had a baby, Karen had a nice house, Karen was married to someone who adored her. She was younger and prettier and slimmer than Emma. My wife's too kind-hearted to say so, but the jealousy had been there since they were kids. As the years passed, it became a festering sore.'

'You didn't get on?'

'I hardly knew her. There was no ill will, we did our best, we invited her to our wedding. She was in Liverpool at the time, but she made an excuse and the best she could do by way of a present for her only close living relative was to send a few Marks & Spencer gift vouchers. When our daughter Sophie was christened, we even invited her to be godmother, but it was the same old story. She said she didn't believe in organised religion. As if that mattered.'

'Was there ever a row between the two of you, Mrs Erskine?'

A shake of the blonde head. 'We were always civil to each other. Emma kept her feelings buttoned up.'

'You were sure she envied you?'

Karen shrugged. 'Emma never quite fitted in anywhere. Sad, really. I thought she might go abroad when she tired of Merseyside. Instead, she came back to the Lakes. She told me she felt homesick, but it was city living that she was sick of. There was nothing for her here.'

'You met her at the museum, I believe?'

'When she returned, Jeremy and I were determined to make an effort.'

'Blood's thicker than water, don't forget,' Jeremy sounded as though he wanted to make Hannah write it out one hundred times after school.

'Was there any suggestion that she live with you?'

'Good Heavens, no.' Jeremy looked as startled as if she'd asked him to open up his home to an asylum seeker. 'At the time we had a tiny semi in Ambleside, near Rothay Park. Very different from this place, I can assure you. I'd started teaching history at Grizedale College, but this was long before I was promoted to head of year. To have taken in Emma would have been impossible, even if she'd suggested it. Which, of course, she did not. She rented a bed-sit for a while and then moved in with the Goddards.'

'Yes, I was going to ask you about that.' Hannah made a show of scratching her head. 'I know it's a small world, but ... it does seem amazing, that, of all the places where she might have found a roof over her head, she finished up with your ex-wife and her new husband?'

'The Lakes *is* a small world, Chief Inspector, haven't you noticed? Thirty miles across, and a population less than Bolton.'

'Even so.'

Jeremy sucked in a breath. 'Vanessa and I met and married not long after I qualified as a teacher. She was a librarian, full of ideals about educating the disadvantaged, people who had never opened a book in their lives. I taught at a comprehensive on the Furness Peninsula. Plenty of deprivation in that neck of the woods, since the steelworks closed and shipbuilding went out of fashion. When you meet Vanessa, Chief Inspector, you see a middle-aged woman with an unsightly birthmark on her face, so you may find this difficult to understand – but I found her passion thrilling.'

'No, I don't find that so difficult to understand,' Hannah said softly and for a moment, despite everything, she warmed to him.

'Within weeks, we were walking down the aisle. Looking back, it was a mistake. I was young, naïve. Vanessa and I could have been such good friends, but ... when I met Karen, I realised she was the woman for me.'

'Love at first sight,' Karen said with a complacent smile. 'It knocked the breath out of both of us.'

'Vanessa took our break-up very hard. She blamed Karen for seducing me, but that was unfair. It was my fault, if you like. My decision, I take full responsibility.'

He gave a defiant nod and then lifted his head, so Hannah could see that the nobility of his profile matched his character. The admiration in Karen's eyes depressed her. It wasn't his adultery that made her cringe, it was his conceit.

Jeremy cleared his throat. 'I was thrilled for Vanessa when she met Francis. He sounds a decent chap and he's certainly made her happy. Even given her a child, the one thing I could

155

never achieve.'

You patronising sod. But Hannah could do hypocrisy too and she coated her smile with sugar.

'I gather their boy is a pupil at Grizedale.'

'We call them students.' He corrected her with a little laugh. Hannah would have found it less offensive if he'd rapped her on the knuckles with a steel rule. 'At present he's a year off senior school, so our paths don't yet cross. When they do, it won't be a problem. Vanessa is a decent woman, I'm sure he's a fine lad.'

Hannah gritted her teeth, and Jeremy sailed on.

'Unfortunately, I suspect Vanessa resents poor Karen to this day. As for taking in Emma as a lodger, well, I don't wish to be unkind...'

'But?'

'I suspect that it suited her to make friends with Emma.'

'Why?'

'Evidently she found out that Emma and Karen were far from close.'

'Are you suggesting there was an attraction between her and Emma?'

'Good grief, no.' He was genuinely amused. 'Vanessa is voraciously heterosexual in her appetites, I can assure you of that.'

Hannah cast a glance at Karen. Could a smirk be coy? If so, hers was.

'What, then?'

'You wish me to be frank?'

'Please.'

'Very well, if I must. I have no wish to be unkind to Vanessa, but in my opinion, she wanted to hear bad things about Karen, to make her feel better about losing me.'

Hannah noticed that, while her husband was talking about his first wife, Karen yawned and stretched out her legs. A woman at ease with herself, confident that she'd got her man exactly where she wanted him.

'Darling, this is old news. None of it matters any more.'

'Don't forget,' her husband said with an unexpected stab at humour, 'my subject is history.'

'And cold case work involves exploring the past,' Hannah said. 'After she left the Goddards, Emma bought her bungalow. How could she afford it?'

'She told us she'd had a big win on the lottery. It was only after she disappeared that we found out from your people she'd lied about that. Goodness knows why.'

'So where did the money really come from?'

Jeremy coughed. 'As it happens, I have an idea.'

He sounded so proud that Hannah had to force herself not to mime applause. She could tell that Maggie was close to bursting with suppressed laughter.

'I'd love to hear it.'

'Well, once Emma's relationship with Alexandra Clough ended, she fell ill. Depression, stress, one of those ailments fashionable among people who don't want to go into work. The Cloughs are wealthy, perhaps she threatened to sue them.'

'They deny it.'

'Is that surprising, if they'd mistreated her?'

'Did Emma tell you that they had?'

'We didn't see anything of her while she was ill.

A quick word on the phone was as close as we came. She may have been poorly, but I'm sure she wasn't at death's door. And of course, she got better.'

'You visited her bungalow?'

Karen nodded. 'The week after she moved in. She was pale, but she told me she'd lost a stone and a half and she was looking all the better for it. I hadn't even known she was interested in reflexology. But that was Emma. She was prone to fits of enthusiasm, but they never lasted. Look at the way she kept changing jobs. That's why I wasn't too surprised when she upped sticks and left the district without a word.'

'Without her car and her passport?'

'She didn't consult me before she moved to Liverpool, either. So she had form, isn't that the word detectives use? And it wasn't so strange if she wanted to start a brand new life. Travel, see the world. After paying out on the bungalow and a new car, there wasn't much cash left. The building society repossessed the house, you know, because she wasn't around to keep up the monthly payments.'

Hannah had already found that out. Pity, it removed a possible motive. She'd wondered if Karen had planned to have Emma declared dead so that, as nearest living relative, she would inherit her sister's estate. But there wasn't much left to inherit.

'Surely she would have contacted you during a period of ten years?'

'Emma could be frustrating. Unreliable. And don't forget, she'd had the benefit of listening to

Vanessa Goddard's opinions of me. Views based on prejudice and envy. Could I help the fact the poor woman had a disfigurement?'

Hannah noticed Maggie's eyes narrowing, sensed her DC was losing patience. Easy to believe in Vanessa's bitterness over the betrayal, but was it credible that she'd poisoned Emma's mind to such an extent that she would break off all contact – not only with Karen but with Vanessa herself and everyone else?

'You saw her the day before she disappeared, Mr Erskine?'

'You've read my statement. It was an entirely innocent visit.'

'Of course. You had a bad back.'

His lips pursed, but if he detected irony, he was too smart to make an issue of it. 'I've been a martyr to my vertebrae over the years. The legacy of an old rugby injury, it flares up every now and then. Karen mentioned it when she called on Emma and Emma reckoned she could help. Admittedly, for a few days after my visit, I felt better. But she didn't achieve a lasting solution. These days I see an osteopath in Keswick, he's first class.'

'What did you talk about while you there?' Maggie asked suddenly.

'Good grief, Constable, you can't expect me to remember a casual conversation at this distance of time.'

Maggie gave him the sort of baleful look her father might reserve for a mongrel worrying sheep. 'She was your sister-in-law and it was the last time you spoke to her. Wouldn't the convers-

159

ation stick in your mind?'

Jeremy folded his arms. 'Not my mind. Even when your people interviewed me before, I couldn't recall details. She was pleasant, without being chatty. As if her mind was far away. On other things.'

Hannah said, 'In your original statement, you suggested that she might have planned to leave the area and do something else.'

'It seems a perfectly rational inference to draw.'

His careful syntax was getting under Hannah's skin. She suspected him of yearning to give her a detention the moment she split an infinitive.

'You said that she seemed – excited about something.'

'Did I? Perhaps, but it is so long ago. Our conversation was superficial, the usual small talk, nothing beyond that.'

'There was no argument between you? No difficulties between Emma and your wife?'

'What would we argue about?' Jeremy asked. 'She lived a very different life from Karen and me. Each to his own, we weren't judgmental.'

'Any further light you can shed on Emma or what might have given rise to her disappearance?'

She asked the question for form's sake, rather than in the hope of eliciting fresh information. The Erskines were hard work. Talk about blood and stones.

'Nothing whatever,' Karen said, as her husband slipped his arm around her shoulder.

No point in probing further without more to go on. Jeremy showed them out and as he led them through the living room, Hannah noticed a

160

familiar glossy hardback on the coffee table. Daniel Kind had written it to accompany his series on BBC Television.

'You're a keen historian in your spare time as well as at work, Mr Erskine?'

'As it happens, I'm this year's chairman of the Grizedale and Satterthwaite Historical Association. The oldest society of its kind in Cumbria.'

'So you know all about the Arsenic Labyrinth?'

He gave a little laugh, probably meant to be self-deprecating. 'Well, I wouldn't claim to be an authority, but of course I am aware of it.'

'Someone was telling me it formed part of an unsuccessful business.'

'Yes, the arsenic works ruined the Inchmores. At one time they were one of the richest families in the county. You only have to look at the hall to see the scale of Clifford Inchmore's ambition. It may lack Brantwood's glamour, but to my mind it's an even more remarkable building. Sir Clifford dreamed of establishing a dynasty. Hubris, perhaps. But his son George blew it.'

'Because of trading in arsenic?'

'Not only that. He fell out with Albert Clough, whom Clifford had taken into partnership. Albert was a consummate businessman and George didn't like the idea of playing second fiddle to him once Clifford retired. The outcome was that Albert left the firm and set up on his own in direct competition, the worst of all possible worlds from the Inchmores' perspective. As their star fell, Albert's rose.'

'Must have been painful for them to sell the hall to Albert.'

'Indeed. No wonder it's been said that Mispickel Scar is cursed. A load of superstitious nonsense, no doubt, but local folk used to take it seriously.'

'What's the story of the curse?'

Jeremy resembled a High Court judge, invited to choose the winner of an end of pier talent show. 'I really could not say. Folklore is scarcely history. You'd need to ask Alban Clough, he's the expert. Of course, he's always revelled in the triumph of his family over the Inchmores.'

'He did give a job to young Tom Inchmore.'

'Humiliating the Inchmores through unforced acts of generosity became a family tradition for the Cloughs. It started when George's son William Inchmore had to accept charity from Armstrong Clough and take up a sinecure in the Cloughs' booming firm. By all accounts, William was an idler, who preferred wine, women and song to the hard graft that made his family's fortune. Yet even he must have found it a bitter pill, to see Cloughs living it up in the house his grandfather built.'

'Clogs to clogs in three generations?'

'Precisely.' He noticed her gaze lingering on the glossy cover of Daniel's book. 'Does your own interest in history extend beyond cold case work, Chief Inspector? Perhaps you saw these programmes? They were quite tolerable, not the dumbed-down rubbish we usually get in return for our licence fee.'

'You know that Daniel Kind has moved to the Lakes? He lives in Brackdale.'

'Really?' An opportunist spark flared in

162

Jeremy's eyes. 'I wonder if he'd be interested in talking to the Association. Do I gather that you are acquainted with him?'

'Our paths have crossed. His father was a police officer, that's the connection.'

'Good Lord. You don't happen to know how I can get in touch with him?'

Hannah was conscious of Maggie's solid presence beside her. Perhaps it was embarrassment that caused her to lie – though this was absurd, what was there to be embarrassed about?

'Sorry, I don't have his number.'

'What do you make of those two, then?' Hannah asked as they were driving back.

Maggie shifted in the passenger seat. You could almost hear wheels turning as she weighed up pros and cons. She didn't do flair, but at this stage of her career she was none the worse for it. Hannah was encouraging her to reason more laterally, whilst desperately striving to avoid Lauren-speak like *thinking outside the box*.

'He wouldn't have lasted five minutes in my old school.'

'Nor mine. And Karen?'

'Thank God she's not *my* sister.'

They both laughed and then Maggie said, 'Can I ask a question?'

'Fire away.'

'It isn't about the Erskines, but Les.'

'Les Bryant?'

'Is he all right?'

'Any reason to believe he isn't?'

'Well, I dunno. He doesn't seem himself to me,

163

that's all.'

'Can't say I'd noticed. Hasn't he always been a grumpy old sod? The time to worry is if he starts singing the ACC's praises and buying the first round when we go to the pub. Then I'll know for sure he's sickening for something.'

'Sorry, perhaps I'm imagining things. Forget I mentioned it.'

Hannah frowned as traffic lights ahead turned to red just as she was tempted to rush through on amber. Maggie didn't imagine things, that was the point. Better keep an eye on Les. Just in case.

Guy and Sarah stayed in bed until mid-day. After she finally got up, he lingered under the warm duvet while she busied herself in the kitchen, making them a scratch lunch. He'd assumed she would be out of condition and her reserves of stamina had come as a surprise. She was never satisfied for long and the endless exertion, coupled with a night broken by memories of the Arsenic Labyrinth, had left him listless and unable to stop yawning. He'd drunk too much the previous evening and his throat was dry. When he moved, his body protested and he worried that he might have put his back out.

When he hobbled downstairs, she flung her arms around his neck, pressing herself into him as they embraced. Her tongue was large and insistent. He caught her glancing at the kitchen table and he wondered if she entertained fantasies of emulating Jessica Lange in *The Postman Always Rings Twice*.

Not this bloody postman, he thought, I'm

164

knackered. As gently as he could, he disengaged from her.

'Thought you'd be hungry,' she said with a provocative smile.

'I wouldn't say no to a couple of slices of toast. Any chance of some soup?'

'Rob Stevenson, what are you like!' She pretended to cuff his ear. 'That's not what I meant at all.'

It was weird, he thought, as he watched her stretching up into the cupboards above her head, mauve leggings so tight over her ample backside that they must be in danger of splitting. The thrill of the chase meant far more than the triumph of conquest and it wouldn't be long before his interest fizzled out. Nothing personal, it had been the same with Megan, with Farfalla, with Maryell and with all the rest.

His head was throbbing, the air was stale. He might be suffering from a touch of claustrophobia, maybe even the early stages of flu. All through lunch, she never stopped chattering about her younger days before the marriage that went wrong. It was as if she were trying to suck him into her existence, make him understand every little thing about her. She didn't seem to appreciate that affairs like theirs were transient. You savoured the moment and then got on with the rest of your life. He hardly spoke, although she hadn't reached the stage of chastising him for having so little to say to her. The blissful look would give way to a reproachful frown and she would click her tongue each time he fell short of expectations. Nobody ever realised how difficult it

165

was, when you made up an identity for yourself. You had to take such care to avoid making a mistake, a careless remark that revealed you were not the man you claimed to be.

As soon as they'd finished eating, he made an excuse about phoning a colleague and hurried out before she could ask any tricky questions. So far his vagueness about his working life had given him the freedom to spend his time as he pleased, but she was starting to take a closer interest. Soon she would be interfering, making demands on his time. She ought to be content to trust him. To allow him, as he liked to say, to do all the worrying for her.

He walked quickly, keen to put distance between himself and the stuffiness of the Glimpse. By the time he'd reached the short, low wooden pier at Monk Coniston, the pain in his back had eased and his head had cleared. He prided himself on being a man who was never cast down for long. Time to look on the bright side.

He stood by the water's edge, remembering. This was where he'd collected a small fortune ten years ago. The world had been at his feet, he'd felt as though he could achieve anything. And now he was back here and about to get lucky again. Sarah was eating out of the palm of his hand. She only harped on because she was happy. He'd made fantastic progress and soon he would be rolling in money. Think of the classy, secluded hotels that he might grace with his presence. He deserved a few treats.

Halfway between Brantwood and Nibthwaite,

he emerged from the forest path and strode towards the shore, feet crunching over the narrow strip of clean shingle in front of the trees. He paused and gazed across the lake towards Torver Beck Common, the Old Man and the Yewdale Fells. The sky was clear and he could make out the silvery water of the White Lady cascade. Impossible to see Mispickel Scar from here, it was masked by familiar peaks. He could almost believe that the Arsenic Labyrinth was one more figment of his vivid imagination.

'So you're fine?' Daniel asked.

Hannah cradled the glass of Sancerre in her hand. The Café d'Art combined a small gallery with a framing workshop and a wine bar. They were sitting at a discreet corner table. The wall behind them was crowded with oils on canvas, purple fells and ochre sunsets. Jacques Brel crooned in the background, the candle burning on their table gave off a subtle lilac fragrance.

'I think so.'

'You look fine.'

'What you mean is, I was an utter wreck when we last met.'

He laughed. They both knew that wasn't what he meant. Her hair was several shades lighter, he noticed. She was changing her look, but by degrees. In five years' time, she'd be a dazzling blonde.

'You'd had a tough time.'

'Not just me. Both of us might have been killed.' She was determined not to spoil their get-together by discussing her miscarriage. No more

167

dwelling on what might have been.

He took his cue. 'That'll teach me to poke my nose in.'

'Didn't you want to follow in Ben's footsteps?'

'I'd seen at first-hand how policing can mess up your home life. He left us for Cheryl when I was a kid, remember? My mum would have keeled over if I'd announced I wanted to become a detective. Besides, I was addicted to history. To be paid money to research it seemed like Heaven.'

'Yet you gave it up.'

'I gave up academic life, the back-biting of the Senior Common Room. I'll never give up history. It's in the blood.'

'A passion for what's dead and gone?'

'Uh-uh.' He grinned. 'The yearning to find out. The detective urge, if you like.'

'Actually, I rather admire the way you walked away from Oxford.'

'What's to admire?' She'd caught him off guard. 'It ought to be a cause for shame, if anything. An admission of defeat. Failure.'

Brel was singing 'If We Only Have Love'. Hannah took another sip of wine, contemplating Daniel. Something about him appealed to her, was it the resemblance to his father? She'd cared a lot about Ben. Although he was dead, killed by a hit and run driver, she'd seen his face many times in her dreams.

'Must have felt liberating, though.'

'Very.' He helped himself to a handful of salty peanuts from a bowl. 'So that is what appeals to you? The notion of escape?'

168

She nodded. 'I love my job, most of the time. When I'm doing what I signed up to do – detecting crime. It's the crap that gets in the way that I can't bear. The politics, the management stuff, the need to keep the right people sweet. Don't get me wrong, I can cope. But my oldest friend, Terri, is always complaining the job eats away at the soul.'

'Ever thought of doing something else?'

'I'm not qualified for anything else.'

'Well, I made the break.'

'For you it was easy.' As the words left her mouth, she regretted their sting. 'I mean, you can write from home. What would I do – become a private detective? A gumshoe in Grasmere, a shamus from Seatoller? I don't think so.'

'Sorry, I didn't mean...'

'Forgive me.' She wanted to reach across the table and touch his hand, but it wasn't a good idea. 'Marc keeps saying I'm too tense, I need to lighten up. Blame it on the job, it's the usual suspect.'

'What are you working on at present?' He needed to steer the conversation to safe water. 'Marc mentioned a case in Coniston.'

'A missing woman. Ten years on, we may be about to find her.'

'Can you talk about it?'

She knew she ought to say no, but it was a distraction from anything more personal. His dad had been the most honest man she'd ever met and she was sure Daniel was to be trusted. And another thing. Emma's story would absorb him, and she wanted him to be absorbed in what

169

she had to say.

'Why not?' She smiled through the candle's flame. 'What do you know about the Arsenic Labyrinth?'

'Jeremy Erskine is a fan of yours,' Hannah said forty minutes later, savouring the last of her wine. 'His interest in history extends beyond teaching at a posh school. He has a copy of your book and he almost swooned when I said you'd moved to the Lakes. He'd love you to talk to his historical society.'

'Not the Grizedale and Satterthwaite?'

'That's the one.'

'I seem to remember an invitation from them whilst I was at Oxford. Shortly after Aimee died; I hadn't got myself together.'

'Takes a long time to get yourself together after something like that.'

Aimee had committed suicide by leaping from the Saxon tower in Cornmarket. A few months later, he'd met Miranda and left Oxford for good. Daniel knew why his sister disapproved. Louise thought he'd got involved on the rebound. He'd wanted to escape by taking up with someone as different from Aimee as he could find.

'Suppose I'd better get in touch with your mate Jeremy.'

'He's no mate of mine. Truth is, he's extra-ordinarily easy to dislike.'

'Not a helpful witness?'

'He'd prefer Emma to be quietly forgotten. All that bothers him is the effect a cold case investigation may have on his career prospects. He may

170

be a fellow historian, but you don't have much else in common.'

'You never know.'

She flushed. 'Sorry, that sounds as though I know you inside out. Very presumptuous. Pay no attention, you and Jeremy may get on like a house on fire.'

He put down his coffee cup. 'When I was a boy, people said I took after my father. How true it was, who knows? But if you think he'd have disliked Jeremy...'

'Ben would have detested him.'

'I'll talk to him. For all I know he's an expert on John Ruskin and I can pick his brains as part of my research.'

'You're working on something new?'

When he explained about his thirst for more information about Ruskin's Coniston years, she shook her head and said, 'I can't offer you any local knowledge. I was taken round Brantwood as a teenager and all I remember is the gorgeous gardens. And that poor old Ruskin was a loser in love.'

'Like Emma Bestwick, by the sound of it. She had all that money – however she came by it – but nobody to love.'

'That's why Sid Thornicroft thought she'd done a runner. He argued that she'd found someone new and followed them, perhaps abroad. Or else gone in search of a new life.'

'Ten years is a long time to maintain radio silence.'

'It does happen. You know all about beginning a new life. Tell me, do you ever yearn for the old

171

days, town and gown?'

'Never.'

'So it's worked out perfectly, starting afresh?'

'Nothing's ever perfect, is it?' He smiled. 'Miranda hated the Lakeland winter. At dead of night, Tarn Fold is too quiet for her. She has trouble sleeping, she's accustomed to London, the eternal rumble of traffic in the distance. Not to worry. Ruskin said imperfection is essential to life; who am I to argue?'

'Did Ruskin have an opinion on everything, then?'

'Pretty much.'

'Any words of wisdom for a hard-pressed law enforcement officer, investigating a suspected murder?'

'You won't be encouraged. He deplored fascination with death, saw it as a sign of the ills of Victorian England. He put the boot into Charles Dickens for being morbid, said far too many respectable characters met grotesque ends in *Bleak House*. God knows what he'd make of late night TV and the vogue for autopsy close-ups. Ruskin reckoned a good society was interested in life, not death.'

'Nothing would please me more than for Emma to walk through that door right now and demand to know what all the fuss is about.'

'Not going to happen, is it?'

'I don't think so.'

'What do you believe went on?'

'Assuming she's dead, we have to look at the possibilities of accident or suicide before ruling them out. If the call to the journalist isn't a hoax

172

and we do find she's buried under the Arsenic Labyrinth, it's hard to imagine that she got there by chance.'

'Sex murder?'

'Perhaps. But not committed by the obvious suspect.'

'The late Tom Inchmore?'

'Yes, some of my colleagues had him in the frame. It would have been quite an end for the Inchmore dynasty, if the last in the line turned out to be a murderer.'

'If Emma is dead, presumably the anonymous caller is the culprit?'

'He might be an accomplice. Or someone the murderer confided in. But yes, the chances are, he killed her. What we don't know is why. Or why he's decided to break his silence. We can't link him to the original investigation. If it was a sexually motivated murder, it doesn't fit the usual pattern. Did she go to the Arsenic Labyrinth of her own free will? And if so, why?'

'You say the place is off the beaten track,' Daniel said. 'Suitable for a secret assignation. A tryst. Perhaps she went to meet someone. Possibly not the person she *actually* met. Maybe she went looking for love and finished up dead.'

Hannah laughed. 'You're incorrigible. A real chip off the old block.'

'The difference is, my father actually became a detective. All I do is speculate from an armchair.'

'He'd have been proud of you,' she said suddenly. 'I wish you'd met him before he died.'

There was a long pause as they looked at each other across the table. As Daniel opened his

173

mouth to speak, Hannah glanced at her watch.

'God, I'm late, I'll have to skedaddle.'

He wanted to protest, even as she rose to her feet, but all he managed to say was, 'Good to see you again.'

Not looking at him, she said, 'Don't leave it so long next time.'

CHAPTER NINE

'Not much of a labyrinth,' Les sniffed.

He was wearing a greatcoat and Cossack hat that made him look like an extra from *Dr Zhivago*. Hannah, Maggie and Giselle Feeney were standing close to him on a long ledge of rock at Mispickel Scar, surveying the hollow that a glacier had scooped out between the fells. Snow had fallen during the night and ice underfoot had made the climb slow and treacherous. For the last half hour Les had lagged behind the three younger women, puffing and grunting and making it plain that he wished he was back home with his feet up in front of the fire. He'd sneezed once or twice and mumbled that he was starting with a cold.

'This was never going to be Hampton Court Maze.' Hannah rubbed her gloved hands together, as much to keep warm as to engender enthusiasm. 'So what exactly do we have here?'

The random scattering of stones was a bleak monument to Mispickel Scar's industrial heritage, but Giselle contemplated the scene as lovingly as if it were a personal Eden.

'Mispickel is another name for arsenopyrite. A silvery-white sulphide of iron and arsenic. I suppose when the works were built, George Inchmore expected it would make him more money than copper had made for his father. But the vein was poor. The cost of digging into the Scar far exceeded the value of what he extracted. His mistake was not to throw in the towel more quickly. He must have had an obstinate streak. The works kept going for six or seven years.'

Maggie opened out a photocopy of an old plan Bob Swindell had found, and jerked a thumb towards a heap of rubble forty yards away.

'So the chimney was over there?'

Giselle nodded. 'It had to be out in the open, far enough away from the face of the fells, so they could get a good draught. Picture plumes of mucky sulphur belching out in the middle of the Lake District. Not very green.'

'Let's get on with it, shall we?' Les grumbled.

Giselle winked at Hannah. 'Next to the stack was a cube-shaped building, designed on a square plan. Two storeys, hipped roof with a ventilator set in. Ore was fed into a big hopper on the top floor and from there it was spread down on top of a pan that rotated slowly inside a small chamber below. The chamber was heated by two coal-fired furnaces to a thousand degrees Fahrenheit, a temperature high enough to draw off the arsenic. It was sucked down a flue attached to the chimney stack. Although the flue was a thousand feet long, it folded back on itself

175

every ten yards or so. That's why it was called an arsenic labyrinth.'

Les stamped his feet. 'Blot on the bleeding landscape if you ask me. No wonder they say it's cursed.'

'Is the lack of vegetation an after-effect of the poison?' Hannah asked.

Maggie nodded. 'I spoke to health and safety and they don't regard the arsenical traces as a serious risk to our people. Everyone will have protective clothing and it'll be incinerated once we're done.'

Les blew his nose loudly and said, 'You can't do better than have a damn good shower.'

Maggie frowned at him and Hannah recalled their conversation in the car. 'The challenge will be shifting all that stone so we can look for a body.'

'Point out the shafts for us, will you?' Hannah asked.

'The whole area is a honeycomb,' Giselle said. 'Don't forget, the Old Man of Coniston is nicknamed the Hollow Mountain. George saw an opportunity to exploit land that was otherwise useless. There were two main shafts here, according to the records. See that large boulder? One of them is underneath it. The stone looks suspiciously like the Sword of Damocles. You see it in old photographs. Until nine or ten years ago the Sword was a pinnacle balancing up on that ridge of rock. Very dangerous, it deterred all but the rashest fell-walkers.'

'So it might have fallen after Emma disappeared?'

176

Silence fell as they digested what this might mean.

Maggie consulted her plan. 'According to the records, there should be another way down into the mines closer to the slope of the fell, but a landslip has covered that up as well. The tunnels were connected. Shall we clear both entrances?'

'I think so,' Hannah said. 'There may have been collapses underground as well. Let's make sure we have good access. Di Venuto's caller didn't give details and we don't want the whole team hanging around here longer than necessary.'

'Too bloody right,' Les said. 'They'll catch their death if it gets any colder.'

'Let's not attract too much attention too soon. Apart from Di Venuto we don't have the Press on our backs, and he's forced to keep his cards close to his chest, for fear he'll lose his exclusive. We're not being mithered by grieving relatives, but if we do find a body, all hell will break loose. Let's make progress before the world and his wife come rubber-necking.'

'Hey, no bugger in his right mind will tramp out to this God-forsaken spot.'

'You'd be surprised. Mispickel may not be as popular as the Old Man or Levens Water, and the warning signs will scare off most people. But even in the depths of winter, a few hardy souls venture out. The minute we start work, the rumour mill down in the village will go into overdrive. We can't hang around.'

'How long are you going to give it?'

'As long as it takes to find out whether Emma is buried here.'

'Wherever she is, she must be warmer than me.'

'So a camera survey is the first step?' Maggie said hastily.

Hannah nodded. 'Before we send the CSIs shinning down ropes, let's shine a light into the shafts. See what we've got.'

Sarah proposed Sunday lunch at a pub she knew near Troutbeck. 'My treat,' she insisted, to Guy's relief. He'd not made a penny since taking the money from Megan's purse.

She drove a rusty old Citroën, painted an embarrassing orange. When, after five minutes of fiddling with the ignition key, she finally got it to start, it hissed and clanked and he wasn't convinced they would make the round trip without breaking down. The heating didn't work and she had the radio tuned to a brass band concert. At the traffic lights in Ambleside he asked how often she changed cars.

'Don bought this little sweetie for me after the divorce. It wasn't new then, of course. But he said it would be fine for my needs.' She did something with the gear lever that sounded chaotic. 'I don't like driving much, I never travel far.'

Just as well. 'How about asking him to replace it?'

'He wouldn't,' she said with flat certainty.

'He has obligations.' Guy was hazy about divorce law, but he'd gained the impression from lads' magazines that it favoured women at the expense of their former husbands. 'Get him to put his hand in his pocket.'

'He has a family to look after.'

178

'You mustn't let him off the hook. Honestly, if you want to give him a call, I can advise you about what to say.'

'Oh, Rob, I couldn't do that. I mean, I'm not proud or anything, but no woman likes to beg.'

He winced as they bounced over a speed bump. 'It's not begging. Simply a matter of making sure you get what is due.'

'Really, I couldn't. We agreed some time ago, we each had to make our own way in the world.'

'But he deserted you after you'd given him the best years of your life.'

She glanced at him. 'Not all the best years, I hope.'

Taking her eye off the road was a mistake. A lorry driver sounded his horn long and hard as the Citroën took a bend at speed and finished up on the other side of the road for twenty yards.

He said urgently, 'You're a woman on your own. Don should pick up more of the bills, it's only right.'

'I think he's hoping I won't be on my own for ever.'

Her complacency bothered him. How likely was it that she'd find a man who offered her a meal ticket for life? She didn't even have much luck recruiting guests for the Glimpse. His concern was unselfish – what would happen to her after he moved on? It was as well that he'd been careful not to make any rash promises. Apart from a few whispered platitudes at moments of greatest intimacy, which obviously didn't count, he'd said not a word to suggest that this was more than a fleeting romance. He didn't want her to get any ideas about a long-term relationship. That wasn't his kind of thing at all.

Miranda was back. Her face shone with excitement when he collected her from the station at Oxenholme. Ethan wanted to appoint her as an associate editor of the magazine and she wanted to know whether Daniel thought she should accept. Whether the new job title involved anything more than an increase in pay wasn't clear, but she left him in no doubt what he was meant to say. Of course he said it.

'Bite his hand off,' he said as they left the grey limestone of Kendal behind. He was glad to see her happy and, besides, what else could he say?

'Even though I'll need to spend more time in London?'

'Doesn't have to be that way. With email and video conferencing, you can work remotely.'

She puffed out her cheeks. 'In theory, fine. But I'm not sure that's what happens in the real world.'

'Give it a go. If you don't enjoy it, you can always take a step down.'

'Ethan wouldn't take kindly to that. The last thing he said to me before I left the office was to think over the offer. If I say yes, I'm making a long-term commitment. He's giving me the chance to put my own imprint on the magazine. But if I mess up, he'll bring in someone else. That's the way he operates, he's a hard-nosed businessman. There will be no going back to the status quo.'

'If you turn him down, you'll regret it.'

'But I want you to be happy with whatever I choose to do.'

As they reached the open road, he put his foot down. 'I'm happy if you're happy.'

She considered this. 'That's a cop-out, darling. I don't want you to be miserable, stuck up here while I'm gadding about in the capital.'

'I can come down and stay with you.'

'Well, yes. But I will be busy most of the time. Don't think I can just sit in the flat and entertain you. The editorial people are busy networking most nights. I'll be able to wangle you an invitation to come to some events. But you once told me you didn't care if you never attended another cocktail party or book launch in the rest of your life.'

'I didn't even enjoy my own book launch,' he said. 'Follow your instinct.'

'You don't want me to do it!'

'I never said that.'

'It's what you meant!'

All of a sudden, she was spoiling for a fight. Not out of malice, but because she craved the buzz of quarrelling. A row energised her as much as it exhausted him. Time to draw a line.

'Darling, I've already said go for it. What more can I add?'

She thrust out her lower lip. 'All right. I'll tell Ethan I'm on board. With your blessing.'

'So tell me about yourself, Rob Stevenson.'

He was tempted to say: *they call me Tusitala, the teller of tales.* But it would sound too much like taking the piss. He caught the eye of a waitress and ordered another glass of wine. Sarah asked for an orange juice because she was driving and he didn't press her to change her mind. The journey here had been hair-raising when she was sober.

'Not much to tell.'

'Now that I don't believe!' She wagged a finger. 'You know, ever since we met, I've talked non-stop about myself. It's time I found out a bit more about you.'

Didn't she understand the deal? She chattered and he listened. It was for the best. There were things in his life she really wouldn't want to know.

'I'd much rather talk about you.'

'You've never mentioned any family. Are your parents alive? Do you have brothers and sisters?'

Funny question. Even funnier, the honest answer was that he didn't know. He'd been put in the Home as a baby and nobody had ever come back to claim him. In his early days this provided endless scope for harmless fantasies. His favourite was that he was the bastard child of a peer of the realm, or a general or a gentleman farmer who owned a good deal of land. But when he told the other kids, their mockery was merciless. Some of them bullied him, a couple went further and did things that even now he preferred not to remember. As the years drifted by, he learned there was more pleasure and profit in making up stories about his own life, rather than someone else's.

'I'm the only one left, I'm afraid.' The drinks arrived, not a moment too soon. 'To be honest,

182

it's something I'd rather not talk about.'

'Oh, I do understand.' Her puzzled expression suggested otherwise, but she was a kind woman, unwilling to hurt. This reluctance to inflict pain was something they had in common. 'Your work, then. Tell me about that.'

'Well, that's where I go wrong.' The wine wasn't bad. He just hoped to God she hadn't forgotten her credit card. 'All work and no play. Makes me a dull boy, I'm afraid.'

As he put down his glass, he felt her hand slide on to his thigh. 'No, Rob, you may take me for a fool, but I'm not. You have hidden depths, you just don't want me to explore them yet, that's all. I mean, I can't help being curious.'

'Honestly, I'm not very interesting.' The modesty of this convenient reply gave him a little jolt of pleasure, but it wasn't enough to satisfy Sarah.

'You're a successful businessman and yet you live out of a single suitcase and never seem to do much work. Put yourself in my position. I can't help adding two and two together.'

Oh shit. 'And what answer do you come up with?'

He held his breath as he waited for her reply. She was stroking his leg through the twill of his trousers. A gentle, sympathetic movement.

'You've been made redundant, haven't you?'

A long silence. Her reply had come out of left field, but no matter. An escape hatch was opening up in front of him. He swallowed rather theatrically. Sometimes he thought he might have made a good living on the stage.

'It's … it's uncanny. How did you guess?'

She blushed. 'You know when you said you were going out to do some business the other day? Well, I followed you.'

He nearly choked on his steak. 'What?'

'You're cross with me, aren't you?'

'No.' He gulped down a mouthful of water. 'Just amazed.'

He'd had no idea. Perhaps he should have noticed, but failing to do so was forgivable. Nobody expected their landlady to start shadowing them when they took walks in the country.

'Oh thank goodness. I've worried ever since that day. You didn't take your laptop with you, not even a mobile as far as I could see. You just walked and walked, as though you were lost in a daze. I tried to stay a safe distance behind, but I'm not that fit and after a mile you were out of sight. Please don't be cross with me. I only did it because I was curious. And because I care.'

He'd underestimated her; not the first time he'd made such a mistake with a lover. Women caught you unawares sometimes, lulled you into a false sense of security with their silliness and then trapped you into an act of self-destruction.

He slipped his hand under the table and rested it on top of hers. 'That was very wicked of you. But very sweet. I ought to tell you the full story, but it's rather painful.'

'If you'd rather say nothing...'

'No, no. You deserve better than that.'

He smiled a soulful smile, buying time as his mind raced. She was leaning closer, her sympathy threatening to turn into a simper.

184

'The company has put me on gardening leave. It's very common in the world of high finance. My contract comes to an end next month and then I'll be out of work. Until then I'm hanging on by my fingertips. It's a cut-throat game I'm in, you see, and my figures for last quarter weren't up to target. All because I wouldn't let clients make investments when the market conditions weren't right for their portfolios.'

'Because you had their best interests at heart!'

A self-deprecating shrug. 'We have a new global chief executive, an American wheeler-dealer. He's only interested in numbers, not people. Ethics are fine, he says, but they don't pay the wages. Unless I bring in more business before the end of the notice period, he'll let me go. A couple of first class investment opportunities have emerged – but he's already switched my clientele to another broker.'

'That's terrible!'

'It goes with the territory. You won't hear me complain.'

'But...'

'No, let's change the subject. Please? It's hard for me to talk about this stuff, after the years I've spent at the top of the tree.'

She took a swig of orange juice. 'I'd like to help.'

Got away with it! His pulse was racing, but he'd not lost his touch. Seriously, this was better than sex.

'You help me just by being you.' He touched her hot hand, trying to keep the triumph out of his voice. 'Thanks for being so understanding. I

185

think you realise – it will take a long time for me to trust someone completely again.'

A light shone in her eyes. He knew she was making up her own happy ending.

At first, Hannah had dismissed Jeremy's suggestion that she consult Alban Clough about the Arsenic Labyrinth, but on reflection it wasn't such a bad idea. She headed back to the Museum of Myth and Legend while Les and the CSIs debated the risk assessment for the exploration of Mispickel Scar. She doubted whether the small print of the Health and Safety at Work Act required a Senior Investigating Officer to check the crime scene for curses. But if you never asked, you never found out.

Alban saw her in his daughter's chilly office, under the watchful eyes of Armstrong and Betty Clough in their gilded frames. What must it be like to belong to a dynasty? Family expectations might be claustrophobic, but inheriting a fortune eased the pressure. Alban didn't seem to have felt any duty to conform. After the sale of the business, he'd been free to pursue his dream. On the phone, Hannah hadn't explained why she wanted to see him and when she asked about the Arsenic Labyrinth, his tufted eyebrows rose.

'Why would a busy police officer investigating a ten-year-old disappearance want to bother her head about a half-forgotten old legend?'

'I was fascinated by your story about Gawain and the Loathly Lady.' Tongue in cheek, but she could play games just like this strange old satyr. 'The labyrinth is associated with the Inchmore

186

family. I thought I should consult the oracle.'

'You are right, Chief Inspector, to proceed on the basis that flattery will get you – *almost* everywhere. But what you say is hardly an answer.'

'I'm afraid that's as close as it gets.' She half-rose from her chair. 'Of course, if you're not able to help, I will quite understand. Apologies again for intruding on your Sunday.'

'Please sit down. You must forgive my curiosity.' He bared his teeth. 'I am really quite insatiable. But of course I'm willing to offer assistance. It's a pleasure to see you once more so soon after our last little chat. Which I much enjoyed, by the way. Besides, I don't want you to arrest me for obstructing you in the course of your duty.'

Hannah gave a tight smile and waited. He breathed in noisily and lifted his head, as if seeking inspiration in the carved ceiling. It occurred to her that he relished having an audience. Was he lonely, this rich man in his castle, despite the presence of his daughter and the vast rooms crammed with displays representing a lifetime's work?

'Do you see me as a foolish, fond old man, Chief Inspector?' His words had a sharp bite. 'I regard myself as more sinn'd against than sinning.'

To me, you'll always be King Leer. 'I'm not so naïve as to regard you as foolish, Mr Clough. And I can't imagine who would dare to sin against you.'

He lifted his head and launched into a speech so fluent that she was sure he'd made it many times before. 'My enemies, Chief Inspector Scarlett, are

187

the social engineers, the dolts who chide me for not making this place more socially inclusive. How absurd. Why should I pander to the unwashed and uneducated masses? What do they care for the lore of our green and pleasant land? And then there are the faceless bureaucrats. The planning authorities, the safety apparatchiks, the council flunkeys who impose pettifogging rules upon us and Draconian penalties for any failure to comply. This is not the V&A, nor even the Abbot Hall, but I am expected to pay out a king's ransom for building insurance, to say nothing of installing a new sprinkler system. My preference for candle-light rather than punitively priced electricity caused such a disagreement with the chief fire officer that I was forced to ask him to leave my home before I threw him out on his ear. After devoting more than half a century to my collection, I am treated as a pariah because I loathe paperwork and tick-boxes as much as I detest the vogue for interactive gadgets to keep tiny minds amused.'

When he paused for breath, she said, 'Isn't paperwork your daughter's department?'

He nodded. 'Without her calm efficiency, the museum would have closed years ago. But not even a woman as astute as Alexandra can cope with everything. This museum celebrates the truth that there is a logic in lore and legend more pertinent than anything to be found in the statute book. Yet the absurdities of modern legislation are such that, if we fail to obtain a substantial grant towards the cost of so-called improvements, we will have to close our doors to the public.'

'You've run out of funds?'

Alban Clough glanced over his shoulder at the stern likeness of his father. 'I was left well provided for after the family business was sold, Chief Inspector, and it has been my proud boast that the museum has made a loss in each year of its existence. Were it otherwise, I would have failed in my duty to educate those who come here to learn something of our magical heritage. We sell neither ice creams nor fridge magnets. As visitor numbers have fallen, I have rejoiced. At least we may concentrate our energies upon those who really care for what we do. The admission fees don't even cover the utilities bill. I confess that, unlike my forbears, I am no businessman. But it would take a Croesus to cope with the demands of the pen-pushers. If I do not call a halt soon, I shall be bankrupt and my daughter will be left not only without a job but also without a penny to her name. It is a scandal! An outrage!'

He closed his eyes, as if raising his voice had exhausted him. Or perhaps he was simply brooding in silence. Hannah coughed, wanting to get back to the point.

'The Arsenic Labyrinth?' she prompted.

'Perhaps it doesn't matter,' he murmured. 'These tales of the past, handed down through the generations. The sophisticates who live in our towns and cities have no truck with the tales and traditions of the countryside. Why should they, when they have broad minds and broadband? England's green and pleasant land is an irrelevance, fast being submerged by cheap houses and shopping malls. But it wasn't always thus,

189

Chief Inspector. Once upon a time, folk recognised the need for balance between progress and preservation of the past. That was what George Inchmore never understood. His folly led to his downfall and that of his family.'

'Tell me.'

He heaved himself upright in his chair. 'Many legends are associated with mining in the fells, Chief Inspector. Think of Simon's Nick, by the Levens Water cascade, named after a Cumbrian Faust who sold his soul for riches in copper. Or the Knockers, little goblins whose tapping was supposed to direct miners towards the profitable ore. They kept quiet at Mispickel Scar, even when a company set up by Quakers dug for copper in the hillside. Different firms tried their luck, until a roof collapsed and killed a couple of men.'

'Was that when the mines were abandoned?'

He nodded. 'Succeeding generations spoke of a jinx upon Mispickel Scar and those who ventured there. Clifford Inchmore was a prudent man who kept a safe distance, but his son thought he knew better. My grandfather warned him that he was deluding himself if he thought he would ever be able to compete with the Cornish arsenic traders. George being George, that made him all the more determined to proceed. He persuaded himself that my grandfather was motivated by envy rather than entrepreneurial wisdom.'

'And George's failure lent credence to talk of the curse?'

Alban nodded. 'In the nineteenth century,

190

arsenic was associated in the popular imagination with malice and murder. Rumour had it that the land in the vicinity of the labyrinth was poisoned. When the works closed, George ordered his few remaining employees to raze the buildings to the ground. A cathartic act of destruction, but it availed him naught. His business was declared insolvent a fortnight later. My grandfather was on hand to buy up the surviving equipment for scrap prices.'

He slumped back in the leather chair and breathed out. Telling the story had drained him, but a mischievous smile danced on the old dry lips.

'One man's curse, I suppose, is another man's good fortune.'

CHAPTER TEN

The mood up on Mispickel Scar reminded Hannah of a school trip. She'd aimed to keep numbers down, with a group of specialists and a helicopter on stand-by in case they found something, but there were still a dozen men and women at the search site, plus a couple of uniformed bobbies policing a cordon whose job was to turn away walkers who fancied sightseeing. With so many outside agencies involved, there were several people she'd not worked with before and although their demeanour was fiercely professional, she sensed excitement fizzing beneath the surface. This was something out of the ordinary, and anticipation sweetened the air. It wasn't often that you had the chance to work with a crime scene team in a place so wild and remote, hunting for a hidden body. Nothing to do with disrespect for the dead, everything to do with being passionate about what you did. They were ready for a long day out in the cold and had packed their kit and brought along drinks and sandwiches. If nothing turned up, there was bound to be disappointment; it was only human nature.

Hannah had briefed the team at first light, everyone chipping in with their own particular bits of expertise. Although it could not be seen from the Arsenic Labyrinth, a mobile command unit – an articulated lorry with a small office on the back – had now been set up at the point where the track gave way to terrain impossible to drive over. She could conduct on-site briefings there, but it wasn't the nerve centre. The incident room had to be based at the station, despite its remoteness from the Scar, because they needed a link straight into the police network computer – as well as a decent canteen.

Already the hours devoted to risk assessment and detailed preparation were paying off. Sooner than she'd dared to hope, after initial video and still photography of the site, the blockages at the access points to the two shafts were cleared and the CSIs were fiddling with battery-powered fluorescent lights to facilitate camera work underground.

By a happy chance, both the CSIs were not

only rope-trained but volunteer members of the Yewdale Fells Mountain Rescue Team. The senior, a ginger-haired Mancunian called Billy, was also a talented photographer whose wife had a small gallery where his pictures were exhibited. For him, taking shots of sleepy tarns and rolling fells made a change from the day job of recording tyre impressions, footprints and teeth marks on bruised bodies. When they broke for coffee, he wandered over and gave Hannah a rueful smile.

'What's the betting we find some bugger's chucked a dead sheep down the hole?'

'Evens?'

'I guess. Reckon we'll strike lucky?'

She shrugged, unsure about *lucky*. If Emma's body had been lying under the Arsenic Labyrinth for the past ten years, there wouldn't be much of it left. Even if she'd been buried deep enough to escape the attention of rats and foxes, hungry little insects would have had time to do a good deal of damage.

He turned back to the shaft. 'Least we've got a nice day for it.'

Yes, it might be freezing, but the sky was clear and blue. The last thing they needed was mist or a heavy fall of snow and the forecast for the next twenty-four hours was encouraging, though Hannah knew better than to rely on it. In these parts, you might need sunglasses in one valley and a waterproof coat and wellies in the next. She spared a few words for a lad with a clipboard whose task was to monitor comings and goings at the scene before spending a few minutes at the cordon. A handful of curious walkers had already

193

been turned away. A drop of sunshine and, even in brass monkey weather, the diehard walkers headed for the fells. Word of the police activity was trickling through the village and before long Candace, the press officer, would be besieged by enquiries. She walked back to the Scar, where Les was blowing his nose and looking a picture of misery.

'Nasty cold you've got there.' She beamed. 'Might be worth trying those Hopi ear candles, after all.'

'A drop of Scotch tonight is the only cure I need.' He interrupted himself with a sneeze so loud Hannah feared it might start a fresh landslide. 'None of that holistic garbage. Hey up, Billy's waving us over.'

Billy was checking the pictures from the camera that he and his colleague had lowered down the shaft nearest the labyrinth. One glance at his pink face told them all they needed to know.

'Looks like we've found something.'

Guy was curious to learn how Tony Di Venuto had used the information that Emma was buried beneath the labyrinth. Of course, it would be foolish to walk up through the Coppermines Valley to Mispickel to see if anyone was undertaking a search. Guy was too astute to give himself away like that. But he expected to read something in the *Post* at any time – after all, exclusives were lifeblood for any journalist, and they didn't come better than this one – and he went on a pilgrimage to the convenience store to buy a copy and see if there was any further mention of Emma.

194

Strolling from the checkout, he rustled through the pages. Not a word. He would, if pressed, have confessed to disappointment that the story had vanished from the newspaper as completely as – well, Emma herself. What were the police playing at? He was sure that he'd convinced Di Venuto that he knew what he was talking about.

He was on his way out of the shop when the elderly woman in front of him stopped short to greet another old crone whose bright auburn wig merely emphasised the leathery texture of her skin.

'Rita, have you heard? There's a lot of police and such-like up by Mispickel Scar. Sally Baines's boy reckons they're looking for a body.'

Guy had to restrain himself from punching the air and shouting, 'Yes!' He loved nothing better than to be taken seriously and Tony Di Venuto must have taken him very seriously indeed. If they were searching around the labyrinth, it surely would not take long to find Emma Bestwick's remains. And then the wretched Karen would learn the truth of her sister's fate and a sad chapter in the life of their family would at last come to a conclusion. Closure for Karen – and for Guy too.

There would be not much left of Emma other than a hunched-up skeleton. The calamity that had bound the two of them together all these years was wretched luck. Thank God he'd had the guts to call the journalist and set the record straight.

''Scuse me.'

He was blocking the doorway. With voluble

195

apologies, he stood aside to allow an old man with a bad cough to squeeze past and buy a packet of Silk Cut. Better be getting back, Sarah would be wondering where he'd got to. She'd become clingy, and this was starting to weary him.

He stopped in front of an estate agent's window. House prices were high enough to bring tears to the eyes of a first-time buyer. The Glimpse had a sizeable back garden, with trees beyond the boundary fence, and that ought to add a premium of a few thousand. Sarah lacked green fingers and there were bicycle tyres and old bricks lingering in the undergrowth. But all it needed was tender loving care. Sarah was sitting on a goldmine.

A makeshift scaffold loomed over the shaft by the labyrinth. The site resembled an eighteenth-century place of execution, hidden away in the snow-dusted fells. The plan was to winch the body up once the CSIs had photographed it *in situ* and combed the subterranean crime scene for whatever trace evidence had survived the passage of time. When dealing with a ten-year-old corpse, Hannah preferred not to rely on a GP to certify death, and she'd lined up Grenville Jepson, Barrow-in-Furness's answer to the late Bernard Spilsbury, to take charge of the post-mortem. No chance of dangling a consultant pathologist so eminent at the end of a rope – though one or two defence counsel would have loved to have him at their mercy – so the corpse would be transferred to the mortuary as soon as it had been dis-interred.

The operation was going to plan, but Hannah felt sombre rather than elated. Entering the presence of death always disturbed her. *Get used to it,* Ben Kind had warned her years ago, but although she'd developed a carapace of calm, in her heart she feared she never would.

She had a coffee with the forensic entomologist, a jolly, red-haired woman who did all the talking. Impossible to share her enthusiasm for poring over insect eggs and larvae on rotting flesh, but it took all sorts. When she'd drained her cup, Hannah wandered towards the scaffold. The CSIs would take a couple more hours to recover the corpse. Even before they reached it, they needed to take pictures of the shaft, in the hope it might yield clues to what had happened. You never knew, perhaps whoever had shoved Emma into the hole had snagged a piece of clothing on a ledge of rock.

Assuming it *was* Emma down there. Assuming that she'd been murdered, probably by the man who had phoned Tony Di Venuto. Though Hannah didn't have much doubt.

She moved her shoulders up and down to relieve the tension in her upper body. She was as keyed up as a callow DC on her first murder case, but to the rest of the team she needed to radiate calm authority. This was what she'd joined the police service for, the adrenaline rush of investigating serious crime. Although she'd risen fast through the ranks, promotion was a mixed blessing. It turned her into a manager when she still hankered after being a detective. For years she'd shared the view that cold case work was a cushy number, somewhere second-raters were put out to grass. But she was doing what she loved best, working in the thick of a criminal inquiry. In a live case, you had to depend on a DS to get a grip of the detail. The SIO had too much to do. Now she could take charge of the whole shooting match, and that was the way she liked it. Not out of control freakery, but because she preferred to take the rap for her own mistakes, not someone else's.

As for mistakes, should she have met up again with Daniel Kind? Her thoughts drifted from Mispickel Scar to the Café d'Art. She'd stayed longer than planned; when she'd checked her watch, she'd panicked that Marc would be fretting. She needn't have worried; when she arrived home, he was absorbed in a novel he'd bought on behalf of a mail order customer in Hexham. If he lost sleep each time she was late, he'd have succumbed to insomnia long ago. She had no reason to feel guilty and of course she told him that she'd seen Daniel for a drink. Marc's only question was whether Daniel had found out anything fresh about John Ruskin.

She liked men who were intelligent and witty and didn't just want to talk about themselves. Because he was Ben's son, detective work fascinated Daniel, unlike Marc, who saw her job as an obstacle to meals on the table at regular intervals and going out to a film or a concert without fear of interruption. He'd asked endless questions about the Emma Bestwick case and his intense curiosity was flattering. He was such a very good listener; she enjoyed capturing his attention.

Seeing him hadn't been wrong, but it wasn't something to repeat too often. Her hands were full, juggling work and her relationship with Marc. She didn't need any further complications in her life.

Yet what could cause complications? She'd had a drink and a chat with the son of a former colleague, simple as that. Nothing secret or hole-in-corner, no spicy chat laced with innuendo. All perfectly innocent and above board.

Sarah extricated herself from a passionate embrace and said, 'You're in a very good humour all of a sudden.'

'I'm always in a very good humour,' Guy murmured, undoing the clips of her bra.

'Not! You were pretty quiet before you went out to the shop.'

They were sprawling on the sofa, scene of several enjoyable encounters over the last few days. He'd opened a bottle of Merlot and was in celebratory mood. With a couple of drinks inside her, she'd be only too willing to help him save his job with the financial conglomerate by taking out a second mortgage on the Glimpse. It wouldn't be a purely altruistic gesture. Naturally, he'd explain that she was looking at a fifteen per cent a year minimum return over a mere eighteen months. You could buy an awful lot of black lingerie with that. To say nothing of a brand new car and a lick of paint for the newly hocked house.

'Oh, I was thinking how nice it would be if I could help you find the money to enjoy life to the full.'

'I don't want money, Rob. People are what matter.'

He pulled her to him and whispered what a wonderful woman she was. Half an hour later, when they were resting in each other's arms, she shifted from under him and gazed into his eyes.

'I was afraid you'd think I was only interested in you because you were a successful businessman.'

This had not occurred to him; he flattered himself that a man with his personality and looks was quite a catch for any woman, let alone a Coniston landlady who'd seen better days. But it didn't trouble him; she'd initiated a line of conversation bursting with promise.

'Just as well that wasn't the reason. If I don't set up a new deal soon, I'll be kissing goodbye to my annual bonus as well as the job.' He hesitated. 'As a matter of fact ... no, it doesn't matter.'

'Yes?' She pulled him closer. 'Tell me!'

He sighed. 'I suppose it can't do any harm. In fact, it would do you a great deal of good in the long run. But I don't think...'

'Darling. We mustn't keep anything from each other, we agreed, remember? Tell me!'

He was a model of reluctance. 'If you insist.'

'Of course I insist.'

It took him less than five minutes to explain. He thought that no woman had ever paid him such close attention as he described the complexities of the scheme that would save his career and net her a handsome profit into the bargain. She wasn't simply admiring his fine profile or smooth chest, she was fascinated by his mastery of high finance.

'Oh, Rob, it sounds so marvellous. If only I could help.'

'I do understand, it's a lot to ask, but thank goodness there's no risk because of the money-back guarantee. This is one scheme that is literally safer than houses. If you were willing to...'

'No.' Her face was the same beetroot shade as the carpet. 'It's not a question of willingness. I'd walk through fire if you asked me to, you know that already. It's just the cash that I can't manage.'

He gave her nipple a playful tweak. 'You'd be surprised. Lenders are falling over themselves to make advances to trustworthy borrowers. Property inflation in Cumbria has shot through...'

'Rob, listen to me.' She dipped her head in shame. 'It's not as simple as that. You see, I have a confession to make.'

Clouds masked the sun, the temperature was slipping. Hannah called at the command unit, talking to Candace from the press office, fine-tuning their media strategy in anticipation of the moment when the body was lifted out of the ground. Lauren Self's PA had been on the phone twice already, wanting to know the best time for a photo-opportunity. Emma could not be named until all the formalities of identification were complete, although after ten years in an ancient mine shaft, there wouldn't be much to identify her by. It was wet down there, so the corpse would not be mummified. Her insides would be eaten away and there wouldn't be much skin left covering the skeleton, though some might

201

remain, trapped in the cuffs of her jacket. Probably her leather walking boots would still contain her feet.

Hannah gritted her teeth. The vague old lady, who had seen Emma in wet-weather gear heading in the direction of Mispickel Scar, hadn't been making it up after all. Chances were, death had occurred within a couple of hours after that sighting. Accident or suicide remained possible, too early to rule them out, but Hannah was sure that Emma had been murdered. Why would someone with no interest in wandering the fells venture up to this grim and isolated spot on a cold and miserable February afternoon? An assignation of some kind, had to be.

She strode back towards the scaffold, trying to make sense of Emma's last movements. In the height of summer, visiting the Arsenic Labyrinth would be easier to understand. Not much risk of Peeping Toms, and if you brought a blanket, the ruggedness of the ground wouldn't be such a problem. Exhilarating to come here with a lover, to take your pleasure in the open under a skin-grilling sun. But Hannah's imagination baulked at the idea of lovers indulging themselves here at the height of winter. Never mind ecstasy, you would die of exposure.

'Ma'am!'

Billy had emerged from the shaft and was slipping out of his safety harness. In his face mask, goggles and nitrile gloves he looked like a creature from another world. But although Hannah could not make out his expression, his wave was unmistakably excited. Frantic, almost.

She broke into a run.

Guy felt sick, physically sick. It was as much as he could do not to vomit all over Sarah's tired Dralon sofa. He wanted to weep and scream and bang his fists. This was so unfair, so fucking unfair. He found it impossible to believe what she was saying. Surely there must be some mistake? After all the care and affection he'd lavished upon her, to be repaid like this was more than a man could bear.

'You're furious with me!' Sarah wailed. 'That's why I didn't dare tell you before. I knew it would spoil everything. What sort of fellow – never mind a go-ahead business executive – would want to marry a woman with an addiction like mine?'

He was too upset even to be startled by the mention of marriage. *Addiction* was right. She didn't just have a problem, she was off her head. How could anyone fritter away the thick end of one hundred and fifty thousand pounds in eighteen months? It was disgusting, it was insane. People committed murder for a pittance and here was a woman who had squandered a fortune, allowed the money to slip through her hands as if it were sand.

'I need help,' she said in a small voice. 'I do realise.'

Well don't look at me, I'm not a trick cyclist. You could have been wealthy, instead you're a church mouse. Aversion therapy, that's what you need. A hundred volts running through you next time you're tempted to switch on the fucking computer. For two pins, I'd press the lever myself.

But he said none of this. He'd always had good manners. Take deep breaths, he told himself.

'So ... it's all gone?'

'Every last penny. Don puts money into my bank account on the first of each month and I've only got ninety pounds to tide me over till the end of February. There are bills to pay, you've no idea. I've never been brave enough to tell Don what I've been up to, he'd blow a gasket. Yesterday I had a final demand from the electric company, last week it was the council tax arrears. They've threatened to call in the bailiffs.' Guy had never paid council tax in his life, but for a householder to default seemed rather shocking. He stuttered the obvious question.

'W... why?'

Her face was ashen. 'It was – so easy.'

What could he say? She'd thrown all her money away, gambling online. Poker, blackjack, you name it. These days no one needed to go to Las Vegas, they could ruin themselves in the comfort of their own homes. Sarah's occasional winnings were paltry, her losses spiralling like Third World debt. She said she needed to escape from the humdrum world of everyday, and with that he could empathise. But you got away from it all by creating a fresh existence for yourself, not by frittering every last penny in internet casinos. Soon not even this horrid house would be hers. The bank would sell it to claw back the loans and she'd finish up living on welfare hand-outs. Psychiatric counselling would come courtesy of Social Services. What a fucking catastrophe.

She pressed his hand to her naked breast,

presumably for comfort. He had seldom felt less aroused. 'Guy, I'm so sorry. Do you despise me now I've let you into my guilty secret?'

'It's OK,' he muttered, because he couldn't bring himself to say what he was thinking. He hated being unkind, even when someone deserved it. 'I was – shocked, that's all.'

'I thought – if the company gives you some severance pay, perhaps I could borrow a few pounds until I get myself sorted. Of course, I'll reimburse you with interest.'

And where do you think you'll find the money to repay me? You must be living on a different planet.

'I don't suppose you can understand me at all?'

His voice was hoarse. 'One thing I do know, Sarah. If you spend your life gambling, you need to win more often than you lose.'

'So, Chief Inspector, the good news or the bad news?'

Billy might be breathless, but he couldn't help playing the showman. One of the perks of his job.

'Good news first. I don't hear it that often.'

'Your tip-off was spot on. The body at the bottom of the shaft – or what's left of it – is clad in a jacket and boots that match the description of clothing that disappeared along with Emma Bestwick.'

Hannah had expected nothing else. All the same, she felt dizzy with relief. The long wait was over. Sid Thornicroft had guessed wrong, the poor woman hadn't done a runner. Her body had been left here to rot for all those years. At last they'd be able to give her a decent burial, and set

about finding whoever was responsible for inter-
ring her beneath the ruins of the weird poison
maze.

'OK, break the bad news to me gently.'

Billy coughed. 'We thought while we were at it,
we ought to take a look along the tunnel that
links with the far shaft. See if we could find a
weapon or anything else that might cast light on
how she came to be down there.'

'Yeah, thanks. Any joy?'

'Yes and no.'

'Meaning?'

'Meaning that we found a rusty old knife, a
kitchen bread knife. The stains on the blade look
like blood.'

'You think she was killed with it?'

'Unlikely, ma'am. You see, the knife is at the
bottom of the other shaft, thirty yards away from
Emma Bestwick's remains.'

She stared at him. 'How come?'

'It's lying next to a second body.'

JOURNAL EXTRACT

I may seem an unlikely person to have committed a perfect murder and yet my crime never
attracted a breath of suspicion. I hope to have
lived a useful life, but now my days are drawing
to a close, I can say this with certainty: I regret
nothing. No, not even the second death, so many
years after the first.

As I swung the knife into his breast, destroying that arrogant sneer forever, I felt as though jolted by an electric shock. Not a current of remorse, but jubilation. How extraordinary. A single blow was all it took, to change my life and end his. When he collapsed to the ground, I stood over him, clutching the haft tight, waiting for his body to twitch, ready to do what was necessary.

He is not moving. It is over.

My breathing is harsh, but I feel light-headed, as though I have consumed a bottle of wine. For a few moments I have a fleeting sense of immortality. I have exercised the power of life and death. I have revenged myself for his betrayal. He is dead, but I shall live on.

And then, I hear a loosening of rubble in the rocks above me. Followed by something worse, far worse. A suppressed cough, little more than a clearing of the throat, yet enough to induce paralysis.

I am not alone.

PART TWO

CHAPTER ELEVEN

Desperate ills called for desperate remedies. Guy regarded himself as a man of his word, yet sometimes you had no choice but to break a promise. Besides, he'd kept to his bargain for long enough. Nothing was forever.

Including, of course, his sojourn at the Coniston Glimpse. It was a tribute to his strength of character that he'd not throttled Sarah, but it was also convenient. He needed a roof over his head until he travelled on, and he couldn't bank on finding another landlady who didn't expect rent. When he'd calmed down enough to think straight, he'd persuaded Sarah to ask her ex-husband for a loan on the pretext of needing to buy a new washing machine. Excellent advice. By a lucky chance she'd bumped into Don in the village early that morning. He was out buying a pricey Valentine's present for his current wife and a combination of guilt and embarrassment prompted him to cough up without demur. He'd even taken her to the cash till and handed over a thick wad of notes.

Guy was still sleeping with Sarah. Despite her shameful behaviour, he didn't fancy exiling himself to that draughty basement. She was pathetically grateful that he hadn't packed his bags and left, and at his insistence had disconnected the computer and confessed all to a sympathetic GP, who had referred her to a gambling therapist for specialist counselling. All in all, Guy thought she'd done very well out of him. He might have made a career out of mentoring people with inadequate personalities, he had a gift for it, but he was destined for better things.

'Lunch in half an hour!' Sarah called from the kitchen. 'Cottage pie, your absolute favourite.'

Actually, he much preferred venison. But Coniston Glimpse was a far cry from the Boscolo Palace, and he was adaptable.

'Any chance of a glass of vino?'

'Sweetheart, your wish is my command. I'll open the Rioja.'

Supermarket plonk, buy-one, get-one-free, but needs must. With a sigh, he bookmarked *David Copperfield*. At this third reading, he'd decided his literary hero was Wilkins Micawber. Guy shared Micawber's optimism; over the years, a belief that something would turn up had served him well. Micawber was underestimated and it was telling that in the end he'd achieved the status of a colonial magistrate. Dickens knew a thing or two, just as Guy knew that one day he'd make his mark. All he needed was a lucky break. Rather than mope because Sarah had proved a broken reed, he intended to think positive.

He was a good man in a crisis. It would have been so easy to panic once he realised the accidental blow on Emma's head hadn't killed her, but he'd kept his nerve. Although it hadn't been pleasant, he'd done what he had to do. Thank goodness he'd learned presence of mind early on. Where he grew up, you kept your wits

212

about you, or you were finished. He'd hated the Home, but with hindsight he recognised that the experience had sharpened him, taught him to cope with the vagaries of Fate.

He'd told stories, long before encountering yarn-spinners like Dumas, Dickens and Rider Haggard. How better to escape the bad stuff? Booze was fine, but he could take it or leave it. Apart from smoking the occasional joint, he wasn't into drugs. Who needed artificial stimulants? Making things up intoxicated him. In his youth, he paid a price for letting his imagination run away with him. He started reading for the first time in prison, allowing himself to be persuaded that he was bright enough to live on his wits without spending the rest of his life under lock and key. But he hadn't been going straight for long before his encounter with Emma on Mispickel Scar led to calamity.

Even then, he reminded himself as he strolled into the kitchen, he'd fallen on his feet. It was a knack.

'You're looking very cheerful, darling.' Sarah dried her hands on a grubby tea towel and gave him a peck on the cheek.

'Always look for the silver lining, that's my motto! Matter of fact, I've been doing a spot of thinking.'

'And?'

'It's time to call in a favour.'

Miranda was in a good mood. She wasn't due back in London just yet and would be at home for Valentine's Day. Daniel's announcement that

213

he fancied writing something fresh about Ruskin had gone down well and they'd spent most of the morning in bed. Over brunch, she quizzed him on his approach to research.

'This is a side of you I've never seen. Remember, since we met, you've barely written a word. Far less a full-length book.'

He munched his toast. 'Like I said on TV, an American called Robin Winks argued the same case long ago. *Every fact must count equally at the beginning of the inquiry, for one may not prejudge the conclusion. To decide at the start whodunit – the middle class, the Fascists, whatever – and why, and What It All Means, is to destroy the historical inquiry.* The historian *is* a detective. Has to be.'

'You ought to call Hannah Scarlett, pick up a few tips.'

'I talked to her while you were down in London. Very interesting.'

He was glad of the chance to slip in a confession to having met Hannah. Yet, what was there to feel guilty about? He and she had chatted over a drink. Nothing had happened. Nothing to be ashamed of, as long as you didn't count the treacherous thoughts that sneaked into his mind every now and then when images of Hannah came into his mind.

'Did she fancy your father?'

He stared. 'What makes you ask that?'

'Just wondered. The way you described it, he was this smart detective, she was a rookie cop he took under his wing. She must have looked up to him.'

'Why do you say that?'

214

Miranda shrugged. 'She's the type.'

She and Hannah had only met once and had conversed for less than five minutes, but Miranda prided herself on her ability to make snap judgments of character. Before he could argue, she added, 'You'd better be careful.'

'What do you mean?'

'If she did like your dad, perhaps she'll take a shine to you.'

There was a mocking light in her eyes and he realised that she didn't rate Hannah as competition. And why should she?

'She told me her latest cold case involved the disappearance of a woman from Coniston ten years ago.'

Miranda's eyebrows lifted. 'That item on the news, about the bodies they have discovered up in the fells.'

'Sounds like they found the woman.'

Each time he'd rung Hannah's mobile over the past couple of days, she'd been engaged on another call and he hadn't left a message. All he'd wanted was to say he'd enjoyed seeing her. Her missing person case must have turned into a murder inquiry. And the news that not one but two corpses had been found up at the back of Coniston suggested she had a lot on her plate. Too much to waste time in idle conversation with her old boss's son.

'So when do you set off?'

'Ten minutes.'

'Good luck.'

His decision to spend the afternoon at the Ruskin Archive had met with her full approval.

He hadn't mentioned that the librarian currently responsible for the Archive was Vanessa Goddard. Self-indulgence on two levels. Historical research and a chance to meet someone who had known Emma Bestwick. Listening to Hannah, he'd become fascinated by Emma's story, intrigued by mention of this Arsenic Labyrinth. If Emma was dead, he was seized by the urge to learn how she had met her fate.

'So, DCI Scarlett, is there any doubt that one of the bodies is that of Emma Bestwick?'

Tony Di Venuto sprawled back in his chair as though he'd just taken over as Chief Constable. Pity he was such a prat, he wasn't a bad journalist. After ten years of nothing, within days he'd conjured up enough interest in Emma's disappearance to prompt his mystery caller to disclose where her body was hidden. Lauren wanted her to throw him a few bones in return for his help, over and above the titbits given out at the press conference. Reasonable enough; if anyone was entitled to be smug about this case, it was Di Venuto. But every time that self-satisfied smile oozed across his dark features, she wanted to scrub it away with a dripping cloth.

'Off the record, not a lot. We haven't received the pathologist's report yet, and there's not much left of Emma, of course, but the clothing we've retrieved from the scene matches descriptions of what she was likely to have been wearing.'

He clenched his fist. 'I knew it!'

'You were sure that the man who rang you up wasn't a time-waster.'

216

A vigorous nod. 'Dead right.'

'Why?'

'Let's just say I have a nose for bullshit.'

Not surprising, he spouted his fair share.

Aloud, she said, 'What can you tell me about him?'

'No more than I said last time. Around my age. Disguised his voice by whispering. Making that call can't have been easy. But he wanted me to think he was ringing to do Karen a favour. As if.'

'Conscience pricking?'

'No way. If you ask me, he didn't even sound like a murderer.'

'And what would a murderer sound like?'

He grimaced. 'You know what I mean.'

'Not sure I do.'

'He wanted me to believe it wasn't his fault that Emma was buried beneath the Arsenic Labyrinth. As it happens, he succeeded. I don't believe he killed her. Somehow – maybe recently, maybe ten years back – he's found out where she was buried, and he's decided not to keep it to himself any longer. Oh no, I don't think your work will be done when you track him down. But perhaps he'll lead you to whoever did murder Emma.'

'Any theories of your own?'

For a rare moment, Tony Di Venuto seemed to be in two minds. Then he said, 'I don't have any evidence, Chief Inspector.'

'But just between us?'

He leaned over the desk. The after-shave was more pungent than ever.

'Jeremy Erskine called on her just before she vanished. Supposedly for the benefit of his bad

217

back. But he's vain, you only have to speak to him for five minutes to realise that. He wouldn't be put off by the fact a woman was a lesbian if he took a shine to her. He'd regard it as a challenge. My theory is, he made a play for her, she told him to fuck off, and he decided to take revenge.'

'He didn't kill her there and then, did he? Bruised self-esteem might explain a heat of the moment murder, but – twenty-four hours later?'

Di Venuto shrugged. 'I told you I don't have any evidence. There may be more to it. But when I interviewed him, he was evasive. All he wanted was for everyone to forget about Emma. Thank God his wish has been denied.'

'One thing I've been meaning to ask. What put you on to the case in the first place? I mean, most people have forgotten all about Emma.'

He folded his arms. 'It was the upcoming anniversary, that's all. We keep an eye on these things in the Press. Pegs to hang stories on, they matter to us.'

'It was quite a story. Not just a rehash of old stuff. Jeremy wasn't happy with the way you tackled it.'

'The *Post* has a complaints procedure and Erskine didn't use it.' The smug smile was back. 'And for good reason, Chief Inspector. All I was doing was trying to get at the truth. Erskine's problem is, the truth hurts.'

Hannah remembered Karen's rare outburst. *This isn't about discovering the truth.* So what was it about?

She stood up. 'When we have more from the pathologist, I'll call another press conference.'

218

'I'd appreciate a nod and a wink in advance, Chief Inspector. Given all the help I've provided.'

Don't push your luck, smarty pants. 'I've already told you more than your colleagues who were at the briefing.'

'Trust me, Chief Inspector.' His wheedling smile suggested the dodgiest used car salesman in Cumbria. 'Take a closer look at Erskine. He may seem like Mr Respectable, but it's a charade. The man is one huge ego. He dumped his first wife the moment he started snuggling up to Karen. Who's to say he wouldn't betray her too?'

Hannah wasn't convinced. Not least because she suspected that the journalist recognised characteristics in Jeremy that he possessed himself. Above all, she yearned to puncture his self-assurance.

'Better be careful, then.'

'What do you mean?'

'Only this. If Jeremy Erskine was willing to kill his sister-in-law because she turned him down, he's a dangerous enemy. Better not let him get wind of your thinking. We don't want to have to spirit you away into a witness protection programme, do we? It's not a glamorous life. Cumbria Constabulary doesn't run to swish gaffs in beach resorts. A bed-sit in a back street in Maryport is as good as it gets.'

Vanessa Goddard was crestfallen. 'I only wish we could help, Mr Kind. But as you can see, our archive is primarily a gathering of Ruskin's writings in different editions, together with background materials, for everyday consultation by members of the public. I feel rather guilty that we don't have much that is unique.'

'Don't worry, you've been very helpful.'

She shut the door behind her and he followed into the office. It occupied the rear of the converted Wesleyan chapel housing the county's Ruskin Archive, and it was full of clutter. Lever arch files were piled high on every available surface and she had to shove a couple of them on to the floor so that he could sit down on the other side of a desk. Behind her head hung a large rectangular cork board covered in staff notices and a trade union calendar. The walls were festooned with book covers and posters advertising library events. On the desk stood family photographs, all depicting a young boy: toddling across the living room carpet, struggling into a school blazer, wielding a cricket bat, dangling a fishing rod into a peaceful tarn. Daniel wondered if his father had kept any pictures of himself and Louise as kids. Or had Ben preferred to draw a line under the past once the divorce was through, and start again in his new job, in his new home, with his new girlfriend?

Vanessa cleared her throat. 'Even if we owned rare manuscripts, we'd probably be told to sell them off to pay for a few more computers in the branches.'

'So you can't tell me anything about Ruskin's relations with the owners of the arsenic works at Coniston?'

'I'm sorry, no. Why do you ask, I wonder?'

'I heard on the news about those bodies up by the Arsenic Labyrinth. Driving here, there seems

220

to be a police vehicle on every street corner.'

'It's very sad.'

She fingered the birthmark on her face. There were dark lines under her eyes and he guessed she hadn't slept. According to Hannah, she had been close to Emma, and part of him shied away from adding to her misery. But curiosity held him captive.

'I read about that woman who went missing ten years ago.' He'd combed through the old cuttings as well as recent stuff by Tony Di Venuto. 'Perhaps she's one of the victims.'

'I expect we'll know soon enough.'

'Poor woman,' he persisted. 'How dreadful, to die like that.'

Her face tightened, as if tempted to scold him for gossiping out of turn. But he was Daniel Kind, the historian, he'd been on TV, for God's sake. For once it was a blessing to be nearly famous. She had to be polite.

'As it happens, Emma Bestwick was a good friend of mine.' Vanessa coughed. 'She was a lovely woman. If – if one of the bodies is hers, then it's an utter tragedy.'

'I'm so sorry.' He felt a pang of genuine remorse. Had his father felt like this, intruding into private grief? Did Hannah?

She took a breath, straightened her shoulders. 'The only consolation is that she lives on, with us. Those of us who knew her, that is. Now, can I help with anything else?'

He couldn't let go just yet. 'Are you familiar with the Arsenic Labyrinth?'

'I've never walked up that far beyond Copper-

221

mines Valley. People say there's not much to see. Just a few lumps of stone dotted around a cold and windswept nook in the fells.'

'I can't believe Ruskin approved of a poison factory in his beloved Lakeland.'

'He once gave a lecture about the fells in Kendal, but I never heard of him writing about the arsenic works. You ought to speak to Alban Clough, he owns the Museum of Myth and Legend down the road.'

'Thanks, I'll call there on my way home.' He paused. 'I've also arranged to meet up with the chairman of the Grizedale and Satterthwaite tomorrow, see if he or his colleagues can cast any light. He sounds very knowledgable, perhaps you know him? His name is Jeremy...'

'Erskine,' she said quickly. 'As a matter of fact, I used to know Jeremy rather well. Though not as well as I thought I did. He was my first husband.'

Daniel felt his cheeks burning. Hannah had forgotten to mention this. 'Sorry, I didn't know.'

'No problem, it was a long time ago. Jeremy went his way, I went mine. It wasn't easy for a while, but in the end things worked out wonderfully well for me.' She gestured towards the photographs. 'It's a long time since I last saw him. Time to bury the hatchet – and I don't mean between his shoulder blades. Will you pass on my regards?'

He nodded. 'Jeremy isn't an expert in Ruskin by any chance?'

Vanessa fiddled with the publishers' catalogues on her desk. 'Not to my knowledge, but that shouldn't stop him sharing his opinions with you.

Jeremy believes he's an expert in everything.'

'So we have two bodies in the shafts below the labyrinth and both of them were buried there at different times – *decades* apart?' Hannah said.

Grenville Jepson fiddled with his bright yellow bow-tie, a habit that irritated Hannah like a flea bite. The bow-tie was a fashion crime; she couldn't believe that anyone would wish to draw attention to the thing.

'No doubt about it, Detective Chief Inspector. No doubt about it whatsoever.'

He was a tiny man with a voice oddly high-pitched, verging on a squeak. This too got on her nerves. But Grenville was as capable as any forensic pathologist she'd ever met. He was never afraid to express a definite opinion, yet he didn't shoot from the hip. Once he formed a conclusion, it took cross-examination worthy of Marshall Hall to shake it.

Les Bryant slurped loudly from a cup of water. 'Could either of them have finished up there by accident? I mean, people are so bloody careless, aren't they? If you're wandering around an area riddled with mineshafts and you don't look where you're going, next thing you know, you're arse over tip and...'

He made a throat-slitting gesture. Grenville turned his pointed nose up in distaste. The pathologist spent his working life in the company of the dead and decaying, but he prided himself on his refinement. He'd been known to hum Vivaldi while conducting a post-mortem.

'With regard to the older corpse, I would say it

223

is out of the question. As to the younger body, it seems highly improbable. The likelihood is that she was forced down the shaft, when either dead or unconscious, breaking an arm and a leg on her way to her resting place.'

'And no doubt that the more recent deceased was Emma Bestwick?' Hannah asked.

Grenville sat back in his chair, swinging his little legs back and forth. He took a packet of Polo mints out of his pocket and popped one in his mouth, as if to aid deliberation. It didn't occur to him to offer them round.

'Of course, we need to do further work on identification for the coroner's benefit. There are no signs of surgical procedures, so we will have to fall back on dental records or DNA evidence. There is a sister, you said? Have the liaison officer take a swab from her. But off the record, this is not so much a working hypothesis, more a racing certainty. Everything fits. The clothing, the size of the bones.'

Hannah picked up a red marker pen and scribbled a couple of notes on the whiteboard. 'How much older is the other corpse?'

'If I were a betting man, I'd say by half a century, give or take. The contrast is stark. Virtually no clothing left, just a few skeletal remains and a tiny amount of skin around the finger ends. We have odds and ends yielding a few scraps of DNA, so identification may be possible one of these fine days. Already I can say with some confidence that the bones belong to a male rather than a female. The murder weapon is sure to be the knife found lying a couple of yards away from

224

the corpse.'

'Two murders fifty years apart, with both victims stuffed down neighbouring mineshafts?' Maggie Eyre asked. 'Beggars belief, doesn't it?'

'Frankly, I don't agree. To my mind, it's not at all surprising.' Grenville crunched his mint noisily, disappointed by the DC's naiveté. 'As you know, most murderers are lamentably lacking in originality and imagination. If one killer stumbles across an ideal location for the disposal of a body, hidden away in a remote corner of the fells, it is entirely within the bounds of possibility that years later, a second murderer might come up with the same bright idea.'

'I suppose.'

'Forgive me, DC Eyre, but this is more than mere supposition. Sixty years ago, the fells were lonely. Not like today, when they seem as crowded as Blackpool beach. One may speculate that the knife was taken to the scene with the express intention of killing the first victim. Regrettably, one presumes that even if we can pick up any identifying material from the knife or the soil surrounding the site where the body was dumped, the culprit is now safely interred in his grave as well.'

'We ought to be glad,' Hannah said. 'Two crimes to clear up rather than one is a pain in the backside, but at least we don't have to worry that we might have a serial killer prowling the Coniston fells.'

'Unless...' Grenville's hand strayed to his bowtie again, setting Hannah's teeth on edge. 'There is always the distant possibility that the first crime was committed by someone in his teens. He might have kept his secret safe for a long time. But what if your Ms Bestwick stumbled across it? There would be a temptation to repeat the success of the earlier crime. But this would require a suspect with the ability and the will to commit murder in, say, his sixties. Unlikely in the extreme, one hopes.'

'Unlikely, yes.' Hannah considered. 'But not impossible.'

CHAPTER TWELVE

'In my younger days, I read a little Ruskin.' Alban Clough waved towards the calfskin-bound tomes surrounding them; a regal gesture, suggestive of a monarch acknowledging his subjects. 'I suspect I am the only Clough who so much as glanced beyond the titles of works such as *Fors Clavigera,* let alone ploughed through the damn things. Nowadays, I lack the patience. You will only catch me returning to Ruskin if in search of a cure for insomnia.'

He and Daniel were in his private library at Inchmore Hall, ensconced in hard leather armchairs opposite a mahogany desk and chair. Glass cases, crammed with enough first editions to make Marc Amos's tongue hang out, lined all four walls, leaving precious little space for the door and a small mullioned window looking out onto the frosty fells.

'Even though Ruskin shared your love of myth?'

'The *dark sayings of nature*, as he called them. But his tastes were classical compared with mine. My own love of ancient lore derives from nothing more sophisticated than a schoolboy's wide-eyed fascination. I confess to a continuing *frisson* at the mere mention of Sunkenkirk Circle or the Fiend's Fell.'

Daniel stretched in his chair and looked around. 'This is an amazing place.'

Despite the stale air, for all the dust and the cobwebs, the idiosyncracies of Inchmore Hall had caught his fancy. To step over the threshold was like entering a time warp. A world of drowned churches and haunted mines, of sea ghosts and giants' graves. Easy to forget that within walking distance was a modern murder scene, marked off with tape and crowded with men and women in white overalls, intent on discovering the names of the dead and how and why they had been killed.

'Thank you, Mr Kind. In the company of an academic historian such as yourself – even a telly academic, if you will forgive me – I claim to be no more than a humble dabbler. A dilettante.'

Daniel offered a smile, but no flattery. Alban Clough's ego was healthy enough without it. He wasn't a historian, but a teller of tales. Lack of evidence didn't worry him. Never let the facts get in the way of a good story.

'I have little patience with the way Ruskin spent so long pondering the Symbolical Grotesque. But on one issue we would have agreed. I men- tioned it last year to another visitor researching

227

Ruskin's Coniston connections. Let me see if I can recall the reference.'

He opened the cabinet and pulled out a book, blinking at the puff of dust as he opened the cover, murmuring to himself as he leafed through the brittle pages.

'Ah yes, I have it.' He cleared his throat. *'Whenever you begin to seek the real authority for legends, you will generally find that the ugly ones have good foundation, and the beautiful ones none. Be prepared for this; and remember that a lovely legend is all the more precious when it has no foundation.'*

'Did the curse of the Mispickel Scar have good foundation?'

'Our little drama has clearly captivated you.' Alban bared his teeth in a fearsome smile. 'The scream of sirens and flashing blue lights almost persuaded me that I had been transported from Coniston to Chicago.'

Daniel rubbed his hands together, for warmth rather than because he shared the old man's amusement. Thank God he'd kept on his outer jacket.

'It isn't every day that two bodies turn up, buried under a strange old site in the fells.'

'How true. One's first assumption is a tragic accident, sadly not uncommon in rocky terrain. Yet village whispers suggest the police are treating their finds as a double murder case. My goodness, if that is so, Coniston will not have seen such excitement since Donald Campbell met his tragic end.'

'And Mispickel Scar?' Daniel persisted.

'Merely to visit Mispickel Scar is supposed to

228

bring bad luck cascading down like Aira Force.' Alban Clough spread his arms. 'As for the origins of the jinx, they are lost in the mists of Lakeland. I doubt whether Collingwood mentions it, let alone Ruskin. Because of its obscurity, we give the story no more than passing mention in our displays, but I am sure it dates back long before George Inchmore's arsenic business failed. It may reflect a yet more ancient fear.'

'Of arsenic itself?'

'Indeed. Arsenic is an extraordinary poison, attracting fear and fascination in equal measure for centuries. As you may know, the peasants of Styria had great faith in its aphrodisiac properties. So did James Maybrick, murder victim and one of the horde suspected of being Jack the Ripper. In Cumberland, the natives were wary of the stuff. Its dangers were common knowledge. No wonder our forebears said the Scar was cursed, even before a roof collapse brought copper mining there to an end. It explains why George found trouble recruiting decent staff for his enterprise, though in part it was due to his unpopularity.'

'Why didn't people take to him?'

'He was spoiled and selfish and a sore disappointment to his father. Neither he nor his descendants were men of character. All were weak-willed and selfish to their bones.'

His voice burned with contempt. Daniel was puzzled. Why so scathing? After all, the Cloughs had profited from the Inchmores' decline and fall.

'I noticed those family trees near the front door.'

'My crude attempt to capture the genealogy of the Inchmores and the Cloughs, indeed.' Alban strode to the desk and rummaged in a drawer, extracting two sheets of paper. 'Take these copies with my compliments. I recall you have written about Victorian dynasties founded by entrepreneurs with half an eye on immortality?'

Daniel nodded. The family trees had been produced on an old-fashioned typewriter with several letters out of alignment. The museum literature, like the rest of the place, was past its sell-by date. He glanced at the Inchmore names and recalled Hannah mentioning that the youngest had been questioned after Emma Bestwick's disappearance.

'So the Inchmore line died out with Tom?'

'Outlived by his grandmother, he failed to marry and had no children. A stupid young fellow – I have no qualms about speaking ill of the dead – but he had one thing in common with my daughter. She too is the last of her line. The Cloughs will be no more when she finally goes to meet her maker.'

The door swung open and Alexandra came in, carrying a tea tray. Her exaggerated blandness of manner made Daniel wonder if she had been listening outside.

'Sorry it took a while.' She set the tray down on the table.

Her father smirked. 'We were discussing your eventual demise, my dear.'

Alex Clough gave Daniel a sidelong look as she poured. 'You must forgive my father. His sense of humour is positively Mephistophelian.'

230

There was an odd note of pride in her voice. She might have been a mother, trying to be self-deprecating about the funny little ways of a favourite child.

'I have disappointed Mr Kind,' the old man confessed. 'I cannot offer any juicy titbits concerning Ruskin's relations with the Inchmores or my grandfather. But at least we have indulged ourselves in topical gossip about – ahem, the Arsenic Labyrinth.'

Alex frowned. 'That's a dreadful business.'

The old man gave a throaty laugh. 'You must wonder why my daughter sounds so dismayed, Mr Kind. As it happens, the Coniston rumour mill indicates that one of the bodies belongs to a young woman who once worked in this very building.'

'Good Lord,' Daniel attempted an Oscar-winning look of amazement. 'The woman who vanished? I read about her in the papers.'

Alex nodded. 'Emma Bestwick.'

'She and my daughter were very good friends,' Alban said.

Daniel made sympathetic noises, but Alex waved them away with a flip of her small white hand.

'It was – a long time ago.'

She was exquisitely made up, but the redness around her eyes made Daniel guess she had been crying. Distressed because Emma was dead – or because the body had been found? A phrase jumped into his head. *Suspect everyone.* The cliché his father amused himself by repeating, whenever young Daniel quizzed him on what a

231

murder detective did.

'And the second body? Someone Emma knew?'

Alban Clough rubbed his sparse stubble. He was struggling to suppress a smile, as if relishing a private joke. 'There was never talk of anyone else disappearing from the village at the same time as Emma.'

'We thought she'd gone of her own free will,' Alex said. 'She'd done it before, just upped and left the area.'

'So who is the second person?'

'Your guess is as good as mine.'

'I'm sorry, Mrs Erskine,' Hannah said.

She and Maggie were back in the Erskines' cosy conservatory. The children had been banished to watch TV in their bedrooms. Jeremy and Karen were squashed together on the sofa, his arm was wrapped tightly around her shoulder. Hannah wasn't sure whether he was comforting her or making sure he kept her under his control.

'How sure are you?' Karen asked.

'We will be asking you to come down and see if you can identify replicas of certain items of clothing discovered on the body. We will also want to compare your DNA with that of the deceased by taking a mouth swab. A straightforward matter of collecting skin cells from the lining of your mouth to obtain a profile.'

Karen flinched and Maggie gave a sympathetic smile. Early on in her career, Maggie had spent six months as a family liaison officer, and since the DC in Thornicroft's team who had acted as FLO to the Erskines had left the force years ago,

Maggie was an ideal successor to the role. It suited her down to the ground, now that her fiancé had taken up a new job and bought a house in Torver. Her brief was to keep an eye on the couple while investigations continued, see if anything emerged to link either of them to the crime. Right now she could play the good cop while her boss asked the difficult questions.

'It's not painful, honestly.' When Karen snorted in disbelief, Maggie added, 'Mild discomfort at worst, I promise. DCI Scarlett and I have both given samples, it's routine for police officers' DNA to be recorded for elimination purposes at crime scenes.'

'How sure are you that Emma is dead?'

Hannah said, 'It's our working assumption. I can't tell you any more.'

Karen exhaled. 'Well, well, well.'

'I'm sorry,' Hannah repeated.

'I don't know what to say, Chief Inspector. Even after all this time, even after I'd come to the conclusion that she must be dead – it's still devastating, to have the truth confirmed.'

Grief did strange things to people. But there wasn't the faintest tremor in Karen's voice, and upper lips seldom came stiffer. If she was telling the truth, she was coping with her devastation with bravery verging on the heroic.

'Was it an accident?' Jeremy asked. 'These things do happen, people go up into the hills unprepared for bad weather and next thing you know they've plunged down a ravine. Emma wasn't an experienced fell-walker, who knows what misfortune may have befallen her?'

233

'We don't think it was an accident, Mr Erskine.'

He wore a faraway look, as if solving a sudoku in his head. 'This other body. Could it be someone whom Emma knew?'

'Unlikely.'

'How can you be sure?'

'I'm afraid I can't discuss that. But we have no reason to believe the two deaths are connected.'

'Coincidence?' A bitten-off laugh. 'Forgive me, Chief Inspector, but that seems pretty hard to swallow.'

'We'll see what the coroner is prepared to swallow in due course,' Hannah murmured. 'In the meantime, we are bound to treat Emma's death as suspicious.'

'Oh no,' Karen said. 'Seriously?'

'It's hard to see how she can have finished up at the bottom of that shaft unaided.'

'Dear God!' Jeremy said. 'As if we haven't had enough to contend with over this whole wretched business.'

Emma's face loomed in Hannah's mind. The pale skin, the slightly parted lips. A woman looking for answers. Whatever she'd been searching for, she hadn't found it beneath the Arsenic Labyrinth. Poor, dead Emma. To Jeremy and Karen, she was little more than a source of continuing irritation.

'May I ask you both a few questions?'

'What on earth for?' Karen demanded. 'I mean, this isn't a good time.'

'If you don't feel up to it, we can talk to each of you tomorrow morning.'

'Listen, I hope this isn't all down to the police

234

wanting to tick a few boxes, to cover their own backs. We're ordinary, decent people, trying to get on with our lives and being subjected to a Spanish Inquisition doesn't help.'

Jeremy patted Karen's white hand. She might have been a five-year-old who'd woken from dreaming of the Bogeyman. 'Please, Chief Inspector. You can see how distressed my wife is at the loss of her sister.'

Hannah assumed a sorrowful expression and said, 'I imagined you might prefer to discuss the situation here and now. We wanted to be helpful, we thought you might not want us to call at your school. But of course if you prefer...'

Jeremy extricated himself from Karen and got to his feet. 'There's absolutely no need for you to come anywhere near the College.'

'Why on earth do you need to speak to my husband, anyway?' Karen snapped. 'We've given every cooperation to the police from day one. Jeremy hardly knew Emma. We're decent, law-abiding folk, what more can we say? Do you realise how damaging it can be to a potential head's career prospects, to have the police turning up at his place of work? Parents don't shell out handsome fees for that sort of thing, you know.'

'This is a murder inquiry,' Hannah said. 'And Mr Erskine was one of the last people known to have seen the victim alive.'

'What are you suggesting?' Jeremy's voice rose. 'I was suffering pain and in need of treatment. The woman was my sister-in-law. Everything was open and above board.'

235

Maggie said, 'Can you remember anything that might help us to understand what happened to Emma? Something she said, did she seem excited or afraid...?'

He pursed his lips. 'I was more interested in what she could do for my back.'

'Surely there was something?'

Jeremy pondered. 'I suppose she was more animated than usual.'

'Yes?' A dogged smile, meant to coax a fatal indiscretion. 'Go on.'

'She never had much conversation. We weren't on the same wavelength. But she asked after Karen and Sophie, made an effort to be pleasant. I had some good news for her. A few days earlier, our doctor had told Karen she was expecting another baby and I thought her sister deserved to know. Emma seemed genuinely thrilled for us, not in the least miserable or depressed. Besides, it must have occurred to her that a self-employed businesswoman needs to keep on the right side of her clients. She'd ploughed her money into the business, she had to work to make a success of it.'

'The money, yes. I keep wondering where it really came from. You didn't help her out with a loan, by any chance?'

'Good God, no.' Jeremy was startled at being suspected of casual generosity. 'Why on earth should we?'

'She was family.' Families meant a lot to Maggie.

'We had our own family to look after. At the time we were hoping for a second child. Emma was footloose and fancy free. Why should we

236

subsidise her lifestyle?'

'She hadn't been well.'

Jeremy made a scoffing noise. 'I'm not accusing her of malingering...'

'But?'

'This stress she'd suffered from. What caused it? She can't have been over-worked at Inchmore Hall. It's not exactly Dove Cottage, the tourists don't come flocking.'

Karen turned to Hannah. 'Where's this leading, Chief Inspector? Surely it must be obvious that we can't help you. Don't forget, Emma isn't the only victim here. We have our own lives to lead. And we have Jeremy's reputation, his whole future, to think of. We really don't want to get involved in a murder case.'

'Your sister is dead, Mrs Erskine. You can't help but be involved.'

'That bloody journalist!' Jeremy said. 'If it hadn't been for him...'

'You still wouldn't know your sister-in-law's fate,' Hannah interrupted. 'Perhaps you owe Mr Di Venuto.'

'Owe him?' Karen's face was red, her voice burning with contempt. 'That preening, arrogant bastard? All he wants to do is to cause trouble.'

Hannah said softly, 'What makes you say he's preening and arrogant?'

Karen stared at her, then at her husband. In the silence, the only sound was the ticking of a black pyramid clock on the radiator shelf.

'Well ... it's obvious, isn't it? Jeremy summed him up in a single conversation.'

Out of the corner of her eye, Hannah noticed

237

Jeremy's brow furrowing. 'You haven't spoken to Mr Di Venuto yourself?'

Karen hesitated. 'No ... no, I haven't.'

'Are you sure?'

'Jeremy told him I wouldn't want to discuss my sister with the Press.'

Time to take a punt. What is there to lose? 'It's just that ... I have the impression there's something personal between Di Venuto and your husband.'

'Nonsense,' Jeremy said. 'I've never even met the fellow. We spoke over the telephone, not face to face. He's a local hack who's grown too big for his boots, that's the top and bottom of it.'

'Is it?' Hannah asked.

Silence.

A clock in the living room chimed the hour, loud as the tolling of a funeral bell. Karen's mouth was clamped shut. Her eyes were glued to her husband, as if imploring him for guidance. But he avoided her gaze.

'You're bound to find out, aren't you?' Karen asked. 'Sooner or later?'

Hannah nodded, suppressing the urge to shout: *Find out what? Get on with it!*

'Years ago,' Karen said slowly, 'Tony Di Venuto and I were ... close.'

Hannah wished she had a camera. A snap of Jeremy's slack-jawed features would have won a prize. Talk about gobsmacked. Obviously he'd had no idea. He made a small, indeterminate mewling noise. It was kinder to pretend not to have heard.

'I'm sorry, darling,' Karen said. 'I should have mentioned it before.'

238

Maggie looked as though she were about to choke. Hannah could read her mind. *Is this woman for real? How can you not mention something like that?*

'I was determined to scrub him out of my life, like a nasty stain on a favourite blouse. And I thought I'd succeeded. I had the shock of my life when he turned up here again.'

'What happened, Mrs Erskine?'

Karen took a breath. 'I met him in a nightclub when we were both twenty-one. He had those Italian good looks and I always adored the Scottish accent. He'd grown up in Glasgow, but come south of the border to train as a journalist. He had the gift of the gab. To listen to him, you'd have thought he was sure to finish up as a special correspondent on the nine o'clock news. You could say I was swept off my feet. Nothing was too good for me. He spent a fortune on presents, treated me like a queen. Of course, I was flattered. This drop-dead gorgeous man, who couldn't get enough of me.'

Jeremy's gaze was locked upon her. For the first time, Hannah found it in her heart to feel sorry for the man. He'd actually believed he was the only man Karen had ever loved.

'But?'

'But it wasn't a healthy relationship. He didn't understand I needed to be my own person. I never met any man so selfish. He expected unquestioning devotion. Obedience. Worship, even. Whenever he didn't get his own way, he had a wicked temper.'

'Is that right?'

'One night we had an argument. He smacked my face, left a horrid mark. I couldn't go out of the house for forty-eight hours, I was so ashamed. Afterwards, he was mortified, swore it was a one-off. A fortnight later, it happened again. That was it. I told him we were finished. He wept and begged me to change my mind. But I stood firm.' She swallowed. Her eyes were fixed on the ceiling as the memories flooded back. 'For a while he stalked me. You know the sort of thing. Silent phone calls, parking his car outside my flat for hours on end. Keeping watch on me. It was a nightmare. And then – hey presto! – he disappeared from my life.'

Jeremy reached for her. An instinctive gesture of shocked compassion. 'I had no idea.'

She didn't take his hand. 'When you and I met, I was determined not to let the past spoil things. By the time we were married and Sophie was born, I'd almost forgotten Tony. But then he came back.'

'When was this?' Hannah asked.

'A week or two before Emma disappeared. One night when Jeremy was out at a parents' evening, I heard a knock on the door. When I saw Tony, I almost fainted. He wanted to come in, but I refused. It turned out the reason he'd vanished from my life was that he'd found some other woman. But they'd split up. He said he couldn't get me out of his head, but the soft soap didn't work any more. I slammed the door in his face.'

'And how did he take that?'

'He stayed in his car outside the house until Jeremy came home. I was shivery, my teeth were

240

chattering, I was so wound up. I pretended I was going down with flu. The next day Tony rang while I was alone with the baby. He said I'd never escape from him. There was a bond between us, we would always be bound together. He sounded creepy. I was terrified.'

Jeremy muttered, 'I remember, you weren't yourself. You were coping with a small child, and you were pregnant. And I put it down to hormones...'

'I told Tony I was expecting another baby. Hoping it would put him off. I don't think he was ever into fatherhood. After that, I didn't hear from him again. A few days later, Emma went missing and there was all that kerfuffle. Being questioned by the police. Stuff in the newspapers. I've never spoken to him since.'

'So telling him you were pregnant worked?' Maggie asked.

'Perhaps.'

Hannah studied Karen's chilly expression. 'Or do you think there was some other reason why he went quiet?'

Karen exhaled. 'This seems a stupid thing to say.'

Jeremy said, 'What is it, darling?'

She turned to him. 'You know, there were days when I wondered whether Tony had something to do with Emma's disappearance. Whether he'd harmed her to get back at me.'

Despite the cold of the afternoon, Guy felt clammy in his fleece. As he turned out of Campbell Road, his walk had lost its swagger. His

241

stomach was churning and he'd needed to empty his bladder twice in the last twenty minutes. He hadn't felt so nervous since that unfortunate incident with the customs officer at Heathrow, how many years back? He wasn't afraid of breaking a promise – he had plenty of experience of that. But this was different. He was going to make a call that would change his life.

He'd rehearsed his lines, knowing the importance of striking the right note. How mortifying to be considered greedy, let alone threatening. He wanted the conversation to be pleasant and painless; this was a request for help, nothing more.

Well, not much more. He'd sworn never to return to the Lakes, but that was the sort of promise you couldn't keep forever. This was his native heath, he'd done remarkably well to stay away for ten years. Was it Fate that had lured him back? He didn't really believe there was a God, but sometimes it was hard not to believe there was some mysterious design to life. If he'd booked into a plusher hotel, he might not have seen Di Venuto's article and none of this would have happened. But he was pleased that it had. Emma would have a decent burial now and her sister could get on with the rest of her life. He'd brought happiness to Sarah and he'd saved her from her gambling habit. Now he deserved something for himself.

The bottom line was that he needed money and he needed it fast. He couldn't live on fresh air. He didn't mean to make a habit of issuing demands, he wasn't unreasonable, far less a parasite. With more luck in the past, he would be swanning around on the Continent now, not scuttling around the chilly streets of Coniston.

A white van's horn sounded angrily as he skipped across Yewdale Road from behind a lorry. He sucked in air, told himself to watch out. How ironic if he was crushed to a pulp when on the brink of getting hold of the cash that would transform his life for the better.

This time he wouldn't squander the money. He'd learn from mistakes of the past. He'd fixed on the sum he would ask for. Realistic, yet sufficiently meaningful to change his life. You didn't need much to make a success of your life. Micawber was spot on.

The phone box was empty. He took out of his pocket the scrap of paper on which he'd written the number, then counted to ten before he dialled. If the wrong person answered, he'd hang up and try again later.

'Hello?'

It was the right person. A voice he'd never forget. Soon his troubles would be over. He wanted to roar with delight.

Instead he said pleasantly, 'This is Guy. Remember me?'

CHAPTER THIRTEEN

At half six the next morning, Hannah padded barefoot into the kitchen, to be greeted by the sight of a dozen roses, the colour of blood. Beside the vase stood an enormous card emblazoned with a pink heart and a box wrapped in gold paper. A dozen balloons, purple, orange, green, were tied to the cupboard doors with sparkly string.

She'd been working in the study until after one o'clock, tapping details of the day's work into her laptop. Falling asleep the instant her head touched the pillow, she'd dreamed of Emma Bestwick, her mouth wide open in a soundless scream, tumbling down, down, down the spiral staircase that led from the tower of Inchmore Hall.

She rubbed the sleep out of her eyes and wondered if her imagination was playing tricks. But when she focused on the message on the card, a torrent of guilt engulfed her.

Shit, shit, shit. How could I forget?

The door swung open behind her. 'Happy Valentine's Day!'

Two sinewy arms seized her and she felt Marc's warm breath on her neck. She could smell toothpaste and jasmine shower gel. He opened her cotton gown and started nuzzling her neck while his hands explored her. His fingers were warm, probing, adventurous. Nails dug gently into her skin. She succumbed to a fit of the giggles even as

244

she wriggled out of his grasp.

'Behave!'

'It's a fair cop,' he murmured. 'A very fair cop.'

'Can't remember when you last gave me roses.'

'You had a narrow escape. I nearly bought you a de luxe edition of *The Kama Sutra.*'

She laughed and told him what he could do with *The Kama Sutra* before confessing. 'I haven't got you a card.'

Never before had her memory betrayed her so badly. How typical that he'd colonised the moral high ground, even though for him Valentine's Day meant little more than an excuse for a meal out in a swish restaurant followed by special occasion sex.

'Know what? You spend too much time worrying about decomposed bodies.'

'Yeah, yeah, it's true, I need to get a life.'

'You said it.' He took a pace towards her and slipped the gown off her shoulders. 'You'll have to find some way to make up to me for your appalling lack of care and attention.'

She skipped out of his reach. 'Tonight, OK? I need to get some clothes on. We have a lot to do.'

'Don't be late. I've booked a table at Gregorio's for seven-thirty.'

He looked like a pleased little boy and she found herself kissing him hard. When they separated again, she read the card and unwrapped the box. Belgian chocolates, her favourites. How come she'd ever doubted him?

'You know, I'm glad you bought me chocolates. I was afraid you might have booked me into a clinic for a boob job to match Vicky's.'

245

He couldn't quite drag his eyes away from her uncovered breasts. Thank God they weren't droopy; not yet, anyway. On the other hand, they were scarcely pneumatic. She was what she was, she didn't want to change. The thought of being cut up for the sake of appearance made her flesh creep. But Marc had this in common with every man she'd ever met: he was dedicated to getting his own way, no matter how long it took.

'I know you don't fancy it,' he said.

His tone was light and bantering. But something in his expression made her pick up the gown and sling it back on.

'I have to go.'

'It's still early. Come back upstairs for half an hour.' When she shook her head, his tone sharpened. 'OK, Hannah. Just remember this. Dead bodies are all very well. But it's living bodies that matter.'

'The property agent texted me last night,' Miranda said.

Daniel snaked his arm around her. He was only half awake. Ten a.m. and they were still in bed, the duvet long since flung on to the floor. There was no danger of their getting cold after two indulgent hours spent celebrating Valentine's. This was the glory of escaping the rat race. You had all the time in the world.

'Uh-huh?'

'Someone's made an offer for my flat.'

He tightened his grip on her, too blissed-out to speak. At last she'd decided to give up on London living and commit. To the Lakes, to Tarn

Cottage, to him.

Miranda disentangled herself and knelt beside him, brushing the silky hair out of her eyes and folding her arms across her chest in a belated gesture of modesty. All of a sudden, her slender body was as taut as a violin string. Her smile was too fixed, too bright. He knew his Miranda. She had more news for him, and it wasn't going to be good.

'The agent talked about something else. There's a flat in Greenwich, not far from the Cutty Sark, I meant to mention it to you, but I kept forgetting. He showed me round while I was down there. It's absolutely lovely and it's just across the river from Canary Wharf, five minutes on the train. The owner's been offered a job in Abu Dhabi and is desperate for a quick sale. The agent's bartered him down so that the asking price is a snip. Would you like to go halves?'

He stared into her eyes, unable to do more than repeat her words like the dullest boy in the class. 'Go halves?'

'Yes, why not? Face it, we just can't afford to jump off the London property ladder. The way prices keep shooting up, we'll never be able to climb back on.'

'Why would we want to? If you need a place to stay while you're working down there, you can rent.'

The blonde mane shook. 'No way. Rent is dead money. I need a place of my own. We both do.'

'Not me.'

'Come on, Daniel. Don't be so – so dogmatic. It's not reasonable. When the time comes, you'll

247

have work to do in London. You can't be a full-time historian up here, that's for sure.'

'Why not? It's not as if we're living north of Vladivostok. We can have the best of both worlds. Live here and sample the delights of London when the mood takes us.'

Somewhere outside, wild geese were crying. He was sure Miranda couldn't hear them, she excelled at shutting her mind to whatever didn't suit.

'No need to be sarcastic.'

'Hey, London's wonderful. I just don't want to live there.'

'Well, I do!' When she saw the look on his face, she said hurriedly, 'I mean, I love the Lakes, of course, but Tarn Fold is a cul-de-sac in more senses than one. This cottage is fine as a hide-away, but we can't bury ourselves in the country-side permanently. There's a world outside Brackdale. It would be crazy to cut ourselves off.'

Daniel lay back and stared at the whitewashed ceiling. It was uneven, like everything in this cottage. Months of building work had trans-formed the place; that was where houses scored over relationships. Easier to paint over the cracks. The room smelled of sex, but the passion of early morning seemed to belong to another life.

'It's not for me.'

She brushed her fingers against the hairs on his chest. Her touch was so light, so delicate. There were moments when he thought she could ask for anything, and he would give it. But it was an illusion, life didn't work like that.

'I want us to spend more time together, darl-ing.'

'Me too.'

'Then why do you insist on going your own sweet way?'

He clasped her hand and sat up. 'Living in the Lakes is what we agreed. And this is perfect, isn't it? Who could ask for anything more?'

Even with tousled hair and not a trace of make-up, she was very beautiful. But as she shook her head and looked into his eyes, he saw nothing but sadness.

'Sorry, darling. It isn't enough.'

Guy and Sarah had exchanged cards bearing protestations of undying devotion, but he'd readily agreed to her suggestion that they shouldn't spend a fortune on presents until their finances were sorted. Sarah was keen to prove that she was capable of behaving responsibly with cash and from his point of view it didn't make sense to waste another penny on her. She'd misled him, and he planned to escape as soon as he'd replenished his coffers.

He'd spun her a yarn about a massive deal that he hoped would save his job and leave him quids in, sprinkling it with jargon he'd gleaned from the *Financial Times* so as to add verisimilitude. The negotiations were bound to be complex and would take him away from Coniston for a couple of weeks, but she shouldn't fret, absence always made the heart grow fonder. She must take in more lodgers to earn a few pounds until he returned to the Glimpse. They could share the future free of debt's shackles.

Sarah was excited, she chattered incessantly

249

about what they might do in the months ahead, places they might visit, holidays they might take. He found it wearisome to pay attention to her fantasies. Of course, she'd be upset when she realised he wasn't coming back, but she only had herself to blame. If she hadn't been so extravagant, she wouldn't have been a bad catch for a bloke of her own age. But he'd given her a lot, more than she deserved. To persuade herself that she had something to offer to a handsome young man with the world at his feet, that really was cloud-cuckoo land.

He was leafing through the *Post*. One story filled the pages, the story that owed its existence to him. He was mystified by the discovery of the second body, but the puzzle didn't faze him. Nothing connected him with Emma Bestwick, no witnesses had spotted him on Mispickel Scar and nobody was going to come forward ten years later to point the finger at him. Di Venuto alluded to Guy's telephone calls as 'a tip-off', implying that it had been teased out as the result of shrewd and resourceful investigative journalism. He'd been lucky enough to be in the right place at the right time, but Guy didn't begrudge him his scoop.

'Penny for them,' Sarah trilled.

She was flicking a feather duster over the surface of the old radio on the sideboard. She had a fondness for Muzak that he found rather common. Abba were singing 'Money, Money, Money'. Of course they were right, it was a rich man's world. Not that he was greedy. He didn't want a fortune, just enough to get by in comfort.

250

'Mmmm. I was just thinking. It's funny how things turn out. Sometimes two people come together and they do each other a huge favour, maybe something that changes both their lives.'

Sarah smiled with delight and said some gooey things, even though he'd had in mind not his relationship with her but the way that he and Di Venuto had scratched each other's backs. By this time tomorrow, he would have money and freedom. Despite the newspaper coverage and the frenetic police activity around the village, he hadn't expected it to be quite so easy. Yet after the initial shock of his call, his old friend had been quick to see the sense in agreeing to his request. And it had been a request, not a demand, no way. He wouldn't stoop so low.

This wasn't blackmail, for Heaven's sake. Nothing more than two decent people doing each other a bit of good.

Marc Amos was sitting behind the cash till when Daniel reached the front of the queue to pay. As he smiled in greeting, he glanced at the title of the fat book in Daniel's hand. Its spine was split and it smelled of damp.

'*Lore of Old Lakeland?* I read it years ago. The author, Herbert Bickerstaff, was a collector of Lake District curiosities. Mind you, as a writer his style was closer to Jeffrey Archer than John Ruskin. And I'm not sure about the reliability of his scholarship. Leisure reading rather than research?'

'I was talking to someone about the curse on Mispickel Scar and I wanted to read up.'

'You'll find it in Bickerstaff, I'm sure. He was no academic, but he loved telling stories. First edition, too. Pity it's such a lousy copy.'

Daniel handed over a ten pound note. 'That's why it's such a bargain.'

'I don't know whether you saw the regional bulletin on the TV last night? You might have caught a long shot of Hannah, looking wind-swept up on Mispickel Scar.'

'Sorry I missed it. She was talking about the bodies they have found?'

'Yes, there was another press conference this morning, but the Assistant Chief Constable was in the chair. She loves the limelight. Hannah would rather get on with her work.' Marc grinned at a burly hiker who had a dog-eared Wainwright in his shovel-like mitt. 'Speaking of which...'

'Good to see you,' Daniel said, stepping to one side. 'Give Hannah my best.'

'Will do.' Marc waited for the hiker to key his PIN into the machine. 'In the unlikely event she gets home tonight before I'm fast asleep.'

'She works too hard?'

'Too bloody right.' As the hiker plodded away, Marc added in a low voice, 'You know something? Last Leap Year Day, I'd arranged to take her out for a slap-up meal. It was a surprise. Between you and me, I was going to propose. We'd been together so long, it seemed like the right thing to do. But she rang to say she'd been caught up with an important suspect interview and wouldn't be back until eleven. That was when I realised, she was married already. To the job.'

252

The *Post's* offices at Broughton-in-Furness occupied a tall Georgian merchant's house overlooking the market square, with its village stocks, slate fish market slabs and obelisk commemorating King George III's Jubilee. Sitting in reception alongside Les Bryant, Hannah skim-read the latest issue of the paper while Les sucked a sweet to ease his sore throat. He reeked of menthol and blackcurrant lozenges and every couple of minutes he blew his nose, making a noise like a honking bird.

'Anything?' he mumbled, nodding at the newspaper.

Hannah shook her head. The Mispickel Scar Mystery, as Tony Di Venuto insisted on calling it, occupied a disproportionate number of column inches, even though he had nothing new to report. The competing stories – a woman mugged for her bingo winnings, vandalism in a graveyard and a street sweeper hanging up his brush after seventeen years' service – were scarcely strong enough to muscle it off the front page. On the walls around them hung framed features from previous issues. Campaigns against the closure of sub-post offices, the cutting of bus routes, the amalgamation of local schools due to falling pupil numbers. The *Post* was one of those Cumbrian newspapers that fought the good fight on behalf of rural England and its people against the countless threats of the twenty-first century. For all her wariness of journalists, Hannah admired their tenacity, though in her heart of hearts she doubted if the battle could ever be won.

The receptionist was busy chatting to a friend on her mobile, complaining about the overweening ego of some mutual acquaintance known as the Diva. The only outside call she took while Hannah waited was from a stringer with a tip-off about the theft of a pensioner's scooter. She was trying to end the call and get back to her gossip when the internal door opened and Tony Di Venuto breezed in, natty and assured as a Sinatra tribute singer called back for another encore.

'DCI Scarlett – good to see you again! And – Mr Bryant, thanks for coming.'

They shook hands; Tony's grip was firm and confident. As the detectives followed him inside, Hannah glanced over her shoulder at the girl behind the desk. She was sticking her tongue out at her colleague's retreating back. With a stab of amusement, Hannah realised who the Diva was. Good name.

The open plan news room hummed with conversation and the click of fingers on half a dozen keyboards. A spiky-haired young woman in a cropped top that insisted *No to Animal Testing* glanced up as Tony strode past. Hannah saw the girl's lip curl. The Diva didn't have too many admirers in his own backyard.

'My desk, Detective Chief Inspector,' he said airily, waving at a tiny workstation festooned with cuttings from stories he had written. Hannah was sure the mention of her rank was for the benefit of his colleague. 'We'll talk in the meeting room. More private there.'

He led her into a tiny room with a window in the door and another above eye level. Four old wooden chairs were grouped around a scratched table. The air was warm and stale. The *Post* didn't run to air-conditioning.

'Do take a seat. Can I offer you coffee?'

Hannah and Les shook their heads in unison. Both of them had eyeballed the receptionist sipping from a paper cup a muddy liquid that resembled goo from a late night horror movie.

'So this is the nerve centre?' Hannah asked.

The journalist smiled. 'Not exactly CNN Tower, eh? Never mind. I don't expect to stay here for long. Off the record, I've been approached by a headhunter. One of the major regionals is interested in talking. Mind you, they'd have to cross my palm with silver to prise me away from the Lakes this time. But if you're ambitious and you get a chance to progress, you need to grab it, that's my philosophy. Anyway, let's cut to the chase. Am I right in thinking you've discovered something?'

Hannah balanced cautiously on her chair. One of its legs seemed shorter than the others. 'We've been talking to Karen Erskine.'

The smile tightened. 'And?'

'I'm wondering why you forgot to mention that you and she were once an item.'

Tony Di Venuto was incapable, she thought, of embarrassment. No beetroot flush, no averting of the eyes. Hides didn't come any thicker. Pursing his lips, he said, 'Because it was irrelevant.'

'You knew the dead woman's sister and you say it was irrelevant?'

'Certainly.' He'd anticipated the question and the words tripped from his tongue, as perfectly choreographed as a West End chorus line. 'I never met Emma. She was living in Merseyside during the brief time that Karen and I were together. So how could our long-ago relationship have any bearing on the matter of Emma's disappearance?'

'She says that you hit her.'

'That's despicable.'

He meant the accusation, rather than the violence. Hannah snapped, 'According to Karen, that's why she dumped you.'

He winced, but his powers of recovery were worthy of a winded boxer. Within moments of taking the blow, he had fixed on a beam and was saying in a hushed voice, 'It was my decision that we split up. Karen wanted to settle down and I wasn't ready for it. I prefer to be footloose and fancy free, Chief Inspector. But she took it badly. No doubt that's why she's telling you these terrible things about me. A woman scorned.'

'She says she finished the relationship after you hit her a second time and then that you stalked her until some other woman caught your eye. By the time that was over, Karen was married, but you threatened that she'd never escape from you.'

'I need hardly tell you, this is slander. Actionable. If she repeats it...'

'The way she explained it, your behaviour sounded like a power thing,' Hannah interrupted. 'You prefer your lovers to swoon at your feet, but you want more. You insist on being in complete control. When they show signs of having a mind of their own, the sparks fly.'

He rolled his eyes. 'Fantasy, sheer fantasy.'

'Is this why you hinted that Jeremy Erskine might know something about Emma Bestwick's fate? As a way of getting back at a woman who had wounded your pride all those years ago?'

256

'My story was a legitimate piece of investigative journalism. A damned good example of it, even if I do say so myself. And may I remind you, Chief Inspector, it got results. Your picture wouldn't be splashed all over the Press if I hadn't tipped you off about where the bodies were buried.'

'Strange as it may seem, I didn't take this job to boost my public profile.'

When she saw his smirk of triumph, she realised she'd walked into a trap. It wouldn't do to write this man off as stupid, as well as unpleasant.

'I suppose not,' he said. 'A hiding place after the fiasco of the Rao trial might be closer to the mark. If you don't mind my saying so.'

Ouch. He was a good enough journalist to have done his homework. And there was a steel fist beneath that velvet glove. Before she could dig herself a deeper hole, Les Bryant cleared his throat and asked a question, broadening his vowels as if in provocation.

'So you had nowt to do with Emma's death?'

Di Venuto stared at Les. 'Don't be absurd. Why on earth would I kill a woman who meant nothing to me?'

'To hurt her sister?'

'You can't be serious.'

Les sneezed, a minor explosion. 'Maybe there was no intention to kill. Perhaps you simply cocked up.'

'You can't be serious. What about the telephone calls? That's the man you need to find, instead of wasting your time harassing me.'

'The calls, yes. Trouble is, we don't have much

detail about them. They weren't recorded. As it happens, we only have your word that this mystery caller told you where to find Emma Bestwick.'

'I made contemporaneous notes.'

'Hang on, we all know about notes made by police officers and journalists, don't we? Sometimes there's a temptation to improve upon reality. Poetic licence.'

Di Venuto's voice rose. 'You're casting aspersions on my integrity as a journalist.'

'Simply testing the information you've supplied to us.'

'Are you seriously accusing me...?'

'We're not accusing you of anything, Mr Di Venuto,' Hannah said. She wondered what Lauren Self would have to say about this conversation if – or when – she ever found out about it. 'But you must realise, these are questions that need to be asked, given that you haven't been entirely frank with us.'

Tony Di Venuto brushed a lock of hair out of his eye. A consciously handsome gesture, which also bought a couple more seconds to decide what to say. When he did speak, his tone was magnanimous.

'Look here, my fling with Karen was a long time ago. Passions ran high. There were faults on both sides. You're a woman of the world, you know what I'm saying? But I've always had her interests at heart. When Emma disappeared, I felt so sorry for Karen. She still meant a lot to me, even though she'd settled down with Erskine. I've never cared for the sound of the man.'

258

'Why?'

'A man like that isn't to be trusted.' The Diva leaned back on his chair, gaze travelling along the ceiling, relishing the chance to play moral censor. 'He began an affair with Karen while he was still married to a plain little librarian. The minute his glamorous blonde girlfriend got pregnant, he left his wife for her. Not exactly honourable. If my kid was a pupil at Grizedale, I'd be asking questions. Who's to say that he didn't take a shine to Emma and then cut up rough when he found she wasn't interested? I was worried for Karen.'

'For Karen?'

'Certainly. Who knew what he might be capable of? I couldn't live with myself if anything ever happened to her, because I'd not bothered to probe. When the ten-year anniversary came along, the story was a natural for the *Post*. I couldn't turn a blind eye, even if I wanted to. I wanted to do her a service, even though so much water had flowed under the bridge. I hoped our campaign would bring out the truth about what happened to Emma. Of course I was careful what I said about her husband. My editor's brother is a shit-hot London libel lawyer and I sought his advice. But I never dreamed of spiking the story. If the finger of guilt pointed at Jeremy, wasn't it about time he paid the price for his crime?'

'You were doing a public service?' Les suggested, his face stripped of expression.

If he caught the sarcasm, Tony Di Venuto gave no hint of it. 'Absolutely. That's what local journalism is all about.'

'So what did you make of that?' Hannah asked, buttoning her jacket as they walked out of the stale air into the flesh-nipping cold.

'Lying toad,' Les muttered.

'No, don't sit on the fence. Tell me what you really think.'

A shadow of a smile. 'Never liked journalists, never will. And he thinks the sun shines out of his arse. But does that make him a murderer?'

'He might be crediting Jeremy with his own motive, his own crime.'

'Maybe.'

'You're not convinced?'

'Just because you're a creep, doesn't mean you're a murderer.'

This was unarguable. Hannah unlocked the car with a click of her remote key. She was about to climb in when she caught a glimpse of Les in profile. Head bowed, wrinkles like ravines around his eyes and mouth.

'You OK?'

'Do I sound like it?'

'I don't mean your cold. I mean...'

He glared at her and pulled open the car door. 'Listen, if you fancy yourself as a trick cyclist, leave me out of it, all right?'

'I was only...' Her voice trailed away. Dourness was par for the course, but she'd never seen Les look as woebegone as he did right now.

He glanced up at the heavens, then closed his eyes. 'If you must know, the wife's left me.'

'Les, I'm sorry.'

'Don't be. I've had a while to get used to the idea. A month since, she packed her bags and

260

went off with someone else. It's not the first time and I thought she'd come running back, like she's done before. My mistake. I've had a letter from her solicitor, telling me she wants a divorce. So she can marry the stupid bastard. Happy bloody Valentine's Day, eh?'

'If I can...'

'Bloke she's run off with, he's my best mate. Well, he *was* my best mate. Can you imagine that?'

Hannah tried to visualise Terri canoodling with Marc. For a moment, she was seized by a wild fantasy, of Marc covertly going online to pick up women and then having the shock of his life when he realised that his date was Hannah's closest friend. The two of them were so different. Terri was loud and funny, Marc quiet and intense. They had never hit it off. At least that was the impression they gave.

For God's sake. She ought to be paying attention to Les as he mused.

'The daft bloody bugger. I only hope he likes trailing round shoe shops.' He sneezed again. 'Come on, then, we'd best be getting back. Lots to do.'

Grizedale College was a throwback in time, reminding Daniel of school stories he'd read as a boy. Black and white buildings and a clock tower, complemented by cloisters, a chapel and a cricket pavilion. A motto in Latin was carved over the imposing entrance to a hall in which he imagined young voices belting out the school song as a warm-up for 'Onward, Christian Soldiers' and

'God Save the Queen'. Easy to picture Billy Bunter en route to the tuck shop, or Mr Chips as he reminisced about succeeding generations of pupils studying Virgil.

The hall was galleried, dark and gloomy even in the middle of the day. The walls were lined with oil paintings of long deceased head teachers resplendent in their caps and gowns. He asked the way to Jeremy Erskine's room, and was helped by a boy and a girl in blazers of a hideous violet hue, suggestive of a bad case of acne. The pupils' diction was so clear, their manners so impeccable, that he suspected they were aliens who had cunningly assumed the form of twenty-first-century teenagers, only for their invasion plans to be betrayed by excessive and unnatural politeness.

Daniel's shoes squeaked as he walked across the parquet floor and he flinched in anticipation of a prefect's reprimand. He rapped on a solid oak door and a lordly voice commanded, 'Come!'

The large, well-upholstered room boasted the warm and comfortable ambience of a Victorian gentlemen's club. On the walls hung framed certificates and photographs of Jeremy standing next to teams of school cricketers and rugby players. The oak desk was covered with pictures of an attractive blonde woman and two young children, together with a pile of essays for mark-ing. History textbooks crowded a glass-fronted bookcase, an ocelot rug stretched across the floor. On a table was spread lunch for two. The cutlery was Sheffield steel, the napkins bore the College crest. There was a hot fire made with fat logs which gurgled and spat.

Jeremy wrung his hand. 'Welcome to Grizedale, Mr Kind! What a pleasure to meet you. Cook has prepared a little something for us, as you can see. Ham, cheese or salmon sandwiches, whatever suits.'

For half an hour they ate and talked history and Daniel found they shared an enthusiasm for exploring the dustier corners of life in Victorian Britain. Jeremy proved a knowledgeable and unexpectedly witty conversationalist, the pomposity Hannah had described melting away as they discussed how historians go about detecting the truth about the past.

'I tell my students to learn to ask the right questions, it's the most important trick of all. Strip out the irrelevancies – the red herrings, as you call them in your book – and focus on what will carry them through to a proper conclusion.'

Ask the right questions. Yes, Daniel preached the same message at Oxford. But it was easier said than done.

'You mentioned your Association purchased several of the lots at the auction where I bought the letters about Ruskin. Do you know what happened to them?'

'We were fortunate to receive a substantial bequest in the will of the late Mrs Elizabeth Clough. Her son Alban founded the Museum of Myth and Legend, you know.'

'I've met him.'

'He isn't a serious historian, I fear, but his mother was a good friend of our Secretary, Sylvia Blacon. Poor Sylvia is very frail these days, but she sent a nephew to bid on the Association's behalf and he came back with a rich haul. Worth peanuts in monetary terms, perhaps, but enormously valuable in giving us a fuller understanding of life in Coniston and its neighbourhood over the past couple of centuries.'

'Where do you store it all?'

'We keep a small archive here in the College library, by kind permission of the Governors. Scarcely the Bodleian, but you would be more than welcome to take a look. Not that what we have can offer you much help with your current project. Occasionally we have inquiries from people researching Ruskin, but we direct them to Brantwood and the specialist collections.'

'I'd love to look over the stuff Sylvia's nephew bought. Ever since the auction, I've regretted not taking a closer look at the lots I didn't bid for. I only decided to turn up at the last minute, so I went in under-prepared. For all I know, I overlooked half a dozen gems.'

'So far we haven't added the auction lots to the collection. They still await cataloguing. Sylvia keeps them at home. During the past few months, she's been unwell and I haven't wanted to press her. She's in her mid-eighties, our longest-serving committee member. Quite a character, she was a history teacher for thirty odd years. She was so anxious to study the materials; her mind is still as sharp as a knife. Unfortunately, when we last spoke, she hadn't made any progress.'

'I wonder if I could talk to her?'

'I remember her saying how much she enjoyed

264

your TV series. Since she was taken poorly, she's not had much to get excited about. I'm sure she'd be thrilled by the prospect of meeting you.'

'There seems to be plenty of excitement around here at present. I read about the bodies the police have discovered up in the fells.'

'Ah.' Jeremy coloured. 'That business is rather close to home, as it happens. The police believe that one of the bodies they have found is my wife's sister.'

Years of swimming through the shark-infested waters of a Senior Common Room in an Oxford college had schooled Daniel in the black arts of disingenuous conversation. His sister had told him more than once that he wasn't as nice as everyone thought he was, and of course she was right. He expressed profound apologies while trying to prise more information out of the bereaved brother-in-law. At least, if Hannah was to be believed, Jeremy wasn't suffering too much grief.

'You know DCI Scarlett, I gather?'

'My father used to work with her.'

'I suppose she's only doing her job.' Jeremy adopted a long-suffering tone.

'The police are treating the case as murder, from what I read in the papers.'

A derisive snort. 'The papers have a lot to answer for, if you ask me. Especially the local rag that has made all the fuss about the tenth anniversary of Emma going missing.'

'At least now your wife knows the truth. Emma can have a proper burial.'

Jeremy shook his head. Now his expression was

265

as bleak as the north face of Great Gable.

'But that won't be the end of it, not by a long chalk. Emma will continue to haunt us like one of Alban Clough's ghosts. Your friend DCI Scarlett won't let Karen or me escape her. Have you seen what the police say about cold case work on their website? They have a proud boast. *An unsolved murder never goes away.*'

CHAPTER FOURTEEN

Who shall I be tomorrow?

Guy smiled at himself in the bathroom mirror. He always had a wet shave; electric razors didn't cut close enough. He liked the sharp touch of the blade on his jaw, slicing away the five o'clock shadow. His hand was steady, he never nicked himself.

Soon he would be out of here. Goodbye threadbare towels liberated from a hotel in Morecambe, farewell rusting Salter scales, kept so that Sarah's conscience could torment her as comfort eating piled on the pounds. He wouldn't miss any of it, not the stink of the disinfectant she kept in the airing cupboard, not the clamminess of damp clothes drying on the hangers suspended over the bath tub.

And he wouldn't miss Sarah, either. Her non-stop prattle was getting on his nerves. The brutal fact was, her best hope was for the bailiffs to come in, take possession of the Glimpse and sell off her worldly goods. Together, hopefully, with that bloody cat – if anyone was stupid enough to give such a cussed animal houseroom. The council would be forced to house a homeless woman, she'd be better off in a little flat, with no access to online betting sites. Bankruptcy might be the making of her.

He couldn't afford to think of anyone but himself. This time, he was determined get it right. Ten years ago, young and naïve, his philosophy was *easy come, easy go.* He'd left the Lakes with a huge wad of cash burning a hole in his wallet. For the first time in his life he felt rich and in his innocence he resolved to spend, spend, spend. No wonder the money had run out so fast and once again he'd needed to resort to living on his wits. Even that became harder as the years scurried by. Each time a relationship ran its course, you were bound to move on. Flying by night, before the woman figured out that you'd taken her purse or not repaid the loan from her rich grandma or whatever. It was no sort of life for anyone with talent. He wanted to take time out. Pamper himself, weigh up his options. Find a lovely lady capable of lasting the course. What was the old joke about the perfect mate: a nymphomaniac whose dad owned a brewery? Someone like that.

'Are you decent?' a voice trilled from the other side of the door.

'Yes,' he said, stroking the blade before he put the razor down.

She walked in and burst into a delighted fit of giggles when she saw that he was naked. 'You said that...'

'Nothing indecent about the human body,' he interrupted. Her tee shirt proclaimed *Tomorrow is the first day of the rest of your life*. He lifted it up. 'God's greatest work of art.'

'Rob Stevenson, you're insatiable!'

He put on a sad spaniel face. 'It is Valentine's Day.'

'Well...'

'And we will be apart for a couple of weeks.'

'How will I bear it?' she breathed, shuddering with pleasure as his hands explored. 'You promise to phone me?'

'As soon as I can. But don't be surprised by a few days of radio silence. I'll be living out of a suitcase, working every hour that God sends. Deals don't come much bigger than this one.'

'I'm praying that it works out for us.'

'Have I ever let you down?'

'Never.'

His hands paused in their adventure. Come to think of it, what she said was extraordinary but true. He hadn't let her down once since arriving back in Coniston. Pity, but there was a first time for everything.

'You don't have to go for another hour yet,' she whispered.

He smiled into her pasty, trusting face and seized her wrist. Might as well give her something to remember him by.

'Sorry I can't give you any more information, Mr Kind.'

'Daniel, please. And I'm very grateful for your help.'

Vanessa Goddard gave him a weary half-smile. Her shoulders were bowed and he guessed she was still struggling to come to terms with the discovery of her friend's body.

'Think nothing of it,' she said with a sigh.

The two of them were standing by the door of the library in the converted chapel and Daniel noticed Vanessa looking over his shoulder, through the glass panes. A green Saab was pulling up outside.

'My husband, Francis,' she explained. 'He arranged to go on early shift at the hospital, so we have plenty of time to enjoy a Valentine's Day meal together this evening. We need to take our minds off what happened to poor Emma, though it isn't easy. Hang on for a moment and say hello to him.'

Francis Goddard turned up his jacket collar against the chill as he flicked the remote to lock his car. When his wife introduced them, he mustered a tense smile, but his mind seemed elsewhere. Hannah had mentioned wondering if there had been something between Francis and Emma Bestwick. Even then, would he have murdered her to stop his wife from finding out?

'Darling, you remember I told you last night, Daniel was asking about the Arsenic Labyrinth? Now he's trying to find out the origins of the curse.'

Francis frowned. 'Why are you interested?'

Daniel said shamelessly, 'I'm researching for a book about Ruskin and I wondered whether he might have had something to say about it. But I've been wading through Bickerstaff's book of

269

Lakeland lore and I can't trace where the story comes from.'

Vanessa said, 'Daniel met Jeremy today and asked him about it. Even Mr Know-all had to confess he didn't know the answer.'

'Wonders never cease.' Francis shrugged bony shoulders. 'You'll have to forgive me, Mr Kind. Although I've lived here all my life, I don't claim any expertise in local history. You may only have arrived here five minutes ago, but I'll bet your knowledge is greater than mine.'

He glanced at his watch. Taking the hint, Daniel thanked Vanessa again and took his leave. As he reversed his car, he caught sight of the Goddards through the glass. Francis was bending to plant a kiss on his wife's disfigured cheek. Daniel eased on to the main road. His father's theory of murder investigation had a snag. Suspecting everybody made you forget that most people caught up in crime deserved to be pitied, not pestered.

Driving along the edge of the lake, he saw reflections of bare trees in the water. Across the road, the ground was covered with reddish-brown bracken. It wasn't dark yet, but the wayside cottages had lights in their windows and smoke drifting from their chimneys. Rounding a corner, he needed to brake sharply to avoid crashing into two horned sheep in the road. They had dark, sad faces and splashes of scarlet dye on their fleeces which made them look as though they'd sustained a gunshot wound.

He parked on a patch of ground fringed by purple crocuses and got out of the car. From the

270

distance came the mechanical hum of someone cutting logs, but there was something reassuring and eternal about the sombre stillness of the lake. Leafless birch trees, stark and bare, made strange, twisted shapes against the backdrop of grey sky and water. His shoes cracked on twigs as he rested his backside on an old dry-stone wall.

He took his mobile out of his pocket and punched in Hannah's number. She answered at once. Simply to hear her cool voice again gave him a lift.

'Am I interrupting you?'

'Of course.' She sounded amused, not angry. 'But don't worry about it.'

'You must be up to your eyes. I'll call another time.'

'No, please. Even a DCI on a murder case deserves a break.'

'So you found Emma Bestwick?'

'The forensics aren't completed, but yes. The real mystery concerns the second body. Not exactly the bonus we expected.'

'Any clue about ID?'

'Beyond that he died somewhere between fifty and seventy-five years ago, we don't have much to go on at present. There are two disused mine-shafts, not far apart. It looks like the first body was shoved down one and Emma down the other.'

'Perfect places to dispose of a corpse.'

'Especially since the shafts are surrounded by unstable rock. Over the years, falls of rock covered the holes in the ground. The bodies would never have been discovered if we hadn't gone in search.'

271

'Were they both murdered?'

'It's early days, and the pathologist is bound to hedge his bets. Off the record, he's certain. We found a blood-stained bread knife near to the older corpse and that's a bit of a giveaway.'

'So no connection between the two deaths?'

'We're keeping an open mind. Police speak for saying we haven't got a clue ... hang on, someone wants me, I'll have to go.'

'Sorry to interrupt.'

'Thanks for calling.' The briefest pause. 'Let's talk again when I have more time. In a day or two, maybe?'

Guy had arranged for a taxi to pick him up from outside the Black Bull at nine o'clock. By then he'd have collected his things from the Glimpse and said goodbye To Sarah. With any luck, he'd get the chance to give her cat a surreptitious kick while its owner wasn't looking. As he closed the front door of her house, he could hear Sarah crying upstairs. Stupid woman. He'd concoct a story to make sure that she didn't start to fret about absence of contact until he was well and truly out of reach. Not too much of a challenge to a mind so fertile. She never doubted a single word he said.

The taxi was booked under the name of Pirrip, to symbolise his hopes for the future. He'd take a one-way ride to a discreet hotel overlooking Ullswater. Four-poster luxury and monogrammed bath towels, somewhere he could get a wonderful night's sleep at long, long last. While he watched a movie in the comfort of his own private suite, he would chew over options about where to go next.

He'd decided not to linger in the Lake District. Becoming sentimental about a place was unwise; he realised now how much better it would be to break with the past. Bad things had happened here, and not just the accident to Emma. He couldn't even pretend his childhood had been anything other than horrible. Besides, he didn't only want to get away from the Glimpse. Tony Di Venuto's articles in the *Post* were becoming repetitive; surely other things were going on in Cumbria, apart from the police investigation? He deplored the way Emma's passing was cheapened by being described as murder.

This was the *quid pro quo* he would offer, a special bonus. It wasn't merely a matter of promising to keep his mouth shut. He was leaving the Lakes and he wouldn't be coming back. Yes, he'd said that before, but this time he meant it. Ten years is a long time, he'd learned his lesson.

Since the fall of darkness, the cold had become bitter and the forecasters promised an overnight dusting of snow. Thank God his outdoor gear was weatherproof. He lengthened his stride.

'Mrs Blacon?'

'If you're selling something, young man...'

'My name is Daniel Kind!' He was almost shouting.

'It's no good, you'll have to speak up, I'm slightly deaf.'

Daniel grinned at the telephone. He liked *slightly*. He liked old people, too, almost without

273

exception. In even the most cantankerous of them, he found something to admire and enjoy. Whatever trials they'd endured, they'd had the spirit to survive. Few crimes, other than those against defenceless children, angered him as much as the murders of Harold Shipman, the doctor who played God with the lives of ageing patients. People whose unnatural deaths went unremarked simply because they'd had a good innings, and so their passing was just one of those things. Even though it wasn't.

After five minutes of bellowing, he'd bonded with Sylvia Blacon and arranged to pay her a visit. As he was about to ring off, she mentioned that he wasn't the first researcher to show an interest in John Ruskin's relations with the villagers of Coniston over the past year or so. Alban Clough and Jeremy Erskine had said the same and this time he had the sense to ask in whose footsteps he was following. Some American woman, Sylvia said. Taking a deep breath, he asked if the name Harriet Costello rang a bell. Sylvia sniffed and said it certainly did.

He put down the receiver and swore in silence. Hattie Costello, the new kid on the block. A svelte and media-savvy graduate of Harvard and the Sorbonne, she'd become the darling of History TV. Her writing was laced with sensationalism, but he admired her gift for engaging readers who otherwise found history a turn-off. Jealousy wasn't one of his vices. But if she beat him to it with a fresh study of Ruskin's life in Coniston, it would be years before a major publisher would be interested in another book treading similar ground. He'd have to start over again, find another subject that excited his interest, and that would take time. Not the end of the world, but Miranda would go up the wall.

'Haven't you changed yet? Didn't you say you'd booked the restaurant for seven-thirty?'

He swung round and drank in the sight of her. In her latest little black dress, she would give even Hattie Costello a run for her money. She pirouetted for him and he put his arms around her.

'We could stay in, if you like,' he murmured into her ear. 'Make it a Valentine's night to remember? We can have a meal out any time. I'll rustle something up...'

'Joking, aren't you?' She wriggled out of his grasp and consulted her Rolex. 'Get a move on, I'm famished and the cab will be here any moment.'

Well, it was worth a try. Admitting defeat, he started up the stairs.

'Who was that on the phone, by the way?'

'The secretary of a history society. I want to talk to her about Ruskin.'

'Terrific, you're getting stuck in at last. But you didn't look too happy with what she told you. There isn't a problem?'

From half-way up the stairs, he blew her a kiss. 'No, there's no problem at all.'

Guy was crossing Campbell Road when a small VW raced round the corner and sent him scurrying to the safety of the pavement on the other side. Rap music blared through the windows of

275

the car and a teenager shouted an obscenity at him. Guy made a rude sign as the vehicle vanished out of sight. Drunken louts, he hoped they would crash into a brick wall, it was what they deserved. How ironic if he'd been killed, this night of all nights, when his life was about to change forever.

But the car hadn't touched him. Catching his breath, he decided it was an omen. He'd given little thought to handling this conversation, but everything would be fine. His style was to relax, no point in over-preparing. So much in life was unpredictable, you had to go with the flow. He intended to be genial yet businesslike, but neither of them would want to mess around with small talk. So much water had flowed under the bridge since their last hastily arranged meeting by the pier at Monk Coniston. It made sense to ignore any temptation to reminisce.

Head up, shoulders back, he strode briskly on. No question of nerves – for what did he have to be nervous about? He'd chosen the same rendezvous as ten years ago. Not out of nostalgia or superstition, but because it was quiet and accessible. All he wanted was a repeat of last time. You scratch my back, and I'll scratch yours – that was the way the world went round.

Passing the bright lights of the Waterhead Hotel, he followed the road around the head of the lake. Beyond the car park, the ground was soft and damp underfoot, but it didn't slow him down. He wasn't in bad condition, though tomorrow morning he'd promised himself an hour in the hotel gym to get himself into shape.

276

And it was a while since he'd had a swim, he was ready to make up for lost time. Look forward, not back. For politicians, a mindless slogan, for him a core belief. Sarah was right about one thing. Tomorrow would be the start of the rest of his life.

The path through the trees was dark and eerie. Was that an owl hooting? He'd never paid much attention to birds, he didn't see the point. Something made a sound as it scurried through the undergrowth. A fox, more than likely, on some savage excursion.

Ahead of him stretched the pier, sleek with the afternoon rain. A sliver of moon was glinting on the wet wood. Ten years ago, the evening after meeting Emma on Mispickel Scar, he'd run all the way here and arrived sweaty and breathless. Tonight he was older and wiser.

As he looked round, a figure detached itself from the trees. He stiffened when he spotted something clasped in the figure's hand. But it wasn't a club, just a torch. He'd kept his penlight in his coat pocket, not wanting to attract attention. The woods might attract one or two courting couples determined to make the most of Valentine's, whatever the weather. The last thing either of them wanted was to bump into a pair of teenagers with their tongues down each other's throats.

'Long time, no see.' His voice, sounded hoarser than he'd expected.

'Yes.'

'Ten years, eh? Amazing.'

'It's passed in the blink of an eye.'

'I hope you don't think... I mean, it's good of you to help me out.'

'And you want to help me, too.'

'You can depend upon it.' But determined cheerfulness sounded wrong on such a dark and desolate evening. 'I mean, I never expected things to pan out like this, but after I came back here, it made sense to get in touch. As for the money, one or two investments have gone sour. I'm on my uppers, actually. That's the only reason I asked...'

'Have you forgotten our agreement?'

'No! Of course not. It's just that ... well, you have no need to worry, honest. After tonight, you'll never hear from me again.'

'Promise?'

'Scout's honour.' He was cross that his laughter sounded forced. 'Not that I ever was a scout, but you know what I mean.'

'I believe you.'

Guy rubbed his hands, not to keep warm but as a reminder that he was in control. 'Shall we get down to brass tacks, then? You'll have the money with you? I won't insult you by counting it ... no, please, I don't think it's wise to switch on your torch. We don't want anyone to see...'

As the dark figure lifted the torch in the air, Guy suddenly realised that he could have held his breath. The light wasn't about to be switched on.

The metal head of the torch crashed down on his head with sufficient force to knock him off balance and his legs gave way beneath him. He barely made a sound as he fell on to a pile of

278

sopping wet, shrivelled leaves. Hurting too much even to scream, he prised his eyes open in time to see the torch swinging down towards his head once more.

Tomorrow wasn't going to be the first day of the rest of his life, after all.

JOURNAL EXTRACT

From that day, high up on Mispickel Scar, my skin has crawled at the very thought of being watched. The spread of security cameras, not merely in our cities but even in the smallest towns, fills me with despair. Few creatures are more deserving of our contempt than the voyeur.

I say this by way of explanation, not excuse. Frankly, I had reached an age of invisibility. People would pass me in the street without a second glance. Old age does that to us. In the eyes of others we become at best insignificant, at worst a burden on the young and productive. Our best days are behind us, we have nothing new to say. I find this lack of interest absurd, yet not altogether displeasing. How many youths dashing by would guess I had murdered one man, and been responsible for the death of another? Anonymity suits me. It has enabled me to survive for so long. And now my only hope is that anyone who may read these words after I am gone will reflect before dismissing the old and infirm. We too were young and passionate once, remember.

And even in old age, the passions of the moment may drive us to terrible deeds.

PART THREE

CHAPTER FIFTEEN

Hannah rubbed sore eyes and switched off the computer screen. She'd been working long hours since the discovery of the bodies and when she finally got to bed each night, sleep never came easily. She diverted her phone and wandered down the corridor to the drinks machine. Her caffeine levels needed to be topped up if she were to keep from nodding off while checking the latest background reports on people linked with Emma Bestwick.

Any lingering doubt as to whether Emma was dead had been settled by the DNA match with the swab taken from Karen. Now the donkey work began. Investigating a cold case meant taking infinite pains and although Gul Khan and Linz Waller were available again, there was much to be done. She'd instructed the team to burrow deep into the lives of possible suspects. The Erskines, the Goddards, father and daughter Clough. They would talk to neighbours, shopkeepers, volunteer museum guides, clients of Emma's reflexology clinic. This must be the way archaeologists worked, sifting through endless rubbish in the hope of chancing across a clue to the past. Although Emma might have been killed by someone who had never featured in the inquiry, you had to start somewhere. Impossible to believe that Emma had come to the Arsenic Labyrinth by chance. If she'd made an appointment, it must have been with someone she knew, or someone she had a very good reason to meet.

The second body still lacked a name. Half a dozen leads following calls from members of the public had fizzled out, though a woman in her eighties had been reunited with the brother she'd become separated from during the war. When Hannah had called to tell her he was still alive, the woman had wept with joy. A moment to savour; good things seldom came out of a murder case.

The office was as cold as Inchmore Hall and Hannah warmed her hands on the plastic coffee cup. Marc gave her a lazy grin from a photograph propped beside the PC. He'd told her Daniel Kind had returned to the bookshop, this time wanting to find out about the legend of Mispickel Scar. She shouldn't encourage Daniel in playing the detective, but she couldn't resist. His energy and intelligence made her spine tingle. Each time she talked to him, she recalled Ben, who was the shrewdest detective she'd ever met.

Her mobile roared the theme to *Mission Impossible*. She'd downloaded the ringtone in a fit of pique when overwhelmed by deadlines for completing performance development reviews for members of her team.

'Hannah Scarlett.'

'It's Daniel. Is this a good time?'

She glanced at the reports stacked on her desk. Buried beneath them was a set of revised resource usage targets and an in-depth confidential briefing on the upcoming force merger. On screen, an

284

email from Lauren had popped up, urging senior detectives to attend a training course about managing time effectively.

'Perfect.'

'I shouldn't interrupt, but this is about Emma Bestwick.'

'Marc told me you're swotting up on Lakeland lore.'

'I visited Alban Clough and asked about the Arsenic Labyrinth. The way he tells it, the curse is an ancient legend, its origins lost in history. After that, I talked with your friend Jeremy Erskine. As a historian, he knows his stuff.'

Hannah grunted. 'He'll have been desperate to impress Daniel Kind, the telly guru.'

'He isn't into legends, so he couldn't help. I've read every page of the book Marc sold me. I've surfed the net and even talked to Vanessa Goddard a couple of times to see if she could cast any light. And you know what? There's more folklore in the Lake District than you can shake a stick at but I can't find one passing mention of a jinx on Mispickel Scar that pre-dates the Second World War.'

'What do you make of that?'

'Dating any legend is next to impossible. Mythology makes historians shudder. No proper sources...'

'You sound like a judge, turning his nose up at hearsay evidence.' Hannah succumbed to the temptation of playing devil's advocate. 'Don't tales often pass from one generation to the next without being written down? Even in Cumbria, with its literary heritage. That's why Alban

285

Clough is obsessed with preserving the region's folklore before it's forgotten, or sanitised out of recognition by the tourist industry.'

'But if the jinx on Mispickel Scar is as ancient as Alban claims, you'd expect to find it recorded *somewhere*. Bickerstaff, an Edwardian expert in the field, had a weakness for dressing up trivia in lurid prose. These days, he'd have been a tabloid reporter. I can't see him missing the chance to embellish a juicy tale about a curse.'

'Where's all this leading?'

He sounded amused. 'Come on, Hannah, you're the detective. You don't need me to spell it out, do you?'

'It's been a long day and it's not half over. Help me out here.'

He took a breath. In her mind, she could see him, grinning with the exuberance of a magician, pulling a flock of white doves from his sleeve.

'A pound to a penny, Alban Clough made the story up.'

Half an hour later, Miranda wandered into the living room of Tarn Cottage. Hair wet, eyes bright, wearing a blue towelling gown and nothing else.

'I'm gonna make you an offer you can't refuse.'

Daniel was stretched out on the sofa, flicking through a new book catalogue. Talking to Hannah had given him a buzz, but what he'd just read had soured his mood. Even so, his bare toes couldn't help tapping the leather cushion in time with the music. Miranda was just back from a shopping trip to Kendal and she'd put on a CD

286

by Corinne Bailey Rae before taking a shower. Mood music to soften him up. She never gave in, he liked that about her. But she'd chosen a bad moment.

'Sorry,' he said absently, 'I'm not buying a half share in a flat I have no intention of using.'

She gazed up to the heavens, a rational woman confronted by mindless intransigence. 'Daniel, you don't ever need to cross the threshold if you're that determined to treat London as a modern Gomorrah. Think of the flat as a pension fund, if it makes you feel better. You'll be sitting on a gold-mine in a few years and you don't need to move a muscle apart from writing the cheque. I'll make all the arrangements.'

'I'd rather use the cash on this place.'

'It's a money pit! Think of how much we've spent doing the place up from top to bottom since we signed the contract.' She sat down next to him, thigh pressing against his, letting the gown fall open. 'Time to draw a line. Spread the investment risk.'

'You're spending too much time with your colleagues on the financial column.'

She raked her nails across his palm. 'Daniel, this is important to me. I'm not prepared to vegetate for the rest of my life.'

'You said it yourself in that article, only the other day. The Lakes are hot.'

She shivered theatrically and pulled the gown tight around her skinny frame. And she had a point; the central heating had developed a fault. All day they'd been waiting for the engineer, but Godot would have been more reliable.

'Poetic licence, OK?'

He squeezed her hand. 'Sorry, I know you're keen.'

'What's eating you?' she asked. 'I mean, it's not just the flat, is it? You're pissed off about something.'

He threw the catalogue on to the floor. 'Publishers, don't you just love them? It's my fault, I should have read this when they sent it a fortnight ago. Look at page seventeen.'

She clambered off the sofa and picked up the booklet. The front cover was adorned with the photograph of a celebrity footballer whose ghosted autobiography was the lead title. Squatting cross-legged on the kilim rug, she started leafing through the pages.

'What's the problem? This is a list of forthcoming publications. But your backlist is out of print and you haven't written for an age, so you can't expect to feature. That's why...'

'But someone else does feature.'

She turned a page and said, 'Oh shit.'

'See what I mean?'

'"*Deep Waters: Ruskin's twilight years at Coniston.* Globally acclaimed historian Hattie Costello lifts the lid on the descent into madness of the sexually tormented Victorian polymath, a man of dark moods and even darker passions."'

'From the blurb, it's juicy enough to be serialised in the *News of the World*. Poor old Ruskin must be revolving in his grave.'

She tossed the catalogue to one side. 'Even for a very different book, the publishers won't give you a decent advance to cover a similar topic?'

'Too right.' Even if they hadn't nearly bankrupted themselves paying the soccer star to have someone else write up his life for him. 'Back to square one.'

Les Bryant walked into Hannah's room without knocking and said, 'Looks like you're stuck with me for a while yet. Her ladyship was busy when I went up to see her, but I've emailed her to say I'll sign that extended contract. It'll keep me off the streets for another year.'

'Terrific.' They shook hands. He still reeked of cough sweets. His eyes were bloodshot and she guessed his sleeping patterns were even worse than hers. 'Will you find a new place to live?'

Stifling a yawn, Les eased his bulky frame into a chair. 'When I get a moment, I might look round for somewhere that isn't next door to a cemetery. I come across enough dead people in the day job.'

'So how are things?'

He cleared his throat noisily. 'When I got back last night, I found another letter from the wife's solicitors. I'll need to find a brief of my own, she'll be wanting to take me for every penny I've got. I might as well splash out on better accommodation while I have the chance. Much as I grudge paying National Park prices.'

'If you need time off to sort things, let me know.'

'I'd rather keep busy, if it's all the same to you.'

She knew better than to nag. 'OK, we need to take another look at Alban Clough. This old wives' tale about a curse on Mispickel Scar may not be as old as we were led to believe.'

He gave her a hard look reserved for unreliable witnesses. 'You've lost me.'

'I've heard from Daniel Kind. The historian, remember?'

'After what happened at Old Sawrey last summer, I'm not likely to forget. His dad was your boss, wasn't he?'

Hannah shifted under his sceptical gaze. 'He's researching nineteenth-century Coniston. He talked to Clough about the Arsenic Labyrinth and the curse of Mispickel Scar.'

'Oh yeah?'

'He isn't convinced it *is* an ancient legend. He thinks Alban Clough may have invented it himself.'

'Invented it?' Les sat up straight, like a puppet whose string she'd jerked. 'How?'

'It helps if you own a museum and people believe you're the fount of all wisdom on local mythology. How difficult can it be? Legends are mostly vague, no one can date them precisely. Even if you know when the first published account appeared, the story may have been around for generations. But Daniel hasn't managed to find a single mention of this supposed curse before the 1950s.'

'Not looking hard enough?' A mischievous smirk. 'C'mon. He's a historian. A professor or summat. Sort of bloke who likes everything cut and dried.'

'Even so. When I first met Alban Clough, he waxed lyrical about the eternal nature of legends. I'm beginning to think he was taking the piss.'

'What would he have to gain?'

'Good question. I want you to find out the answer.'

Les puffed out his cheeks. 'You've got a lot of faith in this Daniel Kind.'

'Not relevant.' As soon as she'd snapped the words, she regretted them. No need to be defensive, no need at all. 'I mean, we have a problem here. We may have identified one of our corpses, but nobody has a clue about the other. All we know is that someone bunged an unknown man down the shaft at least fifty years ago. Alban Clough has spent all his life in that neighbourhood. He knows the fells and he knows their legends. Suppose...'

Mission Impossible interrupted her. She snatched up her mobile. 'What is it?'

'Hannah?' Lauren Self, not accustomed to being greeted so abruptly. 'Do you know your phone's on divert? You need to get back to Coniston right away. There's been a development.'

'ID on our male victim?'

'No, it's getting worse, not better. We have another body.'

Back in Coniston, Hannah headed straight for the incident room. The suspected contemporary murder of an unknown male was a separate inquiry from her investigation into the long ago deaths of the people retrieved from the underworld of Mispickel Scar. Different team, different SIO. But Lauren had instructed them to liaise closely, and the sooner the better, to see if connections could be made between the two cases.

291

The ACC had appointed DCI Fern Larter to head the latest inquiry. Large and jolly with dyed red hair, Fern had a fondness for unsuitably short skirts and a flair for giving good quote. The Press adored her. After the fiasco of the Rao trial, she'd taken Hannah out for a fish and chip supper and helped repair her shattered self-confidence over a couple of bottles of Mateus Rose. Fern didn't do sophistication; it was one of the things Hannah liked about her.

'Help yourself,' Fern said, waving to a packet of chocolate chip cookies on the table.

'Better not.'

'Go on, be a devil.' Fern started chomping. 'They aren't fattening, promise.'

'Get thee behind me, Satan. So what have you got so far?'

Fern pointed a stubby forefinger at a white-board in the corner of the room. Names of people and places were scrawled over it in marker pen of bilious green hue and half a dozen post-it notes had been stuck around the edges. Her team had been busy, knowing that the first 24 hours of a murder inquiry are the most crucial.

'The body was found at seven o'clock this morning. A couple of elderly tourists whose idea of getting up an appetite for breakfast is an early morning walk in the cold and drizzle. Weird, or what?' Fern laughed noisily and treated herself to another cookie. 'Anyway, they were walking along the shore from the pier at Monk Coniston when they spotted a bag of rags just under the surface in shallow water. Only it wasn't a bag of rags, but a dead man.'

'Cause of death?'

'He was clubbed on the head. Chances are, the weapon was a torch. We've found one that someone chucked into the lake near the pier. They didn't hurl it far enough and it drifted back to shore. We need to match up the bloodstains and matted hair on the torch with the victim, but it's a formality. Looks like the killer panicked and tried to weight the body down with a couple of house bricks, but didn't tie them securely. A twenty pound boulder would have done the trick, but we're not talking a professional hitman here. It's possible someone disturbed the murderer and that's why the job was left half done. Lucky for us. At least one murder victim spent twenty years on the bed of the same lake before divers dredged her up.'

Another thing about Fern, she was a mine of information, a unanimous choice to captain the division's pub quiz team.

'When was he killed?'

'Still waiting on Jepson, but the signs are, within the past 48 hours. You know how it works when someone is dumped into the water? The lungs fill up and the body loses its buoyancy. As it decomposes, gases start to inflate the corpse again and it comes back up. Timing depends on water temperature and stuff like that. The warmer the water, the sooner the body will rise.'

Hannah reached into her memories of a long-ago seminar on forensics. 'Didn't someone once tell me Coniston Water is bitterly cold?'

'Dead right, if the murderer had bothered to row the body out in a boat and bung it overboard

293

a hundred metres from the shore, it would have taken much longer for it to be found. By the time we'd dug the victim out of the silt, he'd have been unrecognisable. As it is, we have a clear idea of what he looked like before the side of his head was bashed in.' Fern grinned. 'Quite tasty, provided you use a bit of imagination.'

'Have you managed to ID him?'

'We have a promising lead. A woman called Welsby who runs a B&B on Campbell Road called in here yesterday to report her boyfriend missing. She'd only known him for about a week. He arrived on her doorstep as a paying guest and wormed his way into her bed in next to no time. Two nights ago, he said he was going away on business, but he went out around seven and didn't come back to collect his bag. Causing poor Sarah Welsby to sob her heart out to the PC on the desk yesterday morning. At first he reckoned she was a neurotic time waster, but the moment he heard about the man in the lake, he had second thoughts.'

'Sounds like the chap used Sarah as a meal ticket, then got bored and did a runner.'

'We've found a taxi driver who was supposed to pick him up from the village at nine that evening – but he never showed. Which is where the plot thickens. You don't mind if I have another biscuit? I missed out on lunch and I'm starving.'

'I'll join you, make you feel better.'

Mouth full, Fern made an appreciative noise. 'This chap was known to Sarah Welsby as Robert L. Stevenson. The taxi was hired by someone called Pirrip. His destination was a posh hotel in

Ullswater. He was booked into a de luxe suite for one night only. Not quite what he'd suggested to Sarah. And when we went through his bag, we found an old cheque book in the name of Guy Koenig.'

'A con man with a love of Victorian literature, huh?'

'Yeah, he'll have nicked the name Pirrip out of *Great Expectations*. Not often you come across a corpse with a highly developed sense of irony. He didn't expect to finish up bobbing under Coniston Water, that's for sure. We've done a check and hey presto! Guy Koenig is known to us. Plenty of previous, but nothing recent. A string of convictions on charges of deception. He served sentences in Preston and Haverigg. And this will make you prick up your ears.'

Hannah finished her biscuit. 'Keep talking, the suspense is unbearable.'

Fern beamed, showing a lot of closely packed white teeth. 'Guy Koenig came out of prison for the last time just over ten years ago. A few weeks before your Emma Bestwick disappeared.'

CHAPTER SIXTEEN

Sylvia Blacon was such an assured hostess despite her age and frailty that it came as a shock to Daniel when, twenty minutes into their conversation, she told him that she was almost blind. Her body was twisted with the effects of arthritis and brittle bones and she had to hobble around with a frame, but he admired her determination not to surrender to self-pity. She lived in a large, over-heated bungalow in a quiet cul-de-sac on the outskirts of the village and had a companion called Geraldine, a no-nonsense Geordie with the build and charm of an armoured personnel carrier. Geraldine had served them both with tea and now marched back into the room bearing a plateful of calorie-laden goodies.

'You'll have a cake?'

Black Forest gateau, meringues or profiteroles, Daniel was spoiled for choice. He helped himself to a profiterole. Very tasty and besides, Geraldine looked ready to slap him if he turned up his nose at her home cooking. He relaxed in his armchair. In summer this room would catch the sun in the middle of the day. The pastel colours of the curtains and the floral coverings on the arm-chairs and settee were faded, and even the ebony sideboard and bookcase had lightened in tone. It was an old person's room, but Sylvia was an old person who loved books and history and he'd warmed to her. Uniform editions of Wordsworth and Walpole's *Herries Chronicles* sat above two rows of history books, classics from Macaulay, through Trevor-Roper and on to Simon Schama and Niall Ferguson. There was even one of his own early efforts.

'So you talked to young Jerry Erskine?'

Sylvia's deep voice contrasted with her skeletal frame. Her forehead and hands were covered in bruises. She hadn't been beaten up by Geraldine, she'd explained with a throaty laugh, the marks were caused by minor bumps to skin worn by the years until it was as thin as cellophane.

Nobody else, Daniel suspected, would call the man Jerry, let alone describe him as young. 'Yes, he was very helpful.'

'Competent historian, Jerry. Doesn't mean to be a prig.'

Sylvia had made it clear that she was a Daleswoman who prided herself on plain speaking. After a lifetime telling people what she thought about them, she wasn't about to change now. The late Mr Blacon, who had lured her to the Lakes from her native Leyburn, had passed away thirty years ago, but he'd made a packet from a dental practice in Windermere and left her well provided for. He suspected she'd engaged the intimidating Geraldine because no one else was strong enough to cope with her. Already he'd learned that the grammar school she'd taught in had been swept away by numbskulls who mistakenly despised academic elitism and why almost every reform since the 1944 Education Act had been a retrograde step. She had a degree from Cambridge, but she was prepared to concede that his Oxford pedigree wasn't a bad second best. If she hadn't had a sense of humour, she might have been intolerable. When he complained that Hattie Costello had beaten him to it with the Ruskin book, she said Hattie Costello was a painted trollop and even if now she couldn't see what she looked like, she still *sounded* like a painted trollop.

'So you no longer wish to study the lots my nephew Roger bought with the money Betty Clough left our Association?'

297

'On the contrary, I'm crying out for fresh inspiration. I take it you were friendly with Alban Clough's mother?'

Sylvia sighed. 'Ah, Betty was a lovely woman. When I first met her, she was in her fifties, but when she stepped out, she still turned heads in a way I could only ever dream of. Not that she was a peacock, far from it, she always kept herself to herself. So sad when she died. There is little worse, Mr Kind, than seeing all your old pals shuffle off this mortal coil, one by one. It may seem a wicked thing to say, but I shan't be sorry when my time comes.'

Geraldine had marched in again to tidy away the plates. The clicking of her tongue sounded like the snap of handcuffs.

'You'll see me out, you will.'

'Betty recommended Geraldine to me, Mr Kind. You cooked for Betty at one time, didn't you, dear?'

Geraldine scowled. 'Aye, she was champion.'

She slammed the door behind her and Sylvia said, 'She's a treasure. Absolutely devoted to dear Betty and her family. As for me, I couldn't manage without her.'

'Alban Clough gave me a copy of the family trees for the Cloughs and the Inchmores. Fascinating stuff. Did you know Tom Inchmore, by any chance?'

Sylvia pursed thin, dry lips. 'Tom was a dullard, I'm sorry to say. His grandmother was a friend of mine and she once confided in me that perhaps it was as well that the line had died out. She looked after the boy after he lost his parents, but he was a sad disappointment, sly and unpleasant. If Betty hadn't insisted that Alban give him a job, he would never have found honest employment.'

'So you knew Edith as well as Betty?'

'All my life, as you might expect in a village this size. Edith was always in Betty's shadow, of course. She lacked the money, as well as the looks. All she had was the Inchmore name. She never had much to say for herself, didn't Edith. But she was a proud woman and if she was jealous of Betty, she took care not to let it show.'

'Did the two women have much to do with each other?'

'Not really. Edith always kept herself to herself. She didn't have two pennies to rub together, though I remember Betty once telling me there was a bond between them.'

'Meaning what, exactly?'

'The Hall, I suppose. And the way the families' fortunes had been so intertwined.'

'Which is why Betty insisted that Alban give Tom work?'

'Even though it was common knowledge that Alban had no time for the lad. It must seem very old-fashioned to a young chap like you, Mr Kind, but Betty came from a generation with a sense of duty. That is why she made the bequest to our Association. She felt it incumbent on her to support our work. Also, she wanted to mark our friendship. It didn't matter that she wasn't herself interested in history.'

'Unlike her son?'

Sylvia snorted. 'Myth and legend? Stuff and nonsense, if you ask me. Betty and I didn't discuss Alban or the dusty exhibits he set up in that old mausoleum of theirs. She guessed my opinion and neither of us wanted to fall out. Of course, she thought the sun shone out of his backside. All mothers are the same where their offspring are concerned. Not that I've had any of my own, but I've dealt with enough pupils' parents to know how besotted they are.'

Without much hope, he asked about the curse of Mispickel Scar, but Sylvia sniffed and made it plain she could cast no light on the story's source. A true historian, she only trusted verifiable documentary evidence.

'I suppose you're wondering about these bodies they found in the old mine shafts? Heaven only knows what's going on in this village. They talk about being tough on crime, but it's getting more like downtown Detroit with each passing day. Now I hear that someone else has been found dead.'

Daniel almost choked on his last mouthful of profiterole. 'Another body?'

'Geraldine popped out to the shops earlier on, she'd run out of sugar. The news is all over the village. Apparently some fellow was fished out of Coniston Water this morning.'

'Do you know who?'

'He wasn't a local person, by all accounts, just someone passing through.'

Her tone made it clear that this was a small mercy for which the villagers were thankful. Daniel said, 'Was it an accident?'

Sylvia gave him an old-fashioned look. 'I doubt whether an accident would justify hordes of police officers swarming around the lake. We're not safe in our beds these days, and that's a fact.'

She allowed Daniel a moment to reflect on this before saying, 'So you want to study the material from the auction?'

'Please.'

Sylvia nodded towards a huge ottoman, covered in green velvet, that stood beside his armchair. 'That was overflowing with old knitting patterns and wool and I've made my last cardigan, I'm afraid. So this morning, in readiness for your visit, I asked Geraldine to fill the box with Roger's purchases. Take a look, and if you come across anything of special interest, feel free to borrow it.'

He opened the box and found it full of diaries, notebooks and manuscripts, each neatly preserved and labelled in tiny, cramped handwriting. 'Has your nephew examined the material?'

'Dear me no, Roger is such a busy fellow. Senior partner of an accountancy practice in Whitehaven, you know. When I heard that old books and other mementoes associated with Coniston were to be auctioned, I asked him to bid on our behalf, because I knew he would make good use of our funds. Of course, neither of us had any idea that he would be competing with Mr Daniel Kind.'

He grinned. 'I disciplined myself to bid only for the items I was sure would be of interest. Big mistake. But my partner is always complaining that I hoard too much old rubbish.'

She returned his smile and for a fleeting moment he understood how much charm she'd

301

had when young. 'You'll have to teach her the error of her ways. Nothing from the past is rubbish to the true historian.'

CHAPTER SEVENTEEN

Within ten minutes of walking back into Divisional HQ, Hannah took a call from Fern Larter. Sarah Welsby had identified the dead man as Guy Koenig. Or, as she insisted, a supposed financial services guru called Robert L. Stevenson.

'He was taking the mickey,' Hannah said. 'Maybe the worm turned and Sarah murdered him.'

'Great minds, Hannah. I've asked for a back-up ID of the deceased, in case Sarah is our killer and we can't use her in court to prove identity. But Guy kept himself to himself. No mobile, and he didn't make personal calls from Sarah's place. Maybe he was in hiding. We found an old laptop in his bag, but he used it as a toy, it's given us no clues. As for Sarah, she might have followed him out to the pier. What if she caught him with another woman and the red mist descended?'

'But you don't think so?'

'Can't see her lugging a heavy torch and two chunky bricks all that way on the off chance she might want to biff him on the head, and tether the weights to his corpse so that he'd sink to the bottom of the lake.' A long sigh. 'No, if she wanted to kill him, she'd have done it nearer home. A couch potato like our Sarah wouldn't fancy schlepping over to Monk Coniston.'

'Does she have an alibi?'

'Time of death is so uncertain, we can't rule her out. But if you assume Koenig got his come-uppance before he was due to jump into his taxi, it's hard to see how she can have killed him if he did leave the house at seven, as she says. At ten past, she called at a chippy in Campbell Road for fish and chips and mushy peas. That's corrobor-ated. One of the women behind the counter actually saw Sarah let herself back into her house on the opposite side of the road. Doesn't leave her much time to switch from battered cod to battering Guy Koenig. And why would she report him missing so quickly?'

'Cunning double bluff?'

Fern chortled. 'Sarah Welsby couldn't do cun-ning if her life depended on it. According to her, they had sex half an hour before he left, and he was much rougher than ever before. Sounds to me like he never expected to see her again. But if she was guilty, would she have shared that with us? I don't think so. You know what really hacks me off, Hannah? Koenig was treating her like shit and that poor bloody fool convinced herself the sun shone out of his pretty little arse.'

'Thoughts on motive?'

The door swung open and Les Bryant popped his grizzled head round. When Hannah gestured towards the phone, he mouthed, *Di Venuto is here.*

Fern sighed. 'It's an amateurish crime, but that

303

doesn't mean it wasn't planned in advance. If the bricks weren't lying around near the shore, the murderer must have brought them to the scene for the specific purpose of weighting down the body. Although they weren't heavy enough to do the job properly.'

'You think the murderer was disturbed?'

'Uh-huh. I have a team doing house-to-house, trying to find anyone who may have been hanging around Monk Coniston the night before last. As for why Koenig was killed, it may have something to do with money. From what Sarah tells us, he was skint. I'd bet he was working some kind of scam. Then someone got wise to it, and got angry too.'

The Diva could scarcely conceal his satisfaction that another body had been discovered. One man's tragedy is another man's breaking story. When Les nodded him into the meeting room, he strode up to Hannah and offered the firmest of handshakes. The after-shave was more pungent than ever and self-assurance oozed out of every pore. Their last conversation might never have taken place. With a hide that thick, Tony Di Venuto was surely destined for great things in journalism.

'Good to see you again, Chief Inspector. I realise the investigation at Monk Coniston is separate from your inquiry, but no doubt you share my view that the case is inextricably linked with the bodies found at Mispickel Scar.'

'We're keeping an open mind.'

'Of course, you're bound to say that, but...'

304

'Have you anything to tell us, Mr Di Venuto?'

The Diva smirked. 'Actually, I was expecting you would be more than happy to cooperate, to share information.'

Hannah shook her head. 'It doesn't work like that. As you well know.'

'You disappoint me, Chief Inspector. If not for my investigations on behalf of the *Post*, the maggots would still be snacking on Emma Bestwick in her underground tomb. Never mind. I've already interviewed Sarah Welsby, the dead man's lover.'

Jesus, he was quick off the mark. 'DCI Larter hasn't made any announcement about the identity of the deceased as yet.'

Di Venuto sniggered. 'Me, I like to keep ahead of the pack. Which no doubt is why Ms Welsby contacted me. I gather she's identified the deceased as her lodger, Stevenson? Though I have it on good authority that wasn't his real name and that he was previously known to the police.'

Someone in Fern Larter's team must be earning a few quid on the side by leaking stuff to the *Post*. Shit, that was all they needed. 'I can't confirm that. DCI Larter will call a press conference as soon as she's ready.'

'How long does the public have to wait before it gets answers?' he demanded. 'The *Post* will be running Sarah Welsby's exclusive story tomorrow. I simply wanted to make sure you were the first to know. I've spoken to her at length and I'm convinced that this lodger of hers was the man who called me.'

'What makes you so confident?'

'He slipped out of her house on the day he first arrived. She caught sight of him from an upstairs window. He was only out for a few minutes, but the timing coincided with the first telephone message I received about Emma Bestwick. Same story the second time around. When she lost sight of him each time, he was heading in the direction that would take him to the nearest public call box.'

'She was spying on him?'

'She was a lonely, middle-aged woman. That says it all.'

Hannah suppressed the urge to smack him. 'It's not much to go on.'

'He read my article about Emma Bestwick before he rang the first time. She remembers him borrowing the newspaper and shooting some line about wanting to catch up with the local news after being away for years. That was the day we led on my story about the tenth anniversary of Emma's disappearance. How much more evidence do you need?'

'You can't identify his voice.'

'He spoke in a whisper, what do you expect? I mean, do you want me to give it to you on a plate, or what? Stevenson killed Emma, you can bet on it.'

She stared. 'Why? You're suggesting a sex crime?'

He contrived a theatrical groan. 'Isn't it obvious? Jeremy Erskine wanted Emma dead, but he was determined not to be implicated in her murder. So he hired a hitman to kill her. When his paid assassin came back to the Lakes, he was

306

scared of exposure. Solution – kill the killer.'

Daniel had booked an early table at a seafood restaurant in Staveley as a peace offering. On the drive from Brackdale, neither he nor Miranda spoke and although the food was excellent, their conversation was desultory. Miranda was off to London again the following day and she seemed lost in a world of her own. She insisted that he order a bottle of Chablis, and although he only allowed himself one glass, she'd finished the rest before the end of the dessert course.

His mind kept straying to Sylvia Blacon and the gentleman in the lake. After leaving the old woman's bungalow, he'd checked out the news on Radio Cumbria and learned the police were treating it as murder. The detective leading the inquiry sounded unexpectedly jovial, but gave no hint about any link with the bodies hauled up from beneath the Arsenic Labyrinth.

'Daniel, we need to talk.' Miranda fiddled with a shoulder strap of her little black dress. 'I've come to a decision.'

He considered her flushed face. This wasn't going to be good news.

'About?'

'About us.' She pushed her cup to one side and leaned across the table, keeping her voice low. 'It's not working, is it?'

Two drunken couples at the next table were arguing about how to split their bill and a Scouse waiter was sharing a raucous joke with the girl behind the bar. At the piano, a young man who had hired an ill-fitting tuxedo was playing selections from the Barbra Streisand songbook. The background noise made no impression, he and Miranda might have been alone on a desert island. But she'd built a raft for herself and was planning to sail away.

'No, I suppose not.'

The moment he admitted the truth, relief rippled through him. He wouldn't protest, wouldn't try to urge her to stay. She'd had the courage to say out loud what both of them had known for weeks. Months, maybe.

She reached out and ran her nails over the surface of his hand. 'I'm sorry, Daniel. I so wanted this to work out.'

'Me too.'

She folded her arms, a defensive gesture. 'You think I'm sleeping with Ethan, don't you?'

'I don't think about Ethan.'

'Well, I'm not.' Huge intake of breath. 'But I won't lie to you. I want to, and he wants it too.'

He picked up his napkin, crushing it in his fist. 'What would you like to do about the cottage?'

'I'll move out as soon as I can, if that's OK. I can't bury myself here any longer. For me the Lakes will always mean me and you, and if we aren't to stay together ... as for my half-share, we can sort things out when it suits you. No panic. I've decided against buying the flat in Greenwich, so I won't be desperate for cash.'

'You'll be moving in with Ethan?'

'When he suggested it, I said no way. You know something? I actually said I would be sticking with you, trying to make things work between us. He and I had a blazing row, actually. A hundred

308

times worse than when you and me fell out. Sparks fly off the two of us when we're together, it's a weird relationship. But right now it feels like what I need. While you were out this afternoon, he called me to apologise for putting me under too much pressure too soon. Things seemed to fall into place while he was talking, I couldn't fight my feelings one moment longer. Though if you'd changed your mind about sharing the flat ... well, it might have been different.'

The pianist was humming as he played that song about people who need people. The luckiest people in the world. Daniel fixed the man with a stare, willing him to stop.

'Thanks for telling me.'

She tapped her saucer with a teaspoon, a little *clink* of irritation. 'You're taking this in a very English way. No ranting, no raving. If we don't watch out, we'll finish up acting like characters in a 1940s film.'

'You'd rather I scream blue murder?'

She ventured a smile. 'If I were a suspicious soul, I might wonder if I've played into your hands. Is that what's going through your mind? *I've got rid of the needy cow, I've won back my freedom?*'

He shook his head. 'At this precise moment, my mind is a vast empty void.'

'Louise will be thrilled. She really can't stand me.'

'Feeling's mutual, isn't it?'

'Louise is so protective of you, I'll never measure up. I can understand why, after what happened to Aimee. You were a wreck, you kept

309

blaming yourself, even though it wasn't your fault she jumped from the tower. All I wanted was to make things better for you.'

God, she was so gorgeous. That flawless skin. Those eyes.

'And you did.'

The familiar dreamy look spread across her face. She'd battled through the worst of the conversation, she was ready to rework it, as any good journalist might revise a piece of hasty writing to smooth out the flaws. Create a better impression.

'Whatever you may think, I fell head over heels in love with the Lakes, same as with you. And I don't regret it, please don't imagine I do. But it's a mistake to become infatuated with a place. When I was a kid, I used to love our holidays in Great Yarmouth. When my parents took me there one winter weekend, with the amusements shut up and a gale howling in from the sea, it wasn't the same. The spell was broken forever and I've never gone back since.'

He intercepted the glance of the Scouse waiter, who was running his eye over Miranda's curves, and asked for the bill. 'So it's back to London for good tomorrow?'

She nodded. 'I'll take as many of my things as I can carry. The rest I can leave till I've moved in with Ethan. I suppose you're still determined to stick it out here?'

Why did she have to make it sound like a feat of endurance? 'Me, I'm still infatuated.'

'But with the Lakes, not with me.' She sighed. 'That's the difference, Daniel. The countryside just doesn't do it for me, I need the excitement of

310

city life. Sheepdog trials and ivy-clad coaching inns are fine, but they aren't enough. For me, something always needs to be happening.'

Pictures flickered in his mind. Strap-hanging commuters on the London Underground, glancing nervously at their fellow passengers' rucksacks. Drunken youths smashing bottles outside the doors of a nightclub and pissing in shop doorways. Oxford dons bickering at High Table.

'Depends on what you want to happen, I guess.'

At five to eight, Les put his head round the door and said, 'Time to go home.'

Hannah pulled her eyes away from the columns of figures on the spreadsheet on her screen. She'd spent the last hour juggling overtime and equipment budgets. Even in cold case work, making the numbers add up was more of a challenge for a DCI than detecting crime.

'See you tomorrow.'

'I meant time for you to go home,' he said, stepping into her room. 'For me, it doesn't matter. Long hours are good, it's like the old days, takes me out of myself. It's different for you. Don't make the mistake I made.'

'What was that?'

'Forgetting that there's someone waiting for you at home.'

She felt her cheeks burning. 'Marc is out visiting a customer in Carlisle this evening. Besides, he knows what the job involves.'

'And he's happy about it?'

'He spends all his time with his books, anyway.'

311

Les raised bushy eyebrows. 'I used to say my old lady liked not having me under her feet. She was able to suit herself. Watch trash on telly, natter on the phone to her mates. In the end, it wasn't enough.'

'Yeah, well, thanks for the advice.'

'Don't be huffy. I know it's none of my business.'

'True.'

'All the same, take heed.' He turned to go. 'Goodnight, Hannah.'

She exhaled. 'Sorry, Les, I don't mean to...'

'Listen, you can tell me to piss off, that's fine. Like I said, it's nowt to do with me.'

'I'm not sure I'm doing much good here. I'd feel better equipped for this job if I'd trained as an accountant instead of at police college. I'll pack it in and start fresh tomorrow. We'll drive over to Coniston together.'

He nodded and lumbered off down the corridor. She checked her on-screen diary before switching off her computer. After Di Venuto's departure, they'd agreed that even if someone had hired Guy Koenig to kill Emma, Jeremy wasn't the only candidate. It was a long shot, but there might be some connection between the two bodies buried in the same spot decades apart. The plan was to call on Alban Clough and see what he had to say for himself.

She locked her desk and the door to her office and set off for home. On the CD player, Jimmy Webb crooned about the Wichita lineman. Her mind roamed over the events of the day, but she knew she was too weary to have a hope of making

312

sense of them. Fifteen minutes into the journey, her hands-free phone trilled.

'It's Maggie, ma'am.'

Her DC worked out at the gym every other day, but for once she sounded out of breath. 'Are you OK?'

'Yes, fine, I've just run back to the car. Dave and I were on our way out to a pub in Skelwith Bridge, and as we were approaching Coniston, a fire engine passed us, siren blaring. A couple of miles down the road, we saw why.'

Hannah's pulse quickened. 'What's happened?'

'It's Inchmore Hall, ma'am. The building is on fire.'

Brack village was dozing as Daniel drove through on the way back to Tarn Fold. The church clock was chiming, a few lights shone behind curtained windows. Tarn Fell was a dark shapeless mass in the distance and it was impossible to make out where the fells ended and the sky began. Daniel glanced to his left. Miranda was slumped low in the passenger seat, her eyes half-closed; the Chablis had taken hold. He recalled waking some nights and watching her sleep by his side, telling himself how lucky he was to share her life.

'Hey, you still awake?'

'Mmmm.'

'I'll sleep in the spare room tonight.'

'No need.'

'It's better that way. You have a journey tomorrow and you look knackered.'

Her brow creased, but if tempted to argue, she thought better of it 'Suit yourself,' she murmured.

When they reached the cottage, she said good-night and dragged her weary body up the stairs. He turned on the gas fire and made himself a mug of hot chocolate. For ten minutes he channel-hopped on the TV, but late-night snooker and a re-run of *Friends* did not appeal, so he pulled out the bulging carrier bags that he'd borrowed from Sylvia Blacon and started picking through the auction lots. Might as well make a start, see if he could find something to fire his imagination about an aspect of Lakes history that Hattie Costello had not yet done to death.

There were scrapbooks, diaries and household records of Coniston residents that covered much of the twentieth century. Many of the notebooks were written in the same cramped but legible hand. They had been kept somewhere damp and the paper was brittle to the touch. It wasn't late, but he had to force himself to keep his eyes open as he turned the pages. His arms and legs felt heavy and his throat was dry. He ought to go to bed, but he knew that when he did, he would spend hours tossing and turning. So often it had been like this in Oxford, during the weeks after Aimee committed suicide. Better to keep working, until he was so exhausted that sleep could no longer be denied.

A single sentence snagged his attention. He read them a second time and the words jerked him wide awake.

You'd never believe it to look at me now, but once upon a time I killed a man.

314

CHAPTER EIGHTEEN

Orange-yellow flames writhed like dancers in the night sky as Hannah approached Inchmore Hall. Heart pounding, she'd broken speed limits travelling twenty miles on dark, twisting roads. When she pulled up on the grass verge fifty yards short of the drive, an inferno was raging.

Fire frightened her, she hated its savagery, wanted to shut her ears to its hoarse, greedy roar. She'd never forgotten attending her first arson as a DC. An attack on a supermarket left a security man with cruel burns and a face ruined forever. The arsonist, a bored shelf-stacker, told her later that fire was exciting and passionate, it turned him on like nothing else. He'd licked his lips as he spoke of hot and fast flames, ripping through the building, out of control. Nondescript, spotty, and eighteen years old, he was the most danger-ous young man Hannah had ever met.

Gritting her teeth, she slammed shut the car door. The fire was loud and wild, a monster holding the hall captive, glorying in its power to consume and destroy. The wooden gables were blackened and about to crumble, the blinds at the windows had burnt to nothing. The temperature had sunk below zero, but the night was dry, just when a downpour would have answered prayers. Beyond a cordon, firefighters were striving to tame the beast. From the other side of the road, a huddle of spectators gawped at the spectacle. When Hannah pushed through, a small man in an over-sized ski jacket gave her a dirty look, outraged by the presumptuousness of a latecomer to the evening show. Half a dozen teenagers were giggling, one was taking pictures with her mobile. This was better than Guy Fawkes Night.

Smoke was poisoning the air and as Hannah reached tall gateposts topped with stone pine-apples, she had to fight for breath. She wrapped her scarf around her face to protect her mouth and sinuses from the acrid stench. As she moved forward, she felt the heat on her cheeks.

The old mansion was dying before her eyes, suffocating in the clutches of the raging creature. As she watched, a timber beam fell to the gravelled drive with a deafening crash. A nanosecond of near-silence, then the group of onlookers let out a collective gasp.

Hannah spotted Maggie Eyre, in fleece, jeans and leather boots, talking to a grey-haired fire officer and two uniformed PCs on the lawn. Their eyes met and, with a quick word to the men, Maggie hurried down the drive to meet her.

'So much for your quiet evening down the pub?' Hannah had to shout to make herself heard above the din.

'We'd arranged to meet friends, but Dave's gone off on his own.' Maggie started coughing. 'I had to stop and see if there was anything I could do.'

'Anyone inside?'

'Not sure. It's still too dangerous for anyone to force their way in, even with breathing apparatus and cutting equipment. For all anyone knows, Mr Clough and his daughter are out tonight. I hope to God they are, because we've seen nobody and anyone trapped won't have stood a chance. Their lungs will have choked with fumes inside minutes.'

Hannah's eyes were stinging. 'Any idea what happened?'

'Flames were seen by a passer-by who dialled 999, but even though the station is close by, the fire was so fierce that by the time the first fire engine arrived, they could tell it was going to be a long night. No clue on cause yet, God knows whether this is accident or arson, but I've been talking to the fire officer in charge. He says his boss had a row with Alban Clough about the need to upgrade safety precautions in the Museum. In the end, the old man threw him out. It's with the legal people to take action right now. Too few smoke alarms, let alone a decent sprinkler system. As for the candles...'

In her mind, Hannah heard Alban's sonorous complaints about the pettifoggery of the bureaucrats. No need for m'learned friends to bother now. The fire had done their work for them.

'Alban Clough's a law unto himself.'

'They reckon Inchmore Hall is a deathtrap. This was a disaster waiting to happen.'

'We need to...'

'My God! My God!'

A woman had burst through the cordon and was clattering up the driveway. Alex Clough, in a suede coat and high heels. Thank God she had not been roasted to a cinder inside her blazing

317

home. She wasn't dressed for sprinting and as she drew level with Hannah and Maggie, she stumbled and sank to the ground.

'Is your father inside?' Hannah bellowed.

'I don't know! He was at home this evening. Unless he managed to get out...'

She looked up and saw the look on the two women's faces. Breathing hard, she hauled herself back on to her feet.

'I must try to save him!'

Hannah rushed to her side and grasped her hand. In part to comfort, in part to restrain. 'You can't go in there.'

Alex began to sob. 'My father, my father, my father...'

She repeated the words time after time, even as Hannah and Maggie put their arms around her so that they could lead her to a safer place. Somewhere to wait and watch while the only home she'd ever known burned to ashes.

Hannah wasn't answering her mobile, so Daniel sent her a text asking her to contact him urgently. *I know name of 2nd body.* If that didn't prompt a call, nothing would. After what he had read, he couldn't sleep, so he stayed up all night in his favourite chair, smoothing out the tangles in his mind. When Miranda came downstairs in the blue-striped rugby shirt she wore to bed, she told him he looked knackered. He mumbled something unintelligible, his thoughts far away. They exchanged desultory small talk over toast and coffee in their gleaming new kitchen. He wasn't in the mood to explain what he had discovered.

318

Hannah, he wanted to save it for Hannah.

She called back five minutes after Miranda departed on a shopping trip to Kendal. It was not long after nine, but he heard her stifling a yawn even as she said hello. She sounded as tired as he felt

'Sorry, long night. Inchmore Hall went up in a ball of flame.'

He swore. 'What happened?'

'Remember Manderley ablaze in the final reel of *Rebecca?*' She'd told him once that in her teens this was a favourite film, she'd even had a brief crush on Olivier. 'I could have sworn I saw Mrs Danvers' crazy face at the window. But this time there wasn't a happy ending. Alban Clough was inside. He didn't stand a chance.'

He pictured the old man as he'd last seen him. Smiling slyly, enjoying the thrill of private know-ledge, protesting ignorance of the second body buried below the Arsenic Labyrinth. Of course, he was lying, but that was nothing new. He'd lived a lie for fifty years, hugged his secret close, to the very end.

'Are you still there?'

'Sorry. I was thinking...'

'This text you sent me. What have you found out?'

'The dead man you discovered when you went in search of Emma Bestwick. His name was William Inchmore.'

'William? How can you be sure?'

'Because I've read about his murder.'

'Read about it? You're having a laugh, aren't you?'

319

'He was stabbed to death with a bread knife, wasn't he?'

A sharp intake of breath, then a long pause as she absorbed his news. She hadn't mentioned to him how the man had been killed. Even though she confided in him more than she should, there were limits. And the information hadn't been released to the media. When she spoke again, her tone was wry.

'Tell you what, Daniel. You must have inherited the detective gene. So what exactly is this you've been reading?'

'The murderer's account of the crime.'

'If you tell me you bought it in Marc's shop, I'll scream.'

'No need, the story is in a private journal purchased by Jeremy Erskine's historical society. Not that Jeremy has ever read it. I'm the first.'

'And who is the author? Not Alban Clough, surely?'

'No, although he knew exactly what had happened. His mother was the mistress of William Inchmore. William used the Arsenic Labyrinth as a trysting place, that's where he made love to Betty Clough.'

'Are you saying that Betty murdered him?'

'No, that was Edith Inchmore, William's wife. When she learned about the affair, she lured him to the Labyrinth and went up there herself with a knife. What she didn't know was that Alban was hiding out up there. He witnessed her crime, but he didn't move a muscle to stop her. He kept quiet as he watched Edith kill his mother's lover.'

320

They arranged to meet at a new Bavarian coffee bar in the heart of Kendal. Daniel parked in the multi-storey at Westmorland Shopping Centre and fished a tote bag out of the boot. None of the passers-by in Stricklandgate gave him a second glance, nobody guessed that the bag held a confession to murder.

He'd pieced together the Inchmores' story from Edith's journal. After George wrecked the family business, his son set about ruining their name. What William lacked in wealth, he more than made up for in swaggering self-confidence and raffish good looks. He spent his early adult years sleeping around and squandering what was left of the family fortune at the racecourse, while drifting from job to job. With Inchmore Hall sold to the Cloughs and his parents dead, he had little to keep him in Coniston and during a spell selling silk stockings in Yorkshire, he met and married Edith Sharpe. A plain spinster whose acid tongue belied a dread of being left on the shelf, she was quick to fall under his spell. Above all, she had the inestimable advantage of a father who had made a packet from a leather business in Bradford. William didn't see marriage as an impediment to philandering and gambling, but rather as a means of funding his favourite activities. He faked a heart condition to escape military service and spent the war years selling cosmetics and petrol on the black market. A fortnight before VE Day, he was arrested, and although he managed to talk his way out of a prison sentence, old man Sharpe cut off his daughter's allowance and made Yorkshire County

Cricket Club the main beneficiary of his estate. Edith stood by her husband and never spoke to Daddy again but, after failing to make a go of various improbable business ventures, William was forced to return to Coniston and go cap in hand to Armstrong Clough and ask for work.

What prompted Armstrong Clough, a business-man with a nose as hard as Helvellyn, to offer a job to a slacker who hadn't even made a success out of petty crime? Armstrong was the sort of Englishman who, during the Thirties, argued that Oswald Mosley talked a lot of sense and that Hitler was the sort of leader any nation worth its salt required. War might have changed his tune, but he remained, if Edith's journal was any guide, an old-fashioned bully contemptuous of altruism.

Only one explanation occurred. It must have amused Armstrong to have an Inchmore at his beck and call. Long ago, Albert Clough had to jump when Sir Clifford Inchmore said jump. Now the Cloughs owned the hall and the Inchmores depended upon their goodwill. Armstrong might be a miserable old bugger with a gammy leg, while William was a dashing ladies' man, but it was Armstrong who possessed the money, the mansion and the gorgeous bride, while William had to make do with a cottage in a back street and poor, unlovely Edith. A very satisfactory arrange-ment. The only snag was that William's roving eye soon fell on Betty. A naïve and neglected woman whose son was growing up and whose husband was often away from home was easy prey for an accomplished Lothario.

It was bound to end in tears. William was reckless and left a handful of letters from Betty imperfectly concealed at the bottom of his sock drawer, where Edith chanced upon them. The correspondence made it clear that Betty's conscience tormented her and that she wanted to end the affair, but that William was determined to have her leave Armstrong and extract a hefty sum from him as the price of hushing up the scandal, so that the two of them could run away together. A ludicrous and desperate plan, but Edith knew her husband well enough to realise that he was capable of trying to carry it out, with disastrous consequences for them all. She'd grown accustomed to his infidelities, but this was one betrayal too many. The prospect of being abandoned to penury and forced through shame to leave a village she had come to love was intolerable. She had to act.

She schooled herself in the art of imitating Betty's girlish handwriting and penned a note asking William to come to Mispickel Scar the following afternoon. The letters revealed that the loneliness of the site of the old arsenic works made it a favourite venue for the lovers' couplings. The prospect of William meeting his death in the same spot appealed to Edith's uncompromising sense of justice. She had discovered that Betty arranged for her notes to William to be left in his desk by a young messenger called Vinny who worked at the company's office in Yewdale Road.

Vinny was a simple-minded lad from Liverpool, one of scores of kids who had come as evacuees to Coniston at the start of the Second World War. He'd been billeted at the hall and, after his parents were killed during the Blitz, he was left without a family and any reason to return home when the hostilities came to an end. Vinny had a dog-like devotion to Betty Clough, and she persuaded her husband to employ him out of charity. She was popular in the village for her generous spirit and good works, although Edith confided to her diary her suspicion that so far as Vinny was concerned, Betty had an ulterior motive. Yet Edith harboured no more than a superficial resentment of her husband's lover. She understood how easy it was to succumb to William's charm.

What Edith didn't realise was that someone else knew about Betty's affair. Young Alban Clough detested his father, who regarded him as a good-for-nothing dreamer with no head for business, but he didn't care to think of his mother sleeping with an Inchmore. At his father's insistence, Alban lent a hand in the office. He soon learned that Vinny was acting as go-between. He persuaded Vinny to let him read some of the letters Betty entrusted to him and seized every opportunity, while William was out gallivanting, to snoop round his room. That was how he'd found the letter Edith had placed in her husband's desk. Much more familiar with his mother's hand than William, he recognised it at once as a forgery. Curiosity piqued, he'd trekked up to Mispickel Scar and found a hiding place, overlooking the remains of the labyrinth, an hour before the time stipulated in Edith's message.

Waiting to watch what would happen.

Hannah was slipping on her raincoat when the phone summoned her back from the door. Tempted to ignore it, she hesitated and was lost. Fern Larter greeted her, in cheery mood. Her mouth was full, it sounded as if she was munching her way through a packet of her favourite prawn cocktail flavoured crisps.

'Progress update. We've found a couple of teenagers who saw someone behaving suspiciously at Monk Coniston at about the right time. The kids were going for a romantic walk in the drizzle. Young love, eh? They heard someone in the vicinity of the pier and then caught sight of a figure hurrying off through the trees. Wearing a hooded anorak and Wellingtons.'

'Do you have any more to go on?'

'Are you kidding? Might have been a youngster, could have been a woman, but then again, it might have been a man. And blah, blah, blah. Of course they didn't catch sight of anything useful like a face. I suppose we ought to be grateful to them. If they disturbed the killer, that's why he or she made such a hash of dumping the body in the lake.'

'And the house-to-house continues?'

'Yeah, even with so little to go on, we may jog memories. There must be a chance someone else saw this character. The kids at Monk Coniston say there weren't any vehicles in the car park, which argues that whoever they saw arrived on foot.'

'Someone local, then?'

'Yeah, narrows it down.' Fern sighed. 'So what's this about Alban Clough being burned to a cinder? Not suicide, by any chance?'

'Initial indications are, the fire started by accident. Chances are, we'll never know exactly what happened, but the pathologist and the chief fire officer have come up with a working theory. They think Alban was lighting candles on the second floor landing when he lost his footing. He fell down the steps and fractured his ankle, while the candles fell on to a pile of cardboard boxes that were sitting on the wooden floor. So he couldn't move when the place went up in flames. The hall was a tinder box, waiting for a spark.'

'Bugger.' Fern wasn't one of life's sentimentalists. 'I was wondering if he'd been smitten by remorse.'

'I don't think Alban's conscience ever troubled him.'

'Tell you what, your life and mine would be easier if it turned out he murdered both Emma Bestwick and Guy Koenig.'

'He doesn't really match your description, such as it is.'

Fern grunted. 'ID evidence is usually a load of bollocks, in my book.'

Hannah glanced at her watch. 'Thanks for the update, but I'd better go. Late for a meeting.'

'All right. Have fun.'

Kaffee Kirkus was crammed with Saturday morning shoppers sheltering from the drizzle, but Daniel found a table wedged next to the steamy front window. He wiped a patch of the

326

glass so that he could look out for Hannah. Behind the counter, two skinny girls, one with dreadlocks and studs in her eyebrows, the other with a Mohican haircut, chatted loudly in between serving espressos and blueberry muffins. The world was getting smaller; he might as easily be sitting in Seattle as Stricklandgate. Even the slanting rain seemed much the same.

Edith Inchmore had hated crowds and noise. She'd bared her soul in her journal, confided intimacies to the page that she could never have spoken. Daniel felt like her confidant, her confessor. He pictured her as tall, erect, disapproving, difficult to warm to, yet somehow admirable in refusing to be smothered by the shroud of guilt. She was forthright, old-fashioned, hostile to change. Coniston she loved, and she'd never tried to escape. Perhaps it was a way of expiating her sin, to live in sight of the fells that hid the body of the man she had killed.

He spotted Hannah in the throng on the pavement outside. She was looking out for him, her face set in its familiar searching mould. A fierce curiosity, an urge to keep asking questions, was something they shared. Perhaps it was how to avoid giving too much of themselves away. Moving into the warmth of the coffee bar, she wriggled through the scrum and waved when he caught her eye.

'Sorry to keep you waiting. A colleague rang as I was on my way out.'

She was panting and he guessed she'd raced all the way from the police station. He queued to buy them each a latte and by the time he rejoined

327

her, she'd recovered enough to muster a grin. Warming her hands on the chunky mug, she listened to what he'd discovered about Edith Inchmore's crime. It felt good, having her attention focused on him.

'So Alban let her kill his mother's boyfriend before announcing his presence? He was lucky Edith didn't knife him for good measure.'

He lifted the journal from the bag and put it on the table between them. 'According to this, her first instinct was to kill herself as well. She had nothing left to live for. She'd sunk so deep into despair that she didn't have any sort of plan about disposing of the body. If not for Alban, she would have marched down the fell and given herself up to the nearest policeman. But he wrested the knife from her and persuaded her that she could get away with murder. He had it all worked out. He'd shove the corpse and the knife down the mine shaft, and hope they would never be found.'

'And Edith went along with it?'

'What choice did she have? She protested that Betty would raise the hue and cry, but Alban knew his mother well. Betty might have had an affair with one of her husband's employees, but she'd never intended to run off with him and desert the family. She'd behaved badly, but she was intelligent. She knew William was a rascal, and that he enjoyed the idea of cuckolding the man whose family had usurped his own.'

Hannah leafed through Edith's journal. Daniel had bookmarked several of the most revealing passages and he watched as she read a few sentences. Her concentration was intense. He found himself wanting to reach across the table and stroke her hair. Sucking in air, he forced himself to think about the crime that had brought them here.

'Why did she write all this down, do you think?'

'She reckoned it helped her make sense of everything that had happened in her life. She kept contemporaneous diaries, but they are full of trivia. It was only in the last months before she died that she felt able to write down what drove her to kill her husband, and what happened afterwards.'

'Did Alban tell Betty about the murder?'

'Edith never knew exactly what passed between mother and son. Alban told her to leave everything to him and she had to agree. He was offering her hope, and once she'd calmed down, she decided she didn't want to hang. My guess is that Alban didn't tell Betty the truth in so many words. How much she figured out for herself, who knows? We're talking about the years just after the Second World War, don't forget. Stiff upper lips were still in fashion. Respectable families often left a great deal unsaid. They preferred to keep skeletons safely locked up in their cupboards.'

Hannah drained her mug. 'Alban would never have employed Tom Inchmore if Betty hadn't insisted. You suppose, after all those years, she still felt guilty about her affair with William?'

'You bet. The murder knotted Betty, Edith and Alban together for the rest of their lives. Alban knew what villagers are like. If word got out she'd been having it off with her husband's sidekick in a remote corner of the fells, she'd be regarded as a shameless hussy to her dying day. To protect his mother's good name, he had to protect Edith as well. Easy enough to take some money and make it look like William had been on the fiddle and done a runner to avoid being caught. Armstrong went apeshit, but Betty persuaded him not to involve the police, so the make-believe theft was never subjected to proper scrutiny.'

'And the supposed curse of Mispickel Scar?'

'Alban invented it to discourage people from venturing to the scene of the crime. Must have amused him to concoct a legend of his very own. He was helped by a rock fall that made it unlikely the corpse would ever be discovered. Edith refers to it in her journal as an act of God. Talk about moving in mysterious ways. Alban didn't bargain for the possibility that, decades later, someone else might commit murder within a few yards of where Edith stabbed William.'

'And last night Alban died.'

'Coincidence?'

She told him what she'd told Fern. 'There's nothing so far to suggest suicide.'

'Maybe he was distracted by worry that his secret was out. He'd devoted his life to the museum. If he was afraid that wagging tongues and financial pressures would force him to shut the doors of the hall, he'd have lost his reason for living.'

'How could he know you'd stumbled across the truth?'

'Stumbled?' He switched on an ironic grin. 'I

was expecting you to congratulate me on great detective work.'

She laughed; a musical sound. 'Stumbled is right, I think. Mind you, your Dad once told me all the best detectives are lucky. Now, tell me how Alban found out.'

He described meeting Geraldine at Sylvia's bungalow. 'Geraldine was devoted to the Cloughs and kept in touch with Alban after his mum died. When Sylvia asked her to gather up the auction lots for me to take away, she must have spotted Edith Inchmore's private papers. She wouldn't have had time to read them but my guess is, she spoke to Alban on the phone and mentioned that I'd taken them away.'

'He couldn't know that Edith had written about the murder.'

'No, but he'd known her all his life. He must have feared that she might have written about her crime as a sort of catharsis. What he didn't know was that Edith had another guilty secret. Something she kept hidden even from him.'

Hannah frowned at the cramped handwriting. 'What could make her guiltier than murdering her own husband?'

'Blaming herself for the death of her grandson.'

She stared at him. 'Tom Inchmore fell off a ladder.'

'After he'd been peeping through his grandmother's bedroom window. He was a hopeless lad, pathetic, you told me so yourself. He wanted to see the old lady disrobing for her bath. Edith heard a noise and looked round. When she saw his face pressed against the window, she rushed

331

towards him in a state of rage and horror. He lost his balance and broke his neck on the paving stones below.'

JOURNAL EXTRACT

Men never paid much attention to me. I felt awkward in their company, though I flatter myself that in my youth the fullness of my figure attracted an occasional covetous glance. When William, handsome, dashing William, poured flattery on me like honey, I was in Heaven. I let him have his will, I abandoned all my natural restraint. The slow realisation that it was my father's money, rather than my soft flesh and my caresses, stirring the fire in his loins spread bitterness through me like a cancer. After his death, I renounced intimacy with the opposite sex and kept myself to myself, accepting near-solitude as the price for having evaded the gallows.

I have forgotten what it is to have men casting me a sideways look, as they wonder about the body concealed beneath layers of clothing. They prefer not to think about my flesh. Candidly, neither do I.

That is why it came as a shock to be spied upon for a second time.

A hot July afternoon. I do not care for heatwaves, they make me sweat and struggle for breath. I prefer to go upstairs and lie down. On this occasion, with forecasters talking of temperatures in the nineties, I take a bath to cool down and on returning to my bedroom, consider my wardrobe, searching for clothing that is light and airy.

Suddenly, in the dressing table mirror, I glimpse a reflection. A face, staring in through the window. A face – another! – that once I had loved. But all too easily in my case, it seems that love can turn to scorn.

On this occasion I am not naked, I have the benefit of a fluffy white towel. But I shriek with anger and charge across the room like an old, enraged sow. I need to close the window I had opened to admit a breath of air and draw the curtains to preserve my modesty.

My wrath frightens him. I see terror whiten his stupid face as he jumps away from me. But when you are standing on top of a tall and unsteady ladder, there is nowhere safe for you to jump to.

PART FOUR

CHAPTER NINETEEN

At the door of Kaffee Kirkus, Hannah shook Daniel's hand with careful formality. She'd written out a receipt for the journal, which she'd promised to return to Jeremy once the police were done with it. Once they'd stopped talking about Edith Inchmore and the deaths for which she'd been responsible, their conversation stuttered, as though they were both too embarrassed to venture onto risky ground.

She gripped his hand for a fraction of a second longer than necessary. The story of her life; she was always reluctant to let go. He intrigued her; she felt seized by an urge to learn more about him. Like his father, he had an open manner that made you feel as though you understood what made him tick, but in truth you didn't have a clue. The important things, the personal things, Ben Kind always kept under lock and key. His son was just the same.

'Thanks for your help. I need to speak to Alex Clough, see if she can cast any further light.' She mustered a smile. 'So, having done your detective work for the day, what will you be getting up to now?'

He shrugged. 'An American writer has beaten me to it with a book about Ruskin's Coniston years. It's time for a change. I need to scout for another subject to write about, and...'

'Yes?'

Colouring, he said, 'As a matter of fact, Miranda and I are splitting up.'

After a pause she said, 'I'm sorry.'

'Yeah, well. It's been on the cards for a while. Miranda doesn't want to spend the best part of her life buried away in the countryside. Tarn Fold is a cul-de-sac and, as far as she's concerned, that sums up the Lake District. It's a nice place to spend a few days in summer, but slogging through a wet winter isn't for her.'

'I thought it was Miranda's idea to move here. She talked you into it.'

'I didn't need much persuading. As for Miranda, she changed her mind. It happens, I suppose.'

Hannah wriggled out of the path of a couple of fat women who were coming into the coffee shop for a sit down, a drink, and maybe a muffin or two. Suddenly she wanted to prolong the conversation, but she couldn't think of anything to say that wasn't nosey or crass. Better leave it.

'Thanks again for your help. Let's keep in touch.'

He looked straight at her. 'Yes, please.'

Striding back to Divisional HQ, Hannah tried to airbrush Daniel's face out of her mind. It was a mistake to be distracted, she had more than enough on her plate. He might be out of a relationship, but she wasn't. She and Marc had been together a long time. He wasn't to blame that she felt there must be more to life than what she had. It was her fault. She could hear her dead mother's gentle voice, urging her to count her blessings.

She called in Les Bryant and Bob Swindell and briefed them on the news about William Inchmore. Les scratched his armpit as he studied Edith's handwritten confession.

'Very helpful, that Professor Kind.'

'He's not a professor,' she snapped, hoping that she hadn't blushed.

'Whatever. He's as good at detective work as his old man.'

'There's no comparison,' Hannah said. 'Ben was a professional. Daniel is ... an amateur.'

'Shrewd, though.' His face was straight, but he was teasing her, no question.

'Yes.' Her expression said *drop it*.

With a wary glance at both of them, Bob Swindell launched into an update on the latest from Fern Larter's team. It made sense for both sets of investigators to liaise closely together. If Di Venuto was right and Koenig was the caller who had given the tip-off about the Arsenic Labyrinth, it was hard to believe that there was no connection between his death and the cold case investigation.

'Koenig's mother was a prostitute from Barrow who took an overdose when he was a toddler and there's no father's name on his birth certificate. He had no other family and Social Services took him into care. He turned into a Walter Mitty. But people seem to have liked him and he didn't have any scruples about taking advantage. He would pretend to be a hot-shot entrepreneur and charm older women into investing in get-rich-quick schemes put together on the back of an envelope. But he was nowhere near as smart as he thought he was, and that's why he finished up in the nick. Eventually, he either wised up or turned over a new leaf. For a few weeks he worked in Windermere, but then he upped and left and started travelling. Since then, he's spent several years on the Continent. There are gaps in the story at present, but as far as we can tell, he kept out of trouble.'

'Until someone thumped him with a torch and chucked him in the lake,' Les said.

'He told his landlady he'd just come over from France, but a couple of receipts in his bag indicate he spent time in Wales before he moved back to the Lakes. He liked spending money, doesn't seem to have been too hot at keeping hold of it. He was clueless, a fantasist. If he did kill Emma Bestwick, it's a miracle he ever got away with it.'

Les's cold had gone to his chest and he burst into a fit of coughing. When he'd recovered enough to speak, he said in a throaty wheeze, 'But *why* would he want to kill her?'

'He has no record of violence, all his crimes were about making money.'

'Suppose someone paid him to murder Emma,' Hannah said.

'You're assuming it *was* murder,' Les objected. 'If the guy was that much of a fuckwit, maybe her death was an accident.'

'Then why arrange to meet in the middle of nowhere?'

'We can't answer that until we find something

340

that links him with Emma.'

They turned to Bob, who shook his head. 'Before Inchmore Hall burned down, Alex Clough was asked if Koenig had worked at the museum – as a volunteer guide, maybe – but she denied it. Of course, the records will now be ashes, so even if she was lying, we can't prove it. But she's in the clear for his murder. Her late father, too.'

'Their alibis stack up?' Hannah asked.

'Alban fulfilled a speaking engagement in Grasmere on the night of Koenig's death, addressing the Rotary Club on the topic of barghests and bogies of the Lakes. As for Alex, she went out for dinner with an old school chum and her husband at a swish restaurant in Cartmel. Plenty of witnesses, no chance that they could be mistaken.'

Hannah groaned. The Cloughs had been good suspects. They had money and either father or daughter could have afforded to provide Emma Bestwick with the funds she needed to set up on her own as a reflexologist. Not that Hannah had any idea why they might wish to do so. Unless Emma had somehow discovered the truth behind William Inchmore's death and needed to be kept quiet.

While Bob departed to photocopy Edith's journal, Hannah picked Les's brain on next steps. They decided she should speak again to Alex about Edith's journal, though even if Alex knew the truth about William's murder, there was no chance of her admitting it.

'You think Alban will have confided in her?'

Les shook his head. 'He sounds like a man who

341

enjoyed keeping secrets. He'd have taken this one to his grave if Edith's confession hadn't come to light.'

'Maggie's arranged for me to call on Jeremy and Karen later this afternoon. What do you reckon to their alibis for the night of Koenig's murder?'

A derisive snort. 'Not much.'

Jeremy had told Maggie that he'd been upstairs in his study, marking student essays, while Karen watched TV and their children did their homework in their rooms. Monk Coniston was within walking distance of their house and, in any case, the mere fact that no vehicle had been seen in the car park didn't mean that the murderer couldn't have parked somewhere close by. Either husband or wife could have slipped out, committed the murder and then hurried back under cover of darkness. If a car had been used, it might have been accomplished inside thirty minutes. A return journey on foot would have taken a good hour. Jeremy or Karen might even have killed Koenig without the other realising what they had done. But what was the motive?

Same question for Francis and Vanessa Goddard. They lived even closer to where Koenig had been killed and Fern's team hadn't yet established whether they could provide credible alibis. Hannah couldn't forget that Francis had once been her personal prime suspect. But even if he had had an affair with Emma, would he – or Vanessa, for that matter – first have bought her off and then resorted to hiring Koenig to kill her?

When she asked Les for his opinion, he pinched

342

his nose and said, 'Best take a closer look at Emma. What sort of woman was she? Might she have blackmailed someone? It would explain how she came into so much money.'

'Alex was her lover. She'll have understood her, if anyone did.'

'Maybe.' His expression was bleak and faraway and Hannah was sure he wasn't thinking about Alex. 'But sometimes it doesn't help to be close to someone. You become blind to what's going on inside their head. You think you understand them, when the fact is, you really don't have a bloody clue.'

Alex Clough had taken refuge in a postcard-pretty cottage on the outskirts of Newby Bridge. It belonged to a fiercely protective friend called Mina, a spiky-haired woman in a Greenpeace T-shirt and mud-stained jeans whose hallway book-case overflowed with magazines and guides to self-sufficiency. Mina made it clear that, if it was up to her, the police wouldn't be allowed near Alex until she'd had time to mourn in peace. But Alex, though pale and thinner than ever, was no longer the weeping wreck of the night before and she insisted that she was willing to talk to Hannah.

Even in grief she remained immaculate: black velvet jacket, white blouse and clingy dark trousers. Silently she listened as Hannah explained how her father and grandmother had conspired to cover up the truth about the murder of William Inchmore. When she denied all knowledge of the family's secret, Hannah believed her. And if she was lying, it could never be proved. Nobody was left alive to prosecute. A mystery had been solved by Daniel's discovery, that was all.

Alex pushed her hands deep into her pockets and strolled to the rain-flecked window that looked out over Mina's large working garden, with its damp vegetable patch, hen coop and fruit trees. She pointed to a white bee hive in the distance, near the fence separating Mina's land from a ploughed field.

'If my father were here, he'd say that we should have told the bees everything that's happened. Did you ever hear him recount the legend of Jenkins Syke? It was one of his favourite tales.'

Hannah shook her head, said nothing.

'The Syke is a narrow beck not far from St Andrew's Church. In olden days, folk said that if someone died, the bees must be told. The custom in these parts was to hang a black ribbon on the hives. The bees formed part of the community, and needed to be treated with respect. Failing to do so brought bad luck. The story goes that the coffin bearing the body of a man called Jenkins slipped from the sled on which it was being carried along the old Coniston corpse road and fell into the stream. My father's theory was that his family only had themselves to blame. They must have neglected to tell the bees of his passing.' Her voice broke. 'Perhaps I'd better go outside and put them in the picture.'

Hannah said softly, 'What will you do next?'

Alex cleared her throat. 'Time for a fresh start. The hall was only insured for a fraction of its

344

value, the premiums were crippling. But something nice may be happening between Mina and me. Years ago, long before Emma came on the scene, Mina and I were close, but she and my father never hit it off. Now, well, who knows? We'll take it one day at a time.'

'I wanted to talk to you about Emma. Did she ever mention a man called Guy Koenig?'

Alex frowned. 'Isn't he...?'

'You may have heard on the news, his body was found in the lake. He'd been hit on the head.'

'And there's a connection with Emma?'

'We think so.'

Alex's bewilderment surely couldn't have been feigned. 'His name meant nothing to me. If Emma knew him, she never told me.'

'Any more ideas about how she came into so much cash?'

She lifted her head and stared into the distance. 'It's a mystery to me. I thought I knew her, but I was deceiving myself. We all keep something back, don't we, Chief Inspector? As Edith Inchmore did, as my father and grandmother did. As Mina and I are bound to do. Whatever the reasons, we never allow anyone else to know the whole of our personal history. I suppose we're afraid of what they might think of us. But there's more to it than that. We are terrified of what they might do with the knowledge.'

The rain was easing as Hannah drove past the Blawith Fells, through a landscape of muted greens and browns. Next stop was *chez* Erskine. She'd arranged to meet Maggie there. Jeremy

345

needed to know about Edith's journal, but she also wanted to seek out any connection between the Erskines and Guy Koenig. 'At this Time' was playing on the CD player and, like a detective in anguish, Elvis Costello wanted to know who are these people who keep telling us lies. When her in-car mobile rang and Terri's number showed on the screen, she pulled on to the verge overlooking the lake. A chat with Terri demanded her full attention.

'Just ringing to check you're still OK for tonight.'

Shit. She'd forgotten that Terri had arranged a get-together of girls they'd known in the sixth form. Love Rivals Reunited, Terri called it.

'Actually...'

'Oh, Hannah!'

'Sorry. I mean, I'll see what I can do, but we're still working on this case out at Coniston. I'm on my way into the village right now. We've solved one of the murders, but not the other.'

'Fifty per cent success rate in the space of a few days sounds pretty good to me. Surely you're entitled to a night off?'

'I can't promise to make it to the pizzeria for seven o'clock.'

An exaggerated sigh gusted down the line. 'You know something? I never thought I'd feel sorry for Marc. But I'm starting to think he leads a dog's life. Never knowing from one moment to the next whether you'll be around. No wonder he spends most of his time with his nose stuck in some musty old tome. You'd better watch out. If you don't keep your eye on him, some other

346

woman will start checking out his catalogue.'

Terri must be pissed off if she was taking Marc's side. She'd always maintained that any man who spent his life surrounded by damp and smelly books must be pretty sad. Her preference was for hunks, although with her track record of matrimonial disasters, maybe she wasn't ideally qualified to advise on preserving a relationship. Then again, hers was the voice of bitter experience.

'I'll pop in for a quick drink later on, OK?'

A sulky sniff. 'I suppose that'll have to do.'

'Terri, I didn't mean to mess you about.'

'It's just that ... as a matter of fact, I've got a bit of news for you. I wanted to tell you face to face, but...'

'What is it?'

'Actually, you'll never believe this.'

Hannah waited, watching a lonely gull circle above the lake. Terri enjoyed building suspense. A lifetime of TV soap operas had taught her all the tricks of the trade.

'Go on.'

'Well, have you got your ears pinned back? My date last night just happens to be a millionaire!'

Already the sulkiness had disappeared from her voice and she sounded full of herself. She was never downcast for more than five minutes, it was one of the things Hannah loved about her. She was a make-up artist with her own beauty salon and her moods changed as rapidly as her appearance.

'Wow. Tell me more.'

'Well, he built up a successful business selling

347

artificial limbs and now he's sold out, he wants to enjoy life. He was telling me all about this wonderful house of his up near Blencathra. He's created a brand new garden from scratch. Pergolas and fountains and rare azaleas, blah, blah, blah. It's his way of getting up close and personal with Mother Nature, after too many years in the rat race.'

'I'm sure you'll help him get closer to nature.'

A whoop of laughter exploded in Hannah's ear. 'You bet! Thank God I had the presence of mind to put on my shortest skirt. Not that I mis-behaved, I'll have you know. Other than flashing a glimpse of stocking-top as I climbed into my taxi at the end of the evening. All Denzil got from me was a peck on the cheek and I made it clear that I was otherwise engaged tonight. Of course I didn't mention that I've already lined up four more blokes through the website! Might as well see what's around, eh? Besides, it doesn't do to let a man get too many ideas too soon.'

Hannah laughed. 'Wonderful. So he's hooked?'

'I think so,' Terri said complacently. 'Who knows where it might lead? He told me it was a great sadness that his ex-wife hadn't been able to have children. I felt really sorry for him. He'd make a wonderful father, he has a very gentle way with him.'

Terri had once famously declared that she'd rather have all her teeth pulled out than endure the indignity of childbirth, but Hannah knew better than to remind her.

'And would you...?'

'Look, I know what you're thinking. But the

348

fact is, I've never met the right bloke before. It would be irresponsible to bring a baby into the world when your marriage was on the rocks. I may have been too hasty in what I said. The more time passes, I can't help thinking, it might be quite nice, to have a couple of little kids running around the place. I mean, the clock keeps ticking. I don't want to grow into a frumpy old maid.'

'No danger of that.'

'You know what I'm saying.' Uncharacteristically, Terri paused. 'When you told me about your miscarriage, it set me thinking. I always saw you as a career cop, I never pictured you as a wife and mother. But I could tell how much it meant to you. That sense of loss.'

Typical Terri. She had a scary genius for saying exactly what was in her mind. Hannah gazed out across the grey expanse of water. Sometimes all she wanted was to empty her mind of everything. All the memories, all the frustrated hopes and desires. She didn't speak.

'Anyway, I started to wonder how I might feel if I fell pregnant. And I wasn't as horrified by the idea as I'd expected ... are you still there?'

'Let's talk some more tonight.'

'Come by taxi, so you don't have to worry about how much you drink, OK? I'll make sure they put the Chablis on ice.'

'It's a deal.'

'And I can tell you all about Denzil. I only hope he doesn't think I'm a pushover. If so, he'll be sorely disappointed. I'm going to make him sweat for his rewards, just you wait and see. One thing I've learned about men, they never value anything if you give it to them on a plate.'

Jeremy Erskine was seldom lost for words, but as Hannah described Edith's confession to the murder of her husband, his eyes widened like a child's on seeing a sci-fi monster on TV. Edith's journal belonged to the Association and there was no point in keeping quiet about the involvement of Betty or Alban. As she answered his questions, she could almost see cogs turning in Jeremy's brain. A pamphlet describing the decline and fall of the Inchmore empire would cement his reputation as a local historian.

The climate in the conservatory was Mediterranean. The Erskines' home was smart and secure, this room sealed off from the world outside. At barely four o'clock, already the sky was midnight black. Through the sliding PVC doors, Hannah could see the children, squatting on the carpet in the sitting room beyond, glued to a *Buffy* DVD, hear their muffled shrieks of merriment. Family tableaux didn't come cosier. She felt a stirring of emotion and hoped it wasn't jealousy.

Jeremy was wearing an open-neck sports shirt, slacks with a razor sharp crease and spotless loafers. A man at ease with himself. Hannah yearned to grab him by the arm and shake the smugness out of him. As he listened, he reached out and draped his arm over Karen's tanned shoulder. She was dressed as though for midsummer in a skimpy top and skirt and nestled closer at her husband's touch. If the flimsiness of their alibis for the night of Koenig's murder worried them, Hannah saw no sign of it. Trying to prise the truth out of a happy couple would be a nightmare. To save each other, they would lie through their expensively whitened teeth.

Jeremy made a characteristic *pay-attention* throat-clearing noise. 'So, Chief Inspector, what progress with your investigation? I asked DC Eyre here if the murder of this fellow a couple of days after Emma's body was discovered was simply a coincidence and she refused to be drawn.'

Maggie was sitting in the corner, squashed between the drinks trolley and the portable TV. Her lips were pressed tight together, giving nothing away. But under his sardonic gaze, her fair cheeks coloured, as though she'd failed to come up with a good excuse for not doing her homework on time.

Jeremy smirked at Hannah and said after a theatrical pause, 'So – naturally I deduce there is a link?'

Answer a question with a question. 'You didn't know Guy Koenig?'

'Good heavens, no. There's talk in the village that he was a petty criminal. Spent years in and out of prison. Karen and I are hardly likely to socialise with someone like that.'

'He was a smooth talker, by all accounts. Well read, plausible. You wouldn't necessarily have taken him for a rogue.'

'Even so. We really don't mix in those circles. You could have a word with Vanessa, if you like. She may have come across him.'

Hannah blinked. 'What makes you say that?'

'She worked with prison libraries for a couple of

years. After we separated, she threw herself into outreach work. Vanessa is a thoroughly decent woman, she always likes to think she is doing good. She believes in rehabilitating offenders, though I have to say that in my book, she's naïve. You'll never persuade a young thug to walk the straight and narrow simply by introducing him to Charles Dickens or Thomas Hardy. Let alone Martin Amis or...'

'Which prisons?'

Jeremy freed his arm from Karen's shoulder as he gave the question thought. 'That place at Millom, of course, it's pretty much on the doorstep. Haverigg, isn't that the name? And I seem to recall her mentioning a project at Preston. Did this man Koenig ever serve a sentence there?'

Through the panes, Hannah saw the Erskine children, engrossed in what they were watching. Neat, well-turned out youngsters, with their mother's blonde hair and the long Erskine jaw. Apples of their parents' eyes.

'How long were you married to Vanessa, Mr Erskine?'

Karen frowned, curled herself up into a ball, wrapping her arms around her upper body, as if for protection. Maggie wrinkled her brow, trying to work out where all this was leading.

Jeremy flushed and said, 'Eight years, nine? Possibly less, I can't recall. It was a very long time ago and as a wise man once said, the past is another country. My life is with Karen and the children, that's all I care about. I'm afraid I can't see why you should ask about my previous marriage, it can only cause distress.'

'I don't mean to be intrusive,' Hannah said. 'But something puzzles me. You are obviously a caring father, Mr Erskine. And Mrs Goddard is devoted to her own boy.'

'She dotes on him,' Karen snapped. 'I don't think it's healthy.'

Jeremy put a restraining hand on her knee. 'What's your point, Chief Inspector?'

'I wondered why you and your first wife never had children.'

'I'm not sure it's any of your business.' Jeremy's face had turned lobster-pink. 'How can this have any bearing on Emma's death? Frankly, your question strikes me as prurient.'

Hannah said, 'Did Vanessa have problems, trying to conceive?'

Jeremy cast an anxious glance at his wife. 'If – if you must know, she did. It was a nightmare for us both. We had been anxious to start a family. I can assure you, I was delighted when it turned out that Vanessa was able to have a baby after all. I knew how much it meant to her.'

'But you'd thought it was impossible for her to have children?' Hannah persisted.

'So the doctors told us. We tried IVF, all kinds of alternative stuff, one minute our hopes were raised, next they were dashed. Nothing seemed to work. Nothing.' Jeremy's voice had become hoarse. He swallowed hard. 'When Karen told me she was pregnant, it was the happiest moment of my life. Even though I knew it meant my marriage was finished, even though it crucified me to hurt Vanessa, to treat her so cruelly. She deserved better and I thank God that in the end she got it.

Now – does that satisfy your curiosity, Chief Inspector?'

Slowly, Hannah nodded.

'Fern's line is still busy,' Maggie said.

'Keep trying.'

They were in the car, racing along past the dark gift shops and tea rooms in the direction of Thurston Water House. Hannah almost hit an unlit van as she swung round a corner. Her mind should have been on the road, but was travelling through the years to the time of Emma Best-wick's murder. Her stomach was tight. At last she understood.

'This is about Emma,' she said, almost to her-self, 'about the kind of woman she was.'

'I'm not with you.' Maggie was good at what she did, but one gift she lacked. Ben Kind always said that the best detectives had imagination, they looked beyond what they could see and hear and smell.

They turned into the road that led to the lake and the car jolted on a speed bump. Hannah swore and slammed her foot on the brake. 'She never settled to anything. All her life she spent searching for fulfilment, but she never found it. She fancied becoming a reflexologist, but that required money and she didn't have two pennies to rub together. Luckily, the people she lodged with were willing to fund her. On condition that she gave them a baby.'

'So – she was the mother of the Goddards' child?'

'A surrogacy deal. Conducted in secret because

it's illegal to pay the surrogate mother anything more than expenses. Once she realised how desperate the Goddards were, Emma must have driven a hard bargain. Vanessa and Francis belonged to a small community. They wanted everyone to regard Christopher as theirs – and theirs alone. It must have seemed a perfect plan. Emma lived with them and Francis, as a nurse, could take good care of her. They hid her away to make sure that nothing went wrong and nobody had any idea that it was she, rather than Vanessa, who was pregnant.'

In her head, she heard Vanessa, speaking with passion. *If you ask me, the idea that blood is thicker than water is rubbish.* A curious remark for a devoted mother, she should have paid it closer heed.

'She wasn't stressed out after breaking up with Alex, was she?'

'No, she just couldn't be allowed out once her bump became visible.'

'So what went wrong?'

The dour bulk of Thurston Water House loomed up in the headlights. Hannah swerved off the road and into the driveway, shuddering to a halt in front of the up-and-over garage door. The Goddards were at home. Lights shone behind the curtained windows on the ground and first floors. Somewhere inside, the boy was doubtless lounging around or watching TV. Young Christopher Goddard, innocent cause of death and disaster.

'Remember the last conversation Emma had with Jeremy? She'd changed her mind. After her

355

child was born, she found it impossible to let go. Alex said she was possessive, mentioned her mood swings. The Goddards didn't realise the risk they were running.'

They strode up to the front door and Hannah rang the bell long and hard. A full minute dragged by before anyone answered, although as they shifted impatiently on the step, they could hear hurried movements inside the house. At last the door inched open on a security chain. Vanessa Goddard peered out at them. She looked as nervous as if she thought a pair of ghosts had come calling.

Perhaps that was it, Hannah said to herself. The woman was frightened of a ghost.

'Oh, Chief Inspector, it's you. I wasn't... I mean, on dark nights like this, you can't be too careful.'

'May we come in?'

Vanessa screwed her face into an anxious frown. 'We've already had a young policeman here. Wanting to know where Francis and I were the night that poor man was thrown in the lake.'

She showed no sign of releasing the chain. Why was she playing for time? Hannah said, 'If you wouldn't mind allowing us to come into the house, Mrs Goddard?'

'Oh, I'm sorry. Of course.'

Vanessa fumbled with the chain and finally pulled the door wide open. But when she shooed her visitors into the front room, her haste contrasted with her hesitation before letting them inside her home.

'Christopher is engrossed in his maths homework,' she said. 'He's such a diligent boy, but he needs to concentrate. I wouldn't want him to be disturbed.'

Hannah heard a door bang somewhere in the back of the house. 'May we talk to your husband as well?'

'Francis? I ... I'm not sure...'

'Is he here?'

Vanessa fingered the mark on her face. 'He ... no, I don't think so.'

She's losing the plot. Hannah listened out for an engine starting up, but heard nothing. Besides, if he'd left his car in the garage, they were blocking him in. Gritting her teeth, she said, 'Mrs Goddard, I don't want to waste time. We need to talk to your husband as well.'

Vanessa's expression froze. Suddenly, they heard a young boy's voice, loud and crystal clear, calling from the next room.

'Daddy, come and see this!'

Half a second of silence was snapped by the boy again. He sounded petulant.

'Daddy! Where are you?'

Hannah said, 'Mrs Goddard, you have to tell us, if not your son. Where is your husband?'

Vanessa's brown eyes moistened. 'We saw your car through the curtain. Francis said he had to go.'

'On foot?'

She nodded.

'Do you know where he's heading?'

'I think ... to the lake.' She stifled a sob. 'That's what he said he would do.'

'Tell me.'

357

'He said he'd rather end it all than bring shame and disgrace to Christopher and me.'

Francis couldn't be far away. Hannah and Maggie parked by the trees fringing Coniston Water. The moon was hiding, but they left their headlights on to light a patch of land and lake. The café and the steamship ticket office were shuttered and no living soul was in sight. Hannah's sole coherent thought was that darkness had an infinite number of shades.

They jumped out of the car. Wind was rattling the branches above their heads, water lapped against the shore. As her eyes adjusted to the gloom, Hannah picked out a shape in the murk ahead, caught the rasp of laboured breathing. A man exhausted, close to defeat.

'Mr Goddard!' Hannah cried. 'This is DCI Scarlett and DC Eyre – we need to talk.'

Footsteps pounded across stony ground, then clattered against the wet wooden surface of the L-shaped pier. Francis Goddard wasn't in the mood to talk.

Maggie broke into a run. She was young and fit, with long, loping strides. Hannah followed in her wake. Surely he didn't plan to steal a boat? It was madness, he wouldn't stand a chance.

'Stop!' Maggie screamed. 'Don't do it! You'll never...'

The dark shape seemed to pirouette on the pier. An easy, elegant movement. Hannah remembered that Francis loved dancing, he knew how to move. But then he let out a cry of despair. She heard a loud thud as his body hit the water.

By the time she reached the pier, Maggie was bending over and tearing off her boots.

'I'm going in,' Maggie hissed.

'You can't! It's too cold. Nobody can survive down there.'

Francis was thrashing around in the lake, making a muffled noise that might have meant anything. Did he want to be rescued or just left to drown?

Maggie stood up. 'Sorry, Hannah. It has to be done.'

'No!'

Hannah moved to restrain her, but her shoes slid on the rain-sleeked wood and she lost her footing and pitched forward. Her knees hit the pier with a painful crash. She stretched out her arms, as if in prayer.

Then watched Maggie jump.

CHAPTER TWENTY

'So Francis Goddard is expected to live?'

Hannah couldn't tell from Les Bryant's grimace whether he was glad or disappointed. Hunched over the table in her office, she strove to shut the fan heater's asthmatic roar out of her mind. She wasn't in doubt, she wanted Francis fit and able to talk. Some questions only he could answer.

'They hope so. But the doctors are worried about brain damage.'

Les's nose wrinkled, as though at a dodgy sick note. 'Brain damage? He was only underwater for a couple of minutes before that bloody girl dragged him out.'

That bloody girl. Les was furious with Maggie for having risked her life for a man who had committed one murder and caused another. When Hannah told him that Maggie was going to be OK, he'd come close to shedding tears of relief. Those desperate moments when Maggie grappled with Francis underwater before somehow summoning the strength to drag his inert body on to the shore had been as long as any in Hannah's life. Thank God the ambulance had come so quickly.

'They say it's a case of dive reflex.'

Les curled his lip and leaned back in his chair. His conservatism was ingrained, he was always suspicious of anything he'd never heard of.

'And what's that when it's at home?'

'When you dive into very cold water, sometimes your larynx goes into a reflex spasm, closing up to stop your lungs drowning. The body starts hibernating to protect itself, but the danger is anoxia, being starved of oxygen. That's why the doctors are so concerned, that's what happened to Francis.'

'Let's not beat about the bush. If he doesn't make it, who cares?'

'His wife, his son...' *And me.*

Les snorted. 'Listen, I don't want to dance on the bugger's grave, but what's he got to live for? He's going to spend a long, long time in prison.'

Hannah shrugged.

'Hey, what's up? Lauren's over the moon, you're flavour of the month, we can all move on. Why are you so downbeat?'

'It's just that...'

He wagged a stubby, tobacco-stained finger in her face. 'Forget it. You solved the case. Nothing else matters.'

'Francis wanted a child as much as I did.'

Vanessa Goddard's voice dropped to a whisper, barely loud enough for the tape recorder. Hannah had to lean close to make sure she picked up every word. She and Linz Waller were sitting on either side of Vanessa; the idea was to avoid any hint of confrontation. Hannah had brought in Linz, rather than Les or Bob, in the hope of encouraging Vanessa to open up. Three women together. Like a private chat, except that every word would be taped. And the plan was working; Vanessa was subdued, but far from reticent. She'd hired a solicitor, a local woman and a family friend, to represent Francis if and when he recovered, but she didn't want a lawyer to accompany her when she talked to the police. Even when Hannah pressed the point, she'd remained adamant. She wasn't under arrest, she'd committed no crime. She could handle this on her own.

Deep furrows criss-crossed her brow; she was concentrating with the intensity of a tennis star whose next serve would decide Wimbledon. Her gaze fixed on a point high on the wall of the interview room, her only movement was the fiddling of her fingers with a bracelet. She spoke with as much care as if giving a presentation to library officials. No cue cards, but Hannah was sure she'd memorised a script.

'Jeremy told me you'd been trying for a baby for years.'

'I felt a failure. He said it wasn't my fault, but there was no getting away from the bitter truth. I couldn't give him what he wanted. What I wanted too, more than anything.'

'It must have hurt when you found out that Karen was expecting a baby.'

Vanessa twitched, as if Hannah had yanked her hair. 'You can't imagine the wound. We'd had a good marriage...'

Her voice quavered, she dabbed at her eyes with a lace handkerchief. Hannah gave her a minute to compose herself.

'And then you met Francis.'

Vanessa sat up in her chair and Hannah saw the glimmer of a fond smile. 'A man who loved me for myself. I've always been self-conscious about this mark on my face, but it meant nothing to him, he saw the real woman underneath. I gave him everything I could. But ... he wanted a family and I was afraid he might...'

'Tell us about the surrogacy.'

'After I got to know Emma, she told me Alex had suggested adopting a child. Their relationship was falling apart at the time and Emma refused point blank. Said she'd rather have a nice new car than children. I won't speak ill of the dead, but Emma wasn't really a *giving* person. There was no maternal streak. I mentioned it to Francis, because it was so ironic. Presumably

362

Emma would have no difficulty bearing a child, but she couldn't care less. To us it meant everything, and yet we were thwarted at every turn. We talked about fostering, about adoption, but the agencies put up so many hurdles and, besides, what we wanted was a baby that was *ours*. And then we started wondering – what if we paid Emma to produce a child for us? Nobody else need ever know.'

'But Jeremy knew you couldn't conceive.'

Vanessa's eyes narrowed and Hannah understood the depth of her contempt for the man who had deserted her. 'I knew him well enough to be sure he'd be thrilled to believe I'd found some miracle cure for infertility. It would make him feel less guilty about betraying me.'

'Did it matter that Emma was Karen's sister?'

'Karen stole my first husband by giving him a baby,' Vanessa said. She seemed to measure each word, as if unsure how candid to be. 'How could I not relish the prospect of her sister giving my second marriage the one thing it lacked?'

'And Emma was up for it?'

'Everything went like a dream. She asked for money, lots of it, but that didn't bother us, as long as she did what we wanted. Francis doted on her during the pregnancy, no mother-to-be has ever had such wonderful care. And she presented us with this beautiful baby boy.' Vanessa's voice shook. 'Our son Christopher, a gift from God.'

'Why did she change her mind?'

Vanessa closed her eyes, like a child reciting a poem learned by rote. 'We kept our side of the bargain, we could never understand why Emma broke her word to us. She'd promised faithfully, she'd sworn to us, that she would never make any claim on the baby. We'd paid her enough to buy that nice new car as well as putting down a deposit on her new house. And then she took it upon herself to decide that motherhood might be what she really yearned for, after all. She'd never found a job to satisfy her long term, why pretend that looking after a squealing infant might be any more appealing? It made no sense. But we couldn't reason with her.'

'Did she threaten you?'

'She said she'd go public, she didn't care if she was prosecuted, as long as she had her son back. We could have regular access – can you imagine? Our own son, the son we adored!' A bitten-off laugh. 'She offered to pay back the money in instalments, but that was scarcely relevant. She never gave a toss about hurting Francis or me. Let alone the child. Imagine how confusing it would have been for the little mite, to have two women claiming to be his mother. I couldn't bear the thought.'

Vanessa was shaking in her chair. The birth-mark seemed more livid than ever.

'The selfish, selfish, bitch!'

As Vanessa dissolved into tears, Hannah called the interview to a halt and gave her time to compose herself. There must be no suggestion of improper pressure. But after twenty minutes and a cup of strong sweet tea, Vanessa insisted she was ready to resume. She kept repeating that she wanted to help. This was an utter nightmare, but she needed to do the right thing.

'Guy Koenig,' Hannah prompted when they were back in the room. 'We checked the records. You met him when he was inside.'

'Guy was my greatest success.' Hannah didn't think she'd ever seen a smile so bleak, so bereft of merriment. 'I have this passion for reaching out to people who never had a chance to experience the magic of literature. The government provided a pot of money to support reader development work with prisoners. I love working in partnership with librarians in prisons, mental hospitals, residential care homes. Making a difference to people's lives.'

Hannah could imagine Les Bryant's scepticism. *Yeah, that Guy Koenig certainly made a difference to people's lives.*

'Guy was a member of my very first group. He took to Victorian literature like a duck to water. Gaskell, Hardy, you name it. Charles Dickens, his favourite. Guy was a charmer, I saw that with a bit of luck he could make something worthwhile of his life. I became very fond of him, we talked a lot. But prisons have rules. You're not supposed to get too close.'

'You came across him a second time, we discovered.'

Vanessa sighed. 'In another prison reading group, eighteen months later. He'd been convicted again. A minor offence of deception, but his record was bad and the courts don't understand why most sentences are better served in the community. Guy wanted to go straight, I was

365

sure of it. But he was weak, impatient, that was his downfall. He could never resist the temptation to pretend, he used to say it was because he didn't have a clue who he really was. His mother was on the game, he never knew his father. I tried to explain, it doesn't matter where you come from, what counts is where you're going to. With his gift for persuasion, he could have become a salesman or a spin doctor.'

Sounds like he had you eating out of his palm. 'He was released for the last time a few weeks before Emma disappeared. You remained in touch?'

'Of course it was against the rules, but I wanted him to make something of his life.' For the first time, a hint of colour came to her disfigured face. 'I'd told him, along with everyone else, all about my pregnancy. He was thrilled for me, he even bought a little gift for the baby.'

'Your supposed pregnancy,' Hannah said gently.

'Yes.' Vanessa swallowed. 'When he realised I was stressed out, he thought I was suffering from post-natal depression. I was very low and he was very kind. We met for coffee in the village once or twice. It was all open and above board, please don't misunderstand. Francis knew all about our little get-togethers, there was never anything between Guy and me of *that* sort. But one afternoon, I started to weep and, before I knew what I was doing, I was telling Guy about the disaster that had befallen us. About Emma and how she wanted Christopher for herself. He was appalled by her behaviour, of course.'

As Vanessa examined her short, neat nails,

Hannah glanced at Linz Waller, who arched her elegant eyebrows. If you were going to confide your darkest secret, a flaky drifter wasn't the wisest choice of confidant. But then, who didn't make mistakes?

For some reason, Hannah found herself thinking about Marc and, in a confused way, about Daniel Kind. Oh God. This would never do. Must concentrate on Vanessa's tale of woe.

'Did you ask him to help?' Linz murmured.

Vanessa shook her head. 'He volunteered to have a word with her. Of course, I was bowled over by his kindness. I promised to help him financially, but he said he simply wanted to repay me for all my generosity. He wasn't interested in my money.'

Hannah suppressed a groan. *I bet.*

'Of course, I brushed that aside. I was willing to give him anything, if only he could make Emma see sense. If she didn't have enough put by, we could sort that out somehow. Francis and I aren't rich, but we're comfortable, thanks to family inheritance. It would be better if she left the Lakes for good, so I told Guy that we'd make it worth her while if she promised never to contact us again. This was for Christopher's sake, you understand. What she was proposing was wicked. He was my child, not hers. We'd reached an agreement.'

For Christopher's sake? Hannah told herself not to sit in judgement. Motherhood *was* special, there was something mystical about the bond between a woman and her child. Maybe it was time to admit to herself what she'd tried so hard to ignore. Not a day passed when she didn't think about the baby she'd lost.

'What did Koenig do?' Linz asked.

'He phoned her on the basis Francis and I wanted him to represent our interests. At first Emma refused to meet him, but eventually she gave in. It was never easy to say no to Guy. They arranged to meet in a remote part of the fells above the village, where no one else could see them together or overhear their conversation. He loved a touch of melodrama, and Emma did, too. When I suggested he visit her at home instead, pretend to prying neighbours that he was a client in need of a reflexologist, he wouldn't hear of it. He was supremely confident, he assured me he would talk her round. It would cost, he said, but who cared if Emma left us alone?'

'Did you discuss Guy's proposal with your husband?'

'Naturally. There should never be secrets between husband and wife, that's my motto.'

You're crazy, everyone has secrets, and sometimes secrets keep us safe from harm. Hannah took a deep breath. Was she simply rationalising the way she kept secrets from Marc? Already he'd pushed the miscarriage out of his mind. For him, it was just one of those things. A narrow escape, frankly.

'But it all went wrong?'

Vanessa squeezed her eyes shut, her face folding with the pain of memory. 'Francis took Guy's call. I was feeding Christopher at the time. Guy was pretty incoherent, but he explained that Emma had fallen and hit her head. A freak accident, but fatal. When he realised she was dead, he

368

panicked and shoved the body down an old mine shaft. He said he didn't want to get us into trouble, he was afraid the truth would come out and our life with our baby boy would be ruined. He was thinking of us, not himself.'

Hannah bit back a sarcastic retort. From what she'd heard, Koenig never had an unselfish impulse in his life. If he was naïve, so were those who had asked him to negotiate with Emma, their mutinous surrogate mother. She was sure the truth about Emma's death differed from Koenig's account, but she was equally sure that she would never know precisely what took place that February day ten years ago.

'Did you pay him?'

'Every penny we'd promised, plus the extra money we'd set aside to buy Emma off. We hadn't wanted her to die, it was a terrible misfortune. But at least it meant that we had Christopher to ourselves. Nobody would ever take him away from us.'

So that's all right, then. Hannah exchanged a look with Linz. Sorrowful scorn was written all over her DC's pretty face. Linz was young and free; no need to fret about that ticking clock, kids and responsibilities were years away. For her, Vanessa was a sad old cow with an obsession about a baby that wasn't even hers.

'And Koenig?'

'Francis handled everything. I had my hands full with the baby, he didn't want me upset. He made Guy promise to leave the Lake District and go abroad. In prison, he'd often talked about wanting to travel. When Francis explained the

369

deal he'd struck, I thought it was for the best. Guy would do well with money behind him for the first time in his life. Francis gave him a chance.'

'But Guy couldn't keep away forever.'

Vanessa swallowed. 'That wretched journalist. If only he hadn't...'

'We believe Koenig tipped him off that Emma was buried up on Mispickel Scar. Why would he do that, do you think?'

'Heaven only knows. Guy told me once he believed in living by instinct. I'm afraid it was an excuse for muddled thinking. Of course, we were worried by the publicity, even more by the news that two bodies had been found. Two dead, not one, though we heard rumours that the other corpse is fifty years old, is that right?'

Hannah nodded.

'So, nothing to do with Guy.' Vanessa rubbed tired eyes. 'We didn't have any idea he was back in Coniston until he rang Francis after Emma was discovered. He was in a state, not making much sense. The police presence had spooked him, Francis said, and he wanted money to get away.'

'He blackmailed you,' Hannah said flatly.

'No!' Vanessa rapped the table. 'You don't understand. Guy wasn't like that. I still believed in him, I felt we owed him something. Thanks to Guy, we've had ten wonderful years with Christopher, and no amount of money can buy that happiness. Francis said he would sort it out. All Guy wanted was to get away from here, but he was broke. He wanted a loan. Francis arranged to

370

meet Guy to hand over some cash. He intended it as a gift, no nonsense about interest or paying us back.'

'That's what he said he meant to do?'

Vanessa nodded. 'Absolutely.'

'You had no idea that Francis took a couple of bricks with him to Monk Coniston, hoping to weight down the body? Or a torch, to hit Guy with?'

'I don't believe it, Francis would never hurt a fly. As for the torch, of course he needed it to find his way through the trees.'

'What did Francis tell you about his encounter with Guy?'

Vanessa sipped from a glass of water. 'When he came home that evening, he was in a state of shock. He'd asked Guy to promise never to return to Coniston and for some reason Guy argued. There was a scuffle – Guy started it. But Guy fell over and hit his head on a boulder. Francis checked and found he had no pulse. He was terrified. After all we'd been through, we might still lose Christopher as a result of Guy's death. So he threw the body in the lake. It wasn't nice and he hated doing it. My husband's spent a lifetime caring for others, Chief Inspector, he's an utterly decent man.'

'So it was all an unfortunate mistake?' Hannah strove to keep the cynicism out of her voice.

'I begged him to speak to you, make a clean breast of things. He wouldn't hear of it, didn't want to expose his wife and child to shame. Christopher and I were all he cared about, he didn't want to ruin our lives.' Her voice trembled

371

and she gulped more water. 'I dreaded his doing something – drastic. When the policeman came round to ask if we'd seen anyone heading towards Monk Coniston on the night of the murder, we realised it was only a question of time before you caught up with him.'

She breathed out. 'I must be strong, for Christopher's sake. Are you done with me, Chief Inspector? My son and I really must get back to the hospital. We need to be by his side.'

Hannah nodded and stood up. Chances were, she *was* done with Vanessa Goddard. Her husband might never speak again and Vanessa needed time and space to grieve for what she had lost, as well as summoning the strength to keep caring for the child who meant so much to her. As for her story, if her readers' group were discussing it, they'd be bound to say that it hung together. A prosecutor would say it tallied with the evidence. And Francis Goddard had been her own pet suspect, ten years ago, when everyone else was pissing in the wind, not even sure if Emma was dead. She'd been vindicated, no one now doubted that Francis Goddard was a murderer.

So why couldn't she bring herself to believe it?

CHAPTER TWENTY-ONE

'Your father used to moan that I was never satisfied,' Hannah said. 'He told me all detectives need to learn that every case leaves unanswered questions. You do as much as you can, then move on.'

Daniel laughed. 'I remember him scolding me for being too curious for my own good. Even as a boy, I obsessed about history. I had this crazy idea you could discover everything about the past. He told me there are things it's better not to know. Now I wonder if he was afraid I might find out about his affair with Cheryl.'

'He felt so much guilt about leaving his family,' Hannah said. 'I'm sure at times he realised he'd screwed up.'

Daniel shrugged and took another sip of Chablis. They were back in a warm nook near the bar in the Café d'Art, but Jacques Brel had been supplanted by Francoise Hardy. Hannah had called Daniel and offered to buy him a quick drink after work, a thank you for helping solve the murder of William Inchmore. She couldn't resist telling him about Francis Goddard and the truth about the deaths of Emma Bestwick and Guy Koenig.

Or was it the truth?

'My colleague leading the Koenig investigation is satisfied that Francis committed the murder.

Not that he'll ever stand trial. Or stand for anything else, come to that. They expect he'll need 24/7 care for the rest of his days. But...'

'Francis must have been frightened to death. He knew he was bound to be found out. When you and your DC showed up, he made a run for it and jumped in the lake. What more do you need?'

Hannah traced her finger along the rim of her glass. 'Suppose they planned it, the husband and wife? Francis would take the rap. He'd pretend to attempt suicide, but he didn't mean to die. He was a decent swimmer and intended to make for the shore if we failed to rescue him. Unfortunately, he reckoned without the dive reflex.'

'Why take such a risk?'

'To convince us that he was the killer. To stop the finger pointing at his wife.'

'Vanessa Goddard?' Daniel stared. 'Are you serious?'

'She knew Guy Koenig, Francis didn't. My bet is that she asked him to bargain with Emma and paid him off after Emma died. I can believe the plan wasn't to murder Emma. Something went wrong, we'll never know the full story. When Koenig returned to Coniston, he was penniless. Perhaps in the back of his mind he had the idea of extorting more cash from Vanessa. Even if he didn't think of it like that, it was a convenient fallback when his efforts to exploit his landlady fizzled out. Vanessa must have feared she'd never be rid of him. She and her family would never be safe while he was alive.'

'You think she murdered Guy herself?'

374

'In blind panic, yes. It was a crazy cock-up of a crime. But she was obsessed, she couldn't risk betrayal.'

A picture came into her mind of Alban Clough, that lascivious old misogynist, recounting a favourite tale. *What women most desire is to have their own will.* Not fair. But in the case of Vanessa, perhaps not so far off the mark.

'And she didn't tell Francis in advance?'

'I doubt it. She borrowed his coat and boots, forensic examination links them to the scene. Of course Francis was much taller, so she must have found it tricky. No wonder she couldn't carry anything heavier than a couple of bricks if she was walking all that way to the rendezvous with Koenig. Our only eye-witnesses claimed the person they saw at Monk Coniston was below average height. But we can't build a case on that, any defence counsel worth their salt would tear their testimony apart.'

'When the body was discovered so quickly, I suppose she realised she couldn't get away with it.'

'Exactly. So she talked to Francis and he decided to confess to a crime he hadn't committed. The plan was for him to make an unsuccessful suicide attempt. Given his good character and the fact that Koenig could be portrayed as a serial blackmailer, any judge and jury might be sympathetic. With a manslaughter verdict and our prisons bursting at the seams, he'd have a chance of getting out in time to share a slice of Christopher's late teens.'

Daniel winced. 'He sacrificed himself.'

'To protect his child. And the woman he loved.'

Francis as Gawain, a weird image. With Vanessa as his very own Loathly Lady.

'Maybe you're right.'

'But how can I prove it?'

'Do you want to prove it?'

Hannah swallowed the rest of her drink. 'Good question.'

'I mean – what good would it do? Perhaps the Goddards have suffered enough.'

'But is that justice, to let her get away with it?'

Daniel said, 'Do you really think she's got away with anything?'

Hannah remembered the paramedics by the banks of Coniston Water, loading the inert body of Francis Goddard on to a stretcher. His face had been frozen in an expression of unimaginable terror, as though he'd looked into the heart of the Devil himself. And she remembered catching sight of Vanessa, sobbing uncontrollably in a hospital corridor after the doctors had told her the news.

'I suppose you're right.' She checked her watch. 'I'd better hit the road, I promised Marc I wouldn't be too late. Thanks for sparing your time.'

'A pleasure.'

'I never even asked you ... how are things?'

'Looking up. An American company has offered me a gig on a cruise line, talking history to a party of wealthy tourists as we sail the Caribbean for a month in spring. It's a late opportunity. They booked Hattie Costello ages ago, but last week she fractured her ankle in a celebrity ski-ing show and

376

had to cry off. Shame, huh?'

'And the writing?'

'It'll keep until I return to the UK. But I have the germ of an idea for a new book. Ruskin wasn't the only Lake District literary figure worth writing about.'

'Don't tell me you're falling back on dear old Willie Wordsworth?'

He grinned and reached for the pocket of the coat he'd hung on the chair. With a magician's flourish, pulled out a paperback. When Hannah saw the author and title, she couldn't help laughing.

Thomas de Quincey, *On Murder.*

'Hannah!'

As she walked back along Stricklandgate Hannah was stopped in her tracks by a familiar cry. Glancing across the road, she spotted Terri, in long leather coat and high heels, waving with gusto. She hurried over to join her.

'You're looking very gorgeous.'

It wasn't idle flattery. Terri might be a make-up artist, skilled at dressing mutton as lamb, but in her own case she had the advantage of fantastic bone structure plus thick red hair and a figure to die for.

Terri beamed, showing lots of sharp white teeth. 'Another date.'

'And how is Denzil?'

Terri thrust out her lower lip, a gesture Hannah remembered from the playground, twenty years ago. 'That old fart? He called last night to say he really didn't think we were suited for a long term relationship, but he hoped we could remain good friends. As if! Apparently I didn't show enough excitement about his azaleas, it's how he quality-controls prospective girlfriends. Oh well, easy come, easy go.'

'So who is it tonight?'

'He describes himself as a senior professional. It's all rather mysterious, he doesn't give much away. I'm thinking a barrister, tall, dark and handsome. Possibly a doctor? Or knowing my luck, a serial killer. But I can't come to much harm in the middle of a swish new Russian restaurant, can I? I've taken a peek at the menu. The caviar costs a fortune, but...'

'You're worth it?'

'Dead right.' Terri brushed Hannah's hand with hers. 'By the way, I wanted to apologise. When I was talking about Denzil, I was excited. I suppose what I said about your miscarriage was insensitive. I'm sorry, sweetie.'

'No worries.'

At least not as far as Terri was concerned. Last night in bed, she'd finally got up the nerve to ask Marc how he felt about trying for a baby. He hadn't quite managed to stifle a nervous sigh before whispering that they ought to talk one of these days, but not right now. He was focused on the business, and besides what was the hurry? They had all the time in the world.

'Sure?' Terri asked.

'Promise. As a matter of fact, you pointed me in the right direction. Something you said helped me understand the case I was working on.'

'Seriously?' Terri clapped her hands in delight.

'That's a first, eh? Incidentally, I've forgiven you for not turning up that night. I hope your constable's OK after trying to rescue that feller.'

'Thanks, she's fine.' Hannah pressed her lips against Terri's cheek. 'Have a lovely evening.'

She hurried back across the road but as she passed a home furnishing shop, she saw a familiar figure reflected in the plate glass window. Les Bryant was striding along the opposite pavement, a rolled umbrella in his hand. He had an overcoat slung around his shoulders and underneath she glimpsed a blazer and tie. She'd never seen him looking so natty before, he might have been on his way to a bank managers' reunion.

Suspicion suddenly swelled in her mind. She glanced over her shoulder, towards where she'd left Terri waiting.

As if on cue, Les halted and said something to Terri. Her friend smiled, gracious as royalty, and extended her hand.

Well, well. Hannah turned in the direction of the car park. It wouldn't do for them to see her watching them. With any luck they'd have a great night. Though as a long-term relationship, it didn't have a hope in hell. Did it?

It was a funny thing about relationships. The more she saw, the less she understood why some of them worked and some fell apart.

Wanting to get home, yet not sure why, she broke into a run.

ACKNOWLEDGMENTS

The Lake District is, fortunately, a real place, but this is a work of fiction. At the risk of stating the obvious, I should say that all the characters and incidents are invented, as are all the named organisations that play a part in the story except for the Cumbria Constabulary – my version of it is fictitious, while the real one may change its shape if the much-debated reorganisation of the police service ever comes to fruition. The agencies which Hannah consults about the crime scene investigation at the Arsenic Labyrinth are also imaginary. Any resemblance between people and events in the book and counterparts in real-life is coincidental and unintended. To underline this, I have also taken a few liberties with topo-graphy and local history. Arsenic was mined at Caldbeck, but not, so far as I have been able to discover, at Coniston, and there is no arsenic labyrinth in Cumbria. Nor is there a museum like Alban Clough's, a Ruskin Archive of the kind described, or a Cumbrian newspaper called the *Post*.

I am indebted to a large number of people who have been generous with both time and expertise as I have researched the background to this book. I should like to express particular thanks to John

Prest, for offering insights into the work of a historian, Roger Forsdyke for advice on police procedure, Helen Pepper and Andy Barrett for sharing their crime scene know-how, Kathryn White of the Bagshaw Museum, Adam Sharpe, Cornwall County Council's senior archaeologist, who guided me through the mysterious world of arsenic labyrinths, and Howard Hull, Director of the Brantwood Trust and the Ruskin Foundation for information about Ruskin and his relations with the people of Coniston. Amongst the many authors whose books I have consulted, I should like to express particular appreciation for the work of Eric G. Holland (an intrepid explorer of copper mines), Dinah Birch (an authority on Ruskin), Ian Pepper (husband of Helen and another authority on crime scene work), and the late Robin W. Winks, a historian and detective fiction fan, of whom Daniel Kind is a disciple. I have also consulted websites and newspaper articles too numerous to list, but this is a novel and ultimately the story must take precedence oven the factual background. My colleagues in Murder Squad, my agent Mandy Little and my British and American publishers, Susie Dunlop and Barbara Peters, have offered me enthusiastic support, as always and a final word of thanks go to my wife Helena, my daughter Catherine, and my son Jonathan, who has created a website to be found at *www.martinedwardsbooks.com*.

MARTIN EDWARDS

This Large Print Book for the partially sighted, who cannot read normal print, is published under the auspices of

THE ULVERSCROFT FOUNDATION

THE ULVERSCROFT FOUNDATION

... we hope that you have enjoyed this Large Print Book. Please think for a moment about those people who have worse eyesight problems than you ... and are unable to even read or enjoy Large Print, without great difficulty.

You can help them by sending a donation, large or small to:

The Ulverscroft Foundation, 1, The Green, Bradgate Road, Anstey, Leicestershire, LE7 7FU, England.
or request a copy of our brochure for more details.

The Foundation will use all your help to assist those people who are handicapped by various sight problems and need special attention.

Thank you very much for your help.